MINE TO SAVE

PROTECTION SERIES BOOK 2

KENNEDY L. MITCHELL

*To all those who begged for Chandler's story.
Sorry it took me so long.*

© 2020 Kennedy L. Mitchell

All rights reserved. This book or any portion thereof may not be reproduced or used in any manner whatsoever without the express written permission of the publisher except for the use of brief quotations in a book review.

This book is a work of fiction. Any references to historical events, real people, or real places are used fictitiously. Other names, characters, places and events are products of the author's imagination, and any resemblances to actual events or places or persons, living or dead, is entirely coincidental.

Cover Design: Bookin It Designs

Editing: Hot Tree Editing

Proofreading: All Encompassing Books

❋ Created with Vellum

ABOUT THE AUTHOR

Kennedy L. Mitchell lives outside Dallas with her husband, son and two very large goldendoodles. She began writing in 2016 after a fight with her husband (You can read the fight almost verbatim in Falling for the Chance) and has no plans of stopping.

She would love to hear from you via any of the platforms below or her website www.kennedylmitchell.com You can also stay up to date on future releases through her newsletter or by joining her Facebook readers group - Kennedy's Book Boyfriend Support Group.

Thank you for reading.

PROLOGUE

Unknown

THE REMAINS of long-dead weeds crunched under his bare feet, the blades stabbing into the hardened soles with each step. The small bites of pain were welcomed, amplifying the anticipation that already flooded his veins. His heart raced, thundering against his chest as he drew closer to the dilapidated wooden barn and what was hidden inside: the one thing that would calm the waves of rage that nearly drowned him on a minute-by-minute basis. The one outlet where he could be his true self for a few short hours.

Cold dense steel burned his warm palm as he cradled the lock and slipped the key inside. A small smile tugged at his lips, dried from the whipping fall wind, at the sound of the mechanisms disengaging, offering him access to his prey.

He wet his lips in anticipation. It was almost time. His time to play and allow the stress of the day to slip away with each whimper and cry of anguish.

A forceful gust of wind tugged the rotting wooden door in his hand, nearly pulling it from his grasp. He tightened his hold on the edge to keep it from banging open, possibly alerting others who might be close by. Not that anyone would be since the barn was long forgotten, but he hadn't gone this long without being caught by being careless.

The first step across the threshold eased the built-up stress, draining it from his veins like an open wound, the tainted blood flooding to the hardened dirt floor.

After securing the inside lock and barricade, he turned. Excitement made his throat dry and fingers twitch where they dangled at his side. They itched to be wrapped around the small fragile neck or toy of punishment.

Soon.

Inhaling deep, he calmed his overexcited self and marched across the barn toward the play room. It was once the tack room before being reinforced and outfitted for his playthings. Taking another key from his pocket, he began the tedious task of releasing the four different locks and dragging the chain through the braces.

When the last lock popped and the heavy chain rattled to the floor, he shoved the door open with his shoulder. The stench of human waste, body odor, and infection smacked him in the face. It would worry him, but after so many, the permeating scent of despair was ever present no matter which whore filled the room.

Across the small area, the current filth waited.

Head bowed, scraped and bleeding knees pressed onto the hardwood plank floor, she waited like a good girl. Not that she was one. The ragged hem of the filthy, yellowed shift dress draped across the upper part of her thighs. The threadbare straps barely held on to her bony shoulders, making the front sag. The blisters and lacerations from yesterday's fun decorated her chest, arms, and thighs.

Yesterday had been a particularly difficult day. Much like today, and yesterday, and tomorrow. Every day would be the worst until The One came home. Until she recognized where she belonged and who she belonged to.

Until then, history would repeat itself over and over and over again.

Every toy was nothing more than a filthy, unworthy body to use for his release. Like the trash who trembled before him.

Even from where he stood several feet away, the twitch of her weakened muscles and tremble of her slender shoulders was clear. Outside, the wind gusted a warning that winter was near, but in here, the only sound was his labored, excited breaths. The room wasn't as comfortable as his home, but here he was allowed privacy. Away from curious eyes and ears. The others wouldn't understand this need, the daily urge to inflict pain and the joy it brought him.

That was why he kept this place a secret. For only him and his toys.

Whores. That was the appropriate word for those who came before this one and all the others who would come after. And they would continue to come until The One came home.

Soon.

Soon she would understand they were meant to be together.

Until then.

He paused, the ends of his clean toes brushing against the dark, dirt-streaked skin of hers. Bending at the waist, he withdrew another key and unlocked the steel cuff binding her wrists and keeping her tethered to the rusted, antique bed frame.

"Off." His voice was gruff from the long day and desperation for a release from the anger and rage bubbling inside him.

Her soft whimper was lost to the anticipation thundering in his ears.

He smiled greedily at his handiwork along her skin as she slipped the shift off her shoulders. It puddled around her too-thin waist.

Purple, green, and yellowed bruises littered her stomach and ribs, the aftereffects of the many times he'd disciplined this one. It took her three days of severe punishments and no rewards to understand her place.

And come to terms with her future.

Teeth marks covered each of her tiny breasts, some still raised and seeping clear fluid. He sneered at the small mounds that were barely enough for a mouthful. Unlike The One's full, large chest that begged to be bit and marked.

A large blister from prolonged use of the cattle prod during yesterday's therapy session appeared slightly worse. He would need to treat that before leaving for the night to ensure his fun with this one wasn't cut short due to septic shock.

That was an amateur move. One he hadn't made in years.

What could he say? He was taught by the best, but even the best made mistakes.

Agitation overtook his excitement at her lack of movement. She knew what was expected of her.

"Don't make me ask," he commanded, glaring down at the broken female.

Head still bowed, her shaking, bone-thin fingers crawled up his thighs, avoiding his crotch before blindly tugging at the cotton string that secured his loose pants. Blood caked beneath her jagged nails, a few still bleeding from where she'd bitten them to the quick.

Anger bolted through him, heating his skin.

"You're still biting your nails."

A loud whimper sounded, echoing off the bare walls. He snatched the dirty hand and squeezed. Like a good toy, she held back her scream of pain, but still her face contorted in a silent cry. "I told you that's a dirty habit." He'd thought the thin gag would keep her from gnawing at herself. Throwing her hand down, he sighed and looked to the single overhead light in exasperation. "You'll pay for that later."

Thumb hooked into the damp cotton gag, he yanked it down. It caught the edge of her split lip, making her wince in pain. He held back the urge to roll his eyes. After a week with him, she knew his expectations yet still wasn't acting on her training.

First she would suck his cock, then be punished when she failed to get him hard.

This was the cycle. Yesterday, last month, last year, and the years before. It wasn't until he saw The One that he knew his dick worked without inflicting pain, though he knew he'd enjoy delivering painful pleasure once she was with him once again.

Tired of waiting, he yanked his pants down; they puddled around his bare feet, leaving him in bright white briefs. Gripping both her hands, he forced her to drag the elastic band down his thighs until his underwear was around his ankles.

"Now," he growled, impatience filling his gruff tone. Not waiting for her, he gathered his flaccid cock and balls into her ice-cold hand. Taking a handful of greasy hair, he forced her head forward. "Open."

He closed his eyes, relishing the feel of her hot mouth and soft cries. But it wasn't enough to invoke a single flash of desire. He sneered down at her.

"Look at me." Red, tear-rimmed eyes met his. The disgust and fear that blared through her dark eyes shot a bolt of anger through him. "Am I not good enough? Is that it? Not enough man for you?"

The girl shook her head, panic now alight in her wide eyes.

At the prime of his life, there was no reason she should be disgusted by sucking him off. He was fit, clean. Most women outside of this small room found him attractive. What was her problem? What was The One's problem? Why did she not see him? See they were meant to be together? She was the fix to all of this.

With a roar, he shoved the weak female back, sending her sailing across the room. Her spine slammed against the bed frame, sending it skittering against the floor. She cried out and slumped forward.

Chest heaving, eyes wild, he marched to the toys along the far wall, well out of her reach when chained. His favorite, a cracked, well-used leather belt, caught his eye. At the sound of the metal belt buckle rattling, her panicked eyes whipped upward to meet his.

"No, please," she cried. "I'll be better. Let me make it up to you. Please, please not that again."

"Shut up," he screamed.

Chains scraped and rattled against the floor as she attempted to scurry away until the cuff at her ankle snapped tight. She cried out in terror and pain but was quickly silenced when he wrapped his fingers around her thin throat.

Frantic hands grappled at his wrist as her eyes bulged with lack of oxygen.

A sinister smile tugged at his lips.

He relaxed his hold a fraction, allowing a sliver of air to slip through, keeping his toy alive. The gurgle of her choking, the whimpers, and the tears streaking down her dirty face energized him, causing the soft appendage between his legs to twitch.

But it wasn't enough.

It would never be enough.

Not until The One came back.

The One's return would stop it all.

1

Chandler

THE LOW HUM and gentle vibrations from the jet's engines lulled me into a trancelike state, narrowing my focus to the pictures splayed along the table in front of me. The leather groaned, the smooth fabric of my black suit pants sliding easily along the seat as I adjusted to a more comfortable position. This plane was my second home—a very expensive home that wasn't technically mine.

The FBI had perfected wasting money on frivolous purchases over the years. Not that I would point that out, possibly risking them taking back our team's jet. Unless it meant they'd finally find the funds to hire another profiler to lessen our workload. But that wouldn't happen anytime soon.

"Budget cuts" was always their response when we complained that we were spread too thin and couldn't keep traveling at the drop of a hat to help local law enforcement when the cases were too big, too gruesome—too demented—for them to solve. But a jet to fly us to where we were summoned, sure, that was in the budget.

Fuckers.

Pretty sure flying commercial was more cost-effective.

My muscles protested as I reached back for a quick stretch, the plush headrest molding beneath my fingers as I tightened my grip.

But not nearly as comfortable.

The tense muscles along my spine ached as I arched and twisted one way, then the other. I'd sat in this seat or one of the other twelve too many times over the past year. The solo travel, overtime, and severity of each case was becoming too much. Hell, even my body was protesting at this point. But what would I do? Turn down a case because I needed a lazy weekend, lying naked in bed binge-watching Netflix with enough beer to cause liver damage?

Wouldn't happen.

I couldn't live with myself knowing another innocent was now a victim because I needed a vacation. Maybe it was from my upbringing, all those lessons on selflessness and self-sacrifice, but I'd never be that selfish.

Like now.

One of the reasons I sat on the jet, staring at pictures of half a dozen murdered women, instead of at home enjoying the two weeks' paid time off I had scheduled.

Duty called.

This time I asked for the case that was laid out in gruesome pictures in front of me. My all-female team didn't argue when I raised my hand. Last year we lost a great agent because she went in alone—the team is stretched so thin we can't work as a fucking team and protect our own—to profile a repeat abductor in the Smoky Mountains. We found her body months later.

After that tragedy, I swore to myself that I'd do whatever was needed to ensure no one on our team was in the same situation again. Which was why I was back in the air flying across the country instead of a team member. They appreciated my willingness to go, keeping them out of danger. They each had a family at home to think about.

Not me.

Chapter 1

A deep groan rumbled in my chest as I released the headrest and relaxed back into the seat. The flimsy photograph wavered when I flipped it over to scrutinize the next picture. Cold, slick glass slipped in my palm as I lifted the half-full beer to my lips and took in every detail of the picture, thinking over all the aspects of the case that I knew up to this point.

Seven bodies within a two-year period.

The seventh victim discarded within three weeks of the previous, a first for this unsub to not keep the victim for months before killing them and disposing of their bodies.

But his timeline escalation was only one reason why a profiler was asked to come down to the small Texas town. When surveying the area where the recent victim was found, additional bodies were discovered as well. Within a ten-mile radius, over a dozen old graves were uncovered. The bones found inside were collected and were currently being analyzed at the Dallas FBI office.

We'd known about the case for a few months. After the fifth victim, the team was contacted for help. Unable to get anyone to Texas at the time, we offered a basic profile based on the evidence to help them narrow down a suspect list.

Thirty-five to forty-five, white, low-level job, weak personality, aggressive toward females.

But they never identified the killer, and the bodies kept coming. Then the most recent victim was discovered. This one came with a message. With the escalated time frame between kills and the message, my boss agreed someone was needed on-site to offer hands-on help to the local authorities.

The phone resting beside the now empty beer bottle rattled against the table, drawing my attention from the gruesome picture.

I smirked at the name that flashed across the screen.

Texas Ranger Alec Bronson.

The other reason I asked to be assigned to this particular case. We handled a case together last year in El Paso and worked well together during the two-week span it took for us to identify the suspect. He was good at his job and a good man, both of which made him a potential friend in my book. If only we didn't always have to hang out because of a dead body.

But that was the life and job I chose.

Even if it was slowly eating at my own humanity and soul one case at a time.

Thumb to the screen, I gave it a quick swipe to answer the call and immediately hit the Speaker button.

"I'm on the jet racing to save your ass." Alec's familiar deep chuckle rumbled through the phone. "Should touch down in Dallas in—" I glanced at my watch. "—forty-five minutes or so. I'll grab a Suburban and—"

"I'll stop you right there. That's why I'm calling."

I frowned at the phone, not understanding what he meant. "Okay. Need me to pick up something in Dallas before I head south?"

I could almost see him popping his knuckles as the soft crack of his joints sounded in the background. "No, I meant your choice of transportation. Rent a car. Don't take a Fed vehicle of any kind. Better yet, to fit in down here, rent a truck."

I blinked at the phone. "Why?"

"Seriously? Do you know where you're headed?"

I flipped through the notes on my left. "Orin, Texas. Population 1,432." Damn, the town was small.

"And do you know where Orin, Texas, is?"

I groaned, massaging my brows with a thumb and forefinger. "Straight down Interstate 35 for an hour or so. Listen, I have Waze if I get lost."

"I'm not concerned you'll get lost. The town is sixty miles from Waco. Do you remember what your federal friends did in Waco, oh, thirty years or so ago? I can tell you right now everyone in this town —hell, Texas—remembers. And the locals here won't take too kindly to a Fed showing up and poking his nose around, especially considering the circumstances."

I scoffed. "First of all, didn't you watch the documentary on Netflix? That shit show was ATF's fault. We just—" I waved my hand searching for the word. "—escalated the tragedy. Second, that was about a cult no one understood, not half a dozen brutally assaulted and murdered women."

"Guessing you haven't done your research on the area, then."

A wave of guilt washed over me. Shit. What had I missed? "I was getting to that after looking over all the pictures you sent."

"Well, I'll catch you up, because that's the kind of friend I am." I huffed out a laugh. Lifting the beer bottle, I sighed, setting it back down when I remembered it was already empty. "There's a community out here, The Church. It's about a thousand or so families all living within a fenced-in area. It's all very similar to The Branch Dividians in the way they keep to themselves and stay protected under the 'freedom of religion' banner."

"What does that have to do with the case and me coming to town?" I asked.

"Well, that's a little more to explain and best left for tomorrow. Let's meet tomorrow at the local diner, nine o'clock. I'll explain everything then."

"What aren't you telling me?" I grumbled. I hated not having the full picture. If I didn't, then there would be more victims, more deaths.

"That this case is a fucking mess. An absolute fucking mess that I've spent the last seven months attempting to wrangle while managing other issues in my territory. That's why I need you down here, but having you come to town will also escalate things, and quickly. Between the local authorities being butt hurt that I've called in federal help, the locals not wanting an outsider knowing their business, and then The Church, who will lock the fuck down if they think you're here for them. This is a delicate situation. We need to ease you into the case, not have you show up in a black Escalade with federal plates wearing your 'Look at me, I'm special' FBI jacket."

I smirked at that. He made fun of that jacket daily during the last case.

Then something he said, the way he said it, clicked for me.

"You keep saying 'here.' Are you there already?" The iPad case slid easily across the smooth table as I pulled it close and flipped the cover. I typed in the cult's name and the town into the search bar and hit Enter. Clearly I had zero clue what I was about to walk into, and that was dangerous for me and the case.

"Yeah, I'm here, unfortunately. And I plan on sticking around until we catch this bastard. You know why I asked for you to come down instead of another phone conference, right?"

"He's escalating," I murmured as I swiped through The Church's webpage. Of course they had a webpage. What self-respecting cult didn't have one to constantly recruit for new members? Fucking internet made it easier for the manipulative assholes to target their victims. "I feel like you're leaving more than this cult out, Alec. What aren't you telling me? You know I hate being unprepared."

"It's too much to cover on the phone. Tomorrow morning, nine at the diner. There's someone I want you to meet before we head to the police station and announce your arrival. As soon as that happens, the whole town will know."

"Meet someone?" My ears perked up at that. I paused my scrolling and stared at the phone. "As in a suspect?"

There was a long pause. I leaned closer to the phone, growing anxious for his answer.

"No, not a suspect."

"A victim?" There was no masking the hope in my voice. If we had a living victim, someone who could offer any characteristics about the unsub, then we could solve the case in record time, saving more women from a horrible fate, and get me home to my Netflix binge party for one.

"Not a victim like you're thinking."

I groaned. "Spit it out, Bronson," I snapped. "I'm fucking tired and now have to figure out how in the hell someone rents a damn car from the airport." The last few words were more of a grumble from annoyance from the truth in my words. How long had it been since I had to rent a car on my own?

"Download the damn Budget Rental Car app, you lazy ass. And what I mean is... well... you'll find out tomorrow."

I grunted a goodbye, knowing full well he wouldn't give me any more information until we met, and tapped the red circle with a knuckle, ending the call. Reaching down, I dug through the side pocket of my go bag, feeling around until a hard plastic edge scraped against my fingertips. Tugging the foil-covered gum packet free, I popped two hard white pieces from their encasing and tossed both into my mouth. Jaw working, I inhaled the burst of peppermint, letting the intense smell burn the back of my throat as I gazed at the picture of the recent victim.

Shallow grave. Naked body covered in welts, cuts, and lashes like the other victims. Multiple stab wounds across the chest and sides. But those marks weren't what held my focus as I worked the gum, swiping it from one side of my mouth to the other. No, I couldn't look away from the two words carved into the sunken stomach that stretched from one protruding hip bone to the other.

Come home.

Those words struck my curiosity, urging two questions to circle on a loop.

Who did the unsub want to come home, and where was home?

One thing was for certain: if this case had anything to do with The Church, we were fucked. There wouldn't be a single judge in Texas who would sign a warrant to search the cult's premises unless I had hard evidence. But even then it might be a long shot.

I shook my head, dislodging the thoughts. No need to get ahead of myself.

Land, rent a car, and meet Alec at nine tomorrow morning. Once I was on the ground, working the case, and could submerge myself into the situation, the clues always found a way to rise to the top.

The plane tipped, causing the bottle to slide an inch to the left as we circled. I glanced out the window as we dipped below the clouds, the ground now dancing with lights from downtown Dallas and the surrounding suburbs. Knowing we'd be landing soon, I grabbed my phone to search for a car rental app when an incoming text had me tapping that instead.

I smiled at the picture that appeared on the screen. Alta's wide smile was genuine, her eyes wet. A small snort caught in my throat at

Cas Mathews smiling as much as that bastard could beside her. Snow covered every inch of the background. I flipped to the message, my cheeks aching with the full grin that spread as I read the words.

She said yes.

"Good for you, Mathews," I said to the screen as I typed out a sarcastic but just as congratulatory reply.

A quick tap on the picture had it filling the screen once again. The phone clattered to the table, their smiling faces staring back up at me. So genuine. Happy. Two broken people who found themselves whole through the other. I was happy for them, I really was. But then what was the growing unease in my gut as I continued to stare at the picture of my happy friends? If I didn't know better, I'd say it was akin to jealousy.

I was lying to myself saying I didn't know why I felt the way I did, the two conflicting emotions. I was a profiler, for fuck's sake. Jealousy was the emotion, but the cause wasn't my friends and their happiness. No, it was more than that, so deep rooted that I didn't want to acknowledge the truth. Because if I did, then my fear would be real.

But at this point in my life, how could it not be true? I was thirty-eight years old. That was a long time to search for someone who understood the fucked-up side of me, to understand my brokenness and come up empty-handed. There had been women, lots of women, but none who understood what I needed and why. None who wanted to understand.

"Fuck," I groaned and scrubbed at my face. "I just need to get laid. That's all."

Yeah, that was it.

That was all I needed.

2

Ellie

"Do you remember what it smelled like?" The rounded edge of the wooden bar pressed into my forearms as I leaned closer into Janice's personal space, desperate to catch her every word. I needed her to recall every sense from that moment, hoping I could imagine myself smack in the middle of the memory she was reciting for me.

"Smelled like?" She took a long sip of the white wine spritzer, her signature drink, which I had just refreshed yet was already looking low. "Well, now, Ellie, I don't remember the smell. That was a long time ago, dear."

I nodded with a fake smile to hide the disappointment that I didn't have that one sense to add to the story. She was right, her honeymoon to California was over forty years ago, and asking her to recall the smell of the redwood trees was asking a lot. The woman was sixty-ish, after all. Well, that was how old I assumed she was. And it wasn't like I could ask to see her driver's license to verify she was over twenty-one to drink—she was clearly well over the legal drinking age.

Unlike the two kids who still sulked at the high-top way in the back, nursing the Cokes I served them, sans the Jack Daniel's they asked to have added. I shook my head at the two pouting boys and turned my attention back to Janice, who had now moved on to venting about the leak her husband found in their duplex.

Bar towel in hand, I nodded along as I listened to her complain about the landlord and the terrible living conditions she was forced to put up with while I wiped down the worn bar top. Janice wasn't wrong about the undesirable living conditions of her place, but that could be said about most of the affordable places to live in our small town. It wasn't known for its spacious and modern apartment buildings. We were known for something far more ominous, which drove tourists who were too curious for their own good to our town.

If they knew what went on behind those gates, maybe they wouldn't be so obsessed with The Church. It was located only four miles away, just under the overpass for the highway, but it might as well be a different world once you turned off the main road.

Why cults and their secrecy held such fascination was something I couldn't comprehend. Four miles away from The Church and still I didn't get why tourists made Orin a destination stop. Maybe I didn't understand because I knew firsthand what it was like to live behind those miles of fences and domed homes.

From my perspective, at least. And mine held some weight since I was born into that life and lived it for what I assumed was over twenty years.

"Ellie?"

"Hmm?" I said, shaking off the sense of foreboding thinking about The Church always brought over me.

"I said I brought you something."

I paused and turned from where I'd moved halfway down the bar as I cleaned. The single postcard between her fragile, wrinkled fingers now held my full attention. I tossed the rag into the sink and moved back down the bar, the rubber soles of my Doc Martens

Chapter 2

squeaking against the nonslip mat Carl installed behind the bar last year with each quick step.

"My granddaughter went to Australia with her school for some international study, and she sent me this and a key chain"—she slid the small metal object across the bar toward me—"to give to you."

Teeth digging into the edge of my lower lip, I wiped my damp fingers from the cleaning rag on my snug black jeans before plucking the card from her fingertips.

Towering snowcapped mountains and a quaint little thatched-roofed town at the base with a river running through the middle covered the front of the card. I studied each inch, imagining what it felt like to be standing at the base of those mountains, to walk along the streets bundled up to fend off the cold, or even stand at the peak of either mountain looking down at the world below.

If I imagined hard enough, I could feel the damp cold, the cobblestone street beneath my steps, and smell the....

I frowned. That was the one sense I could never imagine when picturing myself anywhere other than this small town.

With a sigh, I flipped the card over.

ELLIE,
Wish you could be here too. One day.
PS - It smells like fresh rain. Clean and bright with hope of a fresh start.

A SMILE PULLED at my lips as I recited the words in my head, studying the picture once again.

A cold hand patted mine that was balled into a tight fist resting along the bar. "One day, Ellie girl. One day." Janice gave my hand a squeeze until my own relaxed against hers. "You'll see it all."

"I'd settle for seeing Austin," I muttered.

The card stock was smooth beneath my fingertip as I traced the outline of the small houses. A ball of pent-up emotion lodged in my throat. I cleared it and forced a bright smile as I looked up at Janice, whose face was full of concern.

"This," I said, nodding to the postcard, "is perfect. Please tell her how grateful I am. It truly means the world to me." Careful to not crease the edges, I placed it and the key chain on the back counter for safekeeping until closing.

A click of a tongue had me turning back to my best customer. "You deserve so much more than you got in life. You're sweet, beautiful," she paused, her lips pursed as she inspected my new hair color. "Despite this month's choice in hair color." Yeah, this out-of-the-box jet-black wasn't my favorite either. "You worshipping the devil now or something?"

A real laugh burst from me at her narrow-eyed scan from the top of my newly dark hair to my black long-sleeve T-shirt and jeans. It was funny because only Janice would ask such a question. Old people were the best with their zero filter. It was refreshing instead of the others who knew my background and clammed up around me, not sure how to act.

"No, no devil worshipping here. Just trying out a new look. Guess you don't like it?" I arched a blonde brow in her direction and leaned back against the counter.

"Your natural color is so beautiful. Why do you keep changing it?"

Thankfully before I could come up with an excuse—every time she asked that, I came up with a new one, never the true answer—the front door swung open. A burst of cold, damp air blew through the stuffy bar, alerting everyone to the newcomer.

A man I'd never seen before stepped inside, shaking out his black coat as he closed the door behind him. Dressed in nice-looking slacks and a button-down shirt, he moved through the cluster of tables, past the pool table, and sat down on a barstool down the bar from where Janice and I stood gaping.

Okay, I was gaping. Janice was slurping to suck the final drops of her drink.

"Who's that?" I whispered as I pushed off the back counter. Elbow on the bar, I rested my chin on my knuckles, blatantly staring at the

Chapter 2

stranger as he shrugged off his coat and laid it on the empty barstool to his right. When he was situated, he scanned the length of the bar until his gaze landed on me.

I held back the gasp of surprise when those ice blue eyes locked with mine. All the walls I'd built over the years crumbled, the restrained emotions I hid daily from others on full display with a single look from this mystery man. He held me in a trance, never glancing away as he seemed to read every memory, detail, and emotion from where he sat several feet away.

Janice's voice was hollow and sounded far away even though only the bar separated us. He wasn't the normal cult junkie who stopped in every now and again looking for details on what happened across the highway. No, this man was different in more ways than his casual good looks and piercing stare.

"I'll be right back," I muttered to the still talking Janice. My soles squeaked with each step. At the sink, I dunked my hands into the tepid water and retrieved a new bar towel.

I twisted the coarse rag in my hands as I continued my approach, moving slow to take in as much about him as I could. A sad smile lifted the corners of his lips, a sadness I understood. It was mixed with loneliness and maybe a hint of exhaustion, three emotions I knew all too well. That same gaze stared back at me in my own reflection daily.

Yet even with the sad smile, he was striking with his lean, scruffy cheeks, strong nose, and full lips. With the dim lighting and the almost buzz cut of his hair, it was impossible to determine the color. Add his good looks to the confident air about him and that all-seeing stare, and I was at a loss for words.

My lower belly twisted and tingled when I stopped in front of him. Beads of perspiration that weren't there before he entered the bar dotted the back of my neck and turned my hands clammy.

Maybe someone turned on the heat?

I chanced a glance at the thermostat that was on my side of the bar, behind a plastic box that was secured with a lock.

Okay, maybe someone didn't turn up the heat. But then what would cause this sudden hot flash and dry throat?

"Hi," the man said as he interlaced his fingers and placed them palms-down on top of the bar.

"Hello." The coarse weave of the rag scraped between my fingers as I nervously wove it between them beneath the bar.

Nerves had my gaze bouncing from him to the few other locals scattered throughout the small dive bar. Everyone had paused what they were doing, their attention on the man in front of me. One of Farmer Ben's sons was still bent over the pool table, cue ready to strike a ball, frozen in place as he watched our interaction. His playing partner, one of Brett's friends, had his eyes narrowed on the newcomer while he spoke into the phone glued to his ear.

"What do you want?" I asked, nervously wiping along the bar.

Like a switch was flipped, that sad smile changed, now full of humor like he was in on some inside joke I was left out of.

"You might want to work on your greeting skills."

Pausing my wiping, I brought my other hand up to rest on my hip as I leaned against the dark wood of the bar. "Excuse me?"

"Your greeting. It needs work." I arched a brow. Even though I should've been annoyed with his words, they were light with humor, holding zero animosity or anger. He gave me a quick once-over that left me feeling exposed. "You're very hostile." His damn smile grew when I narrowed my eyes at him. "Did I offend you...?"

I watched as his gaze dipped lower, this time more slowly, like he was memorizing every inch of my neck and chest. When his eyes stayed glued to my full chest, I subconsciously hunched my shoulders to make my large breasts seem smaller.

Panic flashed behind his eyes, which were now a bit frantic. "No, sorry. I wasn't looking there, at your—" He waved a hand at my chest, which made me even more self-conscious. "—that. Shit. Sorry, I was looking for your name tag, but you're not wearing one."

"Because everyone knows who I am," I responded, relaxing a fraction at his explanation.

"Benefits of a small town, I guess."

I shrugged. "Benefit or detriment. Depends on the day, I guess."

"Clever." He sighed and slid both hands along the bar, spreading his arms out wide. "I'm in desperate need of a drink. Can we blame my earlier behavior on exhaustion? Hell, I might be sleepwalking right now."

I dipped my chin with a small smile. "Wish I looked that good exhausted," I muttered under my breath as I tossed the bar towel into the dirty rag bucket. Inhaling deeply, I steeled my spine and rolled my shoulders back to stand at my full five-foot-five height. Even with him sitting, he towered over me from his spot across the bar. But for some reason it didn't intimidate me. No, instead it made me... sick?

Sick wasn't the right word. Nervous, but a good nervous that made my stomach go all twisted. Or I was getting sick. That had to be the explanation. I'd never had as much as a single heart race or flash of excitement from a man. The flu or a cold was much more likely an explanation for my sudden onslaught of symptoms.

"Not a problem," I said, wearing the fake smile I reserved for nosy outsiders. "What can I get you?" His lips parted, ready to give his order, when I held up a hand to stop him. "I will warn you that I don't mix drinks unless it has two ingredients, such as vodka tonic or rum and cola, and even then I've been told they're not great. Your best bet is a beer, or I make a killer white wine spritzer per my friend Janice." I inclined my head down the bar where Janice sat clearly listening in.

She raised her empty glass and nodded. "And I'll take a refill of that drink when you can."

I nodded before turning back to the man with an expectant look.

"Beer. Budweiser in a bottle if you have it."

I nodded and slipped the opener from my back pocket. The heavy metal twirled easily around my index finger as I made my way to the cooler.

"So you're a bartender who doesn't know how to make drinks?"

I snorted at his comment and immediately froze at the unconscious slip. Heart racing from the sudden bolt of panic, I stood as still as possible and closed my eyes. Grounding myself to the here and now, I focused all my senses on what surrounded me. The clatter of the pool balls, the low mumbled voices, the smell of bleach and yeast flooded through me as I absorbed the world around me. I was in the bar, not behind those gates with him. No one was here to punish me for that little slip. No one here cared if I snorted or laughed without permission.

A hand wrapped around my bicep and tightened, not to the point of pain but just enough to snap me out of the little cocoon of self-preservation I'd slid into. Opening my lids, I slowly shifted my focus to the man who was leaning half his body over the bar to reach me, his eyes darting between my own, searching for something.

"Hey, you okay?" Those searching eyes and the concern in his lowered voice shredded through my normal defenses.

I blinked, not sure how to respond. Aggression, sympathy, annoyance, I could handle that coming at me, but genuine concern from a stranger? That was a new one. "Yeah, sure, fine." I shook out of his hold and stepped back until I hit the counter, making the shelves of liquor rattle. "Just lost in thought, I guess." Those blue eyes narrowed, almost like he saw straight through the lie. "I'll get you that beer now."

Reluctantly he withdrew to his side of the bar and took his seat, that penetrating gaze never leaving me as I bent to pull a beer from the cooler. The cold glass slipped in my hand as I held the neck to pop the cap. I set it on the bar and gave it a soft push. A line of condensation trailed its path as it slid down the bar right into his waiting hand.

"At least you have that down," he said with a tight smile before taking a long drink. His Adam's apple bobbed with each deep swallow, the sight doing something strange to my breathing.

"The drink thing is more about me not knowing what it tastes like. I either make them too strong or too weak," I explained. "Never really liked the stuff."

"Yet you're a bartender."

I shrugged my thin shoulders and started working on Janice's white wine spritzer. "Carl was hiring, needed help with a few closing shifts a week so he could go to Waco to see his kids." And agreed to pay me under the table in cash. "And no one around here orders anything fancy, so I haven't bothered to study the drink book that he leaves beside the register. Pretty sure it was published in the seventies and its fanciest drink is a Manhattan."

"Carl the owner?"

I nodded and left our little bubble to deliver Janice's new drink. When I returned, he'd slipped back into that sad state, the hint of happiness we'd danced around earlier gone.

"Why are you so sad?" I whispered. Well, meant to whisper. By his reaction, the mystery man heard the random, inappropriate slip of the tongue. Clearing my throat, I gave a fake laugh. "I mean exhausted." No I didn't. I meant sad because it was radiating off him now, and for some reason I wanted to fix it, wanted to make him happy.

He kept his face downturned. "Work. Life. Destiny."

Tongue to the roof of my mouth, I let out a low whistle that drew his attention. "That does sound exhausting. Tell me, why worry about destiny when it's nothing you can change?"

That had him perking up. He leaned forward, the empty beer bottle held between both hands. "You don't think you can change your own destiny?"

"I know you can't." *At least I can't*, I said in my head but kept to myself. He didn't know my background, and that was the way I wanted it.

"That's interesting...." He raised both brows. I narrowed mine, not understanding what he was getting at. "Your name. What's your name? Or I'll have to find a nickname to start calling you."

This time when I snorted, I held the swift race of panic deep down so he wouldn't see just how broken and fucked-up I really was. Not sure when his opinion of me began to matter, but for some reason it did.

"A nickname? You don't even know me."

He tapped his bottom lip with the beer bottle. "I'm sure I could come up with something appropriate. How about 'dark and mysterious'?"

"There is nothing dark and mysterious about me." Well, the dark part, sure, but how would he know that unless he really could see through me to the black spots that were left behind from years of neglect and abuse?

"I disagree," he said, that genuine smile returning. Something brightened in my heart at seeing the sadness washed from his features. "Dark hair, black clothes, and an edge to you that I can't figure out. 'Dark and mysterious' fits from my perspective. And it's kind of what I do, so in my honest but accurate opinion, I say I'm right about the nickname."

"Your honest yet accurate opinion? Who says that?" I huffed out a laugh and bent forward to grab him another beer from the cooler. This time I popped the cap and walked the few steps to stand in front of his barstool.

"I heard a preacher say it one time, and it was so absurd it stuck. I use it to impress the ladies now. How's it working?"

A slight burn crept along my cheeks as a full genuine smile grew so wide it hurt. "I'm sure you do just fine on your own, no lines needed."

"So you're saying there's a chance." At my laugh, a spark flashed behind his gaze, one that wasn't there when he first walked in. "Your name, please." He shook his head like he fought some internal battle.

I opened my mouth but sealed my lips before I could shout out my name when a nagging thought wouldn't go away.

What am I doing? This man wasn't flirting with me, wasn't in to me. No, men didn't flirt with me. One because of Brett, and two because everyone in town knew I wasn't worth it.

Brett's unrelenting comments about my body came roaring to the forefront of my mind. I was too short, too thin, too disproportionate for anyone but him to find attractive.

This man wasn't flirting, he was simply being nice, and here I was taking it the wrong way.

Yes, that made more sense. A man like this guy wouldn't be interested in a nobody like me. What he said about the preacher clicked, and I nodded, understanding now why he was being so nice.

Chapter 2

"Oh, I get it. You're religious." My fake smile fell into place, replacing my genuine one. "The Church. Sorry, I can't help you."

"What?" He choked on the swig of beer he'd just downed.

I held up a hand. "Listen, just be careful with them. They aren't what they seem." I hitched my chin to the beer hovering in midair as he continued to stare at me in shock. "Let me know if you need another one."

As I turned to walk away, my heart heavy with disappointment, he reached over the bar and gripped my elbow, tugging me to a stop.

"What just happened?"

I shook my head, keeping my face toward the floor, not daring to glance up because if I did, he'd see all the emotions this short encounter brought over me.

The awkward silence between us was severed when the front door swung open. It slammed against the wall before rebounding, only for the man walking through the door to hold it back with a palm wrapped around the edge.

Devil's ball sack. What the hell is Brett doing here?

"Who the hell are you?" he yelled from across the bar, finger pointed at the man still holding on to my elbow. Brett's furious gaze zeroed in on the contact before I could tug myself free from the other man's grasp. "Is he harassing you, Ellie?"

Instead of being intimidated, the mystery man smiled. "Ellie. Now, was that so difficult?" There was a lightness to his tone that took out the chiding effect of his words. I immediately missed his touch when he pulled away. Digging into the side pocket of his slacks, he withdrew a wallet, thumbed through some bills, and tossed two on the bar. After taking the final sip of beer number two, he shot me a wink. "No, Ellie, I'm not religious, but I do think I'm done here for the night. Thank you for the distraction."

"I asked you a question," Brett said, now standing directly behind the newcomer as he casually slipped on his coat. Chest puffed out, standing as tall as he could, Brett was still several inches shorter than the other man. His confidence wavered when the stranger turned, towering over him, and met his glare head-on.

Tension weighed heavy in the room as the two stayed locked in their stare-off. For the second time that night, everyone's attention was directed at the man.

"I'm not looking for trouble, just needed a drink. I suggest you step back. I don't do well with people in my personal space."

"Get out of this bar, and stop harassing my girlfriend," Brett spat, pointing across the bar to where I'd scooted as far away from the two men as possible.

The mystery man shot me a quick glance. My heart sank in my chest like a lead weight. Not that I thought I had a chance with the guy, but the idea that I could be with a man like him would've been fun to imagine later tonight.

"I was just leaving. Have a good night."

He didn't look back. Not once.

When the door shut behind him, I deflated, sagging against the register with his two bills crumpled in my fist. It was too much to hope for anyway; better he left now than for me to get my hopes up.

The hard buttons moved beneath my finger as I pressed in the amount for his beers. It was only then that I noticed the amount he left for the two simple drinks. His total added up to eight dollars, which left me with a $192 tip.

I grinned at the two hundred-dollar bills as I carefully smoothed out the wrinkles I'd caused.

"You all right, Ellie?" Brett's words went in one ear and out the other. "Ellie, I'm talking to you."

The annoyance in his tone had me looking up at my ex-boyfriend.

Ex, not current like Brett told the man.

Not that it mattered. I'd never see the stranger again.

Even though the thought made me long for something.

Something I was destined to never have.

3

Chandler

FINGERS WRAPPED around the smooth edge of the chipped porcelain sink, I leaned forward toward the small mirror. A hollow man stared back at me, his eyes vacant and sad. Exactly what that bartender said earlier. Dark circles made my blue eyes more purple than clear. Inflamed red veins streaking through the whites didn't help my strung-out look.

That was exactly how I felt. Strung out. But not on any drug or massive amounts of alcohol. No, I was strung out on life, my job eating at me case by case. The assignment before this was the worst to date. Anything dealing with kids was terrible, but finding them the way we did.... My reflection shook its head in disappointment. I didn't find the bastard soon enough. Didn't save those kids from the horrors they would live with for the rest of their lives.

That was what I had to live with too. The memory of their haunted eyes, blank expressions. Hell, maybe that was why my own gaze was so distant, haunted... sad.

Devastated was a better word.

Destroyed that I was never quick enough, always one step behind these bastards who I profile and help apprehend. Inadequate was how I felt most days. Lost, even.

Lost until those bright blue eyes met mine across the bar. Those eyes saw me, the tortured side I kept locked away. It was fucking unnerving.

I'd been told that was how some people felt under my watchful eye, but I'd never felt the same. Not even my own teammates had that effect. To feel stripped bare, everything I wanted hidden being exposed, left me vulnerable. Whoever this Ellie woman was, she was something special.

Someone special to someone else.

"Fuck," I grumbled and shoved off the sink. "Get it the fuck together, Peters." I attempted to make my inner voice as gruff and commanding as my friend Mathews' for emphasis but fell short.

The hard exterior I had formed to perform in my job, to profile and track down the vilest of criminals across the country, fractured when we almost lost Mathews' girl, Alta. It had been downhill ever since. That was a year ago. Fourteen cases later. Fourteen cases, twenty-five dead men and women, seventeen saved.

But did any of it matter? It was never enough. There was always someone else ready to come up with some new demented way to hurt another.

I scrubbed at my face. I couldn't let myself go there again.

The soles of my feet stuck to the thin motel room carpet as I stalked toward the double bed that had a bedspread that looked older than me. The sudden urge to dig out my black light hit me, but I pushed it away. If I saw exactly what was on the bed, I'd never get any sleep.

And I needed sleep.

The stiff material bunched in my grip as I stripped the bed to put on the fresh set I always brought with me. Careful to keep the contact minimal, I tossed the lump of bedding in the corner.

"You've got to be kidding me." I stared at the bare mattress.

Maybe it was just my eyes playing tricks on me from exhaustion and there really wasn't a dark stain in the middle of it.

After blinking several times, the stain was still there. It was disturbing that annoyance filtered through me instead of surprise. Shit happened in motel rooms—I would know—especially shady, cheap-ass motels like the one which was destined to be my home until we caught the unsub. Destined because it was the only motel within a forty-mile radius from the police station.

Staying local helped submerge me in the case, allowing me to be available at any time for updates or when the next body was found.

Which it would. These killers didn't stop on their own.

A grimace wrinkled my features as I glanced back at the mattress.

Sleep, yes. There, no.

Twisting, I tugged the small plastic chair from under the table and settled into the seat. The table wobbled on uneven legs under the weight of my elbow as I propped my head up and stared out the sheer yellowed curtains to the glowing Vacancy sign just outside the window.

The nights were the worst during solo assignments, which were becoming more frequent. At night there wasn't anyone to commiserate with on the shitty lodging, no one to theorize on why the unsub did what he did. No one to laugh with or share the burden of the job.

A pang of loneliness ached in my chest. Heel of my hand to my pec, I pressed hard to ease the almost hollow sensation. Tonight was like a wake-up call. She showed me what I was missing with just a glance.

Acceptance. Understanding. Seen.

For the first time, a person's brokenness didn't invoke pity.

No, hers called to me.

The neon sign blurred, my lids heavy with sleep.

Not that any of that mattered with Ellie. She had someone else, and I would leave the moment this job was done.

We would never happen.

The last thought that slid through as I fell into a light sleep was of her knowing gaze and the spark of hope it spurred in my desolate soul.

THE DELICIOUS SMELL of bacon and fresh coffee swirled on a gust of bitter wind, making my mouth water before I'd even approached the door. Loose gray gravel crunched under my boots as I wove through the twenty or so trucks parked in the lot beside the diner. Seemed most of the town was here.

The outside wasn't much to look at with its peeling blue paint, dirty windows, and rotting wooden steps that led to an unsteady landing. But none of that mattered if the food was good.

Obeying Alec's strange request, I ditched the suit this morning after a terrible night's sleep and wore jeans, boots, and a long-sleeve Henley beneath my heavy North Face jacket. I didn't fit in, except for the gun strapped to my hip, but at least I didn't stand out as an FBI agent.

The thin glass door rattled beneath my grip as I tugged it open and stepped out of the cruel wind. DC was cold this time of year, but nothing prepared you for the whipping Texas wind. It was constant, biting through your clothes, chilling you to the bone in the winter and being a prick tease in the summer, blowing scorching air across your skin that somehow made you hotter.

I shook out of my jacket, dispelling the cold that had somehow found its way inside, as I scanned the cramped diner. Ten booths, all with faded and cracked red plastic benches, sat along the two walls of the dining room. In the center, eight tables were crowded together so tightly it was a wonder a waitress could slip through the chairs to deliver food.

A raised hand from the far back booth snagged my attention. All eyes were on me as I made my way to where Alec sat, his steaming mug of coffee cupped between his hands. I was used to the stares, mostly out of curiosity, but these felt almost hostile. No doubt everyone wondered who I was, why I was there, and when I was leaving.

I could answer that last part for them now—not anytime soon.

Alec slid from the booth bench and stood to greet me. I clasped his outstretched hand and gave it a hard squeeze, which he returned.

A little taller than me with broad shoulders and commanding presence even without his uniform, the man screamed authority. Much like my friend Mathews. I was the taller, leaner, thinker type. I could hold my own in any fight and was a hell of a shot just like any good Marine, but where I lacked the bulk like some of the other guys, I made up for it in analyzing situations in the blink of an eye and reading people to their core. Hence why I was a profiler for the Behavioral Science Unit division of the FBI.

I'd killed before, would kill again if needed, but helping prevent some sick bastard from collecting more victims was where I excelled.

"Peters," Alec said with a somber grin. It didn't pass my notice that he didn't add the "agent" title. "You look worse for wear." He waved a hand to the opposite side of the booth. "Thanks for coming so fast."

I slid into the booth and shifted to get comfortable. "A message carved into a stomach will do that."

He nodded as he lifted the brown ceramic mug to his lips for a quick sip. "Sick son of a bitch. He's stepped up his fucked-up-ness with that one. Which, I have to admit, surprised the hell out of me."

"Not much surprises me anymore," I said, searching the diner for a server. An older lady in an old-school diner uniform caught my eye across the room. I waved her down and pointed toward Alec's steaming mug of coffee. "Other than that, how've you been, man? We really need to stop meeting under these circumstances," I joked.

"Hell yeah, we do. But I have a feeling after we nab this SOB, another will pop up in his place, bringing you right back to my great state sooner than later." He paused as the waitress approached with an empty mug in one hand and a steaming glass pot in the other. She observed me with suspicion as she filled the mug to the brim.

"Who are you?" she asked while topping off Alec's coffee. "Tourist?"

I held back a laugh. Tourist? Here? What in the hell was there to see in this town besides the largest collection of old beat-up Ford trucks?

"He's with me, Sally. An old friend just stopping in for a while. We'll take two of the specials, please." He glanced around, lips pursed like he was searching for someone. "You here alone today?"

Her stiff hair didn't move with the shake of her head. "Ellie's in the back helping Cook with the rush."

My ears perked up. Was the beautiful blue-eyed bartender from last night here?

"Great, thanks." At the obvious dismissal—well, obvious to me—Sally turned to watch me again. Alec patted her arm. "If you don't mind, we have a lot to catch up on. I haven't seen him in a while, and, well, he's having boyfriend troubles."

Horror washed over her features, eyes wide. I smiled through the flash of annoyance. With a mumbled "I'll pray for your soul," she scurried away.

"Seriously?" I huffed. "What the hell was that all about?" The first sip of the scalding liquid burned the tip of my tongue, but I still forced it down, letting the bitter taste wake me up from the inside out.

Alec stretched his arms out long along the booth's back. "Easiest way to get the biggest gossip in town out of earshot. No way would Sally want to overhear anything that could earmark her for hell in the afterlife."

I shook my head. Smart but annoying. Not that it mattered what she or this town thought of me. Catching the unsub and getting home as fast as possible was most important.

"Catch me up to speed on the case." I took another sip. "You mentioned you've been involved for seven months, now staying here...." I waved a hand between us as a signal for him to fill in the gaps.

Sighing, he rubbed a palm along his scruff-lined jaw. "The case

Chapter 3

was a shit show when I stepped in. The police chief here is... well, there's no nice way to say it. He's an ignorant, incompetent bastard of a man. The only reason he's the chief is because he grew up here and everyone loved his father, who was the police chief before he passed." Shaking his head, Alec looked toward the kitchen, then back to me, his eyes resigned. "Everything in a town like this is closely wrapped together. Nothing is separate. You'll find that out as we dig into the lives of everyone here."

I nodded. "Where are you staying while you're here? I'm at the motel." A part of me hoped he was staying closer to Waco. Maybe somewhere that didn't house an old murder scene.

"Really? The one here in town?" He barked a laugh but quickly reeled it in when he caught my annoyed glare. "Sorry. No, I'm not staying there. I rented a place about ten miles east of here. It's nothing fancy, but it's furnished and has hot water. You should come stay with me."

"No blood on the mattress?"

He grimaced. "Haven't checked. It was an old widower's who recently moved to Waco to be closer to his granddaughter. I offered to rent it from him seeing as no one is moving here with a serial killer on the loose."

"Not any young, high-risk female, that's for sure."

"High-risk? Why do you assume that?"

I relaxed back, shifting when a spring from the cushion pushed into my lower spine. "None of the women have been reported missing. Their DNA isn't in the database from a loved one submitting it hoping one day their lost mother, daughter, friend would be found. These women probably had high-risk occupations or hobbies. Drugs, hitchhikers, prostitutes, that kind of thing."

A sharp gasp had me whipping around. I fought an eye roll and plastered a bland smile across my face to placate the shocked Sally, who'd be clutching her pearls if she was wearing any.

"There's no one like that in this town. None of our men here pay for that kind of thing. They're good Christian men and women. Chief Swann wouldn't allow anyone like that to stick around." After filling my mug, she turned and whispered another slew of scriptures about damned souls and homosexuality.

Great. I groaned and turned back to Alec, who was grinning ear to ear.

"I think she likes you." I laughed and took a sip of my refreshed coffee. "I disagree with her on Chief Swann," he said, practically spitting the name. "He's a tool. But the locals, she was right about that. Anyone with the background you mentioned would've been noticed, and so far, no one has seen these women's faces around town before they turned up dead. They would've been noticed before they were abducted, which solidifies my theory on The Church being key to this case."

"We're getting ahead of ourselves." I sighed and rubbed at my brows. "Let's get our food, go to the police station, then start tossing out ideas on where the victims came from." Closing my eyes, I inhaled deeply through my nose. "But you might as well go ahead and tell me what you know about The Church."

"Knew you were here for them."

The vinyl squeaked under my weight as I twisted in the booth, coming eye to eye with the woman from last night. Sitting like this, I was eye level with those suspicious blue eyes. Hell, she wasn't much over five feet tall. Today she'd ditched the all-black outfit and now sported the same old-school diner waitress uniform as Sally, but hers fit a little different than the older woman's. Ellie's hugged her in all the right places and was a little too short to be considered modest. The Doc Martens didn't really go with the uniform, but somehow she made it work.

Her disappointed gaze shifted from me to Alec, who appeared confused by the whole interaction.

"Two specials. Enjoy." The cream-and-brown plates rattled against the table as she practically threw them down. Before Alec or I could get a word out, she was gone, shoving through the kitchen door like it had personally offended her.

"What was that all about?" Alec asked. "She's normally beyond nice."

Chapter 3

I grimaced. "Ah, well, it might have something to do with last night."

"Explain."

"When I arrived, I needed a drink, so I stopped into the local bar. She and I talked, and for some reason, she assumed I was religious and here for The Church. Based on her reaction last night and just now, she's not a fan of them?"

"Nope." He tipped his face to the ceiling with a groan of frustration. "Damnit, Peters. You just pissed off the person I wanted you to meet this morning. Ellie is the only living example of what I'm talking about, why I suspect The Church is involved in all this." I narrowed my brows and shook my head. "You see, Ellie there, the tiny, beautiful woman who just delivered our breakfast and cut you a go-to-hell look? She doesn't exist."

"Huh?" That was all that came to my mind to say. "Of course she exists." And she looked good doing it, but I didn't add that to the conversation.

"Not on paper or anywhere that 'matters' to the government. She's why I believe The Church is involved, and as much as I don't want it to, it means she's involved in some way too."

"Because she's part of the cult." *Fuck, please say no.*

"No." *Thank fuck.* "But she was." *Damn. Not great.* "Which is why I wanted you to talk to her. For you to understand where these victims could be coming from." Alec grabbed his fork with more force than necessary and dug into his eggs. "Eat up. Then we'll try to talk to her before going to the police station. But we need to ease into it. I'm not sure how she'll take to you being FBI on top of already not liking you."

He smirked at that last bit. Asshole.

I shoveled the food into my mouth, barely tasting the eggs and pancakes. The faster I ate, the faster I'd get to explain to the spunky woman that I wasn't here for The Church and hopefully change her opinion of me. Why I cared so much, hell if I knew. But the idea of her thinking the worst of me made my stomach sour.

Hopefully she wouldn't distrust me once she found out I'm an FBI agent.

Or hold it against me that I had a sudden, absurd crush on her after a thirty-minute encounter from the night before. Because that wasn't creepy at all.

Only one way to find out.

4

Ellie

"I'm a damn fool," I muttered to myself. The rough edges of the zipper pressed into my fingertips as I held the windbreaker tighter, fisting the thin material, hoping it would somehow keep me warmer. Taking my break inside would've been smarter than standing out in the elements, but I wanted to put as much distance between me and the mystery man as possible.

Artificial strawberry flavor coated my tongue as I swirled the Blow Pop along the surface. Others smoked on their breaks, but me, I did this. Not that I was against smoking—didn't care one way or the other—I just didn't crave the nicotine the way others did. No, I craved the sticky-sweet artificial sugary deliciousness candy makers around the world had perfected. Like this Blow Pop.

Perfection.

Would I say that if it was available during my childhood? Who knew. Because it wasn't. Any type of candy or sweets, for that matter.

It would've been a sin to indulge in something that wasn't nourishing to the body Jacob had blessed.

I shuddered at his name. Now candy was my vice, the one thing I could turn to when I needed a reminder that I was free to do whatever I wanted. Well, kind of free.

Shoulder to the edge of the diner's siding, I huddled a little tighter to ward off the chill that had begun to sink to the bone. At my back, the diner door slammed against the frame, signaling someone had joined me, but I didn't turn and put my face to the wind. My cheeks were already wind-burned from the walk to work; I didn't need to add more.

"Ellie."

No, no, no. Devil's balls, why me?

Slowly I turned to face Alec with a fake smile. His friend stood beside him, hands buried in the pockets of a warm-looking jacket. The same man who infiltrated my dreams all night. Dreams I'd never had before of gentle hands, understanding, and pleasure. Yeah, the pleasure was what burned into my memory even still. I'd woken up hot and itchy, tangled in my damn sheets.

Those clear eyes locked with mine, and I found it hard to look away.

"We got off on the wrong foot, it seems," the mystery man said. His features were tight, almost as if this conversation was painful. "I'm Chandler Peters, by the way. I think I left that off last night."

I stared at his extended hand, glancing between it and Alec a few times before I placed my ice-cold fingers in his.

I held back a gasp when his larger hand engulfed my own, chasing the chill from my skin. "Ellie." I swirled the hard candy around my mouth, loving the way he tracked the movement of my lips. "Nice to meet you. You two friends?" I inclined my head toward Alec.

Reluctantly I tugged my hand free from the warm cocoon his offered. Shoving it into my apron, I tightened my fingers into a fist, hoping to hold on to the soft tingle his hand had erupted along my palm.

Chapter 4

Witch's tits, what is wrong with me? Maybe I was coming down with something.

The flu maybe? Wasn't this time of year flu season or something? Then the hot flashes, clammy palms, fitful sleep, and rolling stomach make sense.

I should call Ryan, the local EMT who doubled as the town's makeshift doctor, to see what he thinks of my symptoms.

"How about we talk inside," Alec said with a nod toward the door, his concerned gray eyes focused on my light jacket. Typical Alec. He was too nice for his own good. Great friend to have, protective too, but too nice for someone with jagged edges to her soul like me.

My lips parted, ready to tell him no, that I wanted to stay out here, but I swallowed the words to hold back a gasp as Chandler stepped closer, determination in his gaze. The grind of zipper teeth dragged my focus to those long fingers working the zipper of his expensive jacket down. Now directly in front of me, he shrugged out of the coat and swung it around my back.

A blanket of warmth cocooned around my shoulders, immediately seeping deep and chasing away the early signs of hypothermia. I blinked up at him, not knowing what to say or do. My mind told me to thank him the way Jacob demanded I thank him—on my knees or back—but before I could ask which he wanted, Chandler stepped back to Alec's side and smiled.

"Better?"

I nodded, a little confused. Why was he happy that I was warm? I closed the two sides with one hand while using the other to pop the sucker out of my mouth.

"Ellie." I jerked my attention from Chandler to Alec. "I wanted you to meet Chandler and discuss why he's in town." I slid my gaze back to Chandler. Without the jacket, I could see more of his strong, lean body by the way his shirt clung to his chest and arms. Witch's cunt, there went my stomach again. I was definitely coming down with something. "He's here to help identify the man responsible for the dead women we found outside town."

Like a cold bucket of water was dumped over my head, a shiver raced down my spine, my shoulders shaking with the force. Me needing to find out first couldn't be a good thing.

"Why?" I popped the sucker back in my mouth and moved it from side to side. "What does it have to do with me?"

"Alec didn't want everyone in town to know this yet, but I'm with the FBI," Chandler stated. I could almost feel his reluctance to tell me.

"Okay," I said at the same time Alec cursed and turned, putting his back to me. "I'm guessing Alec thought I'd be scared because of that."

"Guess so." A corner of his lips twitched like he wanted to smile. "Are you?"

"Depends." Alec turned back, his brows raised with surprise at my response. "Are you the good kind or the bad kind?"

That almost-smile grew to a grin. "I'd say the good kind, but I wasn't aware there was a bad. I'm a profiler with the Behavioral Science Unit."

"For real?" I stood taller with the excitement his words invoked. I'd been told my entire childhood that the FBI was bad, but I knew better after everything I'd learned these past four years. Netflix was an incredible teacher. "Like on *Criminal Minds*?"

Chandler laughed and nodded. "Yeah, something like that. You know about what I do?"

Nodding, I pulled the Blow Pop out and rolled it against my lower lip. "Sure, yeah. I binge-watched that show on Netflix last year."

"You're not intimidated by him, or hate him?" Alec asked, stepping back into our little circle. "I figured you'd need some time to warm up to the idea of him helping out."

I debated how to respond. "Anyone else, maybe, but I'm more intrigued than scared. Plus, you seem to trust him. Right?"

"I've worked with Chandler before. He's a good agent and a good guy. Yeah, I trust him."

"Then I do too. As long as we've known each other, you've never put me or the town in harm's way. If the FBI is here to help find the person behind those bodies, then I'm cool."

Alec clapped his hands and rubbed them together. "Perfect. That makes what I'm going to ask that much easier." I arched a brow in response. "We need your help, Ellie."

The lightness of the conversation evaporated, and I knew what he was about to ask. "No." Dread weighed heavy in my stomach, reminding me that I forgot to eat breakfast.

"Ellie. Just one visit, one introduction to help us get past that gate. I think these women are from that community. Hell, maybe even the bastard killing them is in there too. You can help."

"What's all this about?" Chandler asked, looking between us.

"The leader of The Church won't let me past the gate—hell, any law enforcement—to ask questions unless we bring her too." Alec grimaced when he looked my way. "Ellie was raised—"

"I said no, Alec," I snapped before he could divulge my sad little life to the hot FBI agent. I shook my head and popped the sucker back in my mouth. "I've told you before that I'll do anything to help this town except that. Don't ask me to go there, to see him. I can't." I hated that word. It made me feel weak, but it was the truth. I wasn't strong enough to face the community. My parents, Jacob, the others who shunned me when I left.

"It's fine," Chandler said in a calm tone. He should've been furious that I wasn't willing to help, but instead he sounded... understanding. "We'll get what we need another way."

I didn't dare meet his gaze, afraid I might find disappointment in my unwillingness to help. I should've said yes, but I couldn't. Not when the idea of going back made vomit rise up my throat. But if I did, and they found the evidence they needed, maybe they could shut the community down. Then I'd be free.

Free of their constant hold.

But what if they didn't, and I was forced to stay behind those gates?

I wouldn't risk it, even if it was for the greater good. Was it selfish, sure, but who would blame me? I couldn't go back there, back to the hopelessness every new day brought. I had a chance here in this town. As minuscule as it seemed, it was better than having no chance, no hope, no life behind those gates with him.

Jacob Barns.

Leader of The Church.

My husband.

My captor.

My abuser.

"Hey." I turned my face and unseeing gaze to the hand lightly gripping my bicep. This grip felt different than others before. Could a grip have different meanings? Hell yes. Some were to control, some to gain attention, others to demand. But this one, it was strong, in control, yet not controlling or harsh. I blinked at the hand and ran my gaze up the arm to Chandler's concerned face.

I shook my head, dispelling the dark thoughts and memories. What was left of the Blow Pop rolled along my tongue as I attempted to ground myself to the fact that I was free, away from Jacob and his control.

"What?" Did he say something while I was zoned out?

The back door to the diner swung open, sending the stench of cooking meat wafting up my nose.

"Break's over, Ellie. The Rotary Club just got here, and I need your help, doll."

I nodded to Sally, who shot Chandler a death glare before ducking back into the warmth of the diner.

"What was that?" I said with an amused smirk. "How could anyone get on her bad side?"

"Your friend Alec did that." Chandler shot him a fake scowl. "He said it was for privacy, but now I think it was to have someone praying for my lost soul tonight."

A rumbled chuckle from Alec had me smiling in return. "Nah, I just needed a good laugh. Sorry it was at your expense."

"No you're not," Chandler said, shaking his head.

Alec held up his hands. "Guilty."

"What if I could help in other ways?" I asked quickly before I lost the nerve. Both men turned their full, now serious attention to me. I shrank into myself a little at the intensity behind Chandler's stare. "I mean, I know everyone in this town, and if you give me the basic profile or something, I can help. You know, vet people out?"

"All those seasons of *Criminal Minds* didn't make you a cop or profiler, Ellie."

Embarrassment washed over me, heating my cheeks at Alec's admonishment. "And *Mindhunter* and every true crime documentary," I muttered under my breath.

Sure, it wasn't like going to training at Quantico, but it was better than nothing, right?

"She has a point." My head popped up, my focus on Chandler. "About knowing people in town. Being a bartender and diner waitress, she sees everyone from pancake lovers to the town drunk."

Now my cheeks burned with something new. Yep, totally sick. I needed to see Ryan as soon as possible. Maybe Alec could drop me off at the clinic on his way out so I didn't have to walk the four miles.

"This is a terrible idea," Alec said, crossing his arms across his chest. "We can't involve her in the case."

"Isn't that what you tried to do earlier when you asked me to help you get into The Church?" I questioned.

Chandler whistled and raised both brows. "She has you there, man. And good thing I'm here to override you on that decision. Ellie, welcome to the team." He pulled out his wallet and thumbed through a few bills and cards before pulling one out and holding it out to me. "Here's my cell number. Call when you're ready to go over the profile. We're headed to the police station now, so maybe later this afternoon."

I cringed at his mention of going to the station, knowing exactly who he'd see there. Brett wouldn't have forgotten Chandler's interest in me last night. He sure as hell didn't let me forget it. The bastard stuck around until closing trying to talk about the good old days when we were together. Which, if you heard his side of the story, our two years together did sound amazing. Too bad it was all a bunch of shit.

Brett was a manipulative asshole who charmed and talked his

way through life, then turned into Satan himself when things didn't go his way. Why it took me so long to break free from his hold, I had no idea. But I did. I broke free from him, from Jacob, and now I was on my own doing fine. Fine with my three jobs, and now my new side gig of helping the attractive profiler find the serial killer dumping bodies in our town.

I had to remember to keep my distance from this Chandler guy. It wasn't that long ago that I had to start all over with nothing, a second time, because I depended too much on one man. I couldn't do that again, couldn't go back to needing someone to survive.

Nope. Never again would I rely on a man. I was done with being taken advantage of, forced to shove pieces of myself down deep to make room for their likes and needs.

Never again would I lose the freedom to deny a man's access to my body.

Never again would my mind be controlled by someone else.

Never fucking again.

"Thanks for the ride, Alec," I said over my shoulder as I hopped down from the truck.

"Hey, Ellie." On a sigh, I turned and leaned against the open door. "I'm sorry I pushed you earlier. You have your reasons for staying as far away as you can, and I need to respect that." I nodded, accepting his apology. "It might not come to that, anyway. I was getting ahead of myself, hoping we'd catch a fucking lead on this case."

"Why do you think it has something to do with Jacob or someone inside The Church?"

He scrubbed at his scruffy jaw and looked to the dash. "We haven't been able to identify a single victim. Nothing in missing persons, no arrest records from fingerprints, nothing. Chandler thinks the victims were in high-risk professions or floaters of some kind, but I think it's closer to home than that. I've never met a single druggie, prostitute, hitchhiker, or anyone along those lines who didn't have a record. So how have we not been able to identify these women?"

I smacked at my gum, mulling over his assumptions. "So you think because you haven't been able to identify them the normal way, they must have been raised in The Church like me and don't have any records to connect them to." Pinching the sticky substance, I pulled it until it was a long string and wrapped it around a finger. "I can see that, I guess." An idea popped into my head. "What if I could help you in a different way?"

"Chandler already agreed to—"

"No. I'm thinking of something different. What if I could verify your assumptions that these women were from inside the community? I could look at their pictures and see if I recognize any of the victims. It was a big community, but if they grew up there, I'd know their face, especially a female."

Alec's brows furrowed. "Why especially a female?"

"School." Yeah, school. That was a better term than brainwashing camp for the females on how to submit and be a good little wife.

Alec thumped his thumb along the top of the steering wheel, staring out the windshield. "Some of the victims were in bad shape, Ellie. Think you could handle seeing that?"

I swallowed hard, pushing down my nerves. "Yeah. If it helps catch this guy, I'll make myself handle it." And I would if it meant offering what little help I could to protect this town. A town that took me in, loved me, and helped me start a life when they didn't have to. They knew where I came from and accepted me anyway.

A few, like Alec, even go as far as protecting me from the harassment I still receive from Jacob's devout followers who come into town. Apparently the bastard wanted me back. But with the protection from Alec and others, I either had to go back to Jacob willingly or risk the full force of the Texas Rangers if I was taken against my will.

And me going back willingly to that excuse of a man?

Hell. To. The. Fucking. No.

I'd rather suck Satan's dick than go back to that bastard.

"Sound good?"

I shook my head, the ends of my short hair skimming along my neck with the movement. "Huh?"

"Knew you weren't listening. I said I'll talk to Chandler about showing you the pictures, get his take."

"Oh, right. Good idea. Sounds good."

He raised a hand in goodbye. "Great. Hope you feel better." The door wasn't even fully closed before he was shifting the truck into Drive.

A cloud of dust flew up in the truck's wake as it pulled out of the parking lot. Turning into the wind, I held Chandler's coat tighter by wrapping both arms around my chest as I shuffled toward the glass door. A distinctive manly scent infiltrated my nose as I burrowed into the collar and took a sniff.

My stomach twisted as I took another deep inhale.

Yep, I was sick. Had to be the flu.

The cold metal dug into my palm and fingers as I wrapped them around the handle and gave the door a hard tug to offset the heavy wind. I stumbled inside before the door slammed closed, the toe of my too-large boot catching on the threshold. Inside I let out a long breath and stood straight, rolling my shoulders up and back. I blew a bubble, tucking a strand of black hair behind my ear with an air of nonchalance as I scanned the somewhat full waiting room.

Eight sets of eyes glared as I worked my way toward the check-in desk. A worn work boot shot out in an attempt to trip me, but I quickly sidestepped to avoid falling face-first. A small sigh of relief escaped when I reached the counter and tugged a pen from the holder to sign in.

Janice's round, wrinkled face poked around the corner. "What are you doing here, Ellie?" she asked. I felt her concerned gaze sweep over my face even though I kept my attention on the sticker sheet as I wrote my name.

Ellie.

Just Ellie.

No middle name. No last name. Hell, not even a full first name. But it was mine, the one I chose.

Chapter 4

"Not feeling so hot," I whispered. "Wanted to see Ryan to make sure it wasn't anything contagious."

Janice nodded before her eyes went wild. "You're not pregnant, are you?" she whispered, but I was pretty sure everyone in the waiting room heard her. "You did have that date last week."

Devil's balls. This damn town. Loved it. Hated it.

"No, I'm not pregnant," I said loud enough for everyone between here and Dallas to hear. Needed to cover my bases on that one so no one took that rumor back to Jacob. "I think it's the flu."

"Oh, honey, come on back. Let's get you in a room just in case." Shoving away from the desk, Janice rounded the corner to open the door separating the waiting room from the exam rooms.

A few male voices grumbled their annoyance that I was going before them, plus a few snide comments about me that I let flow through one ear and out the other.

"Don't listen to them," Janice said over her shoulder as we walked into a room. After tugging on some gloves, she pulled out a thermometer. "Let's check your temperature first."

I nodded and reluctantly slid Chandler's coat off, draping it over the red plastic chair.

"Where did you get that nice coat? A little big but expensive looking."

"A friend," I lied. "He lent it to me."

"The same boy you went out with last week?"

"No," I groaned. "And that wasn't a real date. It was dinner... at Denny's. It lasted all of an hour."

"A new boy, then."

"No, a friend," I said around the thermometer she pushed between my lips. "Nothing more."

"Well, if you ask me, you need to find a man." She shook her head while watching the numbers tick higher, tracking my temperature. "What about Ryan?" A small knowing smile twitched at her lined lips. Deep creases splayed out from them like rays of sunshine from all those years of smoking.

"We've been over this, Janice." I leaned back, placing my elbows on the exam table.

She pulled the small device from my mouth and checked the front.

"No fever."

"I'm good on my own, and if I weren't, Ryan really isn't my type," I whispered in case he was close. Ryan was a great guy, just not great for me.

"What is your type?" The sound of Velcro separating filled the room before she slid the blood pressure cuff up my thin arm. It swelled as she pumped the rubber bulb.

"I don't know." Another lie. Pretty sure sexy FBI agents were suddenly my type. Damn, two major lies in one day. I was on a one-way route to hell at this rate. "Maybe I'm destined to be alone."

"If you start collecting cats like you do key chains, then I'll be worried." She looked at the dial. "Blood pressure is good too." After pulling the cuff down my arm, she hung it back on the designated hook and grabbed the clipboard. "Tell me your symptoms."

"Hot flashes, clammy palms, and my stomach." I pushed a fist to my belly button. "It feels off. Not all the time though. Just like the hot flashes, it comes and goes."

"Sore throat?"

I swallowed to double-check. "Nope."

"Fatigue?"

"I work three jobs, Janice."

"Right, so that's a yes but normal. Chills?"

"Sometimes, but not really because I'm cold. Just more of like a tingle, I guess?"

The tap, tap, tap of her pen filled the silence as she studied her notes.

"I'm not sure what you have, but I'll leave that to Ryan." Pushing off the wall, she walked to the door and pulled it open. "I'll let him know you're here. I'm sure he'll be right in like always when you're waiting." She shot me a wink before closing the door.

I let out a sigh of relief only to suck it back in as the door rattled beneath a hard knock only moments after Janice left. The person on the other side didn't wait for a reply before swinging the door open.

I held a tight breath to calm the wave of fear that flooded through me.

It wasn't Ryan.

5

Chandler

THE TERRIBLE POLICE station coffee had cooled in the tiny Styrofoam cup, yet still I sipped the motor oil type substance as I surveyed the evidence baggies, notes, and pictures along the long fold-away table. For the tenth time in the last hour, I circled the cheap table, each time snagging something to add to the victim board I'd constructed on the back wall. This was always the first thing I did when starting a case. It helped me visualize the timeline and similarities and differences between each murder.

Under victim seven, I secured the first picture taken of the body. Undisturbed, naked, dumped in the abandoned field like trash. That was exactly how this unsub saw women. At least that was what I initially concluded.

But now with the note carved into her body, I was back to square one.

The physical abuse, vaginal and anal tearing, and raw rings around their wrists and ankles told of a man who used his victims to fulfil his whims. Without knowing when these women were abducted, we had no idea how long they were held and abused before being stabbed in the heart.

That was the cause of death for all the victims, but the recent one was different than the others with the *number* of stab wounds.

Thirty-eight.

The victims all had a single, large blade stab wound to the center of the heart. Meaning their deaths were agonizing, slowly bleeding out and losing the ability to function without blood pumping needed oxygen to their bodies. But with this final victim, only sheer rage would drive this change in signature. Plus the light bruising around each wound was evidence of the anger behind each blow.

But what had pushed him over the edge? And would it happen again?

I shook my head as all the unknowns swirled around me.

"I expect you to clean that up before you're gone."

I didn't turn from the murder wall to acknowledge the fucker who spoke. Of course with my luck, the police chief of this shitty town was the very same boyfriend of Ellie's who harassed me last night at the bar.

"And I won't be gone until I do this." I waved a hand to the wall I'd worked on for well over two hours. "And catch the bastard who abducted and then brutally abused and murdered these women."

"They could've asked for it."

My blood boiled at his words and haughty tone. Inclining my neck one way, then the other, I stretched out the tension building there while cracking my knuckles to prevent myself from committing blatant murder in a police station. Pretty sure that wouldn't win any points with the town if I strangled their asshole police chief with my bare hands. No matter how much I wanted to.

"You think a woman would ask to be abducted, held captive, raped, and murdered?" I didn't try to hide the disgust from my tone. "To be used against their will?"

"I know one who likes it rough." The snark in his voice was like nails on a chalkboard.

Chapter 5

At that I turned, clasping my trembling hands behind my back. If I wasn't careful, they might find their way around his throat.

"Liking it rough and rape are not the same. Quite frankly, you suggesting it could be says more about your lack of sexual expertise and your sexist ego than it does about any woman and their preferences."

The sight of Chief Swann's face turning a nice shade of purple at the nicely constructed verbal slap almost made a smile tug at my lips.

"How'd you know, homo?"

I lifted my gaze to a large water damage spot on the ceiling. "Wow. News spreads fast in this town, doesn't it?"

He puffed out his chest like that was a compliment.

"Swann, stand the fuck down." The asshole stiffened as Alec came up behind him, his glare at the back of Swann's head promising death. "Either help with the case or get out of our way."

Swann held both hands in the air in surrender while turning to face Alec. "I meant no harm." I let out an indignant huff at the obvious lie. "You boys are supposed to be professionals, so I'll leave you to it. Good luck."

Only once Alec slammed the flimsy fake wood door closed did I trust myself to release my tightly clasped fingers.

"I hate that son of a bitch so much," Alec snapped, tossing another hate-filled glare at the closed door. "He doesn't deserve that badge. Gives all officers a bad name the way he flaunts and abuses his power."

I nodded before turning back to the murder wall, staring at a picture of victim number two, but my mind was stuck on what Swann said about Ellie's preferences. "How in the hell does that work?"

"What?" Alec moved to stand beside me, hands on his hips. "The stab wounds? It takes a knife and a hell of a lot of force for that."

"I know how stab wounds work, asshole. I'm talking about your friend Ellie and that waste-of-space police chief being together."

"Oh, that."

When he didn't follow up with any explanation, I turned and faced him, crossing my arms over my chest. Good thing it was warm in the station or I'd be missing the coat I lent Ellie. Call it a good deed or insurance to make sure I saw her again; either way it made something in my chest pulse at the sight of her wearing it.

"Nothing else to add?"

"Yeah, well." He scrubbed his face, drawing his palm along his square jaw. "That's her story to tell, but I can tell you they aren't together anymore."

I swallowed down the rush of relief so he wouldn't see how much that revelation affected me. "Really? That's not what he said last night when he tried to fight me in the bar for talking to her."

Alec turned to face the table, running his fingers along the surface, disturbing the pictures and evidence baggies. "I'm sure he'd say that. Didn't take it well when Ellie finally had the balls to walk away from him." He knocked a knuckle against the wood in quick succession. "I never understood it, honestly." His gray eyes met mine. "How she could leave one abuser for another who teeters on the line between asshole and abusive. I'm guessing you've seen it before and have a theory as to why a woman would do that."

I dipped my chin. Hard plastic dug into my palms as I leaned forward, bracing myself on the back of a cheap chair. "It's common, but the why can vary from woman to woman. Not knowing her background or how she met Swann, I don't want to assume anything. But I can say it is very normal, and if she ever questions it, you should tell her that. Not encourage her to allow that behavior to be directed toward her, but that she isn't a freak or broken because she did."

Alec huffed. "I've told her that. Even done my own research to help support her more than just offering protection from Swann and Jacob."

I tilted my head at the name. "Jacob?"

"The Church's leader."

My knuckles lost their color as my grip tightened on the chair from the building frustration directed at my friend. He knew her, knew her background and her life, and seemed to care for her. That shouldn't piss me off, but it fucking did.

"You seem to know a lot about her. You like her?" *Please no.* Not sure why I was adamantly against him having feelings for Ellie, but jealousy was quickly overtaking my normally rational thoughts.

"Nah." I relaxed, my shoulders falling as I took a calming breath. The way he said the single word, his soft tone, made me believe him. "She's just a sweet girl who had it rough and somehow found the courage to walk away from the only life she'd ever known. I respect the hell out of her and want to help without expecting anything in return. But I can tell you I'm not the norm."

"Meaning?"

"Well, you've seen her. She's beautiful and all alone in the world. Others see that as an opening to take advantage of the situation."

"Like dipshit Swann."

He nodded. "Like dipshit Swann."

"I hate him even more now," I grumbled.

A smirk erased the anger from his features, and a mischievous spark lit his eyes as he hitched his chin my way. "I'll ask you the same question, Chandler. Do you like her? We're friends, worked together before, and this might be the first time you've shown this level of interest in someone who wasn't a suspect or dead."

I rolled my eyes with an indignant huff as I crossed my arms. Realizing what I'd just done, I relaxed them at my side, hoping he didn't catch the defensive reaction to his observation. He was right. I normally reserved this amount of attention to detail to aspects of the case and the victims, not random beautiful locals who had me entranced with a single glance.

"Yeah, well, she's interesting, I guess. That's it." Lie. Such a blatant lie. And by the twitch of Alec's lips, he knew. "Shut the fuck up." I waved a hand, dismissing the entire conversation, and turned back to the victim wall. "Did you run the prints against the federal database too?" I knew he did but didn't know what else to say to divert us back to discussing the case and not my fascination with Ellie.

"Yep. Nothing from the prints or DNA. Still waiting to hear back on the bones they found."

Digging through my bag, I pulled the last two pieces of gum from the plastic casing and popped both into my mouth simultaneously.

"What about towns around here? Do they process fingerprints when someone is arrested?"

"Sure." I glanced over my shoulder at a shuffling sound. Alec stretched his hands high, nearly touching the ceiling, and it wasn't that low. The big fucker was tall, stocky, and a good guy—the perfect cop. "But whether they enter them into a national database?" He dropped his hands and shrugged. "I don't see why they wouldn't."

"Do you think Chief Swann would ever not book someone if they were open to paying him in other ways?"

"Sexually, you mean?"

"You're quick for a Texan."

Alec barked a laugh. "Fucker. So what are you suggesting?"

"Nothing, just tossing ideas out there. What if these women were high-risk, moving from town to town and staying under the radar, but when they were caught, they offered themselves up as payment instead of being processed?"

"Or they could be from The Church."

"Or that." I sighed. "I really don't want that to be the case though."

"Ellie said she'd look at the pictures to see if she recognized any of the women. That's an easy way to test my theory if she won't help us get inside."

I nodded. "Good idea. How long has she been out?"

"Four years or so."

"These women all seem to be about her age. What are the odds they joined The Church between the time she left and now? Are they actively recruiting?"

"Always. You seen their website?"

"Such propaganda bullshit."

"It works. People flock through here wanting to learn more about it. A lot of lost people searching for a place to belong."

His words ran on a loop as I stared at the seven victims.

"What if these aren't high-risk like I thought? What if they were some of the few who came through wanting to learn about The Church?" I paced from one end of the wall to the other, looking at the women in more detail. "They wouldn't be runaways, then, or addicts or prostitutes but young women who went on their own to find a better life."

"That leads us back to Jacob's group, doesn't it?"

"Yes, or someone who preyed on these women before they ever made it into the compound. Is there a waiting period before they'll allow someone entry?"

"Not sure how they work, honestly. We'd have to ask their security about that."

"It's something to consider. Let's put that on our list of possibilities. Once we figure out how he's hunting them, then we're one step closer to finding him." Turning on my heels, I laced both hands behind my head and inhaled deep. "I'm hungry. You?"

"I could always eat. There's a Golden Chick down the way about fifteen minutes." He hooked a thumb over his shoulder without looking away from victim number four. "I can go."

I slapped a hand between his shoulder blades. "Nope, I'm going. I need to get out of here to clear my head. The alone time will help me process all this and strategize our next steps."

"I'll take a number three and six." I laughed. "What? I ran eight miles this morning before meeting you. What did you do, lanky ass?"

I smiled and shook my head. "I slept in a chair last night. I wasn't in the mood to start the morning with a run."

"About that. The house I'm renting has another bedroom. You're welcome to it." I shook my head, ready to say, "Thanks but no thanks," until he cut me off. "I hired Ellie to clean the house. She'll be there daily between four and five."

"How many jobs does that woman have?"

"Too many. It's a hard go when you have to be paid under the table." I raised my brows, not understanding. "Born in the cult, so that means no social, no birth certificate, remember? Ellie doesn't exist, which means everyone here has to pay her in cash."

"And the reason why she hasn't left." Alec nodded solemnly. "Poor girl."

"Don't go feeling bad for her. That would be a quick way to be saddled in the friend zone."

I narrowed my eyes. "Who says I want to be outside the friend zone?"

"The way you get all intense and focused when she's around. Just an observation." His cheeks bunched with a wide smile, crescent moon indentations deepening at the corners of his lips. "Just trying to help a friend out. She deserves someone who looks at her the way you do."

"And how's that?"

His smile dropped. "Protective instead of possessive. She's been possessed her entire life. That woman deserves to have more than me fighting in her corner. So, you want to claim that other room or stay at the motel where a murder-suicide happened last year?"

Fairly positive that was the room I slept in last night. Add in the opportunity to see Ellie daily, and how could I refuse?

After graciously accepting his offer, I left the police station, my stomach growling as I climbed into the rental truck.

I stared out the windshield as the engine warmed, my thoughts on the case. It was proving to be more complex than we initially profiled. And, for the first time, I was okay with the possibility of staying longer. That meant more time with one blue-eyed woman.

Whether she felt the same or not... only time would tell.

One thing was for certain: if—and that was a big if—anything went past pleasantries and discussing the case, I needed to be cautious, take things slow. Based on the slivers of information Alec revealed about her past and what I'd witnessed of her zoning out on occasion, the trauma she'd sustained was deep.

Which didn't scare me. If anything, it made her that much more intriguing.

Maybe I could even help in some way. Show her that a destiny could be altered with some help.

And maybe, if what I felt when she was around stayed true, she could help me too.

Catch a serial killer, help a woman overcome some of her trauma, and make myself feel again.

Sounded like a win-win to me.

6

Ellie

Worst. Day. Ever.

Okay, that wasn't true. I'd had worse in the past.

Fine.

Worst. Day. This. Week.

I chafed my hands up and down both arms, hating even more now that I was out in the elements that the asshole took my coat. Scratch that. Chandler's coat. *Devil's balls, I bet he'll be pissed.* A shiver of apprehension raced down my spine at the thought of someone like him mad with that anger directed at me.

Wait. If I was apprehensive, then why did my stomach go all twisty again? And why would that make the normally dormant area between my thighs pulse? Hell, maybe Ryan's diagnosis of exhaustion was wrong. None of these bodily reactions were normal.

What remained of the dead grass along the road's shoulder twisted beneath my boots as I stomped toward job number two. Sure, I worked a lot, but I enjoyed it, which most people didn't understand.

After breaking things off with Brett, I was alone, penniless, and without anywhere to live. I swore I'd never be that dependent on a man again and picked up every cash-paying job that was offered to support myself. But it was about more than the money. It was nice being busy. Too many hours in my shithole of an apartment reminded me of just how alone I truly was.

No family, no friends. The weight of loneliness became too much to bear at times. Which was why I had so many jobs. That and to support my Netflix and candy addiction. Mostly the Netflix. Candy was cheap. Cheap and delicious.

At least the wind had calmed a little through the day. Now instead of blowing thirty miles an hour, it was at a breezy fifteen. Still chilly but better than the cold air blowing so hard it cut through your clothes and skin.

The broken Golden Chick sign in the distance appeared close, but I knew it was still over a mile away. I sighed and moved to cup my cold fingers over my mouth, but the tight pull of my right bicep halted the motion.

I should've done more when that jackass grabbed me to remind me how displeased Jacob was that I hadn't returned to his side. But besides having memorized every move from several hundred action movies, I had no way to defend myself. So instead of fighting back, I curled in on myself and nodded as he relayed Jacob's message for me.

I really wanted that man to die.

Then I'd be free... right?

Yeah, that was the million-dollar question. Would I ever be free when, according to the world, I was never even born?

A boulder suddenly jutted out from the ground directly in front of my boots, which were slightly too big to begin with since I bought them at a yard sale, catching the toe. A scream lodged in my chest as I whirled my arms to stay upright but failed to defeat gravity.

Loose particles of asphalt, some coyote scat, and glass dug into my bare knees and palms as I fell to the ground. On all fours, I cringed at the tightness in my bicep, turning unbearable as it helped support my weight. Shifting back to my heels, I sat back and lifted my face to the sky, eyes closed.

Destiny was a damn bitch. It wasn't bad enough that I'd already had a bad day, but she had to go and top it off with this. At least no one was around to see the fall.

"Ellie?"

Kill me now. Someone. Anyone. End my misery.

Slowly peeling my lashes apart, I turned to the idling black Chevy truck. From my spot on the ground, I couldn't see who was in the driver seat, but I didn't need to. I'd already memorized his voice. Plus only one man seemed to make my body go haywire at his mere presence.

"Yeah," I said on a groan as I pushed off the ground. Keeping my focus on the road's decaying shoulder, I dusted off my palms and bent forward to do the same with my knees.

"You want a lift?"

I could hug him for not asking why I was kneeling on the road. Maybe he thought I was worshipping the winter landscape. I surveyed said landscape—dry, dusty, dead. Yeah, he probably wouldn't buy that.

I opened my mouth to refuse but thought better of it. "Sure, thanks."

Reaching for the door handle, my fingertips barely brushed the cold metal when the door magically swung open. Confused at what just happened, I glanced between the open door and the man who was quickly infiltrating all my thoughts as he leaned over the center console, hand extended.

"I can get in on my own," I said, still not understanding why his hand was on the seat.

"Oh, I'm sure you can, but where I was raised we open the door for a woman, and I knew you wouldn't give me a chance to round the truck and open it from the outside."

"Okay." That was all I could think to say back. I slid the strap of my bag from my shoulder and tossed it to the floorboard before climbing inside the warm cab.

Once I was inside, he straightened and placed both hands on the wheel, smirking as he stared out the windshield without making a move to put the truck in Drive.

"Where you headed?" he asked.

"Golden Chick."

"Funny. Me too. Lunch for me and Alec." Thumping his thumb on the steering wheel, he continued to stare out the windshield, not turning as he talked. "One of your many jobs, I guess?"

I nodded and reached forward to warm my cold fingers in front of the heater. I hissed as my sore arm stretched, the muscle cramping.

"What happened?" he demanded, turning his full focus on me. Those clear blue eyes scanned from the top of my head down to the scuffed toes of my Doc Martens. "And where's my coat?"

"I, um, left it?" I cringed toward the door, knowing the lie was a terrible one. Lying to a profiler was probably the worst idea I'd ever had. He'd see right through it and be even more mad that I lied to him.

Heavy silence filled the truck's cab, the whirl of the blowing heat the only sound. Biting the corner of his lip, Chandler nodded as a resigned look washed over his features.

"Do you not feel comfortable telling me what really happened?" Disappointment radiated off him, making me question my hesitancy to tell him the truth.

"Honestly?" The armrest dug into my back as I leaned against the door.

"That's all I ask, ever, Ellie. If you want to... work together"—was it just me or did he seem like he wanted to say something other than the word "work"—"then I need you to trust me, and I need to trust you. Think you can do that?"

"What happened today doesn't have anything to do with the case though."

"But it does concern you, and you're working with me." He shrugged like he didn't care one way or another. Very slowly he released the tight grip he had on the steering wheel and reached for the gearshift. After throwing it into Drive with more force than

I'd ever seen anyone use, he returned the hand to the steering wheel.

"Would it help you trust me?" I asked. Chandler dipped his chin in acknowledgment as he started back down the road toward Golden Chick. "Okay, well, someone took it is the short version."

"As in someone stole it?"

"As in someone stole it because it was yours, and I was wearing it."

Fine lines spread from the corners of his narrowed eyes. Flexing one hand and then the other, Chandler readjusted his grip like he needed to stretch out some tension from his long fingers.

"Was it Swann?"

"Ryan?" I chuckled. "No, Ryan wouldn't hurt a fly."

He shot a curious glance my way before refocusing on the road. "No, Chief Swann."

"No. I haven't seen him today. By your tone, I'm guessing he left a lasting impression today at the station?"

"You could say that."

"Yeah, he does that." I eyed him. "Don't think less of me because I dated him, okay? We've been broken up for a while, and... well, the reason we were together is a long story. Plus he's a different person when he needs to be."

"I could see that. It's classic manipulative behavior from a narcissistic asshole."

"Damn, you're good at this profiling stuff." I smiled despite the day I'd had.

"That one wasn't hard to identify." The frown that had turned his lips down lessened before vanishing altogether.

"Am I? Hard to profile, that is." *Where did that come from?* No way in Hades did I want him to see through to what made me... well, me. Yet a small part was excited about the prospect of him digging to my darkest memories, releasing them out into the world.

"You're the toughest one yet." He shot me a wink. "So who was the guy, then."

"The guy?"

"Who stole my coat and somehow hurt your arm." Reflexively, I cradled the injured arm to my chest and grasped the elbow in a gentle hold. "Yep, that one. Don't try to hide things from me, Ellie." An excited gleam seemed to brighten his eyes. "I see more than you realize."

Is it hot? It was definitely hot in the truck. I swallowed against a dry throat and cleared it of the weirdness building there.

"A messenger for Jacob. He doesn't like other people touching his property, apparently."

"You being the property, I'm guessing." I side-eyed him at the deep, menacing tone he'd taken on and nodded. "You know that's not true, right? Women aren't property. *You're* not property."

"Well," I said hesitantly, not wanting to bring this small detail up, "we are married, so I kind of am."

The seat belt jerked, tightening against my chest when the truck came to a screeching halt. The back fishtailed as we skidded along the asphalt. When we finally came to a complete stop, my head popped back against the headrest.

"What the hell was that?" I exclaimed, my heart in my throat. "Did you almost hit something? Was it an armadillo? I bet it was an armadillo. Those assholes are everywhere. Next time just hit the ugly creature. Fuck." My pulse raced with the rush of adrenaline.

At his silence, I stopped searching the side mirror for the animal that almost killed us and twisted toward the driver seat. Face flushed, lips pursed, Chandler had turned in his seat, facing me head-on.

"What?" I questioned. "They're ugly and carry diseases."

"There are too many things about that single statement."

"Are we talking about the armadillo?" I tilted my head, trying to figure out why he looked so upset. Clearly I didn't understand something.

"There wasn't an armadillo, Ellie. I'm talking about what you said about being married and property."

"Oh, that."

Chandler shook his head and massaged his forehead. Once, twice his lips parted like he had something to say but couldn't find the right words. "Did you want to marry him?"

"Um, it was more of a known thing than a choice. I was 'the chosen one,'" I said with air quotes.

"Right," he said, his jaw tight. Clearly this conversation was pissing him off for some reason. Not sure why, since I was the one married to that asshole Jacob. "Did you sign a marriage certificate?"

"Marriage certificate?"

"See?" He waved a hand in my direction like I'd made some kind of groundbreaking point. "If it wasn't your choice and there's no documentation, you're not married, technically. Unless you want to be." I shook my head at his questioning expression. "Good. And the property part, even if you were legally married, that's not how marriage works. You are never property, married or not. You are your own person, have your own choices and consequences. No one owns you. You're free to do what you want. Do you understand that, Ellie?"

I nodded despite the fact that his words battled against my childhood training. What he said made sense, and I knew it was accurate based on what I'd seen on TV shows and with couples around town. But I was different, wasn't I? Our marriage contracts were different in The Church. But did that contract apply outside the community?

"Ellie." I turned from the dash, blinking away the fog that had covered my vision. "You zone out a lot, you know that?"

"Yeah." I dug through my purse, searching for whatever candy I had stashed at the bottom. A fingertip swiped across a flexible plastic wrapper. Gripping the tiny candy, I withdrew the green Jolly Rancher, unwrapped it and popped it in my mouth. "I have a lot going on up here constantly," I said around the hard candy while pointing to my head. "Sometimes I get lost in it. Candy helps though."

"That's normal, considering."

"Yeah?"

Sighing, Chandler turned back to face the windshield. After a moment, the truck shifted as we continued to our destination once again.

"You're a curious one, Ellie."

"Thanks?"

He chuckled at my response. "I like it. It's a nice change. So tell me something about yourself."

"Like what?" I held my breath, hoping he didn't want to hear about my past.

"I don't know. Clearly you don't want to talk about your past." My brows rose with surprise. "You have a very expressive face. Let's start small. Tell me something you want, something you dream about."

I said the first thing that popped into my head. "To live."

His brows furrowed, a thick line forming between them, but he kept his focus on the empty road. "You don't feel like you're living now?"

I huffed a humorless laugh and leaned back against the seat. "I don't think anyone in this town is."

"Point taken." The heel of his hand pressed against the steering wheel, he circled, turning the truck into Golden Chick's parking lot. Only two other cars sat in the lot, both of which I recognized as fellow workers. "Here. How long is your shift?"

"Oh, this won't take me too long." I swirled the apple green hard brick around my tongue. "The GM knows my situation and pays me to come a few times a week to deep clean the bathrooms and eating area." A sense of appreciation swelled at the thought of the man and how he offered this side gig knowing I needed the cash. "He's a good guy."

The canvas strap of my purse dug into my palm, indenting little grooves into my skin as I gripped it tight. Reluctantly I reached for the door, knowing this rare moment was coming to an end. I didn't want to bust the little bubble in the warm truck with us talking, even unboxing my issues and setting the record straight. But he and I, this moment, was over, and no matter how much I wanted this to never end, it wasn't in the cards. I was me and he was him. This was fun, a nice distraction, but time to get back to reality.

A gust of chilled air rushed through the truck when Chandler pushed the driver side door open and stepped out, causing me to shiver. Disappointment gripped my heart, making it ache. He was clearly ready to end the moment I was having a difficult time letting go of. He probably saw through to the mess that I hid beneath a strong, happy exterior. Maybe he'd discovered that I was broken beyond repair.

The sting of rejection made me cringe. I was a fool. This man didn't want someone like me. A no one. Hell, he didn't even ask for a favor in return for driving me to work. Which meant he didn't feel the same... warmth as I did when we were close. Or find me as attractive as I did him.

Now that sucked. The first guy who I liked and wanted to touch me, or to at least reciprocate the attraction, didn't feel the same.

Destiny really was a witch's cold cunt.

I jerked out of my reverie when the door swung open, revealing a smiling Chandler gripping the metal edge.

"Ready?" he asked.

Awesome, now he's rushing me out of the truck to get away from me. Obviously being around me was torture and he couldn't take another minute.

I tightened my grip on the purse strap and swung both legs out the door. My boots met the pavement with a stomp.

"Thanks for the ride," I whispered, keeping my face toward the blacktop, not wanting him to see how much his rejection hurt. "Someone at the front counter will take your order."

I stepped around him, ready to give him the space he obviously wanted, when he placed a gentle hand on my shoulder and slowly turned me to face where he stood with arms crossed.

"Not so fast, Ellie. How bad does that arm hurt?" He hitched his chin toward the bicep that asshole at the clinic nearly snapped in two.

"Not bad," I lied. He arched a blond brow and pursed his lips, clearly not believing me. I rolled my eyes. "Yeah, it hurts, okay? But I'll be fine." Fake smile plastered across my face, I took a step back toward the front door.

Chandler's ice blue eyes sliced through the lie to the truth beneath that I was desperate to keep hidden. I couldn't let him see I needed help. No, I would do this alone. Never again would I be indebted to a man because of a kindness they offered.

Brett Swann taught me that lesson the hard way.

His loud clap startled me. "Well, then I have no choice but to do the gentlemanly thing here." He smiled as he towered over my small frame, the toes of his boots pressing against my own. A soft lovesick sigh caught in my chest as I tipped my head back to take in his handsome face. "Well, I do have a choice, but I'm choosing the one that's selfish on my part."

"What are you talking about?" I took a step back and held my purse close to my chest as a shield from his sexiness.

"I'm talking about telling Alec to get his own damn lunch and me sticking around to help you."

"No, you're not helping me with anything." I shook my head. "I'm fine. And I won't be indebted to you."

Something passed over his face—sadness, disappointment I couldn't tell—which caused his smile to slip.

"Ellie, I want to help because I can, not because I expect anything from you after."

I wet my lips and shifted from one foot to the other. He was incredibly hard to read. First he wanted to get away from me and now he was suggesting he stick around to help? What was in it for him? "You said it was selfish on your part. Why?"

"Didn't miss that slipped confession, did you?" He rubbed at the top of his short, military-style hair.

"Nope," I said, but my heart hammered against my chest, wondering what he was about to admit. "What did you mean?"

"It gives me a reason to hang out with you for a little longer."

"Why would you want that?" I asked, the words shaky from the cold and nerves. *What game is he playing?* "What's in it for you?"

He let out an embarrassed chuckle and turned toward the glass front door. Red bloomed along his cheeks. "I guess I don't want this to end just yet. So how about this. Let me help you here, and then we'll head to Alec's to go over the profile."

I started to nod but stopped when his words sank in. "How do you know Alec's house is where I'm headed next?"

"Alec mentioned you'd be coming by when he offered me the spare bedroom so I don't have to stay at the motel up the road again." He shuddered, revulsion flashing across his features. "After staying there last night and having to sleep in a chair because I couldn't stomach sleeping on the small murder scene on my mattress, I gratefully took him up on his offer. Is that okay?"

"Yeah, sure. Of course that works for me." I chomped on the Jolly Rancher, breaking it into several small pieces. "Um, don't think this is rude or that I'm ungrateful for the help or anything, but I'm not sure someone like you knows how to clean a bathroom."

That smile widened, showing off his straight teeth and transforming his face, somehow making him even more handsome. "Someone like me?"

I waved up and down his clean dark-wash jeans and deep black Henley. "A rich FBI profiler who has better things to do with his time than help a no one like me clean a bathroom."

A gust of wind brushed my chin-length hair across my face, obscuring my view of Chandler. I tucked the stray lock behind my ear and held it as I waited for his response.

"Ah." He glanced down at his attire and shook his head. "Don't let this look fool you. You wouldn't have known this, but before I was a profiler, I served as a Marine."

I furrowed my brows, not understanding the connection between being a Marine and cleaning bathrooms. "That's great, but it still doesn't answer my question. If you want to stay and help, well, knowing how to clean is part of the helping part."

"Sassy. I like it," he said with a wink. *Devil's balls, there goes my twisty stomach again.* "As a Marine, I was trained how to clean a latrine with a single toothbrush and my own spit and make that fucker shine."

I grimaced. "That doesn't sound sanitary. You really should use cleaning products."

Chandler laughed again, this time longer and deeper. I beamed at the accomplishment.

"Come on, dark and mysterious," he said, extending a hand. "Let's get this done so we can move on to catching a killer."

Without a second thought, I raised my hand and placed it in his. For the second time that day, a burst of warmth and a tingle of excitement bloomed from the simple connection and flared within me, making my breath catch when he wrapped those long fingers around my own, engulfing my entire hand.

With his slight tug, I willingly trailed behind him, trusting the man I'd met less than twenty-four hours ago more than any other I'd met in my entire life.

That had to mean something.

Right?

7

Ellie

I'D SEEN attractive men in the movies and on TV shows, but watching a man, in person, on his hands and knees scrubbing a toilet so I didn't have to was the sexiest thing I'd ever witnessed. Cold seeped from the chipped tile through my diner uniform, cooling my overheated skin as I leaned against the bathroom wall watching Chandler finish cleaning the men's bathroom. He already did the lobby and women's bathroom, better than I ever had, which was saying a lot. As a female in The Church, I was trained from an early age how to clean until the house shined like the men deserved.

A perfect ultra-submissive female to fuck, whether they were willing or not, as long as they were of age, and take care of the house chores was what each woman was expected to mold into if they wanted to stay behind those gates long term.

I suspected it was all backward, but it wasn't until I left the cult that I saw how the world outside the community viewed women in a more positive light. We weren't born just to be used and abused. We had rights and dreams. There was equality out in the real world. Maybe not full equality in some areas but still way better than what I was led to believe was normal my entire life. Of course, those two years I stayed with Brett after I escaped Jacob's firm hold didn't help with the conflicting ideals regarding a woman's purpose in life. But watching Chandler sweating, his fingers red and raw from scrubbing grout because he wanted to do something kind for me and not expecting anything in return, discredited those submissive ideals I was taught.

Well, most of them. A part of me was still suspicious that he'd expect something in the end.

They always did.

"And done." Sitting back on the heels of his boots in front of the sink, he shot a proud grin my way. "See? Told you I knew how to clean." He flicked his wrist to illuminate the digital watch screen. "And in less than an hour. Boom. Winning at life."

I laughed, just barely holding in the snort that wanted to erupt, and smirked. "So you're vying for my job now? Pretty sure your job as a profiler is way cooler than doing this."

"Hell no," he exclaimed. "That"—he pointed to the bathroom—"was way too much work."

I shook my head, straight black locks sliding from behind my ear and tickling my face. Annoyed that it wouldn't stay tucked away, I shoved it behind my ear.

Chandler stood with a groan, a hand on his lower back as he arched and twisted. The shirt rose a little with the movement, showing off a sliver of taut muscles beneath. "Let's get out of here. I'm starving."

On the way out, I stopped in the manager's office and grabbed the envelope with my cash for the day's work. I shoved the plain white envelope down to the bottom of my purse as I maneuvered through the small kitchen. Out front, Chandler was busy ordering half the menu as I slipped past the counter, hoping to make it to the front door before he noticed.

"Ellie, you want something?" he asked.

Chapter 7

I paused. Not turning, I shouted over my shoulder, "No, thanks. I'm not hungry."

Shoulders to my ears, I cringed, knowing he read through the lie, and prepared to be called out. But he didn't make a single comment, didn't draw attention to my refusal of the deep-fried murdered chicken. At the door, I zoned out, staring at the soft blues and pinks highlighting the horizon while I waited for Chandler. It was picturesque the way the entire sky was bathed in soft colors. I had heard through others that the Texas sunset was unbeatable in its beauty. I'd have to take their word for it since I'd never have a chance to see another to compare it to.

A protective presence crowded close to my back. Keeping my gaze out the glass, staring past the brand's gold stickers plastered to the door, I exhaled a measured breath.

"Is it true that a Texas sunset can't be beat?" I asked absentmindedly. When he didn't immediately respond, I turned, resting my chin on my shoulder.

"So I've heard."

"Don't you travel a ton to know from experience?"

"I do, but I'd venture to say it's how the person views the sunset or who they view it with that makes it beautiful, not the location. Take me, for instance. I've seen the sun set in almost every state, plus a few different countries, but I've never paid attention to its natural beauty. So right now, for me, a Texas sunset can't be beat because for the first time, I'm really seeing it."

"Devil's balls, that's some line." My high pitch drew his attention from the sunset to me. Smiling despite myself, I pressed my backside to the glass and pushed the door open for him, holding it until he walked through. On the sidewalk, I rubbed at my arms, remembering the coat incident and that I was still wearing the diner waitress uniform from this morning.

"Ready?" Chandler called out from where he stood beside the truck, holding the passenger side door open.

"Yeah, but any chance we can stop by my place before we go to Alec's?" My steps slowed as I approached the truck. Tossing my purse to the floorboard, I gripped his extended hand for help into the tall cab. "I swear I'll be quick, and I can pay you for gas or give you a free pancake tomorrow." I cringed at my rambling. "Please." I gave an exaggerated look to my outfit. "I'd rather not stay in this getup."

My cheeks warmed when he had to rip his attention from the expanse of thigh that the short skirt exposed. I tugged at the hemline, suddenly self-conscious that he didn't like what he saw.

"I don't mind swinging by your place, but I will take that free pancake you offered." A megawatt smile spread across his face, displaying his bright white, straight teeth. "Plus one of whatever you have in there." He tipped his head toward my purse. "I left my stash of gum at the station."

I bit my lower lip to hide a smirk as I shook my head. "My stash is limited at the moment. Long day." I shrugged. "You can go through the candy bowl at my place though." Just as he started to close the door, it hit me. "Wait, how did you know I hoard candy in there?"

"I see everything, remember?"

With that, he double-checked that I was safely tucked into the truck before slamming the door shut. I watched, mouth slightly gaping, as he rounded the hood. *When was the last time someone paid this much attention to me without ulterior motives?*

Back inside the truck, Chandler pressed the start button and shifted into Reverse. Eyes on the video screen displaying the backup camera's view, he maneuvered the truck out of the parking space.

"What do you want from me, really?" I asked, side-eyeing him to watch his reaction. "You know I won't help you get past The Church's gates. So why do all this? Why be so nice when you don't have to?" I held my breath, expecting a selfish or sexual response like others had in the past. Men were men, all the same, right?

He lifted one shoulder in a noncommittal shrug and switched hands on the steering wheel. "Nothing you're thinking, I'm sure, but I can't explain why I can't walk away from this. All I know is I feel happier when I'm around you and don't feel the weight of life pressing on my shoulders. Hanging out with you, it's...."

"Boring? Hard work? Too much?" I responded for him.

"I was going to say real."

"Oh. Well, there's that, I guess."

"Not what you were expecting?"

"No. I'm used to people having ulterior motives."

"And by people, you mean men. Because you seemed friendly with that woman from the bar last night and the other waitress today."

"Right, men. It's a long story. But when you've grown up the way I did, you find it hard to trust people at their word. Because you're a man, I can't process the idea that you did all that today without wanting anything from me in return. That's not the way I was told life worked."

"As in?"

I cleared my throat and fidgeted with the hem of my skirt. "As in you did something nice for me, so now I need to do something for you in return." I turned to look out the window, hoping he got the hint that I didn't want to go into any more detail. How do you tell a guy that you were trained to thank a man by giving him access to your body any way he wanted?

Thankfully he understood my nonverbal response and let the conversation drop.

I directed him toward my apartment complex. Apprehension swelled within me, heating me to the point of sweating as the truck drew closer to the low-rent side of town. Who was I kidding? The entire town was low rent; I just lived in the lower low-rent side, also known as the slums. But I called it home. A lot of great—and a few not-so-great—people called it home.

I caught him watching me out of the corner of his eye as I shifted uneasily in the seat.

"I don't have to go in," he murmured as he pulled into the complex. "I can tell you're nervous."

I swallowed hard, taking in the two-story apartment building and imagining what Chandler was thinking about my home. Rusted metal railings that needed to be painted years ago lined the upper level, outward facing doors spaced close together down the first floor and second, and an empty swimming pool in the center of the parking lot that clearly hadn't held water in years. A few cats, two stray dogs, and people of all ages, sizes, and color mingled along the stairs and sidewalks as he drove through the lot.

"I'm not nervous about you," I whispered. Wiping my sweaty palms down my bare thighs, I swallowed past the rising anxiety. A few spaces away, a familiar neighbor stood from his plastic lawn chair, a deep scowl on his face as he stared down the truck. "Listen, I appreciate you bringing me here, but don't tell anyone you're a federal agent, okay?"

"What is up with everyone hating me because of my employer?" he grumbled.

"And whatever you see or hear, forget it happened."

He paused, a hand hovering over the door handle. Turning, he narrowed his eyes, zeroing his focus in on me. "I don't know if I can do that, Ellie. If I see someone being abused or taking advantage—"

I waved both hands in front of my chest to stop him from thinking the worst. "Oh no, nothing like that. More like... drugs. Low-level ones." His brows rose. "Not me, but maybe a few of my neighbors. Or some people might be 'borrowing' other people's Netflix logins and Wi-Fi passwords." I cringed. "That last part could be me."

Tipping his head back, Chandler laughed, eyes closed in relief. "Well, you don't have to worry about me reporting any of that. I'm not that much of a narc."

Shoving open the door, I held it with the toe of my boot to make sure the wind didn't slam it closed and then slid off the leather seat. The crumbling asphalt ground under my boots as I made my way toward my apartment.

"Hey, Ellie girl," my neighbor called as he swaggered closer.

"Hey, Stan," I yelled with a wave, hoping it would halt his approach.

"Heard you left work early. You good?" He shot a narrowed-eye glare at Chandler and spit a dark wad to the ground. I rolled my eyes. "Who's this guy?"

"A new friend," I said as Chandler stepped to my side. His hot, wide hand pressed to my lower back, somehow boosting my confidence with the simple touch. "I'm all good, promise. I thought I was coming down with something, that's why I left work. But Ryan said it was nothing to worry about."

"Cool. You coming down for a beer before your shift tonight?" Stan motioned to the wide circle of lawn chairs in the far corner of the parking lot where the other neighbors sat, watching this whole exchange.

"No, I actually picked up another side gig."

"Damn, girl, you hustle."

"Like a boss," I said, lifting my hand for a high five. His meaty hand smacked against mine and held on to my fingers to pull me closer.

"Seriously, girl, you good? I could take him," he whispered.

Chandler chuckled but cleared his throat to stop himself. "I don't want any trouble. She's right, I'm just a friend."

The little bubble of hope and excitement that built in the truck of him being attracted to me suddenly deflated, leaving a hollow feeling in my stomach. My shoulders rounded as I folded into myself. I had to stop assuming the attraction went both ways. He was being nice to me, that was all.

I offered Stan a side smile as I nodded and turned toward my door. The sound of rock and glass grinding beneath heavy steps was the only signal Chandler followed close behind. Hand deep in my bag, I rummaged around in search for my keys but came up empty. With an exasperated sigh, I tugged it open and peered down into the dark abyss, sifting through the candy wrappers and wadded-up receipts.

Having made the walk several hundred times before, I thought I'd stepped high enough to clear the small step up from the asphalt to the concrete porch. The stupid too-large boot toe clipped the edge, tipping me forward.

With a silent curse, I free-fell forward, my stomach lifting and twisting at the strange sensation.

A strong arm wrapped around my waist, halting me midair. Chest heaving, breaths quick and shallow, I stood stiff in his hold as he straightened, keeping my back pressed tightly to his hard chest.

Heat radiated off him, slowly relaxing my tense muscles until I was nearly limp in his arms.

"I'm normally not this clumsy," I whispered, the ends of my short hair brushing across my face and sticking to my lips.

Neither of us made a move to pull apart. The sensation of his lips ghosting over the shell of my ear made my entire body shiver with desire. "I don't mind." Behind me, his hips shifted, drawing my awareness to something hard pressing into my back. "You good?"

No, I wanted to scream just so he'd keep me in his tight hold. But we couldn't stay like that forever unfortunately.

Unable to speak with his lips so close, I simply nodded and took a shaky step out of his protective hold. The bite of the winter chill felt like a bucket of ice water when he finally stepped away, leaving my back exposed once again. One by one, he loosened my fingers' death grip on my bag's canvas strap. Before I could protest, Chandler had his hand digging around inside for a moment before grinning and holding up my key chain.

My heavy key chain weighted down by the two dozen or so charms.

He gave it an odd look before holding it out to me.

"Don't judge me. I collect them," I said, sticking out my tongue as I swiped the keys from his extended hand.

"You've been to the Golden Gate Bridge?"

"No." There was no hiding the disappointment in my low tone. "But I know someone who has, and they brought it back for me."

The key slid in easily, but the lock caught, forcing me to shove a shoulder against the door to get it to unlatch. The faded red door finally swung open. Stepping through, I held on to the knob, expecting Chandler to follow me in.

But he didn't. Instead he stopped the door from shutting in his face with a palm to the center.

"What's wrong?" I questioned as I continued inside. The entry table wobbled on its uneven legs under the weight of my purse

Chapter 7

landing on the scuffed top. A quick tug on the laces loosened the boots enough to slide my small feet free without the hassle of undoing each one. Hands on my hips, I waited for his answer. "Either in or out. You're letting out all the heat."

"Doesn't seem that much warmer in here," he muttered under his breath as he crossed the threshold and shut the door behind him. Back against the flimsy wood, he clasped his hands behind his back.

"Why are you being weird?" I asked, eyeing him. "You seem suspicious. Like you're rethinking your plans to murder me."

"What?" he said on a half laugh, half exclamation. "You really need to stop watching crime shows."

I shrugged. "Just saying. You were fine in the truck and now you're acting strange. What gives?"

"I don't want to make you uncomfortable, a stranger being in your space."

"Oh." I waved a hand in dismissal. "I'm good. But I will warn you, I'm not what you might call a clean person."

Chandler shoved off the door and stepped deeper into the apartment. His brows rose up his forehead as he scanned the disheveled—okay, fine, messy living room, sink piled high with dirty dishes, and several opened boxes of sugar cereal on the short counter.

"I see that. How do you live like this?"

I snorted, swallowing down the panic that small sound caused. "Living like this is freeing. It's my space. No one can tell me how to live in here."

"Hmm." I watched as his fingers twitched at his side. "Um, are you going to change?" He didn't look my way as he spoke, only stared down the dirty kitchen like it was about to attack him.

"Yeah, give me five." Instead of turning, I backed out of the main room and into my small bedroom, watching him push his sleeves up his thick forearms.

I swallowed hard and closed the door, leaving a wide crack to peer around. Chandler muttered something to himself and rubbed at his eyebrows. With a huff, he moved to the kitchen and began pulling dishes out of the sink to the counter. Squatting low, he dug around the cabinet and rose with a sponge and soap in hand. Completely engrossed in watching, I slipped the door open a few inches wider as I pressed forward for a better angle.

"You going to watch me clean all this or get changed, Ellie?" His deep voice carried easily across the small living room. "Based on your neighbor's comment, you have to be at the bar later, which means we don't have much time."

Cheek to the edge of the door, I continued to watch as he furiously scrubbed the dishes like he had the bathrooms earlier. My stomach flipped and I smiled. All those shows I'd watched described what it felt like to be attracted to someone, to want to be closer, but this was the first time I'd experienced it myself.

The wanting, almost uncontrollable desire to be close to him.

Late twenties and this was the first time I was turned on by a man's presence alone. How sad was that. I was no virgin—Jacob took care of that the day I turned eighteen on our wedding night. But this, how I felt when I looked at Chandler, this was new and exciting and scary.

"Ellie." Chandler's loud voice snapped me back to reality.

"Right, changing now," I said, hiding halfway behind the door in case he could read the desire and attraction on my warm face. "Five minutes."

"Make it ten," he said, taking in the small apartment. "I should be done by then."

I sank my teeth into my lower lip as I bit back a shy smile and closed the door. The latch clicked, but I didn't bother locking it. Call it habit or brainwashing that wouldn't shake, but being told you were property, that not even privacy was your own, stuck fast. Even though I wasn't under Jacob's control any longer, engaging a simple lock still made me physically ill from the fear of punishment.

The door trembled as I slid down until my ass hit the dingy shag carpet. Face toward the ceiling, I closed my lids and smiled. Chandler might not return the fascination, but that was okay. It didn't take away from this amazing feeling.

Because feelings were the one aspect no one could control.

And right now, I wanted to cherish this sensation of... hell, I didn't know what it was. But I never wanted it to end.

As I stood and stripped off the diner uniform, I tried to pinpoint exactly what it was about Chandler that invoked the new feelings. Sure, he was handsome, kind, funny, smart, but there was something else.

I was halfway through changing when it hit me. The weight of loneliness wasn't weighing me down.

And for the first time ever, I felt valued.

8

Chandler

ELLIE WAS a conundrum of the best kind.

Beautiful, confusing, funny, and that darkness about her was a mystery. A part of her I was desperate to dissect to help her accomplish what she wanted most from life.

To live.

When she said that in the truck, I realized I felt the same. When was the last time I breathed deep and actually saw a sunset before today? I might travel the world, have an amazing job, and have every opportunity at my feet, unlike Ellie, but she and I were still very much the same.

After meeting this woman who'd lived a hell I wasn't sure I could ever comprehend and still wanted to live, now I wanted to as well.

I watched from the small kitchen table, eating cold Golden Chick, as Ellie moved about the rental house cleaning with the efficiency of a Marine. Yet her apartment was trashed. It was also unusual that she didn't mind a strange man in her apartment. Usually women who'd sustained long-term trauma from a man were wary of all males, especially in such a vulnerable space.

Yet she invited me in without a single concern. On the way here, she explained her initial apprehension, that I would judge her because of where she lived. Sure, it wasn't in the best part of town, if there was one, but I knew those "less desirable" apartments typically had a stronger sense of community than high-end neighborhoods. Her neighbor checking in the moment we pulled into the complex spoke to the quality of people living near her.

Not that I cared. Scratch that. I *did* care. Why? Who the hell knew. I had no right to worry about her safety, yet I did. Nor did I have the right to watch her tiny ass with the intensity of committing every inch to memory, yet I was.

"You're staring *again*," Alec said as he passed by. The chair legs scraped across the tile floor as he pulled it out and sat across the table.

"How can you not?" I muttered, shoving another limp, cold fry into my mouth. Stale, disgusting food took the first year on the road to get used to, but now I barely even noticed.

Alec leaned back, tipping the chair onto the hind legs, and interlaced his fingers behind his head. Those gray eyes sparked with a hint of humor and mischief. Bastard was loving watching this. Whatever *this* was I had for Ellie.

"You could say my preferences lean more toward a woman who can handle all this." He waved a hand down his thick chest. "She's just a snack for a guy like me. I'd break that poor girl."

I smiled and shook my head. "Noted."

"Remember you're here to catch a serial killer, not fall head over dick for the pretty local."

"First, I can do both. I'm amazing at multitasking, asshole. Second—"

"Wait, was that multitasking the asshole or—"

I wadded up a used napkin and launched it at his head. He dodged to the left before it hit him between the brows.

"Second, I'm not falling. Just—" I waved a hand as I searched for the word. "—tripped." Smiling at my choice in words, I bit off a chunk of chicken. "And yeah, I can do that too."

Alec tipped his head back and laughed, the sound rumbling through the small galley kitchen.

Ellie glanced up from where she fluffed a throw pillow and smiled.

"What's so funny?" she asked, dropping the pillow to the couch and making her way to the kitchen. Hip against the counter, she crossed both arms over her chest, pushing her generous breasts up higher, demanding my attention.

My throat dried up while every ounce of blood in my body rushed to my cock. "Fuck," I barked at the pain of a steel toe boot nailing my shin. "Fucking bastard," I snarled across the table.

"Tripped, my ass. You're a lost cause." Alec laughed. "Right. Anyway, Ellie, Chandler here was telling me all the ways he can multitask. Helps him achieve the goal faster."

Her blonde brows rose up her forehead as she turned her petite face my way. "Anything you could teach me?"

Fuck. Me.

"I'm going to kill you," I hissed at the smirking dickhead.

"No?" Those arms dropped and her shoulders rounded like I'd just kicked her damn puppy. "That's fine. I just thought—"

"No," I said quickly to make sure she didn't get the wrong idea about my reaction. Not that I wanted her to get the right idea either. What would she think if she knew all the dirty thoughts that raced through my head at showing her all the ways I excelled at multitasking? They sure as hell had nothing to do with work. "Alec's being an ass about something else. But we can multitask now." Not the way I wanted to, but considering I'd only known the woman twenty-four hours, no need to scare her away. "We'll discuss the case while you do what you need to do."

A wide smile bunched her cheeks, and those blue eyes shone with excitement.

Hell. Why wasn't I discussing my sexual multitasking expertise again?

"You were serious earlier today? You'll let me help with the profile?" she asked.

"Not with the profile, per se, but help us identify the unsub once we narrow down the profile." I stood from the small wooden chair that was already making my ass go numb and stepped into the kitchen. Rummaging through the drawers, I searched for the junk drawer every house had. Of course it was the very last one of the row. Tossing a pen and notepad to the counter close to where Ellie stood, I nodded to both. "In case you want to take notes to help you remember the specifics of the profile."

"Oh." That smile turned shy. Tucking a midnight lock of hair behind a tiny ear, she met my expecting gaze. "I'm good. I have a really good memory. I have this thing I do to make sure I don't forget anything." She tapped her temple. "Maybe that's something I could teach you."

My dick twitched beneath my jeans. "I'll be your student anytime," I responded with a wink.

Her eyes widened. "Why did that sound dirty?"

"Because that's the way he meant it," Alec said from where he still sat at the table, smirking as he witnessed the entire interaction. "I brought enlarged photos of the murder wall you constructed like you asked."

"Murder wall?" Ellie followed me back to the table, where I motioned for her to take my chair.

"Thanks, but it's more of a victim timeline." I took the photos from Alec's extended hand. "I put each victim in a column with certain details of their case. This helps me identify the commonality between the bodies and murders. And that helps me narrow down the 'why'."

"Why some guy is murdering women is fairly easy to answer. Because he's fucked in the head, right?" Alec mused, scrubbing at his jaw.

"Yes and no," Ellie answered before I could. "What Chandler is talking about is the trigger, am I right?" I nodded, slightly turned on by her knowledge of how this worked. "Maybe this guy was unstable from a bad childhood or chemical imbalance, but the 'why now' is what we need to figure out. Then we go from there." She turned her face up, clearly seeking confirmation.

"Correct. Not sure what that says about the training at Quantico when she stated exactly what I was going to say based off what she learned watching true crime shows." She grinned and reached for the pictures, but I pulled them out of her reach. "What do you know about the condition of the bodies, Ellie?" I shot a look at Alec, who gave a minuscule head shake, confirming what I thought. "Have you ever seen a picture of a dead body?"

Ellie chewed at her lip, clearly giving my question some thought. "I know nothing about the condition of the bodies, and yes to the dead part. We buried our own at... well, you know." She shook her head like she was dispelling a memory. Fuck, I wanted to crack her brain open and let all the memories spill into the room, cleaning the horrors she'd no doubt witnessed while living with the cult. "How bad is it?" She considered the stack of photos in my hand. "I'm assuming it's bad based on your reaction."

"The women were held captive and assaulted," I said cautiously. "The evidence is on their bodies."

With a deep inhale, she stood and stretched forward to grab the pictures from my hand, bending slightly to reach, offering a clear view down the front of her V-neck T-shirt. But like the motherfucking professional I was, I only glanced—for a long moment—before averting my eyes.

I held a breath as she sat back down and situated the pictures into a clean stack by tapping the bottom onto the table. With a comforting nod toward me, then Alec, she turned her focus to the photos. Only the click of the old-fashioned clock's pendulum filled the quiet house as we watched her scan one picture after the other.

The only small reprieve I had to the worry churning in my gut was that the quality of the photos wasn't as clear as the individual ones I'd taped on the wall. Alec's pictures of the wall itself were just to jog my memory, not focused enough for her to see the detailed trauma.

"Seven women," she whispered more to herself than to us. "These are kind of blurry." Sitting back, she cradled the sore arm with the other. "And I'm not complaining." Those blue eyes lifted, sending my heart hammering in my chest. "Can you tell me what happened to the women? The local gossip says they died by anything from sacrifice for witchcraft to being decapitated." She tapped one of the photos with her pointer finger. "The latter I can tell is false."

Clearing my throat, I pressed both palms to the tile counter and pushed myself up. Keeping my grip on the edge, I pitched forward slightly. "Based on the coroner's findings, we suspect they were held for a length of time, abused physically and sexually before being stabbed in the heart. They were all found naked and disposed in shallow graves. What does that say to you?"

Tapping the end of her tennis shoe against the table base, she held my gaze, but I knew she wasn't really seeing me as she thought through her response.

"He sees them as trash." I nodded, pleased at her ability to pull the clues together. "But the rest...." Ellie shook her head and slipped her fingers through the strands that fell around her face, the motion at the end snagging my attention when she continued raking her fingers like she was used to having longer hair to fiddle with. Interesting. Between the dark hair that was clearly dyed and what seemed to be a shorter haircut, it made me wonder what caused the drastic change.

What was her trigger?

I tipped my chin down to my chest and inhaled deeply. Fuck, I had to stop doing that. Analyzing every subconscious move was an annoying habit to women. Or the women I'd dated lately. But I couldn't shut it off, and honestly, I didn't want to. What I witnessed in their subconscious ticks was how I understood them beyond their words.

I was wrong at the bar last night. Ellie wasn't dark and mysterious. She was amazing and engrossing.

"You know this breaks all kinds of laws, right?" Alec said, bringing me out of my own head. "Telling a civilian the specifics of the case."

I shot him a glare. "Yeah, I know it's not *technically* legal."

"Illegal, really," Ellie said. Alec and I turned our attention to her side of the table. "What? They mention it on cop shows that they can't discuss the details of an ongoing case. That's a real law, right?"

"If you knew that, then why did you suggest helping us?" I asked curiously.

"Honestly?" She huffed out a laugh and waved at the pictures. "I didn't expect all this. I thought maybe you'd give me a heads-up on the profile so I could help you narrow down a list of local suspects. All this?" Using both hands, she motioned like her head is exploding. "It's beyond what I expected and pretty damn cool. But I don't want either of you to get into trouble because of me."

"Eh, I was just busting his balls." Alec waved off her concern. "And I'm hoping that if you see we trust you, then you'll trust us with going to The Church." She started to protest but he cut her off. "If we need it. Who knows? Maybe once we have a more detailed profile to work with, we'll discover the killer to be a local or one close by and all this has nothing to do with The Church."

"But like you said, they're all like me," she whispered. "A nobody."

An overwhelming urge to punch Alec in the damn face for making her sad and then envelop her in a comforting hold slammed into me. The tile and grout molded into my palm under my tightening hold on the counter as I fought to keep myself from lunging forward and wrapping Ellie in my arms.

"Were there other women there like you? Born inside and kept hidden?" Alec questioned.

My blood boiled with rage as I watched Ellie's shoulders round at him pressing an issue she clearly wasn't okay with discussing.

"Alec, back the fuck off," I said through a clenched jaw. "Ellie, if this is too uncomfortable, you don't have to answer any of his questions."

Alec shook his head and shot me a knowing look. Yeah, I got it: my "thing" for the woman was clouding my judgment regarding the case, but I didn't care. He didn't understand this strange connection I felt to her.

Not that I did either.

"It's fine," she whispered and chafed both hands along her forearms. "Yes, there were other girls, women like me. Most of the women who came into the community from the outside world didn't make it long after seeing what the life would be like for them. Do you know their ages, by chance?" She hitched her chin toward the pictures.

"The coroner's report stated anywhere between midtwenties to midthirties." I bit the inside of my cheek to stop me from asking the next question. "How old are you?"

Please be legal.

Of course she was legal. But a long time ago legal or a short time ago was the question. I was almost forty. If Ellie was early twenties, I would kiss this hopeful connection goodbye. I would not date a twentysomething again. Been there, done that, and had no idea what they were even talking about on the date. What the hell was an influencer, anyway, and why the hell did they all care so much? Not that Ellie would be like the typical twentysomething, of course. She didn't seem like the type to care how many followers she had on social media.

"I don't know, actually."

"What?" Alec and I both sat up tall at her revelation.

"What do you mean, you don't know exactly?" I said slowly. Maybe she didn't understand how birthdays worked?

She swallowed hard and hugged herself. Noticing the self-conscious movement, I slid from the counter and strode to my room, dug through my bag, and pulled out a new package of gum. Back in the kitchen, I placed it on the table and slid it over to her. Without hesitating, she pulled a stick free from the pack and folded it into her mouth.

It was like watching the effects of a drug as the tightness in her shoulders lessened and the tension in her spine eased, allowing her to relax against the wooden back of the chair.

Amazing. Truly curious.

"Thanks. How'd you know I needed that?" I smiled and raised both brows. "Right, you see everything. Being that perceptive must make you the best profiler on your team. Speaking of that, where is your team? You guys never go alone."

My smile widened to the point that an ache built in my cheeks. "That part of the show is incorrect. We don't travel around together in big teams. Maybe they used to, but now with so many cases, we're stretched thin. We mostly go in alone these days."

Something like understanding flashed across her face. "That must be exhausting."

"It is."

"And lonely."

"Not having someone to talk to about the case, or hell, how terrible the hotel turned out to be does get hard sometimes. You know a lot about that, Ellie?" I was lost in her, in this simple yet riveting conversation. I didn't care that we weren't alone; it felt like we were by the energy and intensity strung between us.

"You could say that." She chewed on the edge of her lip. "You wanted to know my age to see if it aligned with the ages of the victims. That way if I did know the women, I'd be able to tell you specifics of their personality, their life to see if anything aligned inside The Church or outside. Maybe it was something about the women specifically that was the trigger for each abduction instead of an outside urge."

"You would make one hell of a profiler," I stated, amazement in my tone. How she pieced all that together was shocking. Hell, I didn't even think that when I asked the question, my motives purely selfish and nothing to do with the case. But she made an excellent point.

"Can't happen." Her smile was sad as her focus fell to the floor. "I'd have to exist first."

My own grin fell. "Just because you don't have documentation stating the fact, you do exist, Ellie. The lives we impact with our actions and character are more proof that we've lived than any stupid government bullshit."

"What did you mean by you don't know how old you are?" Alec stared me down in a silent "Get the fuck back on track" before shifting his attention to Ellie, softening his features to appear less hostile.

"We don't—" She shook her head. "*They* don't celebrate birthdays, especially the women. I gauged my age based off how many certain seasons changed, but how old I was when I started tracking that, I don't know." Those light brows furrowed as she focused on the sixties-style linoleum flooring. "When I had to marry Jacob, they said I was eighteen, and that was about ten years ago. So I'm twenty-eight, I think?"

Twenty-eight. I could work with that.

"So around the age of the victims." The scrape of the chair drew my attention to Alec, who stood and stretched his arms high overhead. A few particles of popcorn ceiling fluttered down when his hands brushed against it.

"You're a giant," I said.

"In all the right areas," he shot back, waggling both brows up and down his forehead.

"Seriously," Ellie said on a laugh. "I'm right here, guys. Can we keep the innuendos to a minimum and get back to the case?"

"Alec mentioned you'd be okay seeing the victims faces to see if you recognize them." I stole two pieces of gum from the pack and slid both into my mouth.

"I want to help, but I've been gone for four years. They could've been recent recruits." Grabbing my discarded foil wrapper, she used it to wrap up her chewed gum and grabbed another piece.

"We'll show you the pictures tomorrow," Alec said, rummaging through the fridge. "We need food."

"Only pictures of their faces," I clarified to Alec. "Especially the most recent victim. She doesn't need to see that."

"See what?" Her head tilted with curiosity. "What can't I see, and why?"

I cringed. At my growing desperation to protect Ellie from demented aspects of the case, I piqued her interest instead.

"There was a note," I said while rubbing at my brows. "Carved into her body."

Chapter 8

She winced. "What kind of message?"

"Two simple words that I still haven't figured out. 'Come home,'" I stated, staring her down to monitor her reaction.

Ellie bolted out of the chair so fast that it rocked to the side, crashing against the table with the quick movement. The loud sound made her stumble backward until she slammed against the wall, making the clock rattle with the impact.

Alec and I had our guns drawn in an instant, ready for an attack.

"'Come home'?" Ellie's faint whisper met my ears. "'Come home' was carved into her body?"

"What the hell just happened, Ellie?" Alec asked, his tone deep and menacing. "You scared the shit out of us."

I monitored her shell-shocked look as I holstered the gun. Holding up a hand toward Alec, I cautiously stepped closer. "Does that saying mean something to you?" I asked in a calmer tone than Alec, even though my heart raced, threatening to pound out of my chest.

"Come home," she repeated, her eyes flicking back and forth between Alec and me. "It's a coincidence, right? It has to be a coincidence." Her wide eyes searched mine. "Please tell me it's a coincidence."

"You're safe with us, Ellie." I dared another step closer, careful to keep each movement smooth and nonthreatening. When she flinched away, I placed a hand on her shoulder and tipped her face up to meet mine. "Talk to us. What's a coincidence?"

"Today. Before today. Any day," she rambled.

"I need a little more than that, sweetheart. What about today? Does this have to do with the man who took my jacket and hurt you?"

"What the fuck?" Alec exclaimed. I held up a hand, stopping his next line of questions.

"He asked... he said Jacob wanted to know if I'd gotten the reminders he'd left." Wetness built in her lower lids.

"Okay, have you gotten any reminders?" She shook her head. "What does 'come home' mean to you, Ellie?"

"He said it."

"Who said it?"

"Jacob," she whispered. "When I didn't come back. He told me to come home. He tells me to come home. And today, the man at the clinic, he said it too. He said it was time to return to my husband. That Jacob said it was time to come home. Please tell me this isn't about them, that all this"—she jabbed a finger toward the pictures—"isn't about me."

Tears spilled out the corners of her eyes, dripping down her trembling cheeks. True fear radiated off her. I wanted to lie, to tell her it was a coincidence that the man who she was clearly afraid of wasn't targeting her and leaving dead women as reminders.

But I couldn't.

If I'd learned one thing in this job, it's that there are no coincidences.

9

Ellie

A HIGH-PITCHED squeak emitted from where I scrubbed the damp rag along the pint glass rim. I'd dried this same glass for the last five minutes as I zoned out, only half listening to Janice. Which wasn't like me at all. I always listened, offering my undivided attention so I could live vicariously through her stories, but tonight was different. *He* was here. Sitting at the far corner high-top with Alec, their full focus on the laptop between them. Whatever they were researching, it seemed engrossing; neither had looked up from the screen for a while. I would've noticed since I'd been inconspicuously watching out of the corner of my eye as I worked.

"You're staring at them *again*," Janice said, snapping her thin fingers in front of my face.

Okay, maybe I wasn't as inconspicuous as I thought.

I heaved a resigned sigh and placed the glass on the shelf along the back wall. When I turned, I found myself looking at them again. "What is wrong with me? I can't stop."

"Nothing is wrong with you, honey. Those two handsome men together is enough to get even my old lady parts a-tingling."

I barked out a laugh and threw the rag half-heartedly at Janice; it plopped to the bar a few inches from her glass. "Stop it. That's so gross." I chewed the corner of my lower lip, wishing for the thousandth time since I took this job that I could sneak candy while on shift. But that was Carl's one rule, so I followed it. "Is that normal? The"—I waved a hand below the bar—"tingling down there when someone is attractive?" Janice's wrinkled brow softened with a pity-filled smile. "And the butterflies." I motioned to my lower stomach. "And hot flashes, sweaty armpits, and clammy hands?"

"Which one does that to you?" Janice leaned in close, practically coming over the bar. "Which one has you all flustered? I'd take the big guy." She turned to look over her shoulder. "He looks like he could work me over good, you know what I mean?"

I couldn't help the laughing groan that escaped. "I guess Alec is good-looking, but he's more like a big brother than sexy to me. Now the other one, the new guy?" I whistled and fanned my face.

Sheer horror washed over me, ice flooding through my veins as I watched Janice turn fully on the stool and lean both elbows back along the bar. "I can see that. There's an edge to him, dangerous but not. He has a story lurking in there." I muttered a curse when she circled a finger directly at Chandler, as if I didn't already know who she was referencing. "Now that we know you do have a type, what are you going to do about it?"

"Do about it?" I said with an incredulous huff. "Nothing. I'm... well, me, and he's someone who will leave after his job's done. And I'll still be here. I'll always be here." The dip in my tone made how I felt about that clear. Picking up the rag, I wiped down the clean bar top, hoping the movement would help fight back my rising tears.

Janice turned back around and rested a wrinkled, spotted hand on top of mine, stilling the movement. "Does any of that matter in the short term? I take it this is the first time you've seen a man who you're truly attracted to, not guilted to like or forced." Damn, how much had I revealed to Janice over the years? Apparently she'd been listening

Chapter 9

those nights I rambled on and on, even though I assumed she was napping with her head on the bar. "This is a big deal, honey. You need to act on it."

"What if he doesn't feel the same tingles?" Reaching beneath the bar, I grabbed my bottle of water and took a quick sip to wash back the emotions that clogged my throat. "How are you supposed to know if they feel the same? And if he does, what do I even want? Can I have casual sex? Do I want casual sex? What if—"

"I'm going to stop you there, honey. First off, he's a man. If you're willing, he is too. Who knows? Maybe he'll end up being your knight in shining armor and take you away from this town and give you the life you deserve. But the rest, well, in my day, we didn't have casual sex. Only after you were married did that happen, but nowadays casual sex is accepted. But you have to be fine with the possibility that that's all it will ever be. Does that make sense?"

I nodded even though I wasn't quite sure what she meant. "What if I get attached, and then he just leaves?"

"The bigger question should be, what if you never try and live the rest of your life wondering what would've happened if you did?"

"Wow." I nodded to her empty glass. "The next round is on me."

Janice smiled, showing off the smear of pastel pink lipstick along her two front teeth. After refreshing her drink, I moved down the bar where Chandler had approached, an empty beer bottle in hand.

"Need another?" I asked, taking the sweating brown glass bottle. Our fingers grazed, shooting a bolt of heat straight to the apex of my thighs. I couldn't move, didn't want to break the connection and end this euphoric feeling.

"You okay?" One of Chandler's long fingers brushed small circles along the top of my hand. My breathing hitched as I watched the movement.

I dipped my chin in acknowledgment. "Yeah, sure, I'm fine. Why the stab to the heart, you think?" I blurted.

Awesome. What a way to tell a guy you're interested in having a noncommittal sexual relationship: by bringing up death. Clearly I was terrible at this.

"That's what you're going with right now?" That knowing smile of his grew. I loved it, the resurfaced happiness it displayed. I'd been right last night about him being sad, but this smile was genuine. Genuine for me.

"I'm no one," I said in a hurry. "I know you want to disagree, but listen, I have no family, no real friends. I work too many jobs to get by because I can't get a real one. I don't have a legit education, I have zero clue what the difference is between all the kinds of 'there' or what in the hell geometry is all about—"

"That's most people," he said, cutting off my self-deprecating rambling. "Why are you telling me this, Ellie? It feels like you're warning me away from you."

"I am. I mean, if you were even, you know, interested. Which you probably weren't and it's just me being all tingly and not you."

"Tingly?"

"See, it's just me." I snatched the bottle away and tossed it in the trash. The glass shattered at the bottom. I cringed at the loud noise. "Can we not talk about this ever again? I'm better at the death stuff, it seems."

Chandler tilted his head. Those insightful eyes looking through me the way they did last night and all day today. Seeing past it all. Past the town loner. Past my trauma. Past my dipshit exes. To me. Just me. No-last-name Ellie. The simple girl beneath it all who only wanted to live a life worth remembering.

"You are good at the death stuff." My heart sank into my stomach. "And I was questioning the tingly part because that's not really how it works for guys. It's more of an urgent throb than a tingle." To prove his point, he reached beneath the bar and adjusted himself. "I'm trying to read between the lines here, so help me out if I have this wrong. But it sounds like you're attracted to me."

"Yes." The word was more of a breath than an actual syllable.

"Well, then, that's a good thing, because I'm attracted to you too." He paused, swiping a thumb along his lower lip. Why in devil's balls was that so hot? "More than attracted. Intrigued. Curious. And you don't even want to know how badly I want to bury my face between those thighs your small waitress uniform teased me with all day."

"What?" I squeaked. A trembling hand gently grasped the base of my throat. My pulse pounded against my fingers.

"Too much?" With my heart in my throat, I couldn't answer. "That's fine. Just know when you're ready, I'll be waiting and willing." Reaching to the other side of the bar with his long arms, Chandler opened the fridge door and pulled out a Budweiser. "Can I have the opener?"

The metal felt cool in my hot palm as I handed the opener to him, mouth gaping.

"Thanks." He placed it on the bar and pushed it toward me. "And Alec and I are working a theory on why the single stab wounds to the heart and if we can find any connection to Jacob." His features seemed to darken at the mention of my husband's name. "We'll figure it all out. Don't worry. I'll keep you safe. Thanks for the beer."

Like he didn't just make my panties wetter than a damn swimming pool, Chandler turned with a wink and sauntered back to the high-top where Alec sat smirking. My cheeks heated at his wink.

What if he heard what Chandler said about his face between my thighs?

Chest heaving with my rapid breaths, I turned and faced the wall lined with all the liquors I didn't care to memorize. Both palms pressed to the edge of the back counter, I closed my eyes, attempting to settle my erratic heart rate. It felt like every cell was on fire, my skin crawling with the insistent itch that only he'd be able to scratch.

He said he'd wait. Wait for me to be ready.

Was I ready though?

I'd built a life after breaking free from Brett's suffocating, possessive grip and turning my back on the only family I'd ever known when I didn't return to The Church. Did every man require you to change for them? Were all relationships that slippery slope to losing yourself to their wants and demands?

There was only one way to find out.

Smacking both palms to the shiny surface, I lifted my chin in confidence and stared at myself in the mirror behind the liquor shelf. Gone was the dull look only loneliness and despair caused—a dullness most of the patrons in this bar wore. A new fire flickered behind my eyes, my cheeks flushed with excitement and desire.

The woman staring back at me smiled. The jet-black hair made my naturally tan skin look paler but highlighted my light eyes. The short bob wasn't exactly flattering to my petite features, but it didn't look terrible either. A fresh pink tinted my cheeks. I pressed three fingertips to my cheekbone, mesmerized by the natural blush that had never been there before.

Shifting my focus in the mirror, I studied the man who was quickly turning my world upside down in the matter of a day.

Or was it right side up?

How he was doing it I didn't know or care; all I knew was something in me changed as a direct result to his presence. I didn't grow stronger overnight, but mentally I felt like I could take on the world.

The bar door swung open, and a familiar form stumbled inside.

Take on the world, or a jackass of an ex. Baby steps.

Squaring my shoulders, I turned and crossed both arms over my chest, the earlier ache in my bicep a low throb thanks to the pain meds Chandler and Alec demanded I take. I monitored Brett's weaving form as he careened through the bar. Clearly this wasn't his first stop of the night.

Not that it ever was.

His drinking was always borderline excessive, but ever since that day I left him screaming from the front porch about how I would regret leaving him as I walked away, it had worsened significantly. This scene playing out before me was a familiar one, unfortunately. I eyed him warily as he slid onto the barstool in front of where I stood. He belched, covering his open mouth well after the disgusting bodily function.

How he maintained his job as police chief I hadn't figured out. Maybe it was because the town was stuck in its ways and didn't have a better option for someone in that role. Or because he was still riding on the coattails of his father, who was like a god in this town, so I was told. But that was years ago, and from the stories I'd heard, Brett was nothing like his father. Ryan must have gotten all the good family genes.

Not waiting for him to order his usual, which I wouldn't serve him, I stepped to the well and filled a pint glass with ice water. I clunked the glass onto the bar, the water sloshing over the rim and forming a small puddle around the base.

Before I could pull my hand back, his snapped out and wrapped around my wrist.

"Ellie." He burped again, this time keeping his mouth closed, those red cheeks ballooning out before he could swallow it back down. "I don't need water."

"I beg to differ."

"You know I love hearing you beg." I rolled my eyes and tugged at my hand, but his grip only tightened. Out of the corner of my eye, I saw Janice watching the interaction, and the heavy sense of someone else watching meant Chandler was well aware of Brett's hold too. "But no, Lizzy." I always hated that nickname, and he knew it, only using it when he wanted to get under my skin, put me on the defensive. "I need you. All I want is you to come back. We belong together. Don't you see that?"

"No we don't." I held in the wince as his grip tightened at my rejection. "Let go of my wrist, Brett." His crooked, sinister smile had my stomach sinking. "I mean it. Let go. I have customers to serve."

"Are you saying they're more important than me?"

"It's my job, Brett." I softened my tone and shook the tension from my shoulders. Maybe if I changed my approach, he'd loosen his hold. "Come on now. You know everyone is watching."

At that, his glassy eyes scanned the bar, stopping on the high-top where Alec and Chandler both sat staring. "What are those two doing here?"

"It's a bar. They're having a beer."

"I want a beer."

"You have water," I retorted with a pointed look to the pint glass.

"I want you."

"You have water," I said slower, enunciating each word.

Heels pressed to the rubber mat, I pulled back, putting all of my light weight into slipping my wrist from his hold. Dropping it beneath the bar, I massaged the tender area. Yep, today was going down as one of the worst days. It had been months since Brett pushed the subject of us getting back together. Maybe it was Chandler's presence that provoked this possessive burst to win me back.

The cold air of the beer fridge felt amazing on my warm skin as I grabbed two Budweisers and popped the tops off. Careful to keep them out of arm's reach from my drunk ex, I set both on the bar. I locked eyes with Chandler and tilted my head toward the two glass bottles. He nodded and went back to glaring at the back of Brett's head. I shivered at the intensity behind his gaze, but I wasn't scared of Chandler or what he was capable of.

"Lizzy, are you even listening to me?"

"Nope," I said absentmindedly as I continued to watch Chandler. Pretty sure he was plotting Brett's death at that very moment.

Brett's palm slammed against the bar, causing me to jump an inch in the air at the unexpected loud sound.

"Did all that I did for you mean nothing?" I held a breath knowing exactly what was coming next. It was his go-to tactic, guilting me into remembering the trauma-induced connection we had. He was a manipulating devil of a man. It was surprising that I ended that codependent relationship when I did. "You were always ungrateful for what all I did for you through all that shit and helping you settle into town."

I found myself looking past Brett, staring at nothing as he continued to remind me how he was the best thing that ever happened to me. Would Chandler be the same way? Would he manipulate me into depending on him for survival? Would I lose myself even if he and I were just casual, or could this possibly be best-case scenario considering Chandler would leave as soon as the case was solved, severing whatever connection he had over me? There was no way he'd want to take someone like me back to DC with him.

Maybe it was me. Maybe I attracted men who wanted to dominate me body and soul.

Even with my vision unfocused and my mind lost in itself, a shift of movement caught my attention.

"Thanks for the beers, Ellie." Chandler's deep voice sliced through the heavy fog, bringing me out of my own thoughts and into the present. Only once I offered him a small smile did he shift his focus off me. "Chief Swann, good to see you again." The sound of Chandler's hand smacking between Brett's shoulder blades seemed to echo through the small bar. "We're doing some research on the case if you want to join us."

Brett's lip curled in a snarl. "Haven't figured it out yet?" He burped and pounded a thick fist to the center of his chest. "Of course they'd send the shittiest profiler they had. No respect for a small town."

"Yet you've had this case for almost two years and still have no leads. So does that mean you're the shittiest police chief in a town you don't respect?" Chandler brought one of the bottles to his lips, pausing to arch an eyebrow before taking a long pull.

Brett's face turned a deep shade of red. The meaty hand he had on the bar shook with barely restrained anger before he tightened it into a fist.

"You'll regret those words, Fed. I'll make sure of it." Shoving off the stool, he staggered to the side, catching himself on the bar before he tumbled to the ground. Turning my way, he smiled that fake smile that fooled most of the people in this town. "Come home so we can finish this conversation in private, Lizzy."

I flinched like he'd physically slapped me because of that damn nickname again and his first two words. First Jacob and now Brett using the same phrase that the killer carved into that poor woman's body. What did that mean?

Chandler leaned into Brett's personal space. "What did you just say?"

Brett waved him off and dug in the front pocket of his pearl-snap shirt, pulling out a can of chewing tobacco. "That's between me and her. Stay out of our business."

"That's not my home anymore. Hasn't been for a while now, you know that. How about I call Ryan to pick you up?" I asked nervously, hoping it would snap the two out of their stare-down. The rising tension in the bar was threatening to suffocate me if I didn't put a stop to it.

Brett huffed and scanned the bar with narrowed eyes. "Jake's over there. I'll get a ride from him. We'll finish this conversation later, Ellie. It's time to stop fighting this." He gestured between us. "We were meant to be together. It's time you realized that before you get hurt."

Rapping a knuckle on the bar, he turned, slamming his shoulder right into Chandler's chest before stomping toward his friend.

Before he could get too far, Chandler latched onto his bicep and tugged him to a stop, nearly taking Brett off his feet. "Was that a threat?"

"It was a warning. In case you haven't noticed, women like her are turning up dead. She needs to come back home where I can keep her safe."

"And who would keep me safe from you?" I stood straighter when the two whipped their heads my way. "Brett, thanks for the warning, but I'll be fine."

"You always were oblivious to the shit I protected you from."

Inside, I recoiled at his words, but I held my ground, lifting my chin in defiance. "I discovered the monsters you warned waited in the shadows were less destructive than the one who stood in the light saying he loved me."

"What happened to you?" Brett's face shifted to one of faux concern. To everyone else, it looked genuine, but I knew better. "Why are you so bitter when all I did was love and support you? Held you when you needed it, listened and cared. Why was that so terrible that you now hold it all against me?"

Down the bar, a loud attention-drawing cough had us all turning toward the sound.

"Ellie, sweetheart, can you get me another spritzer?" Janice's penciled-in brows rose up her forehead, her lips pursed in an expectant look. She was one of the only people in this town besides Alec who saw through Brett's mask. Her unwavering support had been the rock I needed the past two years to keep me from running back to him when things were unbearably tough on my own.

"Sure, Janice." Looking to the two men who were back to staring each other down, I tossed a bar rag over my shoulder and pulled the bottle of white wine from the fridge. "And you two take it outside if you need to. I'm exhausted from this shit day and don't need a mess to clean up if you get into it."

As I fixed the drink, I overheard Brett mumble something to Chandler but couldn't make out the words or catch Chandler's response. When I turned back toward their end of the bar, both men were gone, Brett with Jake by the pool table and Chandler back in his seat beside Alec.

With a sigh, I tugged the rag off my shoulder and wiped up the small puddle left by Brett's glass, which he thankfully took with him.

As my shift dragged on, Brett's words stuck with me. *"Women like her are turning up dead."* Maybe I hadn't considered it until today, or didn't put two and two together that no family members had come to town demanding answers, but those women *were* like me.

That should've scared me. Made me run back to the safety Brett offered.

But all I felt was sad.

Sad for them, sad for me. Because no one cared that they were dead. Tossed aside like trash. Missing for months without anyone ever noticing they were gone from this world.

Somehow, I knew, that too was my fate.

To have never existed enough for anyone to care when I was gone.

My destiny was written the day I was born into The Church, then solidified when Jacob chose me as his destined bride. And everyone knows there's no escaping destiny.

Especially for a no one like me.

Only a miracle would shift the trajectory of my life, and I wasn't holding my breath for any of those to come my way.

10

Chandler

I MASSAGED MY BROWS, eyes closed with my head hanging to alleviate the headache I'd had for two days now. Seventy-two hours since I arrived in this small Texas town, and I was nowhere closer to identifying the unsub. Hell, I didn't even have a short list of suspects.

I delivered the profile to the officers, Chief Douchebag Swann, and Ellie, but like me, they came up blank on locals who matched.

Midthirties to midforties, white, unsuccessful, charming, reliable vehicle, anger and aggression toward women.

We also showed Ellie pictures of the victims, hoping she'd identify them as members of the cult and point us in the direction of Jacob or someone else behind those gates, but that was a dead end.

Even with her connecting the message carved into the latest victim to The Church, it wasn't enough to warrant a visit. The moment I showed up at their gate, they'd know I suspected them, giving them the opportunity to destroy evidence or help hide the killer, and there wouldn't be anything I could do until I had a warrant to get inside the compound—or Ellie which wouldn't happen. I needed more evidence than that one saying, which was common, before showing our hand.

"You look like you could use a good cup of coffee." I slowly peeled my lids open, my eyes so dry it felt like sandpaper scraping across the delicate surface as I met Alec's concerned gaze. "You've been working nonstop since you got here."

"And have nothing to fucking show for it." I rubbed a hand over my short hair in frustration.

"Take a break," he said.

I huffed. "Right. Go do something while some woman is missing with no one looking for her, living a nightmare."

"You think he's already grabbed another victim?" Alec sat on the edge of the table, our attention focused on the wall littered with pictures and evidence baggies.

"I do. I think something made him lose control with the last victim. He killed her too fast, and now he has a vacancy. This unsub won't just quit one day. He won't stop until he's caught. There's an obsession in him, one that won't let him go long without a woman to abuse." I stared at victim number three, whose body showed the most abuse. "It's an anger that drives him to do this. But anger at what? What if I'm wrong about the aggression toward women part of the profile, and something different is driving him to take out his rage on the women?"

"Life, maybe. How it didn't turn out the way he wanted. You said this guy would be unsuccessful, so maybe he's angry at that," Alec offered.

I tilted my head left and then right, weighing his words. "I could see that as a possibility. And what's with the wide gap in kills? The report on those bones they found just came in." Blindly reaching behind me, I plucked the manila envelope off the table and slapped it into his awaiting hand. "It was hard for them to narrow down the specific ages. Seemed the bastard covered the bodies in lye, which messed with decomposition. But based on what they can tell, the bones ranged from a few years old to fifteen-plus. If that's the case,

Chapter 10

what made him stop to account for the gap between the older bones and the newer victims? And why not cover these in the lye too, or bury them, for fuck's sake? Why leave them where someone would find them?"

I shook my head. There were too many questions, making everything jumbled and confusing.

"What if he found one who held his attention for that gap between the older set of bones and the new victims, so that urge to take his abuse out on an unwilling victim wasn't needed or maybe subdued?" Alec flipped through the report, skimming the pages before tossing it back to the table. "Victim number one could've been his girlfriend and the one he wants back. The one he wants to come home."

I nodded, liking the way this back-and-forth was helping me work through the never-ending questions. "I like where you're going with that. But why stab her, then?" Alec shrugged and stood to stand in front of victim number one's information. Something he said triggered another thought to snowball. "What if it wasn't victim number one but another woman altogether who held his interest for that gap in time? A girlfriend, maybe, like you suggested?"

"Then she died or left," he added.

"Exactly, making him start his old cycle back again." I stood, excitement thrumming through my veins. This was the first probable scenario we'd come up with. "We need to look into incidences in town from two years ago. This time looking for a couple splitting. Divorces, breakups, wives dying. Anything that was triggered by the woman leaving either by her own accord or not. We know this fucker is a male, so we look at the men who were left angry and bitter after a relationship ended."

Alec cast a meaningful look over his shoulder. "Well, I can ask around, but one stands out in my mind."

"Yeah?" I rubbed my hands together, eager to tackle this lead and possibly get ahead of this bastard. "Who?"

Alec parted his lips to respond when the door to the small room slammed open behind me. By the way Alec's dark brows furrowed and the icy glare he sent over my shoulder, I knew who to expect before I turned.

"They found another one." Chief Swann sneered and shook his head in what looked like disgust. "This is on you," he snapped before turning and stomping down the hall toward the front of the police station.

Alec and I exchanged a quick look before storming from the room, hot on Swann's heels. Guilt ate at my stomach, replacing the earlier excitement. Swann was right. This victim's death was on me.

Palm pressed to the cold glass, I shoved the station door open, putting extra strength into it to negate the strong wind, and jogged down the few steps. Clouds hid the normally brilliant stars and bright moon, the lone lamppost offering the only light in the dark lot as we made our way to Alec's unmarked truck.

Once inside, I slammed the door and secured the seat belt as the truck roared to life.

"I have a bad feeling about this one," Alec muttered as he circled the wheel to make a U-turn and floored it to catch up with Swann's police car, which was already halfway down the dark country road, its lights illuminating the barren landscape in red and blue.

"Me too." Lifting my hips, I dug into my front pocket and pulled out the gum pack I'd stuffed in there earlier today. Popping a piece into my mouth, I leaned against the door and held on to the handle above. "Not sure why. Maybe because I'm here for this one."

"Why didn't he say victim?" Alec asked, fiddling with the radio until country music blared through the speakers. He pressed a button on the steering wheel, turning the volume down to a low background noise.

"Who?"

"Swann. He said 'found another one.' Not 'another woman,' not 'another victim.' Just 'we found another one.' Sounds... detached to me."

I adjusted in the seat, thinking back to Swann's tone and stance when he relayed the information. "Now that you mention it, you're right. Everything about him seemed detached. There wasn't concern or worry or guilt in his demeanor."

"Guilt? You think he did it?"

"Guilt that we haven't caught the bastard yet. Don't you feel it? In the pit of your gut, building with each body we find."

"Of course I feel it. I wouldn't be a good cop if I didn't give a shit that I haven't done my job to catch this guy." He thumped a thumb on the wheel. I held my tongue, waiting for him to continue with whatever he was trying to process through. "Do you think a man like Swann is capable of guilt?"

I watched as the flaring lights turned right down a side street. Tightening my grip, I held firm to the handle as Alec followed, taking the turn without decelerating.

"He's your typical narcissist, so probably not. He's diverting the blame to us that the unsub is still on the loose. He would never think it was his fault. Nothing ever will be."

Alec hummed as the truck slowly approached the group of cop cars. He shifted the truck into Park but kept the engine idling.

"What?" I hovered my hand over the handle when he didn't make a move to exit. "What are you thinking?"

"Swann and Ellie."

A growl rumbled in my chest at the mention of those two together. Nothing had happened between Ellie and me, but after witnessing their interaction at the bar, I felt even more protective over her when it came to that bastard Swann.

"What about them?"

"Two years ago they broke up."

"Okay," I said, not understanding where he was going with that random revelation. "And?"

"Damn, you must be tired." The dome light illuminated the front of the cab when he pushed his door open an inch, highlighting his tight features. "Earlier you said look into relationships severed by the woman as the trigger for this bastard to start his cycle again."

The implication of his words was like a fist to the chest. I sucked in a deep breath and slowly scanned the scene for Swann. Acting like there wasn't a dead woman a few feet away, he sat on the hood of his cruiser with his phone out, thumbs flying across the screen.

"They broke up two years ago?" The way he acted those two incidences at the bar spoke to the fact that he didn't accept her leaving him. Which was typical for a narcissist. They couldn't comprehend why someone would leave them.

"It was a bad scene. That was when I stepped in to help her out, plus a few others too. She'd finally had enough and walked out with nothing but the clothes on her back and a middle finger in the air."

A burst of pride swelled in my chest at that image only to darken with my next thought. "Did he hurt her?" My entire body was still, a predator focused on the fucker still playing on his phone.

"With that look of promised death in your eye, I won't answer that question." I shot a glare at him. "That's her story to tell anyway. Have you seen her since you two talked nonstop while she worked yesterday?"

I shook my head, chewing my gum with more force than needed to shove aside the disappointment. "No. I wasn't there today when she would've come by." I hated missing that hour. I'd come to look forward to us talking, but the case took precedence, and I'd been at the station all day staring at that damn wall.

"Well, now you have a reason to go see her."

"Why's that?"

"First of all, you need a break. I haven't seen you sleep more than a couple hours since you got here, man. That's not healthy. Plus you can ask her what happened two years ago. Tell her it's for the case."

"Using her breakup story as a ruse to get into her apartment. Not the smoothest plan."

"It's better than your damn plan of pouting while you wait for her to come to you."

I crossed my arms. "I'm not a damn two-year-old. I'm not pouting."

"The sexual frustration radiating off you in waves seems like pouting."

I huffed out a laugh, and for the first time today, my lips twitched, wanting to smile. "That might be accurate." I shook my head. Only us two who'd been surrounded by the worst types of crime scenes could talk about my girl problems at a dump site. "There's something about her that I just can't...." I drummed my fingers against my thigh. "It calls to me. Makes me want to dig in her head and pull out all the things that make her, her. I don't know if it's because of her childhood and mine or if it's just her, but there's something so damn intriguing that I want more every time we're together."

He whistled, the high pitch piercing my eardrums. "You have it bad, Chan."

"Chan?" I laughed loud.

"We're at the nickname point in the friendship." He shoved at the door, allowing a gust of cold, dry wind to swirl around the cab. "And think about it. Consider how much you care for Ellie after only knowing her a few days and how Swann felt after having her all to himself for two years, then her walking out on him. That might be a trigger for even a sane man, don't you think?"

The door slammed, rocking the truck with the force, leaving me sitting alone in the dark to process his parting words. Maybe Swann as a suspect wasn't that far off the mark after all.

Climbing out of the truck, I shoved both hands deep into my front pockets to keep frostbite at bay. The skin beneath my long-sleeve T-shirt sprouted goose bumps as the wind cut through the thin cotton, reminding me that I needed to replace the jacket that was stolen sooner rather than later.

The heels of my boots sank into the soft, damp soil as I trudged toward the bright spotlights. Bending low, I maneuvered beneath the yellow crime scene tape that was still being secured on the other side of the large clearing. With every step, my stomach filled with dread. This was always the toughest part when working a case.

This victim's death was on my shoulders. I didn't kill her, but I sure as hell hadn't done anything to stop the bastard who did.

I paused beside Alec, who, without looking my way, slapped a pair of latex gloves between my pecs.

"Well. This is different." He sighed.

My joints cracked as I squatted close to the body. The several bags of chips I ate throughout the day threatened to come back up as I studied the bloody mess that used to be a young woman. It wasn't the bruises and blisters that littered the body that turned my stomach. Nor was it the dozen or so jagged stab wounds across her torso and chest.

No, what made my stomach turn was what was missing.

Her hair.

The victim had been scalped, leaving the top of her head a bloody mess now mixed with dirt and debris.

"Let's get a coroner from the Dallas FBI office down here," I commanded over my shoulder as I stood.

"It'll take a day or so to get someone down here. Do we have that kind of time?" Alec questioned.

"No." I glanced over the body to where Chief Swann was still busy on his phone. "You could take her."

"What?" Alec stepped back, hands out in front of him. "You want me to take the body to Dallas?"

"We need a deeper analysis of the evidence and body. She hasn't been dead long, which means evidence could still be lingering on her. Get her to Dallas, let our coroner pull as much evidence as possible. Have them scour every injury, each of the stab wounds. This one was different." I pointed to the missing fingertips. "This is the first time he's done this too. What if it's because this victim could be identified? What if she wasn't his typical target."

Slowly, Alec lowered his hands, jaw tense as he listened.

Seeing that he was considering my plea, I continued with my reasoning. "The air is cold enough that the evidence won't deteriorate once she's in a body bag."

"You're serious right now."

I nodded and glanced back to the body. "She deserves answers. Our best chance to collect the evidence to help us identify this bastard could be on her right now."

As Alec debated his decision, the coroner from the next town over arrived. The stench of stale whiskey wafted on the wind the moment

Chapter 10

he opened the van door. I tapped Alec on the shoulder and pointed toward the drunk now stumbling toward us, mumbling to himself like a crazy person, to prove my point.

"Fine." Alec sighed. "Let's get the body into a bag. I'll call highway patrol to escort me to Dallas and keep the chain of evidence."

"Take his van." I tilted my head toward the coroner, who'd somehow become tangled up in the crime scene tape. "Clearly he shouldn't have driven here anyway."

Grumbling about bossy FBI agents, Alec flipped me the bird as he stormed off, his phone already at his ear. Pulling out my own, I ignored the few new texts and called my contact at the Dallas FBI office.

After relaying what I needed and starting the process of having our coroner request the cross-county transfer, I pulled the phone from my ear and flipped it over to read the missed texts. Three were from the boss, needing an update and offering suggestions on the profile. The others were from a single number I didn't have programmed into my contacts. I tapped the screen, a smile creeping up my cold cheeks as I read the messages.

UNKNOWN: Hey. It's Ellie. Hope it's okay that Alec gave me your number.
Unknown: And if it's not, sorry. I'll stop texting you.
Unknown: But if it is okay, then hi.
Unknown: I get off work in an hour.
Unknown: Want to come over?

BEFORE I COULD RESPOND, Alec's approaching voice had me shoving the phone back into my pocket and refocusing on the scene. I squinted at the two figures, the coroner and Swann, who stood just inside the yellow tape talking, their heads bowed as if they didn't want their conversation overheard.

"It's all set," Alec announced. "As soon as we get a request from the coroner in Dallas, I can take her."

"Just got off the phone with the Dallas FBI office. They're submitting the order now and will text you directions shortly."

Alec hitched his chin toward Swann, whose focus was back on his phone. "How do you think he'll take it when he finds out?"

"Peters," Swann bellowed, his eyes wild as he scanned the scene. I raised my hand and gave a small wave to help him find me.

Arrogant smirk tugging at my lips, I turned to Alec. "Pissed, I'm guessing. But ask me if I give a flying fuck."

"Do you give a flying fuck?"

Tucking my hands back into my pockets I rocked back on my heels as Swann stormed toward us, steam coming from his ears.

"Nope." I popped the P. "Is it wrong that I'm actually kind of enjoying doing this to him?"

"Nope," he said, popping the P like I did. "That's why we're friends."

"We like instigating men into a fury who deserve it?"

"Exactly."

"What the hell do you think you're doing?" Swann's forehead glistened with sweat despite the cold. "You have no right to take the body. This is my case."

"Due to the current circumstances, I'm officially removing you from the case." Alec adjusted his belt as he stood taller, towering over Swann. "So no, it's not your case." A mischievous twinkle in his gray eyes told me he was enjoying this as much as I was. Swann was now a suspect too, which Alec conveniently left off. "It's mine, and I'm allowing the FBI free reign to do as they see fit."

Swann's hate-filled glare bored into me. Without another word, he stormed off, ripping the crime scene tape off the metal post like a frustrated toddler who didn't get his way.

"I wish he would've tried something," I admitted. "I'd love a reason to punch that fucker in the throat."

"He'll give you one at some point. A dipshit like him won't let this slide without a fight."

Chapter 10

The vibration in my pocket had me pulling my phone free. I read the screen and sighed. "Everything is all set." Gazing down at the woman, another onslaught of guilt slammed into me. "Hopefully she'll be able to tell us something the others couldn't."

Hand on my shoulder, Alec offered a quick hard squeeze. "We'll find him, Chan." I shook my head at the nickname. "Be safe while I'm gone. And keep an eye on Ellie for me. I shouldn't be more than a day or so."

He smacked a hand against the middle of my back, propelling me forward an inch before making his way toward the drunk coroner.

I smirked at the phone screen rereading Ellie's earlier texts. With the invitation to come over tonight, hopefully I'd be keeping more than an eye on her.

11

Ellie

"Ugh," I complained to the ceiling, dragging a hand through my hair in frustration. "This is ridiculous."

After another disgusted look at the cracked full-length mirror, I turned from my reflection and stripped off the Aerosmith 1974 tour T-shirt. Crumpling it into a ball, I chucked it toward the "clean but too lazy to hang back up" pile like it had personally attacked me.

Scavenging through the overflowing laundry basket, I withdrew a dark tank top and sniffed the pits.

Not terrible.

I selected an oversized sweatshirt from the clean pile and slipped both on. Returning to the mirror, I twisted left and then right, making sure my lean hips and small ass looked decent in the ripped leggings I'd thrown on earlier.

"You will not make a big deal out of this," I said, pointing to my reflection with a scowl. "Do not make it awkward. No bringing up dead bodies." Which really sucked because that was why he was here, and it was super interesting. "No murder talk. And for the love of all things holy, do not—"

A knock on the front door paused the short pep talk.

"Be there in a second," I shouted over my shoulder. Turning back, I gave myself one more once-over. "You deserve to have fun. You deserve to want this with him. You deserve this small freedom to do something for yourself." I narrowed my eyes. "Do not do that thing where you talk too much, share too much, and leave yourself open for someone to take control. No matter how cute he is."

Smoothing the sweatshirt down over my hips, I spun around and made my way to the door, snagging a salted caramel sucker from the candy bowl on my way. I stripped the thin plastic wrapper from the candy and popped it into my mouth. Inhaling deep to steady my growing nerves at seeing Chandler, I gripped the doorknob and gave it a twist.

All the air rushed from my lungs and the butterflies that fluttered in my belly died midflight at the sight of the man standing on my stoop.

"Hey, Stan," I said around the sucker, leaning my body weight against the edge of the open door. "What's up?"

"Just checking in on you," he said as he shifted to look over my shoulder into the apartment.

I frowned at the move and stepped closer to the doorframe, closing the door to block the view inside.

"I'm good. You?"

"Good, I guess." He dug both hands into the back pockets of his coveralls and rocked back on his heels. "Been busy with things."

I attempted a smile, but for some reason the disappointment of him standing on my doorstep and not Chandler spoiled my good mood. "Yeah, I get that. Life never stops, does it?" I slid the caramel-coated lollipop from one side of my mouth to the other, not really knowing what to say next. This random visit was odd.

"Listen, I was wondering if you'd, you know...." He pursed his lips and turned his face to the dark, cloudy sky. "Do you want to come over? We could watch that show you're watching on Netflix or something."

Both brows rose up my forehead in suspicion. "Stan, how do you know what I'm watching?" A creeped-out feeling raised the short hairs along the back of my neck. Ever since Chandler delivered the basic profile of the killer, I'd been overanalyzing every white male's subtle movements and words and listening to my gut instincts. And right now, those instincts screamed that something was off about this random visit from my neighbor. Sure, we hung out, and he checked in on me occasionally, but this was the first time he was nervous and strange when asking me to come over.

Stan released a nervous laugh and grasped the back of his neck. "You use my Netflix account, Ellie. It pops up under my 'currently watching' list."

A rush of embarrassment warmed my cheeks. Internally I chastised myself for thinking the worst of my friend. Apparently I was terrible at this profiling thing. Stan wasn't the one being awkward, I was. "Right. Sorry, I'm just—"

"On edge because they found another body?"

"What?" I stood tall, giving him my full attention.

His gaze skirted down the crumbling concrete walkway in a nervous motion. "I got a call from a buddy down at the department. They found another girl earlier tonight. Thought you knew." He squinted out into the parking lot like he was searching for something. Or someone. "Your new friend not tell you?"

"Haven't seen him today. Wait, how'd you—" I cut myself off and shook my head. "Right. Your friend at the department told you about Chandler."

"Chandler, huh?" he grumbled. "First-name basis with a Fed, are you? All them government employees are shady as hell, girl. Best not get too close."

"He's not like that," I said defensively. Popping the sucker from my mouth, I twirled the thin cardboard stick between my thumb and finger.

"They're all like that, Ellie. Don't be a fool." My confidence in Chandler's good nature wavered, my shoulders rounding a bit as I deflated at his remark. Maybe I was a fool like he said. Fooled by Chandler's good looks, deep laugh, and sultry gaze that spoke to my soul. "Listen, you don't understand how this works out here, but I do. And as your friend, I need to warn you about that guy. He'll use you to get what he wants." A quick look to my full chest suggested exactly what Stan thought Chandler wanted from me. "Then he'll toss you to the side. You can't trust them, any of them. Swann, the Fed, that Ranger."

Doubt swarmed my thoughts, making me rethink every comment, every move Chandler had said and done since I met him that night in the bar. But none of it felt deceptive.

"Come on." Stan reached out and lightly gripped my shoulder. Years of being submissive to a man's demands stopped me from moving away even though I didn't want to go with him to his apartment. "We deserve a night of fun."

I didn't want to hang out with him right now even if it was innocent. But I couldn't voice that, couldn't make the words form and force them out of my throat. This was my problem. It would always be my problem. I froze in situations like this. The requirement to shove down my wants and dreams and desires to make sure the man in control of the situation got what he wanted would never fade.

"Ellie?"

Stan's grip faltered at the deep voice from behind his shoulder.

"You expecting him?" Something flashed behind Stan's dark eyes that seemed at odds with his casual stance.

"Yeah, I am." I couldn't meet Chandler's gaze, which I could feel burning through me. "Thanks for the offer, Stan, but I'm just going to hang out here tonight. Another time maybe." *Devil's balls, Ellie. What the fuck is coming out of your mouth?* "Or not." The crestfallen expression that overcame Stan's face had guilt racing through me. "Or yeah, another time. I'm, uh… I need to feed my fish." Turning to the door, I slid through the small crack, my large chest slowing my escape as it caught on the door's edge. "Witch's cunt," I hissed at myself before closing the door.

Chapter 11

Ear pressed to the door, I listened to the muffled voices on the other side while calming my conflicting thoughts regarding the sexy agent. This was what I'd always be. A bit broken, a lot messed up. Constantly at war with the voices in my head and the ones in my heart. I knew what was drilled into me from an early age was backward, but that didn't make not falling back on those teachings and lessons any easier.

In fact, it made it harder. Because when I did stand up for myself, or speak up, or say no to someone, the wave of guilt was almost enough to drown me from the inside out. So which was worse? Dying from guilt or being the perfect submissive woman I was raised to be, even if I hated every second?

The cheap wooden door rattled beneath my cheek, a pounding knock reverberating through the small apartment. Taking in a deep breath, I popped the sucker back into my mouth and forced a wide smile before pulling the door open.

Forearms pressed to either side of the doorframe, Chandler's concerned gaze searched my face, scanning down to my bare feet and back up again. I couldn't breathe with him this close, his upper body inches from me.

"You good?"

I nodded, still unable to speak. With my tongue, I moved the sucker from one side of my mouth to the other. Those light blue eyes tracked the movement.

"Want me to leave?"

I shook my head.

A tentative smile tugged at the corner of his lips. "If I stay, will you talk to me?"

This time the smile I offered him was genuine as I slowly nodded. Shifting back into the apartment, I waved an arm, inviting him inside. Stepping over the threshold, he watched me as he moved past and stood in the middle of the living room. After closing and locking the door, I followed him, tucking my fingers inside the cuffs of the sweatshirt and holding the edges.

"You cleaned," he remarked.

Inside, I beamed at his acknowledgment of the clean apartment. "I hoped you'd like it." A deep line formed between his brows. Shaking his head, he rubbed a hand over the top of his hair. "What's wrong?" I scanned the room, looking for anything I missed. "I can do more if that's what you want."

Turning, Chandler placed his hands on my rounded shoulders. In a quick move, he shifted them back, forcing me to stand tall. A single finger beneath my chin raised my lowered face. "Ellie, you did this for me, not you?"

"For you." My brows pinched, showing my internal confusion. After he cleaned the kitchen last time, I assumed he wanted things clean, which was why I spent an hour picking up. "I wanted to do something that would make you happy."

He sighed, minty breath brushing past my cheek. That finger slipped from my chin to trace along the length of my jaw. My lids shuttered closed at the soft touch and tingles it provoked all throughout my body.

"I appreciate the gesture, but you didn't have to do this for me."

"Is it not enough?" Panic built, making it hard to breathe. Maybe I'd missed something.

"Ellie, you're missing my point."

"What's that?" I swallowed down my thundering heart that seemed to clog my throat.

"You are enough. Just you." I startled when he leaned forward, pressing his forehead to my own. Heat bloomed where our skin touched. The hand on my shoulder slid lower until our fingers interlaced. "Do it because it makes you happy, not me."

"I don't know how to shut it off." My confession was barely a whisper.

"Shut what off?"

"My... training."

Cool air brushed across my forehead. I immediately missed the feel of his skin on mine and the connection it held between us.

"I see." Tightening the hold on my hand, he pulled me toward the secondhand green and red plaid love seat. He dropped to the sagging cushion and leaned back, urging me to sit down beside him. "Is it something you want to talk about?"

I swallowed and slid the sucker from between my lips. "Not really. It's complicated and depressing." I released a humorless laugh. "Plus, that's not why you're here." Stan's earlier remark flashed to the forefront of my mind. "Right?"

"You want to know why I'm here?" Sparks of electricity zapped across my skin where his thumb brushed along my knuckles.

"Desperately," I breathed.

His features softened. "Because you invited me. Because I can't think about the case one more minute or I'll go insane. Because I like hanging out with you. Because you intrigue me, and I can't get enough."

"Oh. Well, that's... unexpected." I popped the sucker back in my mouth and smiled around the white stick.

"I have no expectations for tonight. Honestly, I'm excited you texted, offering me a chance to step away from the police station and that creepy house." He visibly shuddered. "All those religious paintings seem to stare into my soul."

Relaxing against the couch, I laughed at the random comment. "The owner was the preacher at the Church of Christ."

"Well, that explains a lot."

"Explains a lot of what?" I chuckled around the sucker.

"Most religions use fear to encourage a stand-up lifestyle, to be sinless, as if that's possible. Keeping those pictures around the house offered him the constant reminder that he was failing and so was his congregation, which helped motivate him to be harsher, demand more, always thinking of ways they were failing."

"Whoa." I turned on the couch and tucked both feet under my backside. "That's deep symbolism for too many pictures of the crucifixion."

"Just a theory." He surveyed my apartment, his features tight with concentration. "And your pictures tell me you're really into cats."

I laughed and shook my head. "Cats are okay, I guess, but I didn't like the bare walls. They remind me too much of *there*. I bought these on the clearance shelf at the thrift store." Swirling the tip of my tongue around the nearly dissolved caramel, I chastised myself for what I was about to bring up. "I heard there was another body found tonight."

"News travels fast in this town." Chandler rested his head along the back of the couch. "Yes, a new victim was discovered."

"Was she like the others?" I pressed, curious to know if this new victim was also a no one like me.

That deep line formed between his brows. "Honestly, I don't think so." Peeking one eye open, he shot me a weary look. "Do you really want to hear this? We could always talk about something less... morbid."

"I like morbid." I rested my cheek against the scratchy cushion. "Does that make me odd?"

"If it does, then I'm odd with you. The demented mind is fascinating."

"Agreed." Standing from the couch, I inhaled my first deep breath since I found Stan standing outside my door. Tiptoeing to the side table, I snagged the full candy bowl. I placed it in the space between us on the couch and sat, pretzeling my legs. "It's why I watch the crime shows and documentaries rather than girly movies or sitcoms. Just not my jam."

Chandler sat up to pick through the candy, looking all the way to the bottom before choosing a green apple Blow Pop. "And what is your jam?"

I twisted the end of my sucker as I debated my response. "The unusual, figuring out why things are the way they are. The root cause, I guess. Growing up, I loved watching the community go about their daily lives. There were little things I'd notice, like who was fighting or who was unhappy." I tapped the now soggy stick against my lower lip. "I like seeing past the mask." Shrugging, I dug into the candy bowl for my next delicious treat.

"What's with the candy?"

"Partly because it helps remind me that I'm here, free. And then there's... well, have you ever been denied something?" Hand still in the bowl, I peered up through my long dark lashes. "Like really denied something? Where you were forced to watch someone else enjoy something but you weren't allowed to because they said so?"

Chandler's face flushed crimson. "Can't say that I have."

I shrugged and went back to digging. "Well, it sucks, for one, and two, it makes you crave the thing you were denied, so when you get a chance to have it, well—" I raised the bowl an inch off the couch to prove my point. "—you go overboard."

"He would do that? Make you watch him eat something he denied you?"

"I know it sounds absurd. Believe me, I know it does. After watching all those shows and seeing how some people were mistreated, or the kind of abuse that could've been inflicted, it's not that big of a deal."

A large hand engulfed my own. I paused my search for the grape Laffy Taffy I knew was in there somewhere.

"Physical abuse and emotional abuse are two very different things. But they are both abuse. Do you understand that?" I nodded and shrugged at the same time. "He did that to prove his power over you, to control you and take away any thought you had of being able to stop him. Let me guess, he did it as a form of punishment."

Again I nodded. His grip tightened a fraction.

"Was that the only form of punishment?" Chandler's words were sharp, his tone menacing. Even so, not an ounce of fear slithered through me. No. Somehow I knew his anger was toward the man who caused my suffering and not me.

"Pass," I said, swiping my hand between us like I was clearing the board.

He laughed. "So we get a pass on answering questions?"

"I do." Smiling, I pulled the small candy I'd been searching for from the bowl. "What's your jam, Chandler Peters?"

"My jam. That's a tough one."

"Why?"

"I don't know if I've thought about it lately. Work has consumed me as of late. Going from case to case because that's where I'm needed. But is that my jam?" He tilted his head right, then left. "I'd say it's what I do, what I'm good at. The reading people, understanding who they are at the core, is something that, like you, I've done my whole life. Emotions, outside of anger, weren't allowed growing up, so I learned how to read between the lines from an early age."

"They were religious," I said as a statement instead of a question. Not sure where that came from, but something about the underlying passion he had in his tone when he spoke earlier gave away his dislike for religion. "Overly so, I'm guessing."

"Right." Pride radiated off him. "You might have a future with the FBI."

"I don't have a future beyond this." I motioned around the apartment. "This is my destiny. Jacob made sure of that."

"What if that could change?" He sat up and leaned closer, putting only a foot between our faces. "What if you were able to leave here and move on?"

"I'd never look back," I whispered. "That sounds terrible."

"Not to me." For some reason, I believed him. "Tell me what you're thinking, Ellie." His gaze flicked from eye to eye like he was trying to read inside my mind. Hell, maybe he was.

"Don't you already know? You're the profiler."

"I told you before, you're a tough case. And it would be nice for someone to tell me what they were thinking and why instead of having to pick through the clues and subtleties to piece it all together."

I nodded. That made sense. Being told what someone was thinking and the why would be a nice break for him. But did he really want to know what made me tick? The deep, dark, scary thoughts and ungrateful pieces of me? Would he run and hide?

"What if you don't like what I have to say?" I tucked a lock of hair behind my ear only for it to slide loose because of the short strands. "I told myself I wouldn't go down this path with you."

"What path is that?"

"Opening myself up for you to see what makes me, me."

"Why would that be a bad thing?"

"Because it's dark and ugly. Because it gives insight to pieces of me that you could use to control me like others have before. If I keep those dreams of living outside of this town to myself, then they're mine. Only mine. Not for anyone to laugh at or keep just out of my reach. In my head, they're safe."

"All of you is safe with me. Your hopes, dreams, and past. All of it. I want all of it. I want all of you. Not to control but to understand. To unwrap and help you untangle the good from the bad that's been woven into your every thought and action. Let me help, Ellie. If nothing else with our time together, let me help you find a way to live. Live a life you want, not one you feel is destined for you."

Swallowing the last bits of Laffy Taffy, I let myself get lost in his searching gaze. Allow all the unwanted thoughts, the sins of my past and fears of my future to bubble to the surface, putting all my ugly on display for him to see.

With the courage his words created, I squared my shoulders, inhaling deeply for strength to get my biggest, darkest secret out into the world. The one terrible thought that I'd kept hidden all these years.

"This isn't the life I want. But neither was the one I lived before. If my destiny is to continue struggling through life one day at a time, hour by hour, fighting with myself and putting on a brave face, then I don't want a life at all. I'm an ungrateful survivor, and for that, maybe I deserve to going back to being his victim."

I sucked in a breath, prepared for the backlash. Waiting for him to tell me I was ungrateful for the gift of life I was given.

But something unexpected happened instead.

Eyes a bit wild, Chandler reached between us, cupped my face between his hands, and held me steady as he bent forward to seal his lips against my own.

12

Ellie

MY LIDS FLUTTERED CLOSED with the soothing warmth that spread from his lips into mine. Relaxing into his hold, I savored the tart tang of green apple on his smooth full lips as they moved against my own. Too soon the connection was broken. Wanting more, I followed his departing lips as he pulled back.

Forehead pressed against mine, Chandler's heavy breaths brushed against my cheeks.

"You're not ungrateful, you're real, Ellie. It's normal to have those thoughts after going through what you have. Do not think for one minute that this town, this world, would be the same without you in it. Your story is your own. Your future is unwritten. Don't give up because this chapter is harder than you expected."

"The whole damn book has been harder than expected," I muttered.

"And you're still here, fighting every day. And don't be fooled. The best stories are full of heartache and pain. What a boring life it would be if it weren't."

"I think I'd take boring over all this."

"Would you?" Eyes open, he planted a quick kiss to the tip of my nose and leaned back, his hand slowly dropping to the couch. "Think about it. Would you enjoy a boring life?"

"Why did you kiss me?" I asked instead of responding to his question.

"Because I couldn't stop." Sincerity leaked off him. "If I was too forward—"

I shoved the bowl aside. It tumbled to the floor, candy scattered across the room. With the space between us clear, I lunged forward and covered his long lean body with my own, wrapping both arms around his neck.

Surprise was written across his face as I leaned in close, our lips brushing.

"Neither can I."

He closed the small gap before I could, fingers tangling in my hair, holding my head in place as his lips devoured me. A soft moan from the tingling pleasure parted my lips, giving him access to slip inside.

Soft strokes of his tongue built a steady throb between my thighs. Not breaking the connection, I crawled over his lap until I straddled his hips, sinking my knees into the couch on either side. He wrapped both hands around my thin waist, urging me to sink lower until I sat flush against him.

A gasp stole my breath at the amazing sensation of his hardness pressing exactly where I needed. Tentatively I shifted against him, grinding my throbbing center up and down the inseam of his jeans. Bursts of pleasure sparked through me, making my entire body shudder in his possessive hold.

"This is...." My heart raced in my chest.

"Too fast?" he finished for me but didn't stop planting soft kisses down the column of my throat.

"Different." The moment the word left my lips, I wanted to take it back. Now wasn't the time to talk through my fucked-up-ness. What I needed in the past to feel pleasure wasn't needed with Chandler. No, his simple presence, desperate touch, and respectful urgency were more than enough. I was on the brink of falling over that edge and he hadn't even touched an inch of bare skin.

His exploring lips paused against my pulse. "Do you want me to stop?" he asked, harsh breaths pushing past my ear.

"No," I whined. "No, I shouldn't have said—"

The hand in my hair tugged, bringing my face even with his. A fire burned behind his gaze, his jaw working as if he was holding himself back from devouring me whole. "Do you want to talk about it?"

"Later," I whispered, angling my head to give him access to my throat once again. "Please."

Gingerly I ground my center against him. His eyes squeezed shut as if he was in pain, a hiss whistling past his tightly clenched teeth.

"One condition," he demanded. Those lids lifted, blue eyes blazing into mine. "Think only of you. Allow yourself to be selfish for once."

I bit my lip, nostrils flaring with each quick inhale. "I don't... I don't know how."

A cocky smirk played at his lips. "Then I'll help you."

Pulling me closer, he slammed our lips together and lifted his hips off the couch, grinding himself hard into my core.

I melted into him, turning limp as he manipulated my body to give me the maximum pleasure instead of his own. The hand at my waist dipped beneath my sweatshirt. Fire blazed in the wake of his trailing fingers as he stroked them higher and higher.

Surely he felt my hammering heart and erratic breaths as I silently begged him to touch me more, to touch me everywhere. The urge to forget about me and make sure he was taken care of was still there, but the overwhelming heat and tingles took precedence, demanding I lose myself in the flood of pleasure.

An unladylike groan rumbled in my chest as his fingers circled a peaked nipple over my sports bra. Around and around, never brushing across the pebbled tip, keeping me on edge, desperate and eager. Flexing my hips, I slid my hot, damp center up and down, savoring the pressure. Back and forth I worked myself against him, doing exactly what he told me to do—taking what I needed. The hard material of his jeans against the thin cotton of my leggings added a roughness, making me wetter than I'd ever been.

Finally a finger dipped beneath the top of my sports bra, tugging it low until a nipple popped from the top. Sliding his hand over, he did the same to the other. The soft cotton of my tank top scraped against the sensitive nubs. Tipping my head back, I sucked in deep gulps of air.

"Damn, you're beautiful," Chandler said as he watched where I rode his lap. "That's it, baby, chase it."

And I did. I unabashedly rode his straining erection, loving the friction from our clothes, offering maximum pleasure that pulsed from the connection. Talented fingers teased both pebbled nipples, adding to the overwhelming sensations.

Higher and higher I climbed, with only my pleasure in mind.

A dam broke inside me, all the pent-up frustrations and wants spilling out through my soul. A pitiful whimpered plea ghosted past my parted lips as I broke from the inside out. Grinding harder against him, I grasped at the lingering sparks as my orgasm high settled. With a whoosh of air, I crumpled against Chandler, my hot cheek pressed to his shoulder.

Ripples of aftershock swept through me as I inhaled deeply through my nose to calm my thundering heart and quick breaths. At a small shift of my hips, Chandler groaned, his discomfort and frustration evident.

Popping up, I searched his face, recognizing that I got what I wanted but he still sat unsatisfied. I bit my lip as embarrassment nearly swallowed me whole. Knowing what needed to be done to end his discomfort, having done it countless times before—though normally my fingers weren't trembling with lingering bliss and desire—I dipped a hand between us in search for the button of his jeans.

He lashed out and grasped my wrist, halting my movement.

"Stop," he said through gritted teeth.

"But you're...." I nodded to his crotch. "Doesn't that hurt?"

"Yes and no." A feral grin showed all his straight white teeth. "Tonight was for you, not me. Until you can't stop yourself from touching me, when getting me off helps you find your own release, then we only focus on you."

I searched his strained features, trying to figure out what his angle was.

"And—" He shifted on the couch with a hiss. "—I'm a little fucked in the head, Ellie. Restraining myself, not allowing something I desperately want...." He closed his eyes, tipping his face to the ceiling. "It makes it so when it does happen, every touch and look...."

"Is hotter?" I dared.

"Explosive," Chandler clarified, verifying what I suspected.

"Because of your super-religious childhood?" The sharp dip of his chin again confirmed I was correct in my assumption. "You always had to deny yourself, and now it's stuck in your head, and somehow it makes it naughty, wanton." Surprise and understanding shone behind his wide eyes. "Can I tell you a secret, Chandler?"

"I just laid a pretty heavy one of my own on you," he joked. "Of course."

"Until tonight, I couldn't get off unless I convinced myself it was wrong. That what I was doing was a sin or something I had to keep hidden from others." I bit my lip as his eyes seemed to darken with what seemed like understanding. "And pain," I whispered. Tucking a loose dark lock behind my ear, I shifted to look toward my bedroom, unable to hold his intense stare any longer. "That added to it. Knowing I shouldn't find pleasure in the pain, but I did. Not at first. At first it was just pain. But something broke in my head one session with Jacob, and it switched to turning me on." Glancing back to him out of the corner of my eye, I tried to judge his reaction. "I'm broken. My body, my mind, everything."

With a sad sigh, I shook my head and pressed the heel of a hand to the couch back beside his head for leverage to maneuver off his lap. No doubt he was disgusted with me now. Who liked shit like that except serial killers and depraved minds? As a profiler, he knew there was no coming back from the abuse that I'd endured. My physical scars healed, but the emotional ones were too deep to ever recover from the lasting effects.

I'd never be free from Jacob, from my past, from myself.

Two hot palms seared against my cheeks, pausing my retreat. Turning my face, he pulled me close, our noses barely brushing.

"That must be what calls to me. What I can't get enough of."

"My fucked-up-ness?" I snorted and sucked in a breath.

"What if we're not broken but simply searching for the other half that will heal the cracks and fissures? Can what's left of you fit with what's left of me, making us each whole through the other?"

Warm tears pooled in my lower lids. "You're not running away?" I whispered.

"Why would I?"

"Everything right now is the opposite of what I know. You not wanting me to take care of you first, you being focused on me, revealing a peek behind the wall I use to hide my darkness. Why aren't you running?"

A single tear tracked down my hot cheek. He brushed it away with a slow swipe of his thumb.

"Why would I run from my reflection?" With a pointed glance down to my chest, a smirk tugged at the right corner of his slightly swollen lips. "Well, my reflection with amazing tits."

I barked out a startled laugh, breaking the heaviness that was slowly suffocating us both. Sighing, I relaxed against him, nestling my face against his warm neck. Inhaling deeply, I pieced through the varying smells. Green apple, spices of some kind, and a hint of outdoors that reminded me of the winter wind. Engraving this moment with the smells as my reminder, I allowed my lids to slowly close.

With his body heat warming my body and soul, his strong arms banded around my back, keeping me pressed to his chest, I allowed sleep to consume me.

For the first time in years, I felt safe enough to dream.

Chapter 12

To dream of a life worth living.

Soft sunlight filtered through the thin metal blinds, burning through my lids and demanding I wake up. With a groan, I rolled over and tossed a pillow over my head, dousing me in blissful darkness.

A male chuckle had my eyes popping open beneath the pillow. I blinked into the darkness. The previous night's activities and revelations came roaring back, followed quickly by embarrassment.

Damnit, Ellie, why did you have to tell him all that? Now he knew the parts of me that most men enjoyed taking advantage of. Well, when I said most men, I meant Brett. The moment he found out I needed a bit more than the average woman to find release, he abused the information for his own shits and giggles.

"Ellie." The darkness the pillow had encased around me vanished. Bright light had me slamming my lids shut to keep from going blind. "Do you have to work this morning?"

"No. Sunday," I said into the sheet as I hurried my face into the mattress. "Everyone is at church."

"Except us."

I smiled, my lips sliding along the cheap sheet my face was plastered to. "Except us heathens."

A burst of cold air wafted under the blanket. Fingertips trailed down my spine, and my toes curled in response.

Wait, what?

Popping off the bed, I dug my elbows into the mattress and squinted an eye open. "How did we get into my bed?"

Chandler brushed my crazy morning hair out of my face and smiled from where he lay beside me. "After you passed out on my shoulder, I brought you in here. Hope that's okay."

I nodded and fell back to the mattress. "Did you sleep in your clothes?"

"I didn't trust myself otherwise." Turning on my side, I tucked both hands beneath my cheek. "You either. Sorry, I didn't want to attempt getting all that off"—he waved a hand down my still fully clothed body—"except the boots. Which, did you know they're too big?"

"Slim pickings around here, if you haven't noticed. Yard sales and the thrift store are the only places close enough for me to walk to." Not giving it a second thought, I closed my eyes, hoping to get a few more minutes of sleep on my one morning off from the diner.

"You don't have a car."

"Cost and no license, remember? Have to have a birthday to have one of those."

"Your parents never told you when your birth date was?"

I shook my head and huffed, realizing the man in bed with me was sexy as hell but a morning person. Oh well, no one was perfect. "They're devout followers. They'd never break the rules to tell me something specific about myself." At his silence, I peeled my eyes open and blinked back the sleep, sharpening his frowning face. "What?"

"Do you work anywhere else today?"

"No. Sundays are my days off for everything. It's my one day to simply exist." I scooted back along the sheet at his growing calculated grin. "What are you planning?"

"Nothing." I narrowed my brows. "Okay, fine, something. But you'll love it, promise. First, one more question."

Sighing in defeat, I flopped onto my back and smiled at the ceiling. I should've been annoyed, but how could I be when this was the first Sunday in… ever, maybe, that I didn't wake up with the sinking pit of loneliness eating me from the inside out.

"Go ahead."

He pointed toward my stack of worn paperbacks. "Why are you reading parenting books?"

"Devil's balls," I grumbled. "Of course you noticed that."

"I told you—"

"Yeah, yeah, you notice everything." I shot him a glare with zero heat behind it. "The long version or the short version?"

"The truth."

"Touché," I said with a dip of my chin. "I know I didn't have a normal childhood. That what I was taught, what my parents taught me, was backward compared to the world. And when I left The Church, I didn't know exactly what was right."

"Which is why your trauma attached you to Brett."

I swallowed. "Yeah, well, that's part of it. My history with Brett was complicated for several reasons. But the parenting books, well, I thought those would be a great place to start to see how I should've been raised. And I've learned a lot. Learned how I should've been taught instead of brainwashed like I was."

"That's brilliant."

"I was going with desperate, but I like your word better." I smiled and turned to face him. "It helped for me to see how my parents should've raised me. Instead of reading self-help books, reading the parenting books, building confidence in your kids, raising strong girls, things like that helped erase what I thought was the truth and rewrite a new one—the correct one."

Reaching across the bed, he plucked one of the books off the towering stack and held it close to his face as he read the back inscription. "How did you get them?"

"How do you think? Alec has been amazing."

"He's a good man." A wiry smile ghosted his face.

"Shoot!" I shot off the bed. "I bet he's worried about you. Did you call him and let him know you weren't coming back last night? He worries, like really worries. You need to text him—"

Chandler's hold on my shoulder was gentle as he pulled me back to the bed, this time so I was nestled against his chest. "Alec wasn't home either."

"Oh? I thought he was staying in town until... you know."

"Until we found the man abducting, abusing, and killing women?"

"Yep, that one."

His chest rumbled with a soft chuckle beneath my head. "The woman we found last night, she was different, like I mentioned. I didn't want to trust the evidence with the coroner here, so I sent him to Dallas with the body."

"You can do that?" I adjusted so I could look up at his face.

He stared up at the ceiling while running two fingers along my side.

"It takes a few approvals and a request from the coroner to transfer a body across county lines, but with Alec being a Ranger, he's allowed special privileges. He should be back tomorrow. He texted this morning saying he wanted to stay with the body and wait for the results."

"How was this one different?"

His hold tightened almost in a reflexive move, like he involuntarily wanted to protect me from everything outside this room. That small movement crumbled a layer of the wall I'd built around my heart to ensure no man got close enough to control me ever again.

"Well, first she was disposed of within two weeks of the last victim. Which means he's spiraling."

"And could slip up, leaving behind evidence when he was so careful not to before."

"Exactly." I beamed internally at his praise. "Her fingers were sawed off at the second knuckle." I shivered and wrapped an arm around his chest. "Why do you think someone would do that?"

I chewed on my lip. "Fingerprints are the easiest way to identify someone."

"Which means...."

I bolted straight up, my palm sealed to his sternum to steady me in the awkward position. "This one was different because she could be identified."

"Which means...."

My gaze flicked between his eyes as I sorted through what that could mean. "That someone is looking for her."

"And we can narrow down where she was last seen, with who, where she was going. It's information that could tell us how he hunts and give us a rough radius of where he finds his victims."

"Wow," I said.

"And she was missing her hair."

Bile rose up my throat. "Her hair?"

Chandler's eyes turned toward the door. "Yeah, I don't get that one yet. Because we could get DNA from her skin, bone marrow, so why take her hair?"

After a minute of us both considering the question, he shook his head. "Enough of that today. I have other plans."

"Oh." My heart sank into my stomach. "Right, of course. I'll see you later, I guess?"

The smile that crept up his cheeks confused me.

"Plans with you, Ellie. Now come on, get dressed. I need to run by the house to change before we head out of town."

"Out of town?" My words were breathy as I watched him roll off the bed. I was slightly distracted when his taut stomach muscles peeked at me as he stretched his arms high, lifting the hem of his shirt.

"Yep. Now get dressed. And stop looking at me like that or we'll never leave this apartment. And believe me, Ellie, what I have planned for the day, you want to get up and showered."

Leaving me gaping, I watched his backside as he sauntered out of the room and closed the door behind him. The pillow let out a puff as I fell back to the bed and smiled at the ceiling.

Best. Sunday. Ever.

13

Chandler

Microscopic ice pellets clinked against the rental's windshield as I merged onto the highway. The never-ending waves of gray clouds in the sky threatened to unleash more ice and snow, but I wasn't concerned. A Texas ice storm typically vanished as quickly as it formed and left little precipitation in its wake. I relaxed into the heated leather seat and rested my wrist on top of the steering wheel. This early on a Sunday, the interstate was nearly vacant, making the drive to Waco as calm and serene as the wintry weather.

I stole a glance across the cab to where Ellie sat, nose plastered to the window, taking in all the scenes that flashed past. A smile formed for no other reason than seeing her excitement over the least exciting landscape I'd ever seen. But I'd never voice that, taking away from her enjoyment.

She worried when I emerged from my own shower dressed in a pair of slacks and a dress shirt, fearing she was underdressed for whatever surprise I had in store for her. But it was me who was overdressed, though not because I wanted to be. With the strangeness of the case and hostility toward the FBI, I'd stuck to casual clothes, but those were scarce considering I packed mostly suits. This venture out of Orin was as much for me as it was for her. I couldn't keep wearing the same pair of jeans and trading out between the couple black long-sleeve shirts I had with me.

"Can you give me a hint?" Ellie asked, not turning from the window. She wiped away the fog her breath left behind with the sleeve she had tucked into her fist.

"All I'll say is whatever happens, don't put up a fight."

At that she turned, arching a blonde brow, drawing my attention to the difference between her natural hair color and the color it was currently dyed.

"Why do you dye your hair?"

Panic flashed behind her bright eyes before she turned to look out over the barren landscape once again, but this time I could tell she wasn't paying attention to the barns, fields, and businesses whizzing past.

"I don't like what my hair stands for, so I change it fairly often. It was one of Jacob's favorite features about me. He forbade me from cutting it." Taking the ends between two fingers, she tugged it forward and inspected the few strands. "I'm not loving the black though. Red, last month's color, looked okay. Pink has been my all-time favorite though."

"Pink?" I said, my amusement coming through my light tone. "Where in the hell did you get pink hair dye?"

Both her shoulders rose and fell. "Since I don't have a credit card or car, anything needed outside of Orin, I pay others in cash to order or pick up for me."

"Like Alec."

"And Stan. A few times Ryan."

"Stan," I mused. "Last night, did I read the situation wrong when I showed up? It seemed you were uncomfortable."

She leaned back and gazed out the windshield. "No, you didn't read it wrong. Stan was acting out of character last night." Pulling some hair forward, she brushed the ends along her lips. "Could be from the case. He heard from a friend they found another body and was worried about me. Stan's a good friend. He's been there for me since I walked out on Brett." A smile tugged at her lips. "I pay half of his Wi-Fi and Netflix monthly costs since I can't get it on my own. Sometimes we hang out before I head to the bar. Half the time he drives me so I don't have to walk."

"Do you ever get the feeling he wants more than friendship?" I tightened my grip on the steering wheel, hating the idea.

"Sometimes, sure. But I'm careful to not send mixed signals. He knows I'm not ready to move on." Her brows furrowed as if remembering something important.

"What?"

"Oh, nothing. It's just ever since I went on a non-date with a guy from the next town over, Stan's acted more forward, I guess."

Did she say date? "Who was the date with?" There was no mistaking the possessiveness in my low tone, which made no sense. I barely knew the woman, yet I only wanted her to want me, no one else.

Rolling her head along the seat because she was too short for her head to meet the headrest, she leveled me a look that said she knew exactly why I wanted to know this particular detail.

"It wasn't a date. We went to Denny's." She huffed and crossed her arms, pushing those full tits together. The image of me fucking them at some point infiltrated my thoughts. I only caught the last of what she said when I was able to see past the lust fog and focus again. "...just a friend."

I cleared my throat, which came out more like a moan, and channeled my energy into watching the road. "Did he pay?"

"Well, yeah."

"Then it was a date. Why do you feel like it wasn't?"

"Because I wasn't nervous or excited. It was more about...." Her lids slipped closed. "This sounds terrible, but I just didn't want to eat another meal alone." When she blinked, vulnerability shone through, slicing to my core. "He understood. I told him from the beginning not to expect anything. I've seen him at the diner once or twice since, and it hasn't been weird."

Something nagged in the back of my mind, a pounding urge to piece something about what she just said and the case together. I rubbed at my brows in frustration, unable to make the connection.

"What's wrong?" she asked, concern softening her voice.

"I don't know. I feel like I'm missing something with the case."

"How long do we have before we get to where we're going?" she asked curiously.

"Forty minutes, give or take."

"Perfect." Pulling the chest strap forward, she maneuvered along the seat to lean back against the door facing me. "Let's talk through it. That's what they do on all the shows to help make sense of the details."

Apprehension twisted my stomach. Turning the small knob along the dash, I silenced the radio, leaving only the steady hum of the tires as we sped down the interstate. "Now that you mention it, there is something you can help me with. It's a theory Alec and I consider as a strong possibility."

"Great, I'd love to help." I physically cringed. She wouldn't be as enthusiastic when she found out what I needed from her. "Oh crap, I don't like that look," she remarked.

"Based on the gap between the age of the older bones discovered at the dump site and the recent victims, we believe there was a two- to four-year gap between the older victims and the newer ones."

"Okay." Ellie drew out the word and motioned for me to continue.

"We theorized there was a trigger, an incident that forced the unsub to start the cycle again. With the way he dumps women as if they're trash, plus the abuse to the bodies and the single stab wound to the heart, we think a woman was the trigger."

Brushing the ends of her hair against her lip, she nodded. "The single wound to the heart could signify his heartbreak." My brows shot up my forehead at her revelation. Ellie grinned ear to ear. "You two didn't think of that already?"

I shook my head, dumbfounded. "That's brilliant, Ellie. I assumed the location of the stab wound was for maximum pain before their inevitable death."

Pride radiated off her in waves. "There's a saying that heartbreak is like a stab to the heart. I heard something along those lines somewhere." She waved a hand dismissively. "Wherever I heard it, that would confirm your theory that the woman left the killer."

"Unsub."

"Fine." She rolled her eyes, biting her lower lip to hide her grin. "So, what? She hurt him, so he hurts them?"

"Maybe that's how it felt when she left, but that's ultimately not *why* he kills them. Though it may be the answer to why he chose that as part of his signature."

"Then why does he kill them if it's not to inflict pain?"

"Because ultimately they aren't the one he needs. The one he wants to come home. So all this revolves around a single person, a female who left him." I shot a look out of the side of my eye. "Which leads me to what you can help me with. Alec mentioned you and Brett broke up about two years ago."

"Sounds about right."

"Ellie, that's when the first victim was found."

Her eyes widened when understanding hit. "Oh no. No way. Not —" She paused and shook her head, sending strands of hair to brush along her neck. "Sure, he's an asshole who didn't take it well when I left him. But a killer?" Leaning toward to the floorboard, she rummaged through her purse and pulled out a caramel apple pop. The plastic wrapper crinkled when she stripped it off, popping the sucker into her mouth before the trash had fluttered to the floor. Lost in thought, she twisted the white cardboard stick, moving the candy from one side of her mouth to the other.

"The timeline warrants the question," I said after a few minutes of silence.

"Was there a question or just an accusation that my ex is a sick son of a bitch?" Her head thumped against the window.

"The question of why you two broke up." Adjusting my hold on the wheel, I leaned against my own door as I stared at the brake lights of the eighteen-wheeler ahead of us.

"What does that have to do with the case if it's more about the timeline of events and me possibly being the trigger?"

"It doesn't, but I'm curious what your final straw was with him."

A heavy resigned sigh blew past her lips. Ellie popped the sucker from her mouth and stared at the candy. "Because I finally realized what he was—is, rather. You have to understand, he wasn't always the person you've seen. He's able to turn on this—" She waved the sucker in a circle. "—charisma. And when I first met him, it drew me in."

"How did you two meet?" I adjusted in my seat, uncomfortable with this conversation. One, because I had to hear about her relationship with that fucker Swann, and two, the topic was clearly sucking her back into that hypnotic state she sometimes slipped into.

"That's a loaded question that would make me explain the how and why I left Jacob and ended up with Brett. Let's just say he was there when I was healing and vulnerable. That first year away from The Church was terrible, not knowing which end was up, and Brett was there. I see it now. I've watched documentaries, read books, researched online about trauma bonding and now realize that's what it was, not love. It wasn't even lust." Twirling the sucker insider her hollowed cheeks, she pulled it back out and gave me a long look. "I didn't understand that I wasn't even physically attracted to Brett until you walked into the bar."

"What?" I said, surprised.

"The way my body reacted before you even said a word, I'd never had that before."

"Which was why last night was different from other times for you."

"I think so, yeah. I was excited for you to come over. Not for you but for me." She shrugged like it wasn't that big of a deal, but I knew better. "Every time we're together, I get all sick feeling."

"I make you feel sick and that's a good thing?" I questioned with a confused chuckle. This woman was the best kind of confusing I'd ever met.

"Not sick as in sick, but sick as in my stomach is in knots, my palms sweat, and I have this sudden dry throat. It's why I thought I was ill that morning you and Alec met me at the diner."

I nodded, finally understanding. "Trauma bonding is very common in cases like yours, especially with someone like Swann."

"Why especially like Brett?"

"A narcissist can play on others' emotions better than anyone. Brett saw the connection you desperately needed after leaving The Church and gave you just enough to be drawn toward him. He made you depend on him, making you believe he was the one to save you." More ice pelted against the windshield. I flipped the wipers on to help with visibility.

"Looking back, it's clear, but it wasn't at the time." Her voice was small as she shared her confession.

The consistent squeak of the wiper blades against the windshield added to my growing irritation. I hated Swann before, but now hearing all this, I wanted him dead. "Did he initiate the relationship?" I swear the metal steering wheel almost bent under my hold as I waited for her response.

She sat silent for a minute, her gaze unfocused, the sucker held between pursed lips.

"Most locals are aware how the women are raised in The Church. Brett knew that, and looking back, I realize how he took advantage of it. After about six months of him hanging around, understanding and listening when I was lost or upset, he started making comments on how he'd kept Jacob from coming after me again, how he'd kept me safe. Those comments turned into how I was freeloading off him and his brother.

"Due to my upbringing, a deep, insistent need to thank him for everything he'd done for me grew with each comment. One night after dinner—a dinner I'd made but he'd paid for, which he reminded me of—I told him I wanted to repay him. He asked how." Rolling the sucker against her lip, she shook her head. "He knew I didn't have any other way to thank him for everything he and Ryan had done. Which they had. I don't want to negate the good they did to help me right after I left."

I swallowed down the anger coursing through my entire body. Heat burned beneath my skin, making sweat collect along the back of my neck and forehead. "He knew exactly what he was doing from the start. He played on your need to bend to a man's wants and needs. There was nothing you could've done to stop him with where you were in your own healing."

"Still feels like I was to blame for it all."

I wrestled with the urge to slam on the brakes, tug her onto my lap, and wrap my arms around her. "I can see that. Believe me, if anyone understands transferred guilt, it's me. But you were the victim. He was the abuser."

"But then it turned into more," she whispered. "I really thought it was how relationships worked."

"*He* turned it into more. Fed on your feelings and need for comfort and safety, not you." I needed to get out of this damn truck before I exploded. "Was he ever physically abusive?"

"I wanted it." The words were so soft I barely heard them over the heat whooshing through the vents.

"That was your trauma telling you that." Sitting straight in the seat, I cast a wary glance over the center console. "Do you want to talk about this? With me, that is, after last night?"

The fog cleared from her blue eyes, clarity shining through as she nodded. "If it doesn't bother you, yes, I do. I haven't had anyone to talk to about this who understood. Alec tried, but he'd get so angry he couldn't listen long."

"I wouldn't say it doesn't bother me," I said carefully. "Because hearing how someone preyed on you when you were vulnerable makes me want to commit murder." I shot her a tight smile. "But talking with someone who's seen this type of situation through other survivors, like I have, can help. So yeah, I'm listening."

Ellie inhaled deep through her nose and blew it out slow through pressed lips. "That's a very honest answer."

Chapter 13

"You'll only find honesty with me, Ellie. Deception is the root of all evil."

A corner of her lips twitched, attempting a humorless smile. "That sounds like something you were taught in your childhood."

She was perceptive, intuitive even. How she always knew what pieces of me were tied to my past spoke to how she saw through to my core. No one had ever tried, looked hard enough to the reason behind my actions and words.

Like called to like, I guess.

"Correct. It was beaten into me from a very early age, but it doesn't make it any less true."

"Did you have trauma bonding after you left home?" She leaned forward, putting her elbows on the center console. The smell of her sucker wafted over into the driver seat, bringing with it her own sweet scent.

I considered her question for a minute, forming an appropriate response. "I guess you could say that. The minute I turned eighteen, I enlisted in the Marines. What I never told anyone was all the rules during boot camp were nothing new. I made friends with several men, all of us having our own issues, but we formed a bond over a new trauma, not our pasts. That was what helped me the most. I shifted my focus on the future, the new shit I was going through instead of what had happened to me growing up. We all did. After I got out, I got my degree, applied to the FBI, and the rest is history, so to speak."

I furrowed my brow as I thought about all the cases I'd worked on —the successes and failures. "Even still, some of my past comes roaring back, making me question myself. On most cases, it feels like I'll never be enough. I don't know if that's because in my childhood, nothing was ever good enough, clean enough, sinless enough, or if it's because it's truly never enough. There will always be more victims, more people I couldn't save."

A small hand touched my forearm and squeezed. "You're saving me when I thought I was beyond being saved."

"Am I any better than Brett?" I ground out more to myself.

"Because I do want something from you, Ellie. Not in return for all this, but I'm fucking attracted to you, so does the fact that I can barely restrain myself around you mean I'm just as conniving as Brett?"

"Stop." Her hand popped against my own. I arched a brow, looking between the place she smacked and her face. "I told you I was attracted to you the moment you walked into the bar. I never felt that with Brett, or Jacob, for that matter. I was told I was Jacob's from a very early age. Then Brett just held on to me. You've told me it was my decision from the start. I'm glad you want me, because I want you."

I gave a stiff nod, the only action I was capable of in that moment with all the conflicting thoughts and messages swirling in my mind.

"And to answer your earlier question, Brett was never physically abusive in the way most people think about domestic violence." Her hand slipped from my forearm to rest on my thigh. The muscle beneath her touch twitched at the soft contact. "If I tell you something, promise me you won't ever bring it up to Brett. Not even when he's being a witch's cold cunt."

"A what?" I exclaimed with a bark of a laugh. "Where in the hell did you learn your curse words?"

She grinned and shrugged. "We had to get creative growing up. And anything dealing with the devil or witches was like the ultimate curse. So...."

"And the word cunt?" Heat spread across my cheeks at saying the word around her. Not because I hadn't said it before or that I was embarrassed talking about the female anatomy, but the word itself. It was crude, and call me old-school, but I hated using such a crass word around a woman unless it was in bed.

"Oh, well, that was a term widely used growing up. It degraded us and our bodies. They made us believe that part of our anatomy was useless and dirty unless a man was claiming it. Understand?"

"Unfortunately." A flood of rage raced through my veins, boiling my blood. I knew I should keep my mouth shut, shouldn't say what I wanted to say next, but I couldn't stop. "That is all kinds of fucked-up,

Chapter 13

Ellie. I hope you know that now. The female anatomy is beautiful and should be worshipped, not degraded."

Closing the distance, she leaned over the console to brush her lips against the shell of my ear. "Care to worship me later?"

Keeping my eyes on the road, I reached up and gripped her chin, tugging until her lips sealed with mine. "On my knees, face between your thighs, I'll worship you until you scream for me, baby. That's a promise."

Reluctantly, I relaxed my hold and returned my hand to the steering wheel, gripping it tight to stop myself from ripping her clothes off while driving.

Eyes wide, Ellie retreated back to her seat, a stunned look across her petite face. She held that look long enough that worry crept in that I'd upset her with my descriptive wants.

Fuck.

Lifting in the seat, I adjusted the steel rod in my slacks that was doing everything it could to get to her pussy.

I inhaled deep, readying to apologize, when a wide grin spread across her face while a single hand fanned her blushing cheeks.

"Wow, that was hot. I think I just came a little." She shuddered and turned toward the windshield, that grin still in place.

With her anticipating the worshipping of her body as much as me, I debated turning the truck around and heading back to Orin, forgetting the day's plans. But I wouldn't. No, my throbbing dick would just have to wait.

The anticipation was part of the fun, after all.

14

Ellie

HOLY HELLFIRE.

The struggle to play it cool was real. My entire body buzzed with energy similar to the live wire of an electric fence. I forced my breathing to slow; hyperventilating right now would be terrible. I was on fire. My skin itched, heat built beneath my skin, and my center wouldn't stop throbbing. I had no clue he'd respond that way when I boldly whispered in his ear. Who said shit like that? Hot profilers with a dirty mind and mouth, that's who.

Devil's balls, he controlled my arousal with a simple heated glance or naughty word. My breathing sped up again as I pictured his head dipped between my thighs, licking me in a way I'd only seen being done on Netflix. What would it feel like?

"What's this big secret you were about to tell me? The one I couldn't reveal even if Swann is being a witch's tit."

Rotating from staring out the window I shot him a nod at his

"Ellie approved" curse. "Good one." The corner of his lip twitched, but he smothered the hint of a smile to cast me an impatient expression. "Oh, right, sorry. Brett, um, you know, can't do that." I pointed a finger at Chandler's obvious erection. Unable to stop staring blatantly at the length pressing against his slacks, a hot ache built in my lower belly. The urge to touch him there turned unbearable.

In a trance—was being put in a trance by a man's large penis a normal thing?—I stretched a searching hand over the console and placed it high on his thick thigh. Same as earlier when I touched him, that muscle twitched beneath my palm, delighting the part of me that wanted him to be as affected by me as I was him. The smooth material of his slacks caught beneath a short, jagged nail as I trailed a single finger higher.

My lips parted, releasing soft puffs of breath. I needed him more than I needed air in that moment. Maybe ever again.

"Ellie," Chandler groaned but didn't lift a hand to pause my exploration.

"What? I'm curious." Using the sharp edge of a nail, I traced the outline of his erection. At the hiss of air through clenched teeth, I dared a look, peering through my dark lashes to his handsome face. "We haven't even done anything. I'm fully clothed," I whispered. "I thought that just happened on TV shows and movies."

"What?" His voice was strained, facial features tight with concentration—or was that pain?

Daring a handful, I gripped what I could over his slacks and gave his thick, steel dick a squeeze.

"Ellie, you're fucking killing me slowly." His eyes left the road and met mine, lust and heat making the bright blue shine brighter than ever before. "I fucking love it." A honk snapped his attention back to the road. He muttered a few curses before letting out a heavy breath. "You touching me is the best kind of torture a man could ask for, baby, but if we want to survive the drive to Waco, I need you to ease back to your side of the truck."

Biting my lip, I gave him one more squeeze, which earned me a hard, chastising glare, before relaxing back to my side. Our matching heavy breaths sounded over the heater and clinks of ice against the glass.

"I'm nervous to continue this conversation," Chandler said after a few minutes of us collecting ourselves.

The reminder of why I was so curious was like a bucket of ice water to my overheated skin and lusty thoughts. Well, not really ice water; I was still drenched and would hop on his lap if he said the word, so more like warm water. Like shower water. I bet he looked amazing naked in a shower, the water sliding down his lean, muscular body.

Wonder if he has any tattoos.

My breathing increased. Squeezing my thighs together in an attempt to quell the throb, I grimaced when it only made the ache worse.

"Ellie." His tone was full of warning.

"You did something to me," I whimpered like I was in physical pain. Shoving my hand between my squeezed thighs, I pressed the heel of my palm against my throbbing clit, hoping the extra pressure would help ease me. "What did you do to me last night? It's like I can't turn this off," I complained and nodded to where I rubbed between my thighs. "Especially when I'm thinking about you all sexy in the shower."

"Take care of it, then." Chandler's voice dropped an octave, a low rumble adding to the clear order to pleasure myself right here in the truck.

I moaned at the eruption of tingles his dirty idea sent cascading through me.

"But I want you to do it. I want your hands, not mine."

"Pretend it's my hand, my fingers slipping inside that pussy I can't wait to devour."

"Devil's balls," I mumbled. "Please, Chandler. I'm dying over here."

"I can't right now, baby. Either wait until I can pull over or take care of it on your own right here with me watching." Every half second, his eyes flicked from the road to where I grinded my hand against my core. "How about some direction?"

"No," I panted before realizing what he offered. "Wait, yes. Devil's balls, yes."

"Please stop bringing Satan into this conversation. I have a feeling he'd be better than me, being the king of sin and all."

"Chandler," I whined and begged with the single word. "This isn't funny. What did you do to me?"

"Made you horny with my wit and dazzling good looks?"

"Exactly. Now, those directions?" I was possessed. That had to be it. No longer was this body my own but some horny-as-hell devil spawn's. And the words coming out of my mouth couldn't be my own, even though I fully agreed with everything the demon in me was saying.

"Pop that top button." He gave a pointed look to the top button of my jeans. "This would be easier with those leggings you wore last night."

Somehow even more heat flooded my face, this time from embarrassment rather than lust. "Ah, yeah, they were a bit... dirty."

"I bet they were," he responded with a deep, throaty chuckle full of male satisfaction. "Zipper next."

I did as I was told, fingers trembling with excitement instead of fear. How many times had I been instructed to remove my clothing, the commands striking fear and hate through my body, drying up any desire, unlike now, where a damn lake currently pooled in my boy shorts. Chandler had a way with me, turning what I thought I'd hate or not respond to into something I was on the verge of craving more than candy.

And that was saying something. Hell, that was saying a whole lot if I put my current urges above the addiction.

"Where did you go, Ellie?"

I shook my head, dislodging my thoughts. "I was thinking I might be more addicted to you than my Blow Pops."

Chapter 14

"I'll let you have a good suck of me for comparison, how's that sound?" A throaty hum rumbled in my chest, shocking us both. "I'm guessing that's a good sound."

"Another first with you. What next, Chandler? I'm dying here."

"Nothing." I gaped at him, my core throbbing with such an intensity that I wondered if it had its own tiny heart down there. "Those jeans have a little give to them, right?"

"What—oh." My eyes slammed shut at his fingers slipping beneath the elastic band of my underwear. "Yes," I hissed, lifting my hips to allow more room to move.

His hand slid lower, fingers hovering right over my swollen nub. He gave it a quick flick that I felt from the tips of my toes to the top of my head. "I couldn't let you have all the fun, now could I?"

My moan turned into a gasp and then back into a moan when he thrust two fingers past my entrance, pushing deep.

"Fucking hell, you're drenched. You weren't kidding when you said you couldn't wait."

In and out he fucked me with his fingers, adding another thick digit and making the fit deliciously tight. I rode on the sensations exploding in every cell, climbing higher and closer to the peak. Using the heel of his hand, he pressed hard against my swollen clit and circled. Every muscle contracted. Both heels dug into the floorboard to raise my hips high off the seat as I crested and plunged into the deep void of pleasure.

The truck swerved, sending me flying against the door, and a long, loud honk quickly followed. Chandler's fingers tugged out of my pants at the same time my heavy lids blinked open. The rear end of an eighteen-wheeler nearly filling the windshield had a small scream of terror rising up my throat. A string of curses filled the cab as the truck jerked with sudden deceleration. The seat belt snapped tight, keeping me safely against the seat. Another loud honk had me turning to see a huge Dodge Ram speeding past, the driver's middle finger stuck out the window.

Both of us panted, me from the fear of dying and lasting effects of my orgasm, and him, well, I didn't know why he was so worked up. Silence filled the awkward void as we picked up speed once more, merging back onto the highway. Until the most random thing happened.

He laughed. Hard. A full wide-smile, chest-shaking laugh.

Then the next most random thing happened.

I laughed too.

"THIS IS the most amazing thing I've eaten in my life." It was unladylike to talk with my mouth full, but he had to know how much I enjoyed the delicious concoction of egg, cheese, and potato. "We need one of these in Orin."

Chandler nodded his agreement as he shoved the last of his taquito into his mouth. After a long sip of coffee, he leaned against the door and adjusted in the seat until his knee was propped up against the console. "Whataburger is a Texas staple. Every time I'm here, I eat nearly every meal at one. Breakfast is their best though." Taking a long hash brown from the tiny paper sack, he tapped it against the fancy ketchup container. "Why don't you eat meat?"

I cringed, hating that I'd have to tell him the truth. "How'd you guess?"

"When I listed off the different breakfast tacos, your little nose scrunched when I said the ones with meat." Reaching over, he bopped the nose in question and smiled. "And in your fridge, there was jelly, bread, carrots, and peanut butter. You do know peanut butter can stay on the shelf right?"

"Mice," I replied like that said it all. "And your observations are correct once again. It's a combination of things, really. We raised our own chickens, cows, sheep, and a few goats inside the compound, even grew our own vegetables, to make our community as self-sustaining as possible. There were only a few things the men went into town or drove all the way to Waco for. Anyway, long story short, I witnessed them slaughter the animals for our food. It was cruel, and gross, and so, so sad." I huffed and took a small bite of a crispy hash brown. "Which doesn't make sense. I can watch shows that highlight the worst crimes, have seen every true crime documentary out there, but witnessing them killing the animals left a lasting effect on me."

"That makes a lot of sense, Ellie."

"And," I said slowly, knowing he wouldn't like the next reason, "then there's the fact that I was forced to eat raw red meat twice a day that last year before I left."

Chandler blinked at me, then turned and blinked at the shopping center we'd parked in front of. Whispering to himself, he massaged his brows in either concentration or annoyance. Giving him a second to process that oddity that was forced upon me, I unwrapped the still warm taquito and raised it toward my mouth.

"I should stop being stunned by what you reveal, but I can't. I really thought I'd heard it all before meeting you." And he'd seen a lot of shit was what he clearly left off that statement for my benefit. "Do tell, what was the fucking purpose of forcing you to eat raw meat?"

I chewed, giving me a second to debate how to word the honest answer. "Someone in the community told Jacob it would help my menstrual cycle."

His brows furrowed, lips parted like he wanted to say something but was at a loss.

Me too, buddy. Me too.

"It's why I left." I took another bite of taquito and set the uneaten half on my lap before taking a long sip of Coke. "Or why I was kicked out, I guess. After years of doing everything he could to get me pregnant, to give him a perfect heir, I still wasn't. Not even a miscarriage or false positive. Jacob grew more and more frustrated, took… various measures, but still nothing. Between me being defective and my 'insubordination'—" I snorted at the word. I smiled when not even a flicker of fear hit me, and I knew it had everything to do with Chandler's close presence. If he was here, I was safe. I felt that truth in the depth of my wounded soul. "I never stopped wanting more, asking to leave the compound. I'd never left, not once, but I knew there was a different, better life outside the fence." I pressed a hand to my heart. "In here, I knew there was more out there for me than fear, hate, and boredom. Finally one day he snapped. I'd stopped faking orgasms for a long while, stopped being the dutiful wife. That on top of me not giving him a child...." My hand shook as I reached for the orange and white striped Styrofoam cup. "I was publicly punished. The whole community was there watching him list my atrocities against The Church, against him. He told me when I realized who I belonged to that I could come back home, but until then I was to be cast out of the gates and forced to figure out life on my own. Each member got a shot at me. When I woke up, I was tossed outside the gate like I was no one, barely breathing from the punishment I'd received. I haven't been back since."

I raised a lone shoulder like the memory wasn't still a raw, gaping wound. I rubbed at my sternum.

"That's how Janice found me. Dazed with a concussion, bloody, walking alongside the road. Jacob is like Brett in a lot of ways. The more he took that anger out on me, the more excited he became, until soon that was the only way he'd even get hard enough to... well, you know. I think that's why pain turns me on now. It hurt, but I also knew it would hurt worse if I didn't find some pleasure in it to make what came next bearable."

A single tear slipped free. Why did I tell him all that? Surely he wouldn't want me knowing I wasn't just broken, I was unrepairable. But for some reason, just voicing all that lifted a sliver of the darkness that had consumed me since, well, forever.

I startled when the door whipped open, a gust of bitter air rushing inside the warm cab. Wide-eyed, I watched as Chandler leapt out, slamming the door shut so hard the truck rocked. Devastated tears threatened, building in my lower lids, but I willed them back. I couldn't let him see how his rejection wounded me. If he saw how much his acceptance meant, he'd find a way to use it against me.

After steeling my emotions, I twisted to look out the back window.

Chapter 14

Chandler leaned against the tailgate, forearms pressed to the metal, head hanging between his shoulders. As if he sensed my stare, his head lifted. The emotion on his slack features hit me like a smack to the face. There wasn't anger or disgust when he met my gaze.

Devastation.

That was written across his face. Sheer devastation—for me.

Shoving the uneaten food into the trash sack, I hurried out of the truck, tugging the lightweight windbreaker tighter around my chest as I stepped into the cold. The black asphalt was slightly gray with the dusting of snow and ice, some of it crunching beneath my steps. I stopped beside him and pressed my forehead against his bicep, closing my eyes to soak in the minimal contact.

He shifted, and warmth engulfed me as he wrapped me in a lung-constricting bear hug. Soft, dry lips pressed to my temple and lingered. The strength behind his hold made breathing difficult, but I didn't dare say a word, not wanting to disrupt the moment.

"Don't feel bad for me," I whispered, the words swept away on a gust of wind. "Don't let me see pity in your eyes now that you know. Not when, for the first time in my life, someone saw me for me, not my past. Don't you dare take that from me, Chandler."

His solid chest rose and fell with heavy breaths.

"Pity isn't anywhere close to what I feel, Ellie. I don't think I could ever feel that for a fighter like yourself. Understanding, guilt, and wrath war inside me right now, and I don't know... I don't know how to process it. I want to erase everything that was done to you at the hand of that bastard and fucked-up community." At that small confession, he squeezed me tight before releasing his hold and grabbing my hand.

Leading me back around the truck, he opened the passenger side door and lifted me onto the seat with a solid yet gentle grip on my waist. My thighs slid along the leather as I parted my knees, allowing him to settle between my spread legs. A hint of a snowflake fell onto his cheek, immediately melting to a tiny dot of water. I glanced up to the gray sky. Pockets of sunshine now broke through the clouds, suggesting the winter storm would be gone by noon.

"Tell me what to do," Chandler said, drawing my focus back to him. "Tell me you want him dead, or arrested, or missing without a trace." His voice broke at the end. Glancing away, he cleared his throat before trying to speak again. "Tell me to do it so I can make him pay for what he did to you, so I can get all this"—he slammed a fist against his chest—"all this rage out of me. I can't fucking breathe with this anger."

The rough stubble along his jaw scraped beneath the pads of my fingertips as I brushed them along his face, committing each inch to memory. I wanted to remember this, his face in this exact moment. Scooting to the edge of the seat, I pressed a soft kiss to the corner of his lips.

"Don't let his actions destroy you too," I said, letting my lips move across the unblemished skin of his cheekbone. "Breathe for me, Chandler." He sucked in deep, rattling breaths. The grip on my knees tightened, but I didn't flinch. "What's done is done. I'm not holding on to the past, and neither should you. Because you know what today is?"

I leaned back and cupped his face between my hands, forcing his gaze to meet mine.

"What?" he croaked.

"The best day I've *ever* had."

"It's ten." An almost smile tugged at his lips. The deep line between his brows slowly eased, and the flush reddening his neck faded.

"Exactly. That's what you've given me. The best day ever by being you. Don't let your thoughts of premeditated murder ruin the rest of the fun you have planned." I gave him a wide grin and patted his cheek. "I do appreciate the gesture. But if anyone gets to kill Jacob, I'd like it to be me. So get in line."

Shaking his head, he grasped the back of my neck and tugged me close.

"You amaze me," he said against my lips. "You haven't seen the world or met many people, but I have, and Ellie?" He pressed his hot forehead against mine. "You're the strongest person I've ever met."

Before I could deny his claim, he kissed me. Soft and sweet, full of the emotions we both felt in that moment.

Our moment.

It was then that it happened, right there in the middle of the shopping center's parking lot.

I fell for a man I hardly knew.

15

Ellie

My steps faltered just over the metal threshold of the automatic doors, eyes wide and mouth gaping. I'd seen all different types of stores, malls, and buildings in TV shows and movies, but being inside one, well, this was a first. A few people in green collared shirts stared at me awkwardly while Chandler paused a step ahead with a patient smile.

His hand extended between us. I glanced between those wiggling fingers and his face before reluctantly intertwining my fingers with his. With a gentle tug, my feet were set in motion, following Chandler as he weaved down the cluttered path filled with displays of protein bars, weights, and balls for all different types of sports.

I couldn't look fast enough to take it all in. Inhaling deep, I frowned at the smell of... nothing. It didn't smell like the mix of musk, dust, and too much deodorizer like the thrift store, though I guess the nothingness smell was a vast improvement from what I was used to.

A faceless white mannequin with outstretched arms wearing nothing but a pair of tight shorts and a sports bar had me pulling up short. Releasing Chandler's hand, I tapped on her thigh to figure out what she was made of.

"Why are we here again?" I questioned, circling the blank mannequin. "Because I don't look like that or want to. It's kind of disturbing-looking, don't you think?"

My lips twitched at Chandler's laugh. "Yeah, they are creepy. You should see the kid ones." I shuddered, which made him laugh even harder. "We're here, Ellie, because you need a warmer coat than that thing you have on, and so do I." I flicked an apprehensive glance his way. "Don't give me that look. I'm paying, so don't worry about the cost or how you'll pay for it all. I'm sorry it's not somewhere nice like Nordstrom." I cocked my head to the side. He chuckled. "Right. What I mean is it's not fancy by any means, but it's open and they do sell clothes and coats, so we're here. We're limited on our options here in Waco. Now, if we ever go shopping in Dallas, they have anything and everything you could ever want. Will this be okay for now?"

The hesitancy in his voice caught me off guard. This place was amazing already, and I hadn't even looked at a single thing. The rubber soles of my boots twisted the carpet as I swiveled to see the full store. A large dangling price tag with some brand symbol on it caught my attention. My eyes nearly bugged out of my head when I flipped it around and saw the cost.

"Those shorts are seventy dollars," I whisper-yelled while holding up the tag.

Hands stuffed in his pockets, Chandler shrugged like it wasn't that big of a deal. Which it was. I worked my ass off for an entire week to make that kind of money. "Don't worry about the cost, just pick out what you want." At my clear reluctance, he stepped nearer and leaned in. "Didn't I tell you what today is?"

"No. Is it a special day?" A day when they give you all these clothes at 90 percent off would be awesome.

"It is a special day. Today's your birthday." The sheer joy radiating off him had me hiding the reluctance that was keeping me from being ecstatic at his words. "Let me do this for you, okay?" His gaze flicked over my head, and he motioned to someone with a quick wave.

A perky young blonde appeared at my side. "How can I help you two?"

Chandler pointed to me. "It's her birthday."

The woman turned, smiling bright.

"Happy birthday," she said happily.

"Thanks. You too." I bit my tongue and sighed. "I mean, thank you."

Hand pressed to my lower back, Chandler inclined his head my way. "Can you help her find her way through all this? Whatever she wants, we're buying. I'll go check out the coats while you two get started. Is the North Face section upstairs?"

"Yes, and I'd be happy to help her."

With a peck on the top of my head, he turned. Before Chandler took a single step, I lashed out and gripped his hand.

"You're leaving me here?" Panic rose, making my skin hot and voice tremble.

"Give us a second." The pretty woman nodded, still smiling, and stepped away, offering us privacy. "Ellie, you're good. This place is safe, and I won't be far away." He pointed to the second floor. "I'll have my eye on you the entire time, promise."

"I'll go with you."

"No, you can do this on your own. Pick out what you want, try it all on, and I'll be back in no time. This is a big step—a scary one, I'm sure—but I promise you, Ellie, you'll be okay."

I swallowed hard and nodded. He was right. I was overreacting. But this store was so huge, too crowded, and full of strangers. I wasn't worried about Jacob being here, but what about others who might try to hurt me? I didn't want to end up as the victim in one of the documentaries I loved so much.

Two fingers pressed beneath my chin and raised it from where I had lowered my head.

"I believe in you, Ellie. You've got this."

With a quick peck on my forehead, he turned and walked away, our fingers slipping apart as he left. I stood like a statue, absorbing the heaviness of being alone in a new environment. When no one attempted to murder me or ask me to follow them into a random van, the tension in my shoulders and back eased.

"You ready?"

I jumped a little at the too close voice. I twisted to the woman Chandler had spoken to earlier, now standing behind me. I nodded and shoved both hands into the pockets of my windbreaker, searching for an emergency piece of candy.

"Let's head over there." I followed where she pointed. "That's the petite section. With your small frame, that section will be our best bet on finding clothes that fit you."

That would be a nice change. Back home, I had to find clothes in the kids' section.

I offered her a tentative smile.

"Great!" She clapped her hands in excitement and motioned for me to follow her. "We'll make this the best birthday ever."

AFTER SCOURING the racks for a good thirty minutes, the sweet blonde helped me into a dressing room to try everything on. I was on my third outfit when a knock rattled the dressing room door. Expecting the woman helping me, I opened it wide wearing nothing but a pair of shimmery black leggings and a hot pink sports bra.

"I–" I cut myself off at the sight of Chandler leaning against the wall, arms crossed, smirking. "Hey, um, you like these?" I wasn't embarrassed at him seeing me like this—hell, the guy had his fingers inside me just hours ago—but I was turned on. I felt sexy, and the way his heated gaze traveled up and down my body, pausing on my chest, made my temperature spike.

He bit the corner of his lip. "I love it."

"Me too." I shifted from one foot to the other. "So, did you find a coat?"

Chapter 15

"A few," he said, using his elbow to push off the wall. "I asked them to hold them up front while you finished up. After you're done here, we'll find you some shoes that fit."

"I love my boots." My voice was low with my disappointment. Sure, they were a little big, but they were mine, and I was ecstatic when I found them at that yard sale. I didn't even bother looking at the size when I scooped them up and paid the five dollars.

"You're right, I'm sorry. How about instead we buy some insoles that will help them fit a little better? That way you get to keep the boots, and I get to know you won't be tripping along the side the road, in front of your apartment, in parking lots—"

I threw one of the shirts that didn't fit at Chandler's head.

"Ha ha," I mocked. "But yes, that would be great. Thank you."

The woman walked back into the dressing area, arms full of clothes neatly clipped to hangers. She hung them up in the dressing room and rushed out, but not before peeking over her shoulder with a sly grin. "I'll be outside when you're done." With a wink, she disappeared around the corner, leaving Chandler and me alone again.

Closing the door, I began to strip to try on the next ridiculously expensive outfit. How people paid this much just for clothes to work out in was beyond me.

"You never finished your thought in the truck, by the way." Chandler's deep voice carried through the small changing area, making me shiver where I stood naked behind the flimsy dressing room door.

I tugged up the warmest and softest leggings I'd ever felt in my life and almost sighed. Okay, now I understood why people paid this much. No holes, no scratchy fabric, no stains. Turning in the mirror, I checked out my small backside before tugging on one of the long-sleeve tops she'd brought. It hung perfectly over my large chest yet was tapered at the waist, showing off my figure instead of looking boxy.

After ensuring everything important was covered, I tugged the door open and leaned against the wobbly fake wood frame.

"You promise not to say anything?"

Chandler sighed and grumbled something under his breath.

"Fine. I won't say anything to that fucker Swann no matter what he does."

"Okay, well." I poked my head out and glanced right, then left, ensuring we were still alone. "You know how earlier in the truck you were"—I nodded to his crotch—"excited." Almost like to emphasize my point, the crotch in question twitched beneath the thin material of his slacks. Heat built along my cheekbones, as well as other areas. "All without me touching you, kissing, or watching porn."

"What do you know about porn?" He cocked his head to the side.

"Well...." I tucked a lock of hair behind my ear. "Sometimes Stan watches racy shows on Netflix, and it pulls up in his 'recently watched.'" I averted my eyes to stop staring at his crotch. "Sometimes I watch them too."

"We're digressing again. That seems to happen when we talk about my cock, doesn't it?" Humor laced his tone. "Yes, I was turned on by just the thought of touching you, with you simply being in the truck with me so close."

"Brett can't do that."

The rising heat in his eyes vanished. "What do you mean?"

"I mean, Brett has to have a lot of stimulation to get hard," I whispered. "So either me touching him, or him...." I narrowed my eyes. "Don't get mad."

"I'm not mad," he spat.

I pointed to his clenched fists and arched a brow. He huffed in defeat and shook out his hands.

"Pain was one of the things that helped turn him on."

"Please tell me you mean his own pain and not inflicting it," Chandler said through clenched teeth.

I shrugged and stepped backward into the changing room. After closing the door, I leaned against it and closed my eyes. "I'd already been somewhat trained to need it, to want it, like I told you earlier, if I wanted the experience to be enjoyable at all for me. So it was fine. It worked."

"And now?" Chandler asked from the other side of the door.

"Now," I mused. "After last night, and today in the truck...." I pressed my cold hands to my hot cheeks. "You're the first person I've let touch me since Brett. And I like it. I like everything you do. I liked it soft last night, your dirty mouth today, your touch."

Trying not to overthink my confession, I shoved off the door and hooked my thumbs into the waist of the leggings, tugging them to my ankles. The sweater was over my head when the door swung open, nearly hitting my bent arm. I tipped to the side, palm slapping against the mirror secured to the wall to stay upright.

Chandler closed the door behind him and locked it without looking away from where I stood still in shock.

Butterflies erupted in my belly as he trailed his hot gaze along my nearly naked body.

"Tell me, Ellie." He wet his lips, gaze fixed on my heaving chest. "I need to know something before we continue with this." He motioned between us. "Of those racy shows you watched, which turned you on more: the soft and sweet or the dark and dirty?"

My throat felt like the ground on a sweltering August day. "Dark and dirty," I rasped.

A cocky smile split his face.

"We can do both, baby. But I needed to know if the dirty still turned you on. I'm not sweet," he said, taking a controlled step closer. "I'm not gentle." Another step. Witch's cunt, I couldn't breathe. "But I would be for you. But knowing what you like... how are you so perfect for me?"

A hand slid through my hair, fisting a tight hold near the base of my neck. Chandler yanked, forcing my face toward the ceiling. Without my boots on, he towered over me.

"Chandler," I breathed. The temperature in the small square room spiked as his erection pressed into my upper belly. "I want you."

"Not here. I can't—" Before he could finish, I dropped to my knees, my fingers already working on his belt. "Fuck. Ellie, we can't."

"Then stop me." Instead of stepping away, he tightened the grip in my hair, keeping me in place. "I'm doing this for me, Chandler," I breathed. "Because I can't stop thinking about you in my mouth since you mentioned it in the truck earlier."

Chin to his chest, those blue eyes burned through me as he stared down.

The clink of his belt, then the rasp of his zipper filled the small area. Both my thumbs dipped into the waistband of his boxer briefs, pulling both his underwear and slacks down with a hard yank. His long, thick dick jutted out, the damp head directly in front of my lips. Keeping my eyes locked with his, I flicked my tongue out and licked along his slit.

The wall shook when his fist slammed against it. A small smirk played at my lips. If he liked that, well, I was about to bring him to his knees.

Gripping the base, I slipped the head past my lips and pushed forward, taking him fully into my mouth. Only once he pressed against the back of my throat did I pull back, swirling my tongue around the sensitive head. Above me, words of worship and curses were mumbled under his breath. When he was in deep, I tightened my grip. His hips bucked forward, pushing him just past my gagging point.

"Yes," he encouraged. "Tighter."

My knuckles turned white with my grip, but the way his legs trembled and the motion of his hips told me he enjoyed the fine line of pleasure and pain like me.

A thought struck. *If he liked that, then....*

I cupped his balls and squeezed.

That was his tipping point between enjoyment and losing control. The grip in my hair twisted, shooting bites of pain along my scalp. My core dampened and my nipples hardened, nearly poking through the pink sports bra. He thrust his hips, sliding his cock down my throat before pulling out an inch and pushing back in.

His breaths quickened. Swirling my tongue, I urged him deeper, swallowing as he did. With a grunt, he swelled in my mouth. Rotating my wrist, I twisted my still tight hold. He erupted, spilling down my throat as he muffled his curses with a fist between his teeth.

Only after his shudders ceased did I release him, sitting back on my heels and smiling, truly happy that I'd done that for him, and for me. Who knew I could find excitement and pleasure by helping a man find his release?

Lids hooded, Chandler swiped his thumb along my lower lip before slipping it into his mouth. I couldn't stifle the desire-laced groan that dirty little move invoked. With two hands beneath my armpits, he hauled me upright and pressed his lips to mine in a dominating kiss that I willingly submitted to.

The muffled ring of a cell phone sounded somewhere close, but I was too lost in Chandler to care whose. An irritated grunt vibrated my lips before he pulled away, leaving me tipping forward, following his lips. He shot me a shy smile, gave me one more quick peck, and began redressing. After securing his underwear, stuffing his still semi-hard cock into the tight briefs, and pulling up his pants, he dug into the front pocket. Those light brows furrowed as he read the screen. Fully expecting to be left out, I stripped off the sports bra to get my real clothes back on.

"It's Alec," he said, drawing my attention to the screen he'd turned my way. "I can't wait to fuck those," he muttered, eyes on my naked breasts. As if in a trance, completely forgetting about the still ringing phone, he brushed a knuckle down the center of one breast, grazing over the peaked, sensitive nipple.

I sucked in a breath, causing his blue eyes to float up to mine.

"Later." Inspecting the dressing room, he flattened his lips into a thin line. The phone had gone quiet only to start ringing again seconds later. "I need to take this. How about you change, and I'll have that woman help you bring all this to the front."

I opened my mouth to tell him there was no way in hell I would let him buy me all this. Slowly turning in a circle, I added up the cost of what was in the small room in my head. Devil's chode, there was close to a thousand dollars' worth of clothes on the floor and on hangers.

When I finally found the words, I looked up to find myself alone in the dressing room.

"Witch's cold tits," I cursed. Dressing quickly, I left all the clothes on the floor and stormed out of the small dressing stall, ready to tell

Chandler I couldn't be bought, only to be stopped by the overly bubbly woman.

"Your boyfriend told me to clean out the dressing room and bring it all up front." Hands clenched tight, she shook them over her head in excitement and let out a high-pitched squeal. "That's so awesome. What a great birthday present."

"Yeah," I said reluctantly as I pushed a lock of hair behind my ear. "Just seems like a lot, right?" Maybe she saw how strange this was too. I mean, who bought their—

Wait. Did she just say "boyfriend"?

The woman smiled like she was in on some kind of secret. "A man in love doesn't see dollar signs when he's spoiling his girl."

"Love?" I squeaked. First "boyfriend," now "love". This crazy lady was high.

She nodded, her eyes wide like her excitement was about to bust out of her. "Well, yeah. I saw the way he looked at you. And when you were searching through the clothes, I saw him watching from the upper level." She pointed to the second floor. "He couldn't take his eyes off you, and"—she leaned in close like she was about to share a secret—"he was smiling."

"Oh." I absentmindedly dug through the jacket pocket, hoping I'd put more than one piece of emergency candy in there. A thin plastic wrapper grazed my fingers. Absentmindedly, I tugged out the candy and began to unwrap the Jolly Rancher. "And that's a good thing."

"Of course. He was happy seeing you happy. If you ask me, that's love." Her smile faltered. "I've never had that, mind you, but it's what I want to find. You're lucky." Shaking her head, she reinforced that smile, but this time there was a hint of sadness in it. "You go meet him up front. I'll grab all these clothes."

Lucky.

The word stuck with me as I rolled the hard grape candy around my mouth and walked in the direction she'd pointed. No one had ever said I was the lucky one, but that bottle of energy back there thought I was. Was that because she didn't know about my past, only seeing this short, amazing chapter in my life with Chandler?

Chapter 15

She wouldn't think I was so lucky if she found out that I was currently falling for the caring, insightful, dirty man who would leave the moment he caught the killer he was here hunting.

Hearing my name shouted cut through my running thoughts. Scanning the row of registers, I smiled when I found him waving from the counter farthest away from where I stood.

Shuffling toward Chandler, I kept my eyes on the floor but could feel his as I grew closer. The woman who'd helped me hurried past and dumped the pile of clothes onto the counter. The kid behind the register sighed and rolled his eyes at the stack before slowly scanning each tag and dumping them into a waiting plastic bag.

The woman beside him clicked her tongue and came around us, pulling the clothes back out and carefully folding them before placing them into the large green plastic bag. Chandler smiled, his phone pressed to his ear, watching the total tick higher and higher. Embarrassment heated my cheeks as the number rose.

"Well, that's interesting," Chandler said, giving me a pointed look. "No official identification though."

"That'll be $987.63."

I gaped at the kid while Chandler pulled out his credit card and popped the end into the small card reader. My jaw still hung open as Chandler gathered the bags in one hand and nodded toward the automatic doors, indicating it was time to go.

Outside I inhaled deep and tilted my face to the sun, which now shone brightly through the dissipating clouds, warming my face. In typical Chandler fashion, he opened my door even though his hands were full and his shoulder was required to keep the phone glued to his ear.

"Sounds good. Send me the information on her last known location," Chandler said as he slid into the driver seat and slammed the door. "We're already in Waco, so we can check it out." He paused, listening to Alec. "Yep, she's with me." This time he laughed and cut me a nervous glance. "Yeah, I'm taking good care of her. Get your head out of the gutter, fucker. Send me the information and get back to work."

With a chuckle, he disconnected the call and tossed the phone onto the dash.

"Listen, I know it's your birthday," he said and hit the start button for the truck. It instantly rumbled to life. "But I need to do a little work while we're here. After the pet store."

"What does it say about me that I'm more excited about helping with the case than the idea of more shopping?" At his chuckle, I couldn't help but smile. "And why the pet store? That's random."

"For your fish."

"My fish?" *What the hell is he talking about? Is this some kind of kink I've never heard of before?* Staring out the windshield, I racked my brain, trying to figure out what in the hell he was talking about.

"Yeah, last night when you were running away from the confrontation between me and your neighbor, you said you had to feed your fish." He tilted his head. "I figured while we were in town, you could get some fish food."

The giggle started small before turning into a loud, soul-tickling laugh. Every time I glanced at his confused face, another bubble of laughter erupted.

"I don't have a fish. I have no idea why I said that last night." I waved both hands in front of my eyes to dry the laughing-induced tears that were building. "That's sweet though. You wanted to take care of my fictional pet."

Smirking, Chandler shook his head and shifted the truck into Drive. "Well, then, no pet store." A ding from his phone had him inspecting the text. "Good, the address isn't far per Maps."

"Where are we going?" This really was turning out to be the best day ever. First new clothes that actually fit and now working on the case. Obviously I was very easily entertained.

After he tapped the screen a few times, a woman's voice poured from the phone, demanding he turn right.

"The victim we found last night matches the description of a woman reported missing here in Waco. Her roommate said she hasn't been home in two days." I sat up straight. "We knew there had to be a

Chapter 15

reason for the missing fingers and hair. Now we're headed to map out her last steps."

"But the identification isn't confirmed yet," I said, remembering something he'd said while still inside the store.

"No, not a true DNA match. They're working on it now. But based on the picture the roommate sent over, we're almost positive it's the same woman. She went missing at a popular college nightclub here in Waco. I need to get their surveillance footage, search for her car, talk to her friends. This is the first hint we've had to his hunting ground. It's huge for the case."

"Yes and no," I mused as I thought through everything I remembered about the case and profile.

"What do you mean?"

"You said hunting ground, but isn't it just this one so far?" Chandler dipped his chin. "So this is more of a one-off. This victim is an anomaly, which points to someone in Orin being responsible instead of an outsider. If it was an outsider, the anomaly would be victims we couldn't identify, but it's the opposite in this case. The other victims haven't been reported missing or have DNA in the system. This one does. So I'd be asking the question, why was she different?"

He rubbed a palm along his jaw, his head tilting one way and then the other as he thought it through.

"You're right," he said. I sat up straighter in the seat, pride roaring through me with those two words. "Don't look so shocked. You're good at this. That begs the question, then, where is his hunting ground? He has transportation to take a victim all the way from Waco to Orin, so the radius could be huge. If the other victims weren't from The Church—"

I held out a hand, stopping him. "Just because I didn't recognize the victims' faces doesn't mean they weren't from the community. Women came and left the compound often. They were sold a utopia way of life, then found out what they'd have to give up to have it and left. So maybe these women we can't identify weren't a part of The Church but weren't reported missing because their loved ones thought they were still inside the compound... happy." I swallowed the remaining sliver of grape candy. "Only those of us born into that life were too scared to leave. We were more held captive by our own fears and disillusions of the outside world than anyone preventing us from leaving."

"Except you."

I set an elbow on the door ledge and sighed. How did I explain there was always this voice that told me throughout my time in The Church that the life I was living wasn't right? How would a child who'd never seen the outside world know she was being fed lies?

And even stranger, how did I have dreams that seemed more like memories of a happy blonde-haired, blue-eyed girl held in the loving arms of a woman who looked just like her?

How did I explain the feeling of wrongness I lived with every day until I woke up broken and bruised outside those gates? And, even stranger, that I didn't feel hope for more than barely living until he walked into the bar?

16

Chandler

Ellie's soft snores from the other side of the truck warmed me from the inside out. A semitruck's headlights flashed from the other side of the interstate, and I narrowed my eyes to keep from being momentarily blinded. Fuck, I hated driving at night.

The sharp ring of an incoming call jolted me into action, swiping the screen to answer before the sound could wake my sleeping beauty.

My?

Hell, Alec was right about me falling and not tripping.

"Hey," I said softly. "Hold on a second while I get my earbuds in." One hand on the wheel, I blindly dug around the center console, retrieving the small plastic square case. I waited for the connection to click over once both were in place. "There. Sorry, driving back from Waco now."

"It's nearly ten," Alec stated from the other end of the line. "You've been there all day?"

"Your observation skills are uncanny. No wonder you're a Ranger." A deep rumbled laugh seemed to vibrate the buds in my ear. "What did you find out?"

"You first."

Sighing, I switched hands on the wheel and leaned against the door. "The surveillance footage showed nothing we could use. She was there alone, then left alone. Her car is still in the parking lot. We had it opened, but again, nothing. Her friends said she'd just broken up with a boyfriend and was at the bar that night to drink her anger away."

"Why didn't they go with her?"

"They have exams coming up, they said." I rolled my eyes. Who let their upset friend go out to drink alone? "To their credit, it's not like we've spread the news of a man abducting women and killing them since we had zero clue where he was hunting his victims. But I have a feeling the media will pick up on it now."

"Yep. We just positively ID'd her. The parents are on the way to Dallas to collect the body, and I'm already fielding calls from multiple news outlets in Waco."

Guilt gnawed, making the Whataburger cheeseburger I ate for dinner sit heavy in my stomach. "Ellie had a thought that this victim is an anomaly. We shouldn't consider Waco his hunting ground now. Instead, still consider someone local or inside The Church."

"Smart girl."

"That she is."

"Oh hell." Alec cackled. "You've got it bad. I swear I heard a teen girl lovesick sigh at the end of that."

"Did not," I denied gruffly.

"Anyway, I agree with her. All of this is pointing toward that place or a local. That's how he knows which victims to target, knows they won't be missed."

"Why this latest victim though?" I thumped my thumb on the steering wheel. "Why go from unidentifiable victims to snatching a woman at a bar, a college student no less? The age doesn't even fit with the other victims."

Chapter 16

"Desperation?"

"Maybe. We should focus on why this one was special to make him bypass his normal target. So we're back to thinking a local or someone inside The Church as our unsub."

"The local part is hard for me to comprehend. We've gone over your profile and compared it to the local residents and came up empty, remember? But...," he said, drawing out the word. "Okay, here's an idea. Not everyone in Orin comes into town frequently. There are lots of loners. So it could be one of them, someone I'm not thinking of because I've never met them personally or seen them around town. The Jacob angle is the strongest possibility to me. Everything points to him. Hell, he already makes it known he wants Ellie to come back to him. Or maybe a member's wife left when she realized the type of utopia wasn't what she wanted."

"You mean turning women into nothing but mindless, submissive sex toys."

"Exactly. What woman from the outside would agree to that unless they were already in an abusive relationship?"

"Okay, I see what you're saying. The woman came with the husband, or boyfriend, stayed a few years, realized it wasn't what she wanted after all, and left, leaving our unsub desperate to have her back." I nodded. "That sounds plausible. Between that scenario or Jacob himself, we need to get in there and ask questions, and start looking at some of those loners you mentioned and compare them to the profile."

Alec let out a heavy sigh. "There's only one way Jacob will let us through the gates."

I glanced to the other side of the truck. Her lips had parted, lashes fluttering with the movement behind her lids. "That's not going to happen. I won't use her as our key to get into the compound."

"Can you get a warrant?"

Sighing, I rubbed my brows. "No. Especially not with this new victim being from Waco. I can't justify breaking their freedom of religion on a gut feeling."

"What did she say about that fucker Swann and the timeline of current victims starting up when she walked out on him? He patrols that area, would see the women leaving the community. Maybe picked them up in his squad car saying he would help them get somewhere safe."

"She said it's not him." What she revealed about Swann's impotence flashed in my mind, making a question surface. "Was the recent victim raped?"

"Yes," Alec growled. "The ME confirmed both vaginal and anal tearing."

"Is there a way he can tell if it was done… organically?" I rolled my eyes at myself.

"What? What are you getting at."

"I need to know if the unsub raped them himself or if he used other objects." Silence carried over the phone. Alec was too smart for his own good. He knew I was holding something back. And I was, but now that I was on this line of thinking, something else occurred to me. "What if he stabs them not because they're done being useful, but because they can't give him what he wants?"

"A boner?"

"Exactly. Impotence is high in men like this. It could be why he started abducting women in the beginning. To test out different ways to help him get hard."

"I'm disturbed by the information that you store in that head of yours, Chan."

I chuckled. "Me too."

"I'll ask the ME to look for evidence of objects used. This case just keeps getting more fucked-up the deeper we dig."

"I've never had a case that doesn't," I admitted. It was the truth too. The deeper you dug into the disturbed mind to find out the why, shit got fucking crazy.

"Moving off disturbing shit. What were you and Ellie already doing in Waco when I called this morning?"

I shrugged even though he couldn't see me. "She needed a new coat and so did I, and then, well…." I sighed. "Did you know they never told her a birth date?"

"Get the fuck out. I thought they just didn't tell her the year or didn't have a calendar when she said she didn't know how old she was."

"Same. So she's never had a birthday."

"Please tell me you rectified that today. I'll taser your ass if you didn't."

"Of course I did." I held a breath, not wanting to admit what was sitting heavy on my chest.

"But?" he drew out, indicating he wanted me to fill in the blanks I was obviously leaving out.

"Fuck, you're observant. I had fun today, real fun watching her and just hanging out." I left getting the best head I'd ever had in my life out. Didn't want to make him jealous. "This is getting real, and I don't know how I'll let her go when all this is done." I swallowed hard. "When I'm with her, it all doesn't seem so bad."

"What doesn't."

"Life. Living. My job. The world."

He whistled, nearly shattering my eardrums. "Don't fuck this up, Chan."

"Stop it with the fucking Chan shit."

"Never. Especially now that I know you hate it." I could hear the smile in his voice. "If you've found someone who understands your dark, fucked-up head and helps lift some of the weight our jobs press on our shoulders daily, well, then, I'm damn jealous."

"But it can't go past this, right?" I relaxed back against the seat, suddenly realizing I was sitting up straight, tension tightening my spine.

"That's all up to you and her. I will tell you one truth." He paused, leaving me hanging for his next words. "You fuck this up and hurt her, I will kill you."

The seriousness in his tone had me sitting straight in the seat once again. "I have a feeling you mean that."

"She's a good woman who's been through hell. I wouldn't be much of a man if I sat back and watched her get hurt again." His sigh filled the earbuds. "I'll go talk to the ME, then head out. Should be back in Orin by morning. Don't wake me until Tuesday unless something big happens in the case."

Concern for my friend grew as his loud yawn filled my ears. "How about you get a hotel, put it on the FBI's tab. I don't want you falling asleep at the wheel."

"Aw, Chan Chan, you do care."

"Seriously? Now you're saying it twice."

"I'll be fine, but thanks for the offer. You're a good friend. Later."

Flicking my blinker, I slowed to take the single exit to the small town of Orin, Texas. The light at the main intersection blinked red in all directions. With zero other cars on the road for miles, I rolled through, foregoing coming to a complete stop. I hadn't even crossed the intersection when blue and red lights flashed in the rearview.

"Fucking hell," I muttered under my breath as I pulled to the shoulder and slammed the truck into Park. I grimaced when the noise had Ellie shifting in the seat. I held a breath until she settled and fell back asleep. I loved that she felt safe with me to sleep that soundly, to know I'd protect her from all dangers.

Tearing my gaze away from her, I squinted at the side mirror. With the glaring lights, there was no way to see the face of the officer approaching, but I certainly recognized the cocky-ass swagger and stocky stature.

Fucking Swann.

Him pulling me over the second I turned into town couldn't be a coincidence. It was almost like he was waiting for me. Alec's reasoning behind keeping Swann as a suspect lingered in the back of my head as the fucker stopped beside the driver side window. The window I had yet to roll down. I smiled through the tinted glass, and his annoyed scowl deepened.

With the end of a blue ballpoint pen, he tapped against the window. Once it was halfway down, he leaned closer. The smell of stale booze wafted off him like it was clinging to his pores. "Do you know why I pulled you over?" he said with an unfriendly smile that made his full cheeks bunch.

"Because you're a cocky prick who feels the need to prove his power by preying on the innocent and unassuming?" I raised both brows like I expected him to agree to my pointedly accurate statement.

"Get out of the truck," he growled and took a step back, fully expecting me to obey his direct order.

"That's a solid no." Using my heels against the floorboard as leverage, I raised off the seat and pulled out my badge. Flipping the leather covering down, I pointed toward my papers. "Mine's bigger than yours."

I shouldn't goad this manipulative asshat. I really shouldn't, but I couldn't help it.

"You think you're tough shit, don't you?"

I nodded and gave a pointed look to my still raised papers. "This is proof."

"You can't even find the man behind the case you're here to solve." Okay, he had a point there. "You're nothing more than a posturing Fed leaving all the hard work to us locals." No point there. "Where have you been?"

I didn't miss the way he shifted to see through to the passenger seat. I angled my shoulders so he couldn't see Ellie without making it obvious.

"Well now, Chief Swann, it's none of your business where I've been. I don't have to report my whereabouts to you."

"You can't save her," Swann snarled, some of his spit flicking on the tinted window.

My hackles rose at the clear threat. "Save who from what?"

"This is her life. She belongs with me. After everything I did for her, she's mine."

Disgusted and furious at his words of ownership over another person, I reached for the door handle, ready to kick his ass all the way to Dallas.

"I don't belong to anyone."

Keeping my gaze on Swann in case he tried to do something stupid like taser me, I leaned back against the seat. The now awake

Ellie kneeled in the seat, both hands on her hips, glaring the promise of death at the idiot police chief.

"Oh, hey there, Lizzy. You okay? I was worried about you." He dropped the asshole stance and stepped toward the truck. "What were you doing leaving town? It's not safe, not for someone like you."

"You don't own me, Brett." Her words were hard, but I heard the tremble in her voice. Standing up to one's abuser took guts, but even the strongest person would feel distress during the confrontation. "I've told you before, I'm not coming back. I'm not coming back to you, to Jacob, no one."

"So, what, you're with him now?" he mocked. "The gay Fed who'll use you and leave? I'm here for you. I've always been there for you."

"No," she said, shaking her head, sending dark short locks brushing against her neck. "You've been there for you. Leave me alone, Brett. Let me go."

"No," he snapped before regaining some of his composure. "You're just confused. You'll see soon that you're better with me than with anyone else. We understand each other. We were meant to be together." Sliding that hard gaze to me, he attempted to stab me with his beady brown eyes. "This isn't over. Watch your back, Fed."

In the side mirror, I tracked each of his steps as he sauntered back to the squad car. Even after he'd sped away, clearly going over the thirty-five mile per hour speed limit, I sat staring into the dark, barren landscape.

Who threatens a federal agent? The same asshole who won't take no for an answer from the woman he supposedly loves. Clearly something was off in his head, as it was with most narcissists. Was it enough to drive him to murder though? Could he be the man I was hunting, my unsub hidden cleverly in a police uniform?

"I take it back," Ellie said, bringing me out of my own thoughts. "You can totally make fun of his limp dick."

Despite it all, I tipped my head back and laughed.

This woman. I'd be a fool to ever let her go.

Chapter 16

"Thank you for an amazing day," she said on a yawn as we turned into her apartment complex. She stretched her arms high above her head, hooking two fingers together in an exaggerated stretch. "Best birthday ever."

"Investigating a murder victim's last steps and a little shopping at a sporting goods store." I clicked my tongue. "I really know how to make a girl feel special."

I slowed to avoid missing a cat that dashed in front of the truck, then stopped to not hit the dog chasing the cat, and paused even longer to avoid the person chasing the dog. I shook my head at the entire scene while smiling.

"If you'd like to make me feel really special, you could—" Ellie sat up straight in the seat and leaned forward, resting her elbows on the dash as she squinted through the windshield. "Witch's tits."

"What?" I scanned the parking lot on high alert. "What do you see?"

"Not what. Who." The groan in her voice caught me off guard. I followed her pointer finger through the darkened parking lot. My headlights swept the area as I pulled into a parking spot, illuminating two figures standing in front of her door. "My parents."

Oh hell.

My face between her thighs, making her scream my name before burying myself balls deep into that tight pussy I was teased with earlier—that was what I was hoping for to end the night, not an awkward meet-up with the parents who you want to strangle for giving their child to an abuser.

I slid the gearshift into Park and cut the engine. The man who I assumed was her father narrowed his eyes at me, a look of contempt passing over his weathered face. A tall full-figured woman with stringy brown hair and dark eyes smiled, but there was no joy behind it. She stood beside Ellie's father holding a small brown box between her hands.

"I can run them over," I said out of the corner of my mouth. "All you have to say is yes. Or code word 'Chandler's dick tastes better than my Blow Pops.'"

With a lopsided smile, Ellie shook her head. "Even though that statement is accurate, I'll pass. They're not too terrible. It's their quarterly visit to remind me how I'm a disappointment, tell me I should come back to the community, or that I'll rot in hell for not attending to my husband." She sliced a hand through the air like she was physically cutting herself off. "You know, typical parent guilt stuff."

"I don't think it's typical, but I do understand." I tightened my hands on the wheel. "I'm told on a regular basis that since I don't attend church three times a week and didn't rise to my parents' aspirations of being a preacher that I'm doomed to burn for all eternity." I shot her a look and shrugged. "Parents. Am I right?"

Hand on the door handle, she turned to look over her shoulder. A strange expression washed over her features as she looked at me, really looked as if trying to convey something words could never explain. The moment I was alone in the truck, what that look meant hit me in the heart like a powerful punch.

That beautiful, strong woman was falling for me.

And what that revelation did to the dark, broken parts of me solidified one thing.

I was falling hard too.

17

Ellie

OF ALL THE DAMN NIGHTS, they chose *tonight* for a visit. A nagging thought whispered that this was no coincidence. Somehow, just like Brett, the Orin rumor mill notified everyone in a twenty-mile radius that I ventured out of town, with Chandler no less.

The horror. How dare I be so selfish.

With a deep inhale for courage, I leapt from the seat, my boots stamping to the crumbling asphalt. Desperate to get this visit over with, I set my feet in motion, my steps quick in the direction of the people who raised me. Pointless pleasantries bypassed, I maneuvered around the two to unlock the door.

"Elizabeth." Dad's deep voice shot a shiver of repulsion down my spine. Devil's ball sack, I hoped they didn't feel the need to enlighten Chandler on all the ways I was fucked-up in the head. With any luck, they had some lingering self-respect to not divulge all our dark family secrets. "You're to come home with us. This rebellion has gone on long enough."

Rebellion. Right. That was what they called me not returning to the sick asshole who kicked me out of the only home I ever knew all to teach me a lesson, so sure I'd crawl back to him. Jacob or anyone behind those gates never expected me to figure out the real world on my own.

With a dramatic sigh, I shoved a shoulder to the center of the door, wincing slightly at the impact, forcing it to swing open. "Can we *not* do this where all my neighbors can hear?" I waved in the direction of a few curious faces who'd peered out their doors, Stan being one of them. Gesturing into the apartment, I gave them a wide berth as they passed through the open door.

The bags from my shopping trip, and the store we stopped in for him to purchase a few pairs of jeans, hung from Chandler's fingers, colliding against his thighs with each step he took toward my apartment. He paused at the threshold, his face a mask of calm.

"You don't have to stay for this," I whispered so my parents wouldn't hear. "I'll call you?"

"What if I want to stay?" he asked. "I won't say a word, just be there for emotional support." When I didn't respond, he glanced over his shoulder at the truck. "Or I can go. But I'd prefer not to leave you alone with them. I know they're your parents, but I know from experience the mental shit that parents can spew in the matter of minutes that will fuck with your head for days."

"Our parents should never meet," I said. Dad's impatient voice rumbled through the apartment, ordering me to hurry up. "If you stay, don't let what they say affect how you think of me."

Chandler considered my words. "When I was eleven, my mother caught me jacking off. She washed my hands with bleach, then tied them behind my back for two days. I was then forced to watch documentaries on the sexually perverted mind to make sure I knew that sex was from the devil."

"Whoa." Why did that make me feel better rather than worse? He was abused, yet I found comfort in the story.

"Do you now feel differently about me, Ellie?"

Chapter 17

"Well, no, not at all. It makes me feel... understood."

"Well, there you have it. I promise not to pass judgment no matter what I hear inside. And I also promise to not kill them. Tonight."

"But another day is on the table?" I laughed, somehow in this fucked-up situation after his awful childhood story and finding my parents on my stoop.

"Well, yeah. My restraint only goes so far." He peered over my shoulder, and his almost smile vanished. "So what will it be, Ellie? Can I come in, or should I go wait in the truck until they leave?"

Biting the corner of my lip, I stepped aside and gestured into the apartment.

"Don't say I didn't warn you," I muttered to his back as he passed by.

Dread rolled in my belly as I shut and locked the door. Steeling my spine, I pushed my shoulders back and lifted my chin, then immediately rushed to my candy bowl for the necessary sugar support.

They will not have power over me. Their words will not hurt, their reminders will not scare, and their actions will not affect.

Not today, Satan. Not fucking today.

"Your soul will be damned for sleeping with another man's wife." That was what I heard when I rounded the corner, sucking on a Blow Pop—which I'd never be able to eat again without remembering Chandler fucking my mouth. My dad was practically spitting in Chandler's face. But to Chandler's credit, he didn't react, just stepped around my imposing father toward the single bedroom, bags gripped tightly in both hands.

"Can we just assume we're all damned to hell for breathing and move on to you telling me to come back to the compound so I can refuse and you can leave? It's been a long day." And because I knew it would piss them both off, I added, "It is my birthday, after all."

Mother's eyes widened while Dad's face turned a bright shade of red.

"You're a disgrace to this family." I nodded as I swirled the cherry-flavored candy coating along my tongue. "We raised you better than this."

"Yep. Disgrace. Raised me better." Hell, where did this attitude come from? Normally I listened without interruption, then ate an entire tub of ice cream to fill the dark void their words had caused after they left.

The man responsible for this change, encouraging me to be the independent, strong woman with a damn backbone I always wanted, walked back into the room. Crossing both arms over his chest, he leaned against the far wall where he could observe the entire room.

"How could you, Elizabeth? Your beautiful hair." Mom pressed the tips of her fingers against quivering lips. "He loves your hair." Dad rested his hand on her shoulder, his fingers tightening in a silent command. "Sorry," she whispered. "Won't happen again."

"Look at what you're doing to your mother." His dark, soulless eyes slid from me to Chandler. "Whores suffer the most in the depths of hell."

"Well, we haven't gone all the way yet, so maybe I'll have a chance at scoring one of the upper-level rooms." I popped the sucker back between my lips and smirked. Okay, Chandler's game of goading assholes had clearly rubbed off. I liked it.

A slow sinister smile crept up Dad's thin lips. I knew what was coming and braced myself for the wave of disgust that would surely pass over Chandler's face when he learned how disturbed my childhood really was. How could he not be disgusted when he finds out most of what I learned sexually was from watching my parents?

Bile burned up my throat, but I swallowed the revulsion down and swirled the sucker that now tasted like ash.

"Don't," I rasped.

"Don't do what, Elizabeth? Don't tell him the sexual acts he's enjoyed thus far were perfected by my tutelage." Turning with that same conniving smile, he stroked Mother's hair in a placating motion. "Jacob expected Elizabeth to be pure," he explained. "But how would she please him without training?"

Chapter 17

"Porn would've been a better option, in my opinion," Chandler said, his voice tight. "It was a great teacher for me."

Clearly that was not the response Dad expected. His fingers tightened in Mother's hair, but she didn't flinch, only turned those adoring eyes up to him.

"He's done waiting," Dad said with force. "Jacob commands you to come home."

I felt the blood drain from my face. To hide the tremble, I clasped both shaky hands behind my back.

"Have there been new women coming around to placate him?" I kept my gaze glued on the fucked-up couple. Hopefully I could get them to reveal small bits of information that Chandler could use for the case.

"Of course, but you're special, Elizabeth. Not some distraction like the others. You are the chosen one for him." Mother leaned against my father's side. "You are the one he truly wants."

"Let me guess. Those women left the moment they realized the fucked-up life they'd be forced—" I gasped, my next words gone as Dad stepped forward, hand raised high in the air. I didn't shrink from the blow I knew would come next. No way in Hades would I give him the satisfaction of seeing me cower.

But the hit never came. Instead a grunt of pain reached my ears.

I blinked at the scene. Dad's hand was no longer raised ready to strike but secured behind his back by a stone-faced Chandler.

My insides went all squishy and tingly, heat building between my thighs at the sight. He protected me. Intervened on my behalf.

Swoon.

"I will say this once, and only once. Touch her and I will break every finger on the offending hand. Hurt her and I will shove the barrel of my gun up your ass and pull the trigger with zero remorse as your insides splatter against the walls. Do you understand?"

"Don't touch me," Dad bellowed, clearly not happy being the submissive one. A howl of pain echoed around the apartment. His chest rose and fell with rapid breaths.

"I said. Do. You. Understand?"

The menace in Chandler's quiet words sent a shiver down my spine. The thought of that commanding tone directed at me did all sorts of strange things to my body. Sweat beaded along my brow and slicked my palms while my breaths turned to short pants.

"Yes," Dad ground out. The fury behind his eyes was almost enough to send me shrinking back.

Almost.

"It's time you two leave. I've heard your case, and like all the times before, I won't go back. Ever. And as a reminder, if I am taken against my will, or come up missing, the full force of the Texas law enforcement community—"

"And FBI," Chandler added.

"And FBI will be at the gates, armed and willing to search every house to find me. That is not what your fearless leader would want, now is it?" A bit of Chandler's tenacity rolled through me. "Do you understand?" I cocked an eyebrow.

The rage pumping through my father's veins was palpable.

"One day you will pay for this," he spat. "Pray for his forgiveness, but either way, his punishments will be severe."

"Not if I can help it," Chandler nearly growled as he slammed the heel of his hand between Dad's shoulder blades, propelling him forward a couple feet. Dad stumbled to stay upright before shooting a death glare over his shoulder. "She asked you to leave, so leave."

Dad stormed out the door, leaving Mother alone in the middle of the apartment. In what looked like a daze, she shuffled to the kitchen and set the box she held onto the counter. Turning, she took her time surveying the walls, Chandler, then me.

"That was on your front porch when we arrived." Her hair swayed as she nodded toward the box. "Be careful the game you're playing, child. Your words and actions have hurt others. His attention will only be diverted for so long." Her feet barely lifted from the floor as she hurried out of sight.

I jumped when the door slammed shut, the cheap frames around the cat pictures rattling against the wall. My backside cushioned my fall as I slid down the wall until I sat on the floor. Their sour smell lingered in the apartment, making me wish I'd bought that half-burned cinnamon candle at the thrift store last week.

"I'm sorry," Chandler said from where he paced along the other side of the room.

"For what?" I laughed around the Blow Pop. "For standing up for me? I think what you mean is 'you're welcome.'"

"I told you I wouldn't say anything, and I did. I intervened when you didn't ask me to." Rubbing the back of his neck, he paused, staring at the wall. "Tell me he didn't touch you."

I leaned my head back until it hit the wall. Chandler didn't need to clarify what he meant. "He didn't."

His shoulders eased an inch from his ears. "Okay." His voice was strained.

"They made me watch them together. It was a special request from Jacob for his future bride." I studied Chandler's back as it rose and fell with each deep breath. "My father is a gem, as I'm sure you noticed. He took a perverse satisfaction in making me watch as he talked me through my mother's—"

His rage-filled bellow startled me, sucking the next words right out of my throat. The crunch of drywall and wood filled my ears. I scrambled to my feet, tossed the half-eaten sucker toward the kitchen, and darted to where Chandler reared back, ready to assault the wall again. I grasped his bicep, my fingers barely touching around the taut muscle already in forward motion. I cringed, bracing myself to be flung against the wall with the momentum of his punch.

"Ellie," Chandler croaked. His muscles melted, the once fisted hand unfurling to pull me to his chest. Up and down I moved with the cadence of his breaths as his heart pounded beneath my ear. For several minutes we stood sealed together. I cherished the quiet moment, the protection he offered from everything outside the little cocoon of warmth he created around us.

"I want to torture every person who's ever hurt you." He trailed long, comforting strokes up and down my spine, causing me to melt even further into him. "And after all I've seen, I could be very creative."

Unsealing myself from his chest, I rested my chin on his sternum. "Thank you, but I can defeat my own monsters. But knowing I have you as backup makes me stand taller." I tilted my head toward the hole in the wall. "Especially if I'm ever threatened by thirty-year-old drywall."

"How do you do it?" A sense of wonder highlighted his voice.

"One day at a time," I said. "One thing I learned through all the shows and books I've read is that none of what happened was my fault. It happened, and it sucked, but I have the choice to either dwell on it or move on. Every day I choose to move on instead of dwelling. That's how I do it."

"You amaze me," he whispered before brushing his lips against my own. I sighed and molded my body against his. "Every aspect of you sucks me in and holds me captive." Lips to my ear, he nipped at my lobe. "Don't ever stop."

"Never."

He herded me backward until my ass hit the wall, his full weight pressed against me. I lost myself in the sensation of being engulfed by him. Warm, wet lips pressed against the column of my throat, sucking against my throbbing pulse.

"I should go," he muttered against my skin, goose bumps flaring up in the brush of his breath.

"Why, when I want you to stay?"

Pulling back, he stared deep into me, his eyes shifting as if he was reading my thoughts.

"If I stay, I won't keep my hands off you."

"Even after hearing what...." I rolled my eyes, hating myself for bringing it up again. "You know."

"Just because I'm shredded on the inside because of what happened to you doesn't change that I want you. But I was planning to take the high road and let you have some time to yourself if you needed it."

Chapter 17

"I don't need it," I murmured.

His bright blue eyes seemed to darken. "What do you need, Ellie?"

"You."

As if that word was a knife cutting the tether he had on his restraint, Chandler snapped into motion. One hand slipped into my hair, fisting at the base of my neck and holding me captive. A hard thigh wedged between my own and pressed against my throbbing core.

"Dark and dirty, right?" he muttered as he nipped at my collarbone.

"Yes," I begged. "Do your worst, Fed." I don't know why I tossed that slur out, but it added to the naughty nature of what we were about to do. "We shouldn't do this," I moaned, my own words spiking my already heated blood thrumming through me. "Darkest levels of hell, remember?"

A mischievous chuckle tickled the skin of my chest. "At least we'll be there together. It's wrong on so many levels how I want to destroy this tiny body." Releasing my hair, he gripped the hem of my vintage T-shirt and yanked it over my head. With a little help, the sports bra concealing my full chest followed the T-shirt. Chandler stepped back, his rapt attention on my bare chest.

Biting the corner of his lip, he cupped both breasts, thumbs harshly dragging over their pebbled nipples. I sucked in a tight breath and closed my lids, focusing every cell on his dominating touch. I jolted against the wall when his flattened tongue dragged over one before switching to the other. Wetness collected between my thighs, no doubt dampening his dark slacks.

A flash of pain that quickly morphed into pleasure had my eyes flaring open to watch him nibble and bite the full flesh of my breast while his expert fingers tweaked and pulled the nipple on the other. Unable to stop, I slid both hands over his short-cropped hair, urging him to take more, to make it hurt in the best way possible.

"Nope." Tilting back, Chandler dropped his hands to his belt and worked the clasp. Pulling the thin leather through, he held it in one hand and gathered both of mine behind my back. After securing both together with the belt, the efficiency of his quick movements signaling this wasn't his first time, he gazed down at his work. "Better. But not quite." His short nails scraped along my hip bones, dipping into my jeans before sliding them down to my feet. Boots first, then socks, and finally pants were tossed to the side. "Perfect."

The single word was said more to my pussy than to my face. Falling to his knees, he pressed his nose to my center and inhaled deep. My legs wobbled as a surge of desire pounded through me at the erotic scene.

"Chandler," I said, chest heaving up and down as I stared at him. "I've never…. No one has ever…."

Nodding, he placed a tender kiss to my inner thigh before taking a quick nip. I squealed and tried to shuffle away, but his firm grip on my hip stopped my retreat.

"Well, that will change tonight. Come on." Hand clasped against the back of my neck, he guided me to the couch and positioned me on the hard armrest. I squirmed on the rough material, a soft moan escaping at the scrape along my sensitive folds. He clicked his tongue. "No playing without me, baby." With a quick shove between my breasts, I fell backward, a gasp of shock whispering past my lips.

A cloud of dust burst from the cushion at my impact. Chin to my chest, I stared up at the grinning Chandler, not understanding. With a harsh tug, my ass, still positioned on the armrest, lifted and was dragged closer to the edge. Widening my knees, he stood between my spread legs.

"How dirty?" he rasped.

I shouldn't enjoy this side of him, the pure dominance and desire pulsing off him in waves. But I did. And I wanted more of it.

No, fuck that. I wanted it all. This between us would be over soon, and I didn't want to waste a minute of what little time we had.

For the first time in my life, I *wanted* it to hurt instead of *needed* it to. I wanted him. My body demanded him and all the detestable things he had planned.

I was going straight to hell for this.

Chapter 17

"I want it all," I panted. "Don't hold back."

His eyes flared as a smile that promised pain and pleasure spread across his face, bunching his cheeks.

I swallowed, my mouth suddenly scratchy and parched.

There was no going back now.

18

Ellie

Scorching hot palms slid up my naked waist, roughly cupping both breasts and pushing them together. With one hand, he kept them pressed together while the other shoved between them. I gasped at the tug of his skin against my own.

"I want to fuck these later." I nodded. "You'd like that, wouldn't you, baby? To lick my head as it slipped in and out of these huge-ass tits. Marking you as I exploded coating your neck and face."

"This is terrible," I groaned, loving each filthy word.

His dark chuckle drew my focus up to him. "If you think that's bad, wait until we make it here." For emphasis, he pressed against my back hole. I arched my back, lifting my ass off the armrest, giving him more access. He tsked. "Not yet, baby. First I'm going to eat you, lick up what's dripping all over the couch for me." He released my breasts and gave the hardened nipples a quick pinch. After untying my hands, he secured them in front of my chest. "Play with yourself. My attention will be elsewhere." He dragged a thumb through my wet slit. On their own, my hands obeyed his command, grasping handfuls of my breasts. "That's it. Do you play with yourself when you're alone at night?"

Insecurity tried to sweep in, diminishing the pleasure coursing through me. "No. I can't."

"Can't or won't?" he asked casually as he continued sweeping that devilish thumb between my lower lips.

"Won't," I whimpered. "It's never enough."

"What about toys?"

I glared up at him. *Why in the hell is he talking?* "Where would I get those?"

He nodded. "Good point. Pinch like this." Bending forward, he pinched a nipple between his thumb and forefinger and tugged, twisting until I cried out. "We might have to get creative later, then."

Before I could ask what he meant, three fingers edged at my entrance, cutting off all thoughts and words. Again my hips arched off the armrest as his fingers slid easily inside. The tight fit filled me just enough to be a damn tease.

Every thought, every cell zeroed in on his touch and the sparks it sent through my lower belly and beyond. A warm blow of air sent a shiver racing up my spine. Lids hooded, I watched as he blew another soft current of air over my swollen bundle of nerves.

My heels slipped against the side of the couch, desperate for traction but failing.

Blue eyes locked on my own, he flicked the tip of his tongue against my oversensitive clit. I groaned and tugged at the belt, needing to reach up and push his head harder between my thighs, forcing him to apply more pressure.

Over and over he flicked that tongue. I mimicked the move, pinching and teasing my one nipple and then the other until the pain tipped over to pleasure. A scream of ecstasy passed my parted lips when his finally sealed around me and sucked in quick succession. With the pump of his hand and the warmth of his mouth and suction, I shattered.

Back arched off the couch, I flexed my hips as best I could, riding out the most intense orgasm I'd ever had. My breasts jiggled with each of my labored breaths. Still licking, drawing out the aftershocks, his focus was on my swaying breasts.

"More," I said greedily.

"Yes, ma'am." He scraped his teeth against my sensitive nub before flattening his tongue and sweeping a long lick from my entrance upward. After the third swipe, his tongue swirled before slipping inside. With his tongue thrusting inside my channel, he flicked a thumb against my clit. Higher and higher I rose, the two too much before I broke again, this time with a full-body shudder that seemed to travel from toe to crown.

Panting, I attempted to back away from him, but a firm grip on my hip bone held me in place.

"One more." He arched a brow at my whimper. With a wicked gleam in his eyes, he slipped a thumb inside, coating it with my wetness that was no doubt leaving a mark on the couch. Not that I gave two shits. I held in a gasp as he trailed that wet thumb to my back entrance. He swirled the rim, coating it before pressing, demanding entrance. At my squirming, he shushed me. "Relax. You wanted this, remember?"

"Yes, I want it," I begged.

He tugged me farther forward so the edge of my feet dangled in the air, my core now raised high, giving him full access to all of me. I blew out a harsh breath as his thumb slipped fully inside. I closed my lids, enjoying the burn, relishing the foreign, dirty feeling.

"That's it." His lips closed around my clit once again, this time sucking hard, causing more pain than pleasure. My scream turned into a moan as he released and a wave of ecstasy washed through me. Over and over he danced me along the edge of too much pain and rushes of pleasure.

The orgasm consumed me, chasing away any thought other than Chandler.

With zero energy left, I wilted against the couch, attempting to steady my quick breaths. Lids open to thin slits, I watched him stand tall and lick his lips. One by one he worked his way down the buttons of his dress shirt. After tugging the cuffs open, he slipped it from his shoulders and draped it over the back of the couch. Reaching back, he stripped off the white undershirt and tossed it to the floor.

I licked my lips as I visually consumed every bare inch he'd displayed. A narrow, defined chest, lean waist, and rippled stomach. A line of dirty-blond hair trailed down from his belly button, dipping beneath the waistband of his slacks. When I finally dragged my sluggish gaze back up to his, I offered a lazy smile.

"If you're able to smile, I haven't done my job right," he said, casually stroking his hard length over his slacks.

"Well, I guess you better try harder next time," I teased.

His narrowed eyes were like a lightning strike to my desire, flaring it back into a raging inferno.

"Is that a challenge? I—" He stopped and frowned. Slipping a phone out of his slacks, he cursed when he looked at the screen. "It's Alec." A conflicted expression crossed his features.

"Take it. It's why you're here, after all." I didn't mean for my disappointment to leak through, but the bite in my tone snuck free. His brows furrowed. "I'm serious. But first." I held up my secured wrists. "Can you untie me?"

Groaning in defeat, Chandler unfastened the belt around my wrists and helped situate me in a more comfortable position along the couch. After answering the still vibrating phone, he pushed it to his ear.

"What?" he growled. I giggled at his obvious frustration at Alec's timing, which earned me a quick smack to my bare breast. I hissed and grabbed myself, my breasts overflowing in my small hands. Again Chandler groaned, but this time it sounded painful. "Stop that," he snapped. "No, not you, fucker. What do you want?"

I snuggled against Chandler, savoring the feel of his bare chest against my own. An arm draped over my shoulders, securing me even tighter against his side.

"Okay, well, that puts a new spin on things." I shifted back to look up at his strong jaw. "It was a hunch, but it might offer a new set of suspects. I'll ask the FBI analyst at Quantico to run prescriptions for

Chapter 18

erectile dysfunction in a hundred-mile radius, or organic meds if HIPAA prevents her from seeing prescription records. Then we'll narrow it down from there based on other parameters we already know."

I pressed a hand to his hard chest to put some space between us. "What are you talking about?" I asked.

Chandler's index finger pressed hard against my lips and shook his head. Annoyance had me gritting my teeth and nipping at the pad of the finger he shushed me with. Taking advantage of the opportunity, he slipped that single digit between my lips.

"I'm going tomorrow," Chandler said into the mouthpiece, but his entire focus was on his finger pumping between my pressed lips. "No, she's won't be with me." I narrowed my eyes and pulled back until his finger popped free. "I'll work on revising the profile tonight. With the impotence angle, the stabbing could be from sexual frustration, needing to penetrate the victim one last time but frustrated that it can't be him." He paused and rolled his eyes. "Yes, you did interrupt something." Another pause, Alec's deep muffled voice barely filtering past Chandler's ear. "No, unfortunately you killed the mood." He cringed. "Poor choice of words. Great, see you in a few hours."

Tossing the phone to the floor, he groaned and rested his head against the back of the couch, closing his eyes, but the strain on his features remained.

"You're going to the compound tomorrow," I stated after piecing together what I could of the one-sided conversation. " You think it's Jacob or someone inside?" Unable to resist, I skimmed a finger along his hard stomach, savoring the way the muscles twitched under my touch.

"No. Yes. Hell." He groaned and rubbed at his brows. "I don't know. Everything points to the unsub being from here, but how could someone keep this hidden this long? It's not like we're talking about a huge population. Someone would've noticed something."

"Which leads us back to The Church, since they could hide in plain sight there."

He nodded. "Which is why I'm going to talk to them tomorrow. See if I can secure a meeting with their security team."

"But the impotence aspect makes you think it's Brett."

"Or someone like him. But just because this fucker used objects to assault his victims doesn't mean he's impotent. Maybe he does it to not leave evidence."

"If it was Jacob or Brett," I whispered, my breath brushing against his pec, "then that message on the body was for me."

"That saying is very common, and we still don't know who it was referring to. But there is a chance." His hand slipped higher and clasped my bare shoulder, holding me tighter. "So far there isn't anything tying you directly to the case, which is good."

"But your gut tells you something, doesn't it?"

He pressed a kiss to my forehead. "My gut tells me I'm missing something. I just hope like hell it's not something that ends up putting you in danger."

"I can protect myself if it comes to that." There was little conviction in my voice. To be honest, I was worried. There was this ominous weight in the air that seemed to mount with each passing day. At some point, it would erupt, but what did that mean for him? For me? "I haven't been much help, have I?"

"Sure you have. You've offered a different perspective on several aspects, making me question and look deeper. I would've never thought to ask about object rape until you mentioned Brett's limp dick."

Despite the topic, I grinned. A sudden chill made my shoulders shake. I curled more of my naked body against him for his body heat.

"I should get dressed." My lips brushed along his sternum as I spoke.

He grunted in annoyed agreement. "Fucking Alec."

I smiled as I stood and stretched both hands high overhead.

Chandler's warm palms burned against the skin of my waist, his touch gentle and possessive. He pitched forward to press a single kiss just below my belly button. "We'll pick this up another time." Stand-

Chapter 18

ing, he adjusted himself and bent to retrieve the cell phone he'd tossed. "I need to call the analyst at Quantico and my boss."

"Yeah, sure, go ahead. I'm going to take a quick shower."

He smiled and dragged his fingers through my short hair. A deep line appeared between his brows as he played with the ends. "You're perfection personified, Ellie. Not because of your beautiful body"—he ran a knuckle down my breast for emphasis—"but because of who you are despite the challenges you've faced." His features softened as he cupped my face. "I'm in awe of you."

"Same," I whispered.

After a soft kiss, his hand slipped away.

With a sheepish smile, I turned toward the kitchen and grabbed the box my mother left on the counter. Chandler was already talking to whomever as I shut the bedroom door. After tossing the box onto the bed, I made my way to the shower and turned the handle all the way left. Fingers dancing in the cold spray, I waited for the water to warm, staring at myself in the mirror.

The pink highlighting my cheeks, flushed splotched skin, mussed hair. I was anything but beautiful, but I felt like I was. For the first time in my life, I saw past my imperfections in the mirror to the strong, beautiful woman beneath. It was because of him. I was beginning to see myself like he saw me. Unlike with Jacob and Brett, who tore me down until all I saw were my many flaws, Chandler's words and touch made me feel beautiful, sexy even.

With the water warm, I stepped into the spray. I gasped when I slid a hand over my breast, my abused nipple sore to even the gentlest of touches. Smiling into the spray, I finished rinsing off the soap and shut off the water, knowing it would turn icy cold quickly if I didn't rush.

Threadbare towel secured around my chest and my spare tied like a turban around my head, I stepped from the bathroom, steam billowing into the bedroom the moment I opened the door. The simple brown box lying in the middle of my bed held my attention, my curiosity growing while I pulled out clean underwear and pajamas. I tossed the clothes onto the bed and sighed.

Might as well go ahead and get this over with.

The soft mattress gave as I kneeled on the bed and stretched, pulling the package closer. No return address was given, or even my own address or name written across the front, meaning someone dropped off the package personally instead of sending it through the mail. Alarm bells rang in the back of my head, but I ignored the warning, ready to open the box and see what was inside. Using the edge of a jagged nail, I sliced through the single layer of clear packing tape securing the top.

I stared at the package, unease making my heart race. Glancing toward the closed bedroom door, I strained to hear Chandler's voice. Relief settled some of my nerves at his muffled words, knowing he was close if I needed him. But I wouldn't, because this was nothing. Probably just another ploy by my parents or Jacob to convince me to come home. I was clearly overreacting because of the case. I wasn't in danger any more than I normally was as a single woman.

And I didn't need Chandler. I could open this stupid, simple box on my own. I wouldn't allow myself to depend on him. This would end soon, and I wouldn't let myself be lost without him once he left. No, I was on my own in life, and I needed to remember that.

I could do this. It was nothing, and I was simply overreacting.

Despite the reassuring thoughts, my fingers trembled as I lifted a hand, giving away to the adrenaline thrumming through me. The edges of the thin cardboard pressed into my fingertips as I peeled apart the top flaps. A foul smell floated up from the inside. Gagging, I smacked a hand over my nose and scurried off the bed, leaving the package in the middle of the mattress.

Turning to call for Chandler, I stopped when his voice drifted from beneath the bedroom door, signaling he was still on the call with Quantico. I shouldn't distract him.

Pressing my lips into a thin line, I looked back to the bed.

It was fine. Probably something dead that Mom or Dad sacrificed to help atone my sins. Sure, they'd never done that before, but who knew what they were into nowadays?

Chapter 18

Using the tips of two fingers, I pulled the half-opened box to the edge of the bed, the smell worsening with each inch it drew closer.

Holding a breath, I again pulled apart the first two flaps and held them open with my wrists as I worked to move the inside two. I squinted at the item nestled in the bottom, not understanding at first. Then relief washed through me when I finally registered what the box held.

A blonde wig. Fucking parents scaring the shit out of me with their fucked-up reminders of the parts of me Jacob loved.

But the smell. That seemed... off.

I frowned and reached inside, pulling the wig out by a chunk of long blonde strands.

When I'd lifted it halfway, the spatter of red on the ends caught my eye first, then the jagged edges along what looked to be pale skin.

A scream lodged in my throat as everything clicked.

Dropping the human hair, I stumbled backward, my back slamming to the wall. Still I tried to retreat, scooting along the wall until I came to the bedroom door. I fumbled with the knob, the metal slipping in my sweat-slick palm. Finally the scream that had been silent erupted in a high-pitched wail, piercing my eardrums.

The floor beneath my bare feet shook before the door slammed open. The force sent me soaring to the opposite wall. Chandler's eyes widened as I smacked against the drywall and crumbled to the ground.

"Fuck," he yelled while rushing to my side. "What's going—"

Nose twitching, he swiveled on the balls of his feet, scrutinizing every inch of the room. His all-seeing gaze paused at the open box and ball of blonde hair on the bed.

A string of curses fell on deaf ears, the ringing too loud to understand a word he said. Next thing I knew, I was scooped into a strong hold, and we raced from the room. Not stopping, he practically yanked the front door off its hinges as he forced it open, then jogged to the truck. Only after I was nestled against the cold leather seat did awareness settle in.

"I'm in a towel." My voice sounded odd, distant.

"I'll grab some clothes and shoes. Ellie—" He cut himself off and looked back to my apartment, his brows furrowed.

"I know," I whispered and curled my knees to my chest, not caring that I was flashing my lady bits for the world to see.

Heavy silence enveloped us, neither wanting to voice what we were thinking.

The human scalp inside my apartment solidified one thing.

Our hope of me not being tied to this case was gone.

Whether we liked it or not.

19

Chandler

"I NEED you to stay right here. Do *not* move or open the door for anyone but me. I'm locking you in."

After ensuring she was tucked safely into the truck, I slammed the door and pressed the lock button on the key fob. Before returning to the apartment, I cast one last look through the passenger window.

Ellie was as still as a statue, eyes wide and unblinking, hair still damp from the shower, her only movement the slight tremble in that lower lip. Clearly in shock and barely hanging on to her sanity. Then again, who wouldn't be after receiving a rotting human scalp?

Forcing myself into action, I stormed back to retrieve the cell phone I dropped the moment her terrified scream filled the apartment. Once inside, I paused outside her room, my gaze locked on the grisly package still lying in the same spot from moments earlier as I retrieved the small device from the floor.

I tapped a few buttons and pressed the phone to my ear.

"I'm sorry I cockblocked you earlier, but I won't help you finish."

The lightness in Alec's tone pissed me the fuck off, for no other reason than my endless frustration at myself and the fucker who was tormenting my girl.

"The fucker sent her the missing scalp," I gritted out through clenched teeth. Massaging my brows, I stepped toward the bedroom but halted when the smell became too intense. "Plain brown box, no return address. Just that victim's full scalp, hair still attached."

In the background, the roar of a large diesel engine filled the tense quiet. "You gotta be fucking kidding me. I'll be there as soon as I can."

"I need to get the evidence secured and gathered."

"I'll handle that. There's a guy in Waco whose cell I have on speed dial, unfortunately."

A heavy pause held between us, neither of us knowing what to say.

"She was a blonde," I stated, those four words heavy with meaning.

"Yeah," Alec said. "I saw the picture her parents used when she went missing."

"Long blonde." My concern for Ellie made all the aspects of the case and questions blur. But something her mother said just a few hours earlier snapped to the forefront of my mind. "Ellie used to have long blonde hair, right?"

"Yes. She started cutting it and dying it after she left Brett. Said she didn't like what it stood for."

"It had something to do with Jacob."

"Which, if this gift was long blonde hair when Ellie dyes hers the complete opposite...."

"This is more evidence that the cult is involved in some way."

"But why now?" Alec asked. "She's been dying her hair for two years now. Maybe he really hates the new color?" I tilted my head one way and then the other, debating his question. "You think it's Jacob, then?" he asked before I could respond.

"If not him directly, then he's orchestrating it somehow. Or maybe it's one of the other men within the compound who wanted her, but

Chapter 19

she was given to that bastard Jacob instead." I paced. "One thing is for certain, Ellie is at the heart of it all."

Alec cursed. "Hasn't that poor girl been through enough? And now she has a sick motherfucker thinking she's his and needs to come back to him?" He let out a resigned sigh. "I don't know how you do this every day."

"It's normally not this—" I searched my scattered brain for the right word. "—personal. I've always taken what happens after I arrive as my fault, letting the weight of the guilt push me to do more, see more. But now?" I leaned against the wall and let my head thump against it, closing my eyes, hating what I was about to admit. "Now I can't think clearly. All I can focus on is getting her somewhere safe and not on the case. I don't think I can protect her and do my job to the best of my ability at the same time." Casting a long look out the front door, I groaned. "Now I'm no good to her or this town."

"Hold off on berating yourself too much there, Chan Chan." I rolled my eyes, but a fraction of the weight on my shoulders lifted at his attempt at breaking through to me. "None of this is your fault unless you're the killer we're searching for." I let out an incredulous huff. "Well, then, there you go. And no one would be able to think clearly right now. You have her there, vulnerable, a scalp in the other room, and I'm guessing she's a bit distressed at what was in the box and the realization that she's this psycho's target."

"You're right," I groaned. "But it still sounds like an excuse."

"Get her to our place. Make sure she's safe and taken care of. I'll make the necessary calls and meet you back at the house in about forty minutes. We'll powwow then and come up with new suspects. Don't think this is all on your shoulders. I'm here, and once Ellie shakes out of her shock, she'll help too. With her being the center of all this, we now have a base. We go through her past, match up dates with her life, and circle out from there. This is actually a good thing."

"Seriously?"

"Once you're not in the midst of it all, you'll see that too. This fucker made a mistake tonight."

"Showing us the 'who,'" I mused.

"And making this personal to two scary bastards who are set on protecting that woman no matter the cost."

"Damn right."

"That's the spirit. Forty minutes. See you at the house."

The line went dead.

Inhaling deep, I immediately regretted it as the stench of decay infiltrated my nose. Shaking out my self-doubt and heavy guilt, I swiped my undershirt off the floor and pulled it over my head, grabbing my dress shirt at the last second. Holding my breath, I slipped into her room, grabbed the bags of new clothes and her favorite boots.

The moment I stepped over the threshold heading outside, I inhaled a deep breath of clean evening air. Some of the tension eased until movement around the truck caught my eye. A man stood beside the passenger side door, hands pressed to the window.

"Hey," I shouted, striding toward the truck, the bags swaying awkwardly against my knees. The man turned, and the one working security light highlighted Stan's face. "What the hell do you think you're doing?"

Stan pressed a shoulder against the truck's black paint and crossed his arms, effectively blocking my access to Ellie. The thin plastic of the clothing bags dug into my fingers, cutting off circulation as my grip tightened.

"I'm making sure she's okay. I heard a scream, and now she's locked in your truck. The fuck you doing to her?" Popping off the truck, he took a menacing step closer. A cocky laugh rumbled in my chest at the thought of him trying to fight me. "Where you taking her?"

"I didn't do anything to Ellie." When I passed by, my shoulder happened to slam into his chest, sending him stumbling back. I dropped the bags to the pavement beside the back door. "And where I'm taking her is none of your concern."

"Sure as fuck is. We watch out for each other around here, and I don't know you."

"I'm a fully background-checked federal agent who only has the

Chapter 19

best intentions for that woman sitting nearly traumatized in the truck. She's safe."

"Says you. Seems like the opposite to me."

I didn't flinch when his words hit home, pouring salt on the gash my own doubt and guilt inflicted. "Better with me than you."

"Ellie." Stan turned and yelled at the window. "You don't have to go with him."

She didn't move, simply kept that unseeing stare toward the now closed door of her apartment.

"I don't have time for this." I fished a business card out of my pocket and tossed it to him. He fumbled to catch it before it fluttered to the ground. "That's my cell. Call me if you have any information about who left a package on her front step earlier tonight. Ask around, see if anyone can describe who left it or when it was dropped it off." He eyed the card suspiciously. "But right now she's in shock and needs to get out of here."

He looked over his shoulder, those big bushy brows furrowing in concentration.

"This isn't the first box to be left."

"What?" I roared in his face. "And you didn't think to tell her, or me?"

Stan flicked his gaze nervously around the parking lot, licking his lips. "It's only been a few times, or maybe a little more. I knew she wouldn't want them, so I picked them up before she saw they were left for her. I never saw who left them though. They just appeared."

I held a breath to keep myself from killing the man who'd tampered with evidence. "Where are they?"

"I tossed them." His response was soft. But was that remorse for throwing away evidence or because he didn't want competition from Jacob?

"What was in them?"

"I... I didn't look. I just threw them in the dumpster out back." He sighed and glanced to Ellie. "I know that cult wants her to come back. It's why I do it. She doesn't belong with them. This is her home."

"With you?" I questioned.

"With us. Not in there dying each day. Everyone around here knows what goes on behind them fences. Ellie is special. She doesn't deserve that."

This was going nowhere, and I still had a semi-catatonic Ellie to think about. "Someone will be by soon to collect evidence inside the apartment. Do not let anyone inside until they arrive. Are we clear?" Not waiting for an answer, I unlocked the doors, tossed the bags into the back seat, and slammed the door closed. "Call me if you think of anything or anyone suspicious lately."

At that, I rounded the hood and climbed into the truck, hitting the start button before the door was closed. The engine roared to life, pumping warm air through the vents, the engine still somewhat warm from the earlier road trip.

Ellie stayed silent, completely still besides her trembling shoulders as I backed out of the parking spot. Goose bumps covered her bare skin, and her lips were a soft shade of blue.

"Damnit," I muttered to myself. Shifting into Park, I reached into the back, pulling my dress shirt over to the front seat. Careful to make my movements slow, I draped the shirt over her shoulders and tucked the ends beneath her thighs. After securing her seat belt, I leaned back to my seat and put the truck back in gear.

She stayed silent the entire ride, not that I said anything either. What was there to say? Casual conversation about the weather seemed silly when the night had taken a dark turn. So instead of saying anything, I reached over the center console and slid my fingers into hers, offering her the little comfort I could while driving.

But it wasn't enough. None of what I could do was enough. Once again I was failing when others needed me most. I wasn't asking the right questions or putting the information together fast enough, and now the one woman who made me feel less broken was the one in danger.

I had to find the unsub before it was too late.

For Ellie, and for me. If something happened to her because I couldn't solve the puzzle in time, I'd never forgive myself. I'd drown in the ocean of guilt that I'd barely kept at bay this past year.

Chapter 19

So there I had it.
Save Ellie and save myself.
I would not fail her.
No matter the cost.

THE SLAM of the garage door rattled through the house, all the way to the bedroom where I lay staring at the ceiling. Alec was back. Rolling off the bed, I swung my legs over the edge and braced both elbows on my knees.

"Where are you going?" Ellie's voice was quiet, heavy with exhaustion.

"Alec is back. We need to... plan." The handmade quilt twisted with my movement as I turned toward the other side of the bed where she lay. "We'll be right down the hall if you need us. But don't be scared. We've got you."

"Chandler," she said as she pushed up to her elbows. "I'm not scared."

Surprise lifted both brows high on my forehead. "You're not?"

Short dark locks shifted along her neck. "Shocked, sure. But scared, no. I know you're here." Her timid smile warmed my soul. "And you'll find him before anything can happen to me." Twisting out of the piles of blankets I'd covered her with earlier she mimicked my stance, her toes dangled just over the carpet. "I want to help."

"Ellie," I groaned. "Give yourself tonight."

"You're not," she countered, raising her chin defiantly. "And I feel —" She rubbed at her sternum with a small fist. "—guilty."

"Guilty?" I countered. "That's my job. I'm the one who hasn't caught the bastard."

"And I'm the one he's after. All those women." Tears built in her lower lids. "All those women died because of me."

I was across the bed in an instant, gripping her chin between two fingers and forcing her to look up to where I towered over her small frame. "He's the one responsible for all this, not you. Do you hear me,

Ellie?" I cocked my head to the side, a sudden realization hitting me. "I don't know your last name."

"I don't have one."

"What?"

She shrugged. "I didn't want to keep Jacob's and never came up with another one. Besides, last names are familiar, showing a family line and where you belong. I don't belong anywhere."

I angled my head right, then left, inspecting each inch of her face. "Well, maybe one day we can fix that. But right now," I said, an idea already running through my head, "we have an unsub to profile."

Standing, I extended a hand and helped her off the high bed. The movement made her tits bounce beneath my dress shirt, now slightly sheer from her wet hair. I pursed my lips.

"Would you mind putting on something a little more...?" I waved a hand, drawing her attention to her nipples pointing straight at me. "I really don't want to kick Alec's ass for staring at those gorgeous tits of yours."

"He wouldn't," she said with fake audacity.

"He's a guy, and you're beautiful and mostly naked, so yes, yes he would."

She chewed on her lip, reminding me of something else.

"Oh, and I dumped what was left of your candy bowl into one of those big green bags on my way out of your apartment." Her eyes lit up again, warming a part of me that had turned gray with the night's events. "I'll meet you out there when you're ready."

She nodded, tucking a damp strand of hair behind her ear. "Chandler," she said when I was halfway through the door. "I hope this doesn't dampen our, um, rain check on the earlier festivities."

A shot her a wink. "Let's narrow down the list of suspects. Then we'll talk about finishing what we started."

Crossing her arms over her ample chest, she huffed. "I hate this guy even more now."

"Same, baby, same."

With a smile on my lips, I closed the door, giving her privacy to change. I'd already secured the window and checked the closet and under the bed—twice—so I knew she was safe alone.

When I rounded the corner, only Alec's wide ass was visible, the rest of his bulky frame hidden behind the opened refrigerator door.

"I can hear you thinking." His voice was muffled. "How is she?"

"Better than I would be, I think." The wooden chair legs scraped along the floor as I pulled it away from the table. Falling into the hard seat, I pressed an elbow onto the table and rested my head on my fisted knuckles. Something about her parents' earlier visit that wouldn't stop bothering me nagged at me again. "Have you ever met her parents?"

"Those fuckheads don't deserve the title, but yeah. Why?"

"They were there tonight when we pulled up to her apartment." The contents of the fridge rattled, glass jars clinking with the slam of the door. "Did anything ever bother you about them, besides how they raised her and gave her to that asshole Jacob?"

Alec ripped the thin plastic off the block of cheese in his hand and took a huge bite. I shook my head, fighting a laugh.

"What? I was hungry, and we have shit here. One of us needs to go grocery shopping."

"You mean go through what's on the shelves at the Food Mart that might have expired in 2018?"

"Better than nothing. And besides them being the two worst people I've ever met—mind you, I know Brett and have met Jacob—nothing stands out. Why, something bothering you about those two?"

I nodded and dropped my hand to the table. "I've seen so many different families all across the US and even some abroad. And I've always been able to see at least one similarity. Whether it's in the color of their hair, or eyes, or build. Sometimes it's even the texture of the hair. But they all have something similar." Leaning the chair back on two legs, I looked down the hall for Ellie in case she was eavesdropping. "She looks nothing like them. Not a single similar quality. Not one. Considering how they treated her, what they forced her to watch, and how easily they seemed to give her away, I don't know. It raises my suspicion."

Alec tore another bite of cheese off the block and chewed while looking past me, deep in thought. "I wouldn't put it past them to switch around babies so no one is attached. That would explain the detachment and zero similarities."

I deflated a little. He was right. And it made more sense than the way my imagination was taking me. But still, the inkling that something wasn't right wouldn't go away.

Lost in thought, I failed to notice Ellie until she was standing directly in front of me.

"Hey, you good?" Alec asked. Tossing the half-eaten cheese block into the fridge, he made his way to the table and pulled her into a tight hug. "Don't worry. You're safe with us."

"I know," she said with an eye roll. I fought a grin. "And I can take care of myself too." Alec and I shared a look. "What?" she exclaimed, pushing out of his hold and resting her small backside on my thigh. I adjusted, widening my legs to make it more comfortable for her. "I can take care of myself."

"It's not that we don't believe you, Ellie. It's just... this man who's clearly fixated on you...." Alec waved to me. "You explain it to her."

Wrapping an arm around her waist, I urged her higher up my thigh. "What Alec is trying to say is this guy is strong. It takes an enormous amount of force to break through the upper rib cage with a blade. The bruising around the wound was deep too. We're not saying you can't take care of yourself, but this is an anomaly."

"Fine." She sighed, a little deflated. "But I won't let myself become dependent on you guys, let you have power over me. I can't go back to that."

"We're nothing like Brett or Jacob," I said with bite to my tone. My hackles rose at even the suggestion.

"I know. I mean, I think I know. It's just... I've worked hard to be okay on my own, and I don't want to go back to needing someone else."

I nodded, hating it but understanding.

"So." She pulled a Blow Pop from a hidden side pocket of the new leggings. "Where do we start on catching this asshole?"

I shouldn't have felt relief, not with me failing her so terribly, but I did.

That half smirk, the hope shining in her eyes, and the excitement clearly rushing through her veins were enough to ease my overprotective urges. She was handling this better than I was. Pride grew for my girl in how strong she was in the face of all this.

I tugged her closer, and she leaned against my chest and nestled her head in the crook of my neck.

And that solidified it for me.

Her strength yet vulnerability in my arms.

I would never let her go.

20

Chandler

Finally the house was quiet.

After nodding off twice at the table while creating a list of suspects, Ellie begrudgingly went to bed and was asleep within minutes of her head hitting the pillow. Alec was quick to follow, having been up for almost forty-eight hours.

Now it was just me, the case, and the various Jesus portraits that seemed to stare into my soul with their tracking gazes. It was as if they knew what I'd done to Ellie earlier and were condemning me with their solemn expressions. I physically shook off the eerie sense of being watched.

With Ellie's suspect list laid out in front of me, timeline of events next to it, and a fresh pot of coffee brewing, I could finally focus on identifying this bastard. Having Ellie's input and Alec's assistance was beneficial, making me consider aspects I wouldn't have before, but working alone was how I pulled all the pieces together.

Now it was time to solve this case, catch the unsub, and ensure Ellie was safe.

The reminder that I wouldn't be here to protect her after the case was solved threatened to disrupt my focus, but I pushed that problem to the back of my mind to resolve at another time. The gurgle of the brewing coffee filled the silence as I stared at her list.

A few names I recognized, some I didn't.

It was a good list, but I needed to make my own too based on my years of experience with the FBI and what I'd witnessed since arriving in Orin. Knowing she was the focus of the unsub made narrowing down the list quick and short, pared down to those who'd inserted themselves into the case or had been impactful in her life.

I scribbled the names as they came to mind.

Jacob.

Swann.

Stan.

Guy she went on a date with.

Someone inside The Church—not Jacob.

I tapped the end of a blue ballpoint pen against the yellow legal pad, staring at the list in hopes the clues would all magically fuse together, pointing me toward the killer. Sighing, I pushed from the table to make the cup of coffee I desperately needed. I filled the large mug to the brim and reclaimed my still warm chair.

First I needed to narrow down what I knew about each of the suspects on my list. The three I knew fit one or more aspects of the profile, and they all had a personal connection to Ellie. But what about opportunity, or motive? It didn't matter if they checked every aspect of the profile, because if they didn't have the opportunity or motive, then I was back to square one.

I needed to dig deeper into each suspect to determine who had both. In past cases, this was the point when I'd pass my suspect list off to the detective to find out the answer to those two imposing questions. But this case was different. One of the suspects was the chief of police, and plus, like I told Alec earlier, this case was personal.

Chapter 20

So no, I wouldn't hand this list off. I'd handle the investigation from here.

Focusing on the first name on the list, I racked my brain on everything I knew about the bastard Jacob. Forced Ellie to marry him at eighteen, considered her property, saw women as objects to be used, kicked her out when she disobeyed. Why was he silent those two years Ellie was with Brett? If he was the killer, wouldn't he be outraged that she was with someone else, pushing him to up his game during that time, not go dormant?

My attention flicked to the second to last victim. Something about the timeline kept irking me.

She was the first to have a message, the first to have several anger-fueled stab wounds, and she wasn't kept as long as the others. That was almost three weeks ago now. What happened three weeks ago with this guy, or even Ellie, that made him so enraged that he killed the victim before using her for a longer period like the others? Why stab her thirty-eight times instead of the single stab wound?

The answer hit me like a slap to the balls.

Slumping back in the chair, mouth gaping, I stared into the darkened living room.

Wasn't it three weeks ago that Ellie had the date she considered not a date but really was?

That would've been enough of a trigger to cause his downward spiral. She was moving on in his eyes, and not with him.

That led to another question.

Who knew she had that date?

I'd have to ask Ellie tomorrow after she woke up and had her unhealthy dose of sugar.

Sitting back upright, I debated the names again with this new piece to the case.

I scratched out the second to last person. If the guy who took Ellie out on that date was our unsub, he would've been happy that she went out with him, not enraged. She even mentioned he'd come into the diner a few times and was pleasant.

Now my list was down to four.

The bitter flavor of the dark coffee settled on my tongue as I took a tentative sip.

The latest victim was picked up in Waco, so who had the means to get to Waco and bring the body back here? I made a note to check DMV records to see who on the list owned a car. One did for sure—Brett. And if the latest victim was drunk, who wouldn't take a ride home with a charismatic police officer, especially if it was in a cruiser?

Groaning, I tossed the pen and massaged my brows.

I was talking myself in circles. There were too many questions and not enough answers. I needed more, and the only way I'd get that was asking the tough questions myself. But that would mean leaving Ellie behind while I conducted the interrogations—I meant interviews. It wasn't ideal, but Alec was here and could watch her at the diner, even though I hated that it wasn't me protecting her.

I grinned despite myself remembering the argument a few hours earlier when I suggested—okay, maybe demanded—that she forgo work until the bastard fixated on her was caught. The debate ended with her still going to work with the compromise that Alec or I went with her.

Ellie was a feisty little woman, and I loved that about her. Where was the fun in a woman who gave in to your every word, who didn't have a backbone to voice her own thoughts and demands? Not Ellie. It was even more impressive considering her background.

Which reminded me....

Palms to the table, I shoved the chair back. Keeping my footsteps silent, I crept down the darkened hallway toward the bedrooms. Her snores filled the room as I slipped inside. Pausing at her bedside, I took a moment for my eyes to adjust to the dark room. The faint light streaming from the cracked door highlighted her parted lips, and her short hair fanned around her pillow. Her petite features and sweet button nose made her appear innocent, unscathed by the life she'd lived.

Now to get what I snuck in here for.

Silky strands of hair glided through my fingers. Hand held toward

Chapter 20

the light, I smirked at the few dark stands that dangled from my fingers. Attention on the sleeping beauty, I backed out of the room, softly closing the door behind me.

Letting out a relieved, heavy breath, I glanced at the hair between my fingers.

Next order of business—find an evidence baggie.

"Everyone," Ellie said while brushing out her hair. "Janice knew about the date that wasn't really a date. And so did Sally, I guess, so with those two, yeah, anyone with ears knew Sam asked me to dinner."

I nodded from where I sat on the bed, hiding my disappointment.

"Hey, did you come in the room last night and pet me?" I kept my breathing even, not giving away how my heart rate stuttered with her question. When I didn't respond, she shrugged. "I couldn't remember if that was a dream or what."

"Huh," I said, my answer intentionally vague. "You sure you want to go to the diner? You could stay here with Alec while I—"

"I told you two already. I have to work, and I won't let this guy stop me from living the life I've worked my ass off to build." Tossing the brush to the bed, she crossed her arms. "And besides, this"—she pointed a finger to me, then her—"will be done the minute you leave. Then what would I do? No, I'm making my own way. As exhausting as it is, it's all mine."

She scrunched her features into an exaggerated fake scowl as she backed out of the room. Alec's deep voice and her laugh drifted down the short hall moments later.

Elbows pressed to my knees, I inhaled deep and stood to finish getting dressed. With the day full of official interviews for the case, I opted to wear slacks and a button-up, going for a more professional impression. Before leaving the room, I snagged the navy jacket with "FBI" printed in bold yellow on the back.

Ellie's laugh as I walked into the kitchen made my own lips tweak up. She truly was amazing. Laughing despite the hell she had lived and was living. Truly exceptional in all ways. But was that enough to ask her to leave this life and move to DC, give up everything she knew for me? I'd be back on the road, leaving her alone 90 percent of the time if she did say yes.

"Why the serious face?" Alec asked, snapping me out of my internal dilemma.

"Nothing, just focused on what needs to be done today." At the table, I leaned my thigh against the edge. "The Church first, then Brett and Stan. Hopefully I can get them all done today, which means I'll be back late. You sure you're good?"

Alec nodded. "Yep. We'll be fine." Holding up a single finger to pause the conversation, he dug into the front pocket of his jeans and pulled out his phone. As he read the screen, his dark brows raised in surprise.

"Bronson," he said in greeting to the caller, curiosity in his tone. "What?" he exclaimed. "You've got to be fucking with me. We'll be there in fifteen."

"What happened?" Ellie and I asked at the same time when he ended the call. She rose from her chair, a hand wrapped around her dainty throat.

"Ellie," he started but stopped, rubbing a hand across his mouth. Dread made my stomach drop. Instinctively I stepped closer and draped a protective arm around her shoulder. "Your place is on fire."

THE RESIDENTS of the entire dilapidated complex crowded the parking lot, sectioned off by a single fire engine, keeping them a good distance from the smoldering remains. I laid on the horn to move the gawkers and get as close to the barricade as possible. Once I got us as far as I could, we hopped out and raced toward the fire truck.

Ellie gasped, stopping in her tracks when what used to be her small apartment came into view. Tightening my grip on her hand, I

Chapter 20

urged her forward, determined to figure out what the hell was going on.

A potbellied man in fire pants but no coat or helmet stood talking to my favorite police chief.

Brett's cold stare found us as we drew closer, and if I wasn't mistaken, a ghost of a smile appeared.

"What the hell happened?" Alec demanded, his hard tone and intimidating stance making the two men take a step back.

"We got a call about smoke. When we got here, smoke poured through the windows and beneath the doorframe of apartment seven," the fireman stated. "We contained it to that apartment and the ones on either side but evacuated the others just in case. With these old buildings, they usually all go up in flames once one does."

"Cause?" I asked.

"It appears an accelerant was doused around the living room, most of it concentrated on a couch or chair maybe."

I focused on the smoldering remains. Water dripped from the blackened wood.

"Chandler," Ellie said and squeezed my hand, drawing my attention away from the apartment. "The couch?"

It took a moment to understand what she referred to. It couldn't be an accident that the couch where I pleasured Ellie just last night was the ignition point. That meant either someone had cameras set up inside her apartment or was peeking through the windows. Anger simmered just beneath my skin at the thought of either. If there were cameras, then this would've happened after we made out on the couch two nights ago. So that left some pervert—our killer, more than likely—watching from the shadows.

"Where were you, Ellie?" Brett's voice raked on my already thin nerves.

"Did they get the evidence out before this?" I asked Alec, completely ignoring Brett. Alec nodded. "He was probably waiting to see how she reacted to the gift and got a show instead."

"What evidence? What gift and show?" Brett stepped close. Using my own body as a shield, I wedged between him and Ellie. "What the fuck is going on in my case?"

"My case now, remember?" Smirking, I turned my full attention back to Alec, a clear dismissal of the furious police chief. "So this was either set because of what Ellie and I did on that couch"—her hard yank on my hand and kick to my calf told me she wasn't happy about that announcement—"or because she wasn't happy with his gift."

"Or because that couch was hideous to begin with." Alec rocked back on his heels, smiling even though the strain was obvious. I liked that he always did his best to ease mounting tension with ill-placed humor.

"Hey," Ellie shouted behind me. "I loved that couch."

"You haven't answered my question, Ellie," Brett demanded like a pouting three-year-old. "If you weren't here, then where were you?"

I pressed a hand to Swann's chest and pushed him back a step, giving me some breathing room. Fuck, I hated it when people invaded my personal space. "She doesn't have to answer anything."

While Alec and Swann bickered about who had the authority in the arson case, the feeling of being watched raised the hairs on the back of my neck. I found myself subconsciously scanning the crowd.

He was here. Watching.

But I didn't know what Jacob looked like to say if he was there or not. Another reason I needed to go meet the bastard, so I knew who to shoot... I meant be on the lookout for.

"Do you see anyone from The Church here?" I asked Ellie. A look of confusion scrunched her small features. "In the crowd. Do you see anyone or even Jacob?"

I kept silent as she inspected the crowd. "A couple faces seem familiar. Then, of course, there's Stan." She raised her hand and waved. The man waved back, smiling until he saw me. Then that wide smile fell to a frown. "And the entire town seems to be here."

Of course they were.

"Witch's tits," she exclaimed and tossed her hands in the air. "My uniform was in there for the diner. I had asked Alec to swing by here on my way to work to pick it up." Groaning, she dug through her purse. After popping a peppermint into her mouth, she pulled her cell phone out and flipped it open.

That's right. Flipped.

Snatching it from her hand, I inspected the relic with awe.

"Give that back." She yanked it away. "Don't judge my phone. It makes calls and can send texts. Not that I use it much," she grumbled. Holding it to her ear, she turned and began talking to the person on the other end of the line. I kept one ear on her conversation and the other on the argument still happening between Alec and Swann.

My eyes widened when Alec patted the top of Swann's head in a condescending brush-off. He swatted Alec's hand away and stormed off, shoving his way through the crowd like he was on a mission. I tracked him until he was swallowed up by the small swarm of people.

"He doesn't have a spare in my size," Ellie said beside me with a huff.

"And the last one was?" I remarked. She smacked my arm like I said something inappropriate. "What? It was tiny. So does that mean no work today?" My voice lifted with hope. It would make my day easier knowing she was safe at the house behind a locked door with Alec standing guard, firearm at the ready.

"No, I'll just work in this." She waved to the leggings and oversized sweatshirt. "At least it's all black. No need to worry about grease stains."

I nodded along like I was listening, but I wasn't. All I could focus on was the crowd, a sense of foreboding growing in the pit of my stomach. "We should get you to the diner, then." I shouted to Alec that we were leaving. He wrapped up the conversation with the fireman and connected with us halfway to the truck.

As we made our way through the crowd, Ellie saying hello to every person we passed, I couldn't shake the uneasy feeling like we were walking into a trap of some kind. But that didn't make sense. This unsub didn't want to hurt Ellie, he wanted her for his own.

Two feet from the truck, I stopped dead in my tracks. Alec and Ellie stopped on either side of me, their confusion indicating they didn't see what I saw.

A small rectangular white card tucked beneath the passenger side windshield wiper.

A note.

"Stay here. Alec, watch her," I said, my voice as distant as I felt. Leaning against the truck, I plucked the paper from the glass using the tips of my fingers on a small edge of a corner. Using the truck's hood, I flipped the paper over to read what was scribbled on the other side.

"What does it say?" Alec called out.

A glance their way showed him holding on to Ellie by her shoulders, her body leaning toward me like she'd tried to get closer. Cringing, I turned back to the note, hating what I had to say out loud.

"Nowhere else to go. Come home."

21

Ellie

Worst. Morning. Ever.

I could say that with absolute fact. Of course the asshat who thought I was his left a note, after burning down my place and my neighbors'. And that couch. I really didn't love that couch, but I did after last night's activities.

"Order up, Ellie." The loud ding after Cook's gruff voice snapped me to attention.

The warm plate of steaming food slid along the steel shelf. I grabbed it before the plate could slide off the edge. I shot a look into the kitchen. What was Cook's deal today? He seemed gruffer, more on edge than usual. Shrugging it off, I turned and used my ass to open the swinging door.

The murmur of various conversations and a few cackles of laughter enveloped me as I weaved through the full tables. I hitched my chin, acknowledging Alec where he sat in a far back booth, laptop open and eyes on me. As much as I didn't want to admit it, I felt safer having him here even though I fought him and Chandler on it last night. After the scalp incident and now the fire, it was obvious the killer was escalating.

I smiled at Rancher Joe, patting his broad shoulder after dropping off his overflowing plate. He smiled, those brown spotted teeth from years of dipping showing. Sally stood across the diner, steaming coffee pot in hand as she talked with a table of four regulars.

Taking the moment, I scanned the dining room. How could someone I knew, someone from this town, be responsible for all this? The things he did to those women... my shoulders shook at the thought. I'd probably delivered him pancakes or served him a few drinks at the bar. This man, whoever he was, was part of our community. Yet none of us knew who it was.

I took in the various faces, trying to see behind the mask like I used to do in the compound. But everyone seemed... ordinary. Not a vile face, set of dark ominous eyes, or wave of ick from anyone in here. It wasn't the entire town but most. A part of me wanted the killer to be Jacob or someone within The Church. That way they would have a reason to shut it down. There wouldn't be any legal red tape if that group was harboring a serial killer.

"Hey, Ellie." I turned to the familiar voice. Ryan, Brett's older brother, stood at the door, hands shoved deep in the back pockets of his maroon scrubs.

"Hey, yourself. Good to see you." I turned, looking for a free table, but came up empty. "Do you mind waiting for a table, or you want something to go?"

He smiled, those straight white teeth sparkling. How he was related to Brett was a mystery. The two were polar opposites.

"I'll just get a cup of coffee to go, if that's okay. I need to get to the clinic. It's my day without Janice's help."

I held up a single finger, indicating for him to hold that thought. After grabbing a large Styrofoam cup, I filled it to the brim, stirred in three sugars, and popped a lid on the top.

"Thanks," he said when I handed him the cup. "Hey, sorry about your place, by the way."

Chapter 21

I groaned, having forgotten about it for a split second. "Thanks. It's more of a hassle than anything. I'm just glad no one was hurt."

"Yeah, extensive burns would've been beyond my fixing." He sighed and took a quick sip. "I wish I could do more sometimes."

Reaching out, I grabbed his bicep and gave it a squeeze. "You're doing what you can. And we all appreciate it."

"How are you feeling, by the way? Any more symptoms?"

"No," I said, feeling a blush heat my cheeks. "I figured out what was causing it."

"And?"

I waved him off. "It was nothing." My name being called had me turning. A man wearing coveralls had his cup raised in the air. "Listen, I gotta get back to it. But I'll stop by sometime, we can catch up?"

"Sounds good." Before he turned to the door, Ryan raised his coffee in the air, acknowledging someone. Alec raised his hand in the back before turning his attention back to the laptop. "He seems to be hanging around a lot. You seeing him too?"

"Too?" I squeaked.

"Janice," Ryan said sheepishly. "She told me about you and that FBI guy."

"I'm going to kill her." My name was called again. Sighing, I offered Ryan a sad smile. "No, Alec is just here as my bodyguard. Listen, I'll explain it all later. Gotta go."

Turning before he could say anything else, I rushed toward the table with the now frowning customer. "Hold your horses," I said to the regular.

"Horses are gone. You know that," he joked. "Sold them years back."

I nodded as he continued talking about the good old days when his land held hundreds of horses. It wasn't until the terrible drought three years ago that he sold them all.

An idea popped in my head. Bouncing on my toes, I refilled his mug, a bit of the near boiling liquid splashing over the edge with the jostling movement. With a hasty apology, I wiped up the spill with the rag on my shoulder and raced to Alec's booth.

"Ellie, something wrong?" He raised his brows, not looking up from his computer screen.

"We're assuming this person lives here, right? If this person knows me well enough to want me to come home.... Where did he do it?" That got his attention. Turning in the booth, he rested an ankle over top of the opposite knee. "The women. If he held them, did all that terrible stuff, that takes space. Private space. So where did he do it?"

His lips parted, then closed. With a nod, he grabbed his phone resting on the table. "That's a good question. Chan had—"

I held up a hand, a laugh caught in my throat. "Did you just say Chan?"

"Yep. You should use it too. He hates it."

"No, thanks, I like being on his good side." For the second time in a matter of minutes, my cheeks heated. This time I pressed my cold fingers to the warm skin, trying to calm the flush.

"I bet you do." His chuckle was deep and full of secret humor. "Anyway, Chandler had mentioned this guy needing a place to hold the women, but that was before we narrowed the suspects down to a local with the ability to get to and from Waco. I have his list of suspects that I'm already running through the DMV for him. I'll look for property in their names too. I highly doubt this person would use some forgotten barn or shack that didn't belong to him. This fucker is too cautious, too calculated for that. Good idea, Ellie. I'll look into it."

Smiling like a fool, one because of the reminder of Chandler and two because I just helped a little with the case, I weaved through the tables, topping off coffee and taking orders. For over an hour, I was in the zone, doing my job with zero issues or complaints until *he* walked through the door.

The breakfast rush had thinned, leaving nearly all the tables open for him to choose from. Tugging at the utility belt weighing down his uniform pants, Brett strutted to the booth on the opposite side of the diner from Alec and stuffed himself into the bench seat.

Internally I groaned again, wishing he could be more like his brother. Kind, caring, not an asshole.

His raised hand and flick of his fingers was more of a command

Chapter 21

than a polite request for my attention. My boots dragged against the floor, almost like the dread that was weighing in my stomach had also turned my feet to the heaviest of lead.

"What can I get for you?" I asked, plastering my fakest smile across my face.

"Oh, come on now, Lizzy." My grip tightened so much that the pencil in my hand nearly snapped. "Is that any way to greet me?" Tipping his face up, he tried for his most charming smile. Good thing I knew better. "After what all we've been through together? I at least deserve a 'Good morning' or a real smile, don't you think?"

His words ignited an internal war. An all-out battle between knowing he was manipulating me and wondering if I was wrong for being so rude. Clearing my throat, I stepped out of reach of his hand, which had risen in search of my own. Reaching into my apron, I desperately searched for a piece of candy to ground me but came up empty.

"Good morning," I gritted out, balling my hand into a fist in the apron, nails making crescent moon indentions in my palm. "Now, what do you want?"

"What I want is for you to stop making me out as the bad guy." I sighed as he leaned back against the booth, stretching his arms out wide along the back. His growing beer belly pushed at the table's edge. "You were the one who left. Shouldn't I be the one that's upset?"

"I'm not falling for this, Brett." I took another retreating step, hating that his words were hitting a healing raw spot in my soul. "What do you want to eat?"

"You're being really ungrateful for what I did for you."

"You mean Ryan," I corrected.

He snorted and gave me a once-over. "That outfit looks terrible on you." My shoulders rounded in on themselves despite my internal voice screaming at me to stand up to him. "You always were a little too skinny in all the wrong places. But I overlooked that and took care of you when you needed it."

Did he? It was so long ago it was hard to remember now. He was there that first year when I was a complete mess. A year of taking care of me without asking for anything in return. But then he did. He found my weak spot and capitalized on my need for comfort and companionship. Those didn't come free. He took from me, just like Jacob. They both took what I wasn't knowingly willing to give. They took from me and never gave anything in return.

Unlike a sexy-as-hell, caring, selfless, protective FBI agent I was in love with.

A real smile tugged at my lips.

"There's that smile. I knew you'd see the truth. I just had to remind you, like usual."

I shook my head. "This smile isn't for you. It's not because of you." Brett's smug grin fell into a scowl. "It's because of him. I know what you're doing, and I'm stronger now. I won't fall for it. You can go fuck yourself, Brett Swann, because I sure as hell won't ever do it again."

"You're a damn fool," he sneered, all his vileness poured into those words. "He'll leave you. Leave you here where you'll be a nothing again. No family, no friends, not even a full damn name." The tears I wasn't willing to let him see burned in my throat. "You will be mine again. I just have to wait for you to see that without me you're nothing. Nothing, Ellie. And will never be anything more than a body to use. Because that's all you're good for."

Quick movement in my periphery had me staggering back, the suddenness causing a bolt of panic to send my heart racing. But it wasn't Brett reaching for me. No, it was an enormous body moving around my own. The smack of skin and a hard crack echoed through the diner. I blinked and Alec now stood between me and Brett, his shoulders rising and falling with heavy, quick breaths.

"You broke my nose," Brett screamed. "You fucking broke my nose."

Peering around Alec's waist, I couldn't help but giggle at Brett holding both hands over his nose, blood pouring between his fingers.

"I did not. I fucking held back so I wouldn't break that or your thick damn skull." Gripping the back of Brett's uniform, Alec dragged him out of the booth. Brett's utility belt slammed to the floor, causing the salt and pepper shakers on neighboring tables to rattle with the impact. "You're done talking to her like that. Any woman for that matter," Alec snapped as he dragged Brett behind him, moving toward the door. At the front, Alec yanked Brett upright and pulled his face close. "If I were you, I'd be terrified of what Agent Peters will do when he finds out how you talked to his girl."

"Mine." Blood sprayed as Brett hissed the word. "She's not his."

"She's whoever's she wants to be. Get the fuck out." With his free hand, Alec pulled the door open and shoved Brett out, who stumbled to stay upright. His back slammed against the wooden railing on the other side of the small landing. "And I'm not joking around. Peters can be scary as hell when he wants to be. Run."

The bell above the door crashed to the floor with Alec's hard shove. He grimaced.

"I'll buy the place a new one." He inspected the trail of blood along the stained floor. "And clean this up."

"I've got it. Thank you." Against my better judgment, I glanced out the window. Brett stood leaning against his cruiser, those dark eyes filled with hate and anger glaring into my soul. "I'll never be free of him or Jacob, will I?"

"Hey." He laid a large hand on my shoulder. "Don't let that asshole get you down. We'll figure it out. One step at a time."

I laughed and wiped away the rogue tear that had escaped. "Right. I need to survive all this first before I start thinking about the future."

"I didn't mean—"

"I know. I know what you meant. But it doesn't make it any less true." Squaring my shoulders, I tilted my chin to look up at my large friend. "Surviving a serial killer's obsession shouldn't be tougher than what I've been through already in life, right?"

Alec laughed and patted between my shoulder blades in an awkward, fully platonic attempt at comfort. "Right. Now, where's the mop? Looks like a damn crime scene in here."

As I made my way to the utility closet, I fought the urge to text Chandler. The desperate need to hear from him was eating at my rational thinking. This was my problem to handle, not his. I would not depend on him for any kind of support. Even if I desperately wanted it. Because there was a bit of truth in Brett's words.

Chandler would leave.

And I'd be left here, alone.

A forgotten small-town nobody once again.

22

Chandler

My stomach twisted and tightened with anticipation as the above overpass doused the truck's cab in shadows. At the four-way stop, I inhaled a full breath and held it before releasing it slowly through pursed lips. Two miles west, I turned the wheel, directing the truck down an unmarked gravel road. A quarter of a mile down, the front gates and stretching high fences guarding a seemingly never-ending cluster of dome homes became clear.

Stopping several feet from the gate, I surveyed the fence, wondering if it was there to ensure others stayed out or to keep his followers inside.

Based on what Ellie shared the night before, it might be a little bit of both. As she compiled her own suspect list, she cleared up a few misconceptions Alec and I had derived based off her stories.

Seemed not everyone was subjected to learning about sex by watching their parents; that was specific to Ellie at Jacob's request.

Other kids who weren't selected as a child to be the bride of the leader lived a relatively normal life. Well, as normal as any kid in a cult could.

All children were taught the devil and US government were evil and out to hurt them. Of course, they were also taught about eternal damnation and the differences between heaven and hell. As they grew older, the boys and girls were split for school. The boys were taught they were the providers, the workers, and commanders of their homes. The girls, well, that wasn't much different than what I had already surmised from Ellie's way of thinking. They were taught they should be submissive in every way, their bodies not their own after marriage, and to never question a man.

What did surprise me was to find out some of the couples swapped. Which made me wonder if couples were drawn here to live a swinger-type lifestyle. I'd asked Ellie how it was wrong for me to be in a relationship with her, in her father's eyes, since she was still "married" to Jacob, but those who swapped spouses weren't condemned to damnation.

She couldn't explain it, but it seemed that, based on what she remembered, if the man offered his wife to another, then it was okay because it would make him happy.

Fucked. Up.

I didn't have the courage to ask her if Jacob swapped her during her time, but she alluded to being a commodity and also being used as one. That was when Alec had wrapped an arm around my neck in a choke hold to keep me from storming The Church guns blazing.

Two men, each holding an assault rifle and another sidearm on their hips, moved to stand in the middle of the gate. Resentment and hate pinched both their features.

Seemed like someone warned them that I'd be coming by.

Awesome. This should go well.

Broken fragments of gray rock crunched under my polished dress shoes, dust already collecting on the shiny toes, with each cautious step I took toward the two men. Hands casually slack at my side, I

Chapter 22

kept them in clear view as I rounded the hood of the truck and leaned my ass against the grill. Tilting my face to the clear blue sky and warm morning sun, I smiled. Yesterday it snowed and spit ice; today it was a pleasant forty-nine degrees, the breeze calm and pleasant.

"Nice day, isn't it?" I said in way of greeting. With the warmer temperature, I left the FBI jacket folded in the passenger seat.

"Your kind isn't welcome here," one of the guards shouted through the bars. Disdain dripped from his tone. "Leave before we make you."

"I need to speak to Jacob." I laid both hands on top of my thighs, still keeping them in clear view so they didn't get trigger-happy and fill me full of those large rounds. "I need to ask him a few questions about some missing women."

"Everyone here is accounted for."

The nontalkative guard shot the other an unsure glance. That was the confirmation I needed. Some of the victims must have come from here. Either taken from inside the compound or maybe on their way home when they realized how fucked-up it was behind the fence.

"I need to talk to Jacob," I stated with authority.

"Not going to happen."

I shrugged. "Okay. He's too busy doing...." I squinted and glanced down the length of the fence. "What does he do, actually?"

"He leads us, like his father before he passed." I nodded. "We won't help the federal government find reasons to infiltrate our community. Leave."

"Those are great guns. Where did you get them?" I asked, nodding toward the ARs in their hands.

"They're legal, and we have our LTC. That's all you need to know."

"That's not what I asked. How did you get them? Hell, how do you get anything inside this compound?"

"The men provide for the females," the one who hadn't spoken stated.

"Does everyone have access to the vehicles to get supplies?" I picked at my nails, acting as nonchalant as possible. When I didn't get an answer, I glanced up, both brows high on my forehead as I waited for a response.

"No. That's a privilege."

Hmm, so maybe only the long-term members had the freedom to go into town. Which would narrow down the suspects list of those inside The Church. Only those with access to a car or truck could be the killer.

Time for a different tactic, even if it left a bad taste in my mouth bringing her into the conversation.

"Did you know Ellie?" The two shared a look. The name her father used yesterday sparked in my mind. "Elizabeth, Jacob's...." I couldn't bring myself to say "wife."

"She was a disgrace to how we live and what Jacob provided. She's not welcome until she repents and begs for his forgiveness."

Steady, confident footsteps drew my gaze past the guards. The man approaching was forty-ish, wearing soft flowing pants and a matching loose shirt, his hands gently clasped in front of him in a genial appearance. At the gate he gave me a slow once-over. A cocky vibe rolled off him, and the way the other two looked to him in reverence pointed to one thing.

This fucker was Jacob. He looked as excited to see me as I was to see him.

A growl of rage grew in my chest as I took in the scrawny prick. His long blond hair floated on the soft breeze, a mask of serenity hiding the evil man I knew lurked inside. The bastard thought he was present-day Jesus, or hell, maybe even God himself. He warped the minds of his followers one manipulation, one lie at a time, and now he had all this at his fingertips.

But I had the one thing he wanted most.

"Thank you for greeting our guest," Jacob said to the two guards. One even blushed at the leader's attention. I fought an eye roll. "I'll handle this from here. He's clearly confused on what he hopes to accomplish by harassing my most loyal guards."

Chapter 22

He motioned for one of them to hand over his rifle, which he slung on his back, and then turned to me, staying a foot behind the closed gate.

Wonderful. Now the leader of the crazies had a weapon. This was a terrible idea.

"How is my wife?" His conniving smile raked at my frayed nerves. "I hear you're enjoying the best parts of her. Which I don't mind, just need something in return. What have you come to give me for access to what's mine?"

I clenched my teeth so hard the muscles along my jaw cramped. This was why I left my guns in the truck. Even so, the urge to jab the pocketknife I always had on me into his jugular was overwhelming. He said that on purpose to throw me off course. Getting me riled up so I wouldn't ask the right questions, or possibly throwing me off his trail. What serial killer would be obsessed with wanting a woman to come home if he was open to sharing her?

Fuck him. He had no idea that his menial mind games wouldn't work on someone like me. Someone with my training and who grew up with parents just as conniving and manipulative wasn't susceptible to this shit like his followers.

After calming the urge to kill the bastard, I cleared my throat and looked him dead in the eye. "What do you know about the women missing from your compound?"

"What missing women? All of our followers are here." He waved behind him toward the expansive community. "Those who choose to leave, to step back into the world where evil and hate are prevalent, they are not my community nor my concern."

"Who behind the gate has access to a vehicle?" I asked.

Jacob's grin widened to a full sinister smile. "Bring my wife to me and I'll tell you everything."

"Not a chance."

He shrugged. "Even though more women will die? On your watch, no less?" I held in a tight breath, trying my best to not let his words hit home. The fucker was good at reading people, I'd give him that. "Bring me Elizabeth, just for a few hours, and I'll give you full access to the compound. You can ask any questions, look into any house or building, while she is with me."

I shook my head, anger at myself sweeping over me. This was a dead end. I would need to gather the information a different way. Hopefully the DMV check Alec said he'd run would narrow down who behind the gate had access to the vehicles that went to Waco for the compound supplies.

"You'll never lay a hand on her again. And she's not your wife." Putting my back to him was a terrible idea, but I needed the appearance of dismissal, to show him I didn't give a fuck how important he thought he was. "One day she might be mine though. Ellie Peters. That has a nice ring to it, don't you think? Oh, and you can believe I'll take her back to DC with me. Far, far away from here." I looked over my shoulder. "Far away from you."

The rattle of the metal gate was like the ring of victory in my ears. The bastard was falling for my goading. I was always good at pushing the assholes into showing their hands.

A bar gripped between each hand, Jacob pressed his face between the two. "You will not take my wife. She is mine."

I tilted my head one way and then the other like I was considering his statement. "That's for me and her to decide. Nothing to do with you."

"You can't give her what she needs."

"And what's that?" *Damn, this asshole is off his rocker.* The overwhelming need to destroy this compound from the inside out ballooned in my chest. If only there was notable criminal activity, something that would circumvent the religious statute they used to keep the authorities at bay.

"Me. I'm her husband, her world. This is her home, always has been and always will be." My ears perked up at the word "home," but it didn't hold the edge of wrath that I would expect the unsub to have. "She's safe here with me."

I shook my head. "She doesn't want you, doesn't want this oppressive life you forced her into. Leave her alone. And stop having your brainwashed followers harass her."

Chapter 22

"Or what?" He held his arms out wide. "You can't get inside here. Not without her. So tell me, Agent Peters, which is more important to you, catching this killer or having my wife?"

"Are you saying the man I'm after is behind those gates?" Excitement raced through my heart, making it thunder against my chest. *Did he just slip up? Does he know who murdered all those women and wants Ellie?*

He shrugged. "You'll have to bring her back to find out for sure, won't you?"

"Bastard." I took a menacing step toward him, causing him to back away from the gate and swing the gun around.

He flexed his hands around the grip. "Bring her home and all this will stop."

He was playing me. It was there in his too-confident voice, in the shine of victory in his gaze. He already knew I wouldn't find anything behind those fences even if I brought her to him. If he thought for a moment that someone in his community was guilty, he'd cover up the evidence. Hell, if it was him, he'd ensure I wouldn't find a speck of evidence. Because if I did, that would be enough to bring the weight of the FBI on their heads, disrupting the utopic fucked-up-ness he'd created.

"Why do you care so much?" I asked, hoping to draw more information out of him. I was grasping at straws, sure, but in my gut, I knew this place was a dead end. "And why didn't you demand her to return to the compound when she was with the police chief? She mentioned you didn't start harassing her until after she left Swann."

A sly grin tugged at his thin lips. It was the kind of smile someone gave when they had a dirty little secret and was about to disrupt someone's world.

"What would you say if I said we had an agreement of sorts?"

I huffed. "That bastard wouldn't negotiate with you." But even I knew my words held no weight. Of course Swann would negotiate with this bastard if it got him what he wanted—Ellie.

"Wouldn't he, though?" Fuck, nothing made sense. He talked in circles to confuse me. "He has attachment issues with my wife, I will admit that. And I'd hate to see her hurt at his hands. Which will happen if someone doesn't... intervene."

"So now you're pointing me in the direction of him as the killer?" I scoffed. "You take me for a damn fool."

"Or killing two birds with one stone."

"How so?"

"When you find out I'm telling the truth about Chief Swann's obsession with my wife and how depraved he really is, well, then you'll believe me when I say you can have unrestricted access to the compound if you bring my wife to me."

"I think you're playing me."

"Think what you want." He considered me for a moment. "Ask him what he offered me in exchange for uninterrupted access to my wife. You know I'm always willing to share if it benefits the community. Go ask the chief yourself and see how he responds. If you need to press him for the truth, tell him I kept the evidence and still enjoy the gifts he sent." The gate rattled as he shoved off. "Don't come back without my wife, or I'll shoot you the moment you step on to my property."

Turning, he gracefully shuffled away.

With no other way to release the inferno of rage about to erupt, I jammed both middle fingers in the air and shook them at his retreating back.

Fucker.

Once inside the truck, I detonated. "Fuck," I bellowed and slammed a tight fist against the steering wheel over and over again. Chest heaving, breaths quick and shallow, I glared at the gate, making a promise to myself that one way or another, I'd make this man pay for what he did to Ellie. I just had to bide my time until the moment was right.

But now I had another man to find and question.

Chapter 22

THE COP WORKING the front desk at the police station said Swann was at the diner, and then Sally told me he went to the clinic to get his nose checked. That one made me pause as I turned for the door and ask what was wrong with his nose. And now, as I drove toward the small makeshift clinic, I couldn't hide my smile as I recounted the story Sally had told me. The bastard deserved what he got and worse, if you ask me. Which he would receive by my hand the moment I was done interrogating him.

Brett held many of the characteristics detailed in the profile, except the menial job. Which honestly didn't fit Jacob or Brett. Jacob thought highly of himself and convinced others to see him that way too. And Brett, well a badge gave many wrong men a sense of self-worth when it was never earned.

I thumped my thumb on the steering wheel as I flipped the turn signal. Not that it mattered considering I hadn't seen another car or truck in a while.

In the clinic parking lot, I pulled beside Brett's cruiser and parked. The bright red handprint along the edge of the door made me smirk as I passed by.

No doubt he was pissed having to admit he had his ass handed to him.

I tugged the glass door, but the empty waiting room had me pulling up short. Not even a receptionist greeted me from the front desk when I approached. I opened my mouth to call out when arguing male voices floated down the hall, snapping my lips closed. The voices grew louder by the second. Ignoring the "Employees Only" sign, I shoved through the side door and stalked down the hall.

The voices grew as I stalked down the short hall of exam rooms. One door was partially open, and two male voices poured through the slight opening.

"You have no idea what she wants," a voice that sounded similar to Brett's said.

"She belongs with me," Brett said. "You should know that. You saw us together."

"She's not yours, brother."

"I know how she likes it, what she wants. Me, not you, and sure as fuck not that gay FBI fucker." I held a breath and dared an inch closer to not miss a single word. "Once I get rid of him and the Ranger, she won't have anywhere else to go."

"Someone made sure of that," the man said with a sigh.

As I continued to listen to their back-and-forth, I sorted through the conversation and how it pertained to the case. Yes, Brett wanted Ellie to be his again, to be under his unrelenting control, but was he the unsub? My gut tensed, telling me off, but was that because Brett and Jacob were both master manipulators or because I was suspicious of the wrong men?

"I—" Brett cut himself off abruptly. By their low whispers, I knew I was caught. The exam room door swung open and the barrel of a gun came out first, ready to sweep down the hall.

Sighing at this shit of a day, I gripped the middle of the gun, twisted the barrel the opposite direction of where I stood, and pressed on Swann's wrist. He let out a very feminine shriek and relaxed his hold on the weapon. Following through, I twisted his arm behind his back and tugged it high, inflicting significant pain.

I moved the confiscated gun and tucked it against my lower back for safekeeping. The other man in the room didn't move as I wrangled the unruly and cursing Swann, but his gaze tracked my every move. The resemblance was there, the nose and cunning eyes, but Brett's brother didn't have the same rage and hate burning behind his.

No, this man was calm, collected, and in control.

"Agent Peters," the brother said. The room was so small it only took him two steps to be close. "What brings you to the clinic?"

"Let me go, you motherfucking piece of shit." Brett bucked in my hold, but I held my ground barely moving.

"I came to ask him a few questions about the case."

Brett's brother nodded. "I'm Ryan Swann, by the way. The town EMT, medic, and go-between for real medical help."

"Knock it off," I growled in Brett's ear before shoving him across

Chapter 22

the room. Once he'd regained his footing, he squatted low, preparing to rush me. I rolled my eyes, withdrew his own gun from my lower back, and leveled the barrel at his head. "Stay." Turning my attention back to the better Swann, I smiled. "I see you patched him up okay." I angled my head toward the pouting man, who was glaring at me even though I had a gun pointed to his head.

"Yeah, I can do the basics, have the supplies here. Antibiotics, any type of compound breaks that need to be reset, things like that I have to send people to Waco for. Since I'm not a licensed doctor, there's only so much I can do."

A defeated look caused his features to droop, making pity for the man calm some of my anger. This guy was doing the best he could with the shit situation. Ellie mentioned one day when she was cleaning the house that Ryan had left for undergrad but didn't get to finish because his dad died. Tough luck.

"Why are you questioning my little brother?" I couldn't mask my shock. This guy looked years younger than Brett. The surprise must have shown on my face, because Ryan chuckled. "Drinking, poor decisions, and being an all-around asshole will age you quick, it seems."

I smiled wide. "So it seems. And to answer your initial question, I can't tell you. It's regarding the case."

Ryan whistled, and Brett huffed in annoyance. "How's that going, by the way? I know a few of the details from overhearing my brother talk on the phone. How terrible."

"Sorry, I can't discuss an active case." Unless you were just shy of five foot five, spunky, and broken like me. Then I'd tell you every damn detail. "Is there somewhere he and I can talk, or do we need to take it down to the station?"

Ryan waved a hand, indicating the small room. "Here is fine. But try to keep him from yelling and disrupting anyone who might come in."

After the door shut behind him, I lowered Brett's gun and tucked it into my waistband for quick access if needed.

Arms crossed over his chest, shoulder pressed against the far wall, Brett glared as best he could around the tape and gauze.

"I'm not your killer, if that's what you're here to ask," he said, his voice nasally from what was stuffed up his nose to stop the bleeding. "Sure, I want Ellie back with me. It's where she belongs, where she's safe. But I'm not out getting my rocks off doing that shit to women who aren't willing. I'm not the sick son of a bitch who tortures women, then kills them."

"I'm not convinced." I said that, yet I believed him. There was still more I needed to know, such as what he traded with Jacob to have access to Ellie those couple of years.

The asshole shrugged like we were talking about the weather. "Not my problem you're terrible at your job. Am I seriously the best suspect you have?" He scoffed.

"Where were you the night the recent victim was taken from a bar in Waco?"

Brett huffed. "Drunk, at home, sleeping off a hangover—one of those three. Doesn't matter which night you're asking about, that would be what I was doing." He nodded to the door. "Just ask my brother."

"Your brother is your alibi?" I shook my head. "If you're drunk or hungover most of the time, when do you work?"

"As little as possible. I'm the chief, which means I'm allotted certain exceptions."

I shook my head. "You mean having the officers who report to you do all the work."

"Yep." He stood tall and dusted off his hands in a signal that the conversation was through. But he wasn't going anywhere. I wasn't anywhere close done with this guy. "Speaking of which, I gotta run, seeing as my girlfriend's apartment was set on fire last night. Need to figure out who did that, and shouldn't you be following up on real suspects?"

When he attempted to open the door, I slammed a palm to the center, shutting it once again.

"You're not going anywhere until I say so. Sit your ass down and

Chapter 22

listen the fuck up. I need some damn answers, and we're not leaving until I have everything I need. And for clarification purposes, for the last time she is not your girlfriend now nor ever will be."

With a disconcerted harrumph he slumped down into the single chair in the room.

Time to ask the hard questions.

23

Ellie

The soft *whoosh* of the door opening had my eyes flaring wide. I'd crawled in bed only moments before, disappointed, after waiting up well past midnight for Chandler to come home. Twisting along the mattress, I peered through the dark to the tall, lean silhouette of a man moving through the room. A loud crash followed by a whispered curse interrupted the quiet. Hand pressed to my mouth, I laughed. The muffled sound made Chandler turn toward the bed.

"Damn wall." His voice was gruff from prolonged use. "When did that get there?"

"Pretty sure it's always been there." Rising, I pressed both elbows into my pillow. "You're back late."

His features were doused in darkness, preventing me from seeing his expression, but the sluggish and careless way he moved about the room signaled his exhaustion.

"Long day, and I have shit to show for it." The whisper of clothes and a clink of metal had my ears perking up. The soft sheets suddenly felt rough against my warm skin while my heart rate kicked into overdrive.

"Nothing pan out from your questioning?"

The bed dipped beside my knees. One shoe clattered to the floor followed by another. An almost silent *rustle* caught my ear as his pants puddled to the floor. I yelped when cold air blasted against my skin before a hot, solid body snuggled against me.

"A few things came out of the questioning, but not what I was hoping for. The more I dig the more questions I have. I'm nowhere closer to identifying the unsub than I was when I first got here." Guilt and disappointment weighed in his tone, making my heart hurt for him.

"You'll figure it out," I whispered as he nuzzled against my neck. A contented sigh brushed against the sensitive skin of my throat, kicking my libido up another notch. I squirmed along the sheets, pressing my thighs together to keep them from swinging over Chandler's hips and straddling him. "I believe in you."

He pressed a tender kiss just beneath my ear. "What if I asked you to move with me?"

I stilled. Surely I didn't hear him right. "What do you mean?"

His hold around my waist squeezed. "I mean, after all this is done, move to DC with me."

Excitement and sadness mixed, confusing the hell out of me. "Chandler, I can't. I'm a nobody, remember? Stuck in this town, staying one step ahead of Jacob and dodging Brett's advances for the rest of my life is my destiny. There's no changing that, no matter how badly I want it to be different."

"Give us a chance, Ellie." Pushing onto an elbow, he hovered over me, the faint light from under the door highlighting the sincerity on his face. "Give me a chance to show you this isn't all that's out there for you. We'll figure out the papers, name, all that. Just give me a chance."

My lips parted, ready to tell him that no matter how desperately I wanted to say yes, I couldn't, but his mouth pressed to mine in a hard kiss.

Chapter 23

"I've been thinking," he said, his lips moving over my own. A hint of spearmint wafted up with each of his tight breaths. "We could use someone like you."

"Who?"

"The FBI. You could partner with the BSU when there's a survivor who's too intimidated to talk to us. It happens more than you think. You could help make them feel comfortable, help them open up and possibly reveal details that could help the case. You could help be their voice when they're too scared to do it on their own."

"Chandler, that would be amazing, but I don't have a degree. I don't even have a high school diploma. They would never—"

"Just think about it, okay? I don't want this between us to end when I leave. And maybe a part of me isn't piecing together the clues as quickly as I normally do because subconsciously I know that means I'll leave, that I'll go home. Come with me. Make me your home."

Fresh tears dripped down my face, disappearing into my hairline. "I don't know if I can."

"Maybe you just need more convincing."

Despite the heartrending sorrow eating at me, I smiled and nodded, my hair sliding against the pillow. "Most definitely."

This time when his lips touched my own, it was soft, caring, almost like he was attempting to cherish the moment. Reaching up, I gripped his bare bicep and held on tight. Rolling the rest of the way, he positioned both knees on either side of my thighs.

Interlocking my fingers behind his neck, I pulled him closer, demanding more. Understanding the subtle hint, the soft kiss turned demanding. Pulling back, he nipped at my lower lip and along my jawline.

"Are you sure?" he whispered into my ear before tugging the lobe between his teeth.

"Yes, please." Embarrassment slammed the brakes on my desire. "But, um, do you have a condom?" His head tilted to the side. "I don't, and, well, I'm not really sure... I've never had blood work, you know?" Oh hell, here I was ruining the moment.

But instead of leaping off me like I had the plague, he smiled. "I do."

I sank into the bed in relief.

Stretching toward his bag, half his body suspended midair while his lower half dug against me, he tossed out a few clothes before shifting his body back over mine. He held up a foil packet, then scissored his fingers, turning the one into two. He tossed the two packets to the bed and returned that intense focus to me.

A hand snaked lower and gripped the edge of his T-shirt that I tossed on before bed. I wiggled out of the shirt as he pulled it over my head. Hovering over me, he dipped his head, catching a peaked nipple between his teeth. I sucked in a sharp breath when he tugged, the pain spiking before morphing into pleasure. A loud moan vibrated in my chest. I held the back of his head as he switched to the other breast, repeating the torture I desperately needed.

When he started trailing nips and kisses down the center of my stomach, I gripped the short ends of his hair and tugged him back up to me.

My hair slid beneath me as I shook my head. "No, I need you. You. Now." I was desperate for him to fill me, to give me what my body had begged for since he walked into the bar.

A dark, humorless chuckle sounded above me. Without taking his eyes off mine, he slipped a hand into my panties. He groaned when he found my core slick and ready for him. "Were you thinking about me before I came home, baby?" I nearly screamed when he flicked my swollen nub. "You're soaked."

I wouldn't lie even though my cheeks now warmed with embarrassment instead of lust. "Yes."

"Tell me," he demanded. Again he flicked my clit, causing tremors to rack through my entire body.

"I imagined you exactly like this," I said between breaths, "and the feel of you inside me." I groaned, thrashing my head when he thrust two fingers past my entrance.

"Did I feel good in your dirty little wet fantasy, baby?"

"Yes," I moaned. "Please, Chandler. I need you."

Chapter 23

"Begging will get you everywhere."

A pathetic whimper slipped from my pouting lips when his hand disappeared and his body vanished from above me. Frantic, I searched the dark. My vision adapted just as his boxers slid down his thighs.

"Hand me one," he said and pointed toward the condoms. I patted along the bed, the thin metal wrapper poking into my palm. With great interest, I watched as he ripped the small packet open with his teeth and slowly rolled the sheer rubber down his twitching length.

"Last chance, Ellie. You sure?"

Instead of answering, I swiveled on the bed, allowing my legs to dangle off the side, and widened my knees. With zero hesitation, he stepped between my spread legs and pushed them wider to accommodate his hips. With a strong tug, I nearly fell off the bed, only held up by his grip beneath my bent knees. Ass floating in the air, I rocked forward until the head of his dick barely brushed against my center.

I gasped in pure delight as he pressed against my entrance. Agonizingly slow, he pushed inside me inch by inch, stretching me fuller than I'd ever felt. Fisting the sheets, I held tight to keep from sliding backward along the bed. Another blissful whimper poured out of me when he pulled out, leaving me hollow and desperate for more.

"Hold on" was all the warning I had before he slammed into me. My grip slipped, but I adjusted my hold to stay exactly where I was. Over and over he thrust into me, pulling out to the tip before rocking forward again.

Sweat glistened along my forehead, breaths turning into wheezes. Each time he thrust deep, a burst of tingles and quivers spasmed in my lower half. I twisted my hips to the right, and he quickened his pace.

"Oh fuck," I nearly yelled as a full-body, mind-exploding orgasm ripped me apart. Everything tightened and loosened and tightened again as he continued to pound into me, elongating my pleasure.

Swallowing past a dry throat, I forced my lids to open. Still thick and hard inside me, Chandler smirked, full of male pride as he slowly slid himself in and out.

"Wow," I breathed. "Did you not...?" I didn't finish the sentence; we both knew what I left off.

"I will, maybe next round. Or the next."

"Or the next?" I squeaked.

"Yes, baby. Or maybe the next. I've waited for this moment, and I sure as hell won't rush it. Now." He slapped my still raised ass. "Flip over."

24

Chandler

My raw, scabbed knuckles split open again as I gripped the handle of the coffeepot like a lifeline. I stared at my hand, the abrasions and sting a memento of what I did. Never had I lost my temper like that, but after hearing what that worthless piece of shit Swann revealed, there was no holding back my rage. He was lucky I left him breathing.

The bitter taste of too strong coffee was just what I needed to snap me out of my reverie. With another sip, I sat at the table and stared at the pictures, notes, and other papers strewn along the top. As I drank my morning fuel, I studied the names listed on my initial suspect list.

Shit.

It was all shit.

The only likely suspect after yesterday's questioning was Jacob, or at least someone within the compound. But that was a dead end unless I could find a way to get beyond those gates without using Ellie as a negotiation tool.

"Morning." I grunted in acknowledgment to Alec's greeting. "What's eating you? You're usually a morning person. And after last night—"

"Fucking hell, shut up." I rubbed at my brows and held out my coffee mug as he shuffled by wearing nothing but a pair of gray sweatpants. "Fill me up, would you?"

Grumbling something under his breath, he snatched the mug. What remained at the bottom sloshed over the rim and dripped down the side.

"Seriously, what's eating you? You're in a sour-ass mood for someone who got laid last night."

"Nothing is adding up with the case," I admitted. Taking the now full mug from his outstretched hand, I dipped my chin in thanks. "And something happened yesterday with Swann."

"Oh," Alec said as he slumped into the wooden chair on the opposite side of the table.

"I don't want Ellie to know." Brows raised, Alec leaned forward, resting his forearms on the table, full attention on me. "When I spoke with Jacob yesterday, he mentioned he and Swann had some kind of agreement during those years Ellie was with him."

"Sounds suspicious. Probably trying to divert attention off himself."

"That's what I thought, but then I talked to Swann. The first hour or so, he was combative, ignoring my questions and demanding his innocence regarding the killings. He stated over and over that he wasn't a sick fuck who would do that to people. His confidence, the anger, it wasn't forced. So either he's the best manipulator I've ever encountered, or he was telling the truth about his innocence. Well, about the killing part, at least."

"Go on."

I leaned back in the chair to look down the dark hall. It was still early for Ellie, the sun just now peeking over the horizon, outside still more dark than light with the fading of the night, but I needed to make sure she wasn't eavesdropping.

"When I asked about his agreement with Jacob, he clammed up.

Chapter 24

His confidence wavered, and he started deflecting, which made me realize that scrawny-ass wannabe Jesus was right. So I pressed Swann." I cleared my throat. "Hard."

"Is he alive?" Gratitude swelled within me when there was zero judgment in my friend's tone.

I nodded. "I think so. It worked though. He admitted to what he agreed to give Jacob in exchange for him being with her."

Alec blanched. "I have a feeling I don't want to know."

Bile rose up my throat, hating that I had to say the words out loud. "He taped the two of them, Swann did. And sent those to Jacob as... payment or collateral, in a way, to be with who Jacob believes in his dark fucked-up soul is his wife."

Alec's jaw dropped, followed by a rush of red that washed across his face. "I'm going to kill him." He slammed his fist to the table. Using the leverage, he stood and started for the door.

I leapt from the chair, sending it crashing to the floor behind me, to prevent Alec from leaving. "I might have taken care of that already." His bushy brows rose. "I lost it. Really lost it." I shook my head and righted my chair. Slouching into the seat I took a long sip of coffee. The mug trembled in my grip. "When I left him, he was breathing."

"You know, even though I'm an officer of the law serving this amazing state, I'm still the friend who you can call to help bury a body. As long as the fuckstick deserved it, that is." His tight smile told me he was trying like hell to calm himself down.

"Thanks. I'll keep that in mind for the next time." Silence engulfed the room, both of us lost in thought. "Jacob won't let me beyond the gate without Ellie."

"Do you think it's him or someone behind that fence?"

I nodded, then shook my head with a sigh and shrugged. Heavy bare footsteps smacked against the floor as Alec returned to the table and slouched back into his chair. "I'm not convinced enough to make me use Ellie as bait. What if while I'm talking to the others, he takes her and disappears, or kills her? Or if it's not him, I'd put Ellie within arm's length of the unsub who's hiding among the brainwashed followers."

"You think we're missing something."

"I know we are. Or I am." I shook my head and pressed a hand to my sternum to ease the guilt weighing on my chest.

"How'd it go with her neighbor, Stan?"

"Not him. He did admit to leaving shows on his 'currently watching' list in hopes of making Ellie hot so she'd come running to him." The corner of my lip lifted with a snarl. "But he's been watching out for her by intercepting packages he thought were from The Church. What sucks is he tossed the packages before opening them, so they could've been from the unsub. Which makes sense that he would've tried to communicate directly with her like with the scalp. But we'll never know."

Again a heavy silence settled between us.

"I wish we could shut that place down," Alec muttered a few minutes later.

A subtle shift, a quiet breath down the hall, snagged my attention. Clearing my throat, I gave Alec a pointed look and tilted my head toward the darkened hall.

He nodded in understanding. "So where does that leave us today with the case?"

"I need to think, look at the victim wall for a few hours and see if anything jumps out at me in the timeline. The profile is strong. A bit vague, sure, but it's who we're looking for. Where are we on the DMV records and property maps?"

"Working on it more today. What about the objects used to rape the victims and things that could've left those marks on the bodies? Can your analyst run recent purchases for anything that could've been used for the torture or rape?"

I smiled at Alec, grateful for his input. "That's a good idea. Once I have the list of locals narrowed down, I'll have her look into past purchases that would fit that bill."

Both our heads turned when a tiny body rounded the corner. Hair a mess, wearing one of my long T-shirts that hung past her

Chapter 24

knees, mouth opened wide with a yawn, Ellie entered the kitchen. "Hi," she mumbled. She bit back a shy smile when her eyes connected with my own. "Good morning."

"Morning, baby." Before she could shuffle past, I hooked an arm around her waist and tugged her onto my lap. "How much of that did you hear?"

"Nothing really, just that we're back to square one on the suspect list." Picking up my now room temp coffee, she took a sip. Holding it between her hands, she kept it close to her chest. "I can help with that. With you starting fresh with the suspect list, I can give you insight into the locals. Like Farmer Ben matches your profile, but he's been in a cast for the last six weeks on his dominant hand. There's no way he'd be able to drag a body around."

"I like that," I admitted. "And that would mean you're with me all day instead of vulnerable at work." I gave her a triumphant smile.

"And then we can go to The Church," she stated nonchalantly.

Alec choked on his swig of coffee. Coughing and hitting his sternum, he narrowed his gaze at Ellie. "What?"

"Listen, I know it's not what I want, but neither is another woman being abducted, tortured, and murdered. I can deal with Jacob if that's the only way he'll let you inside the gate." She nodded almost like she was trying to convince herself. "I can do it."

"You heard more than you let on," I mused. Rubbing down her spine, I kissed her shoulder. "Let's start with the list and victim wall. Hopefully we won't need to go that route."

When she stood, I couldn't help myself with her tiny ass right there. The smack I landed echoed around the kitchen. Her small hand flew to the spot I'd struck, her dropped jaw sitting on her shoulder as she gawked at me.

"That's my cue," Alec mumbled. "I'll be in my room with my earbuds in and the music turned up really loud. Again."

Before he had disappeared around the corner, I pulled Ellie back to my lap, lifting her by the waist and helping her straddle my thighs. I wove my fingers through her hair, fisting at the base. With the other hand at the top of her ass, I forced her closer until her weight settled just over my stiffening cock.

The hem of the black T-shirt had ridden up her thighs, stopping just an inch shy of showing off her pussy to me. With a smirk, I slid it up that remaining inch. My smirk fell when I found her pussy bare, no underwear hiding the heaven I was quickly becoming devout to.

In the overhead lights, a glimmer shone between her spread lips, a welcoming beacon begging me to have a taste. I stood, the chair toppling to the floor with the force. Those blue eyes never left mine as I laid her back on the table, gently resting her head among the sea of photos. Not wasting a second, I dropped to my knees. Nipping a line up her inner thigh, I paused, my lips brushing against her swollen clit.

"Chandler," Ellie moaned, her hands gripping the opposite edge of the table near her head.

Flattening my tongue, I gave her center a hard lick from entrance to swollen nub, pausing to suck it between my lips. Flicking the sensitive tip with my tongue, I pushed three fingers inside, pumping in and out hard and fast. She wiggled beneath me, trying to squirm away from my harsh and demanding treatment, but I held her to the table with a hand pressed to her lower belly.

Torturing her, I'd bring her to the brink and then slow, only to repeat the action over and over again.

Only when delirious begs fell from her lips did I give her what she needed most. On a silent scream, Ellie shook beneath me, a flood of her juices seeping between my fingers. Gathering some of the slick fluid, I dragged it toward her back entrance and slipped a single finger inside, adding another after she relaxed.

"How dirty this morning, baby?" I asked, nipping along her inner thigh.

Hooded eyes met mine over her heaving chest. "Do your worst," she breathed. Her eyes closed on a moan when I slipped another finger inside. "Yes, Chandler, please."

"You know I can't say no when you beg," I said darkly. "Bend over the table."

Chapter 24

I LEANED against the cool tile, allowing the hot water to pound on my chest. With the quiet of the moment, alone in the bathroom, the guilt of not telling Ellie what her asshole of an ex did while they were dating ate at me. Was I saving her from more hurt or causing more because she didn't know?

But did she need to know?

Pounding a fist against the wall in frustration, I finished rinsing off and jerked the metal handle to the left, cutting off the stream of water. At the sink, I wiped away the layer of condensation and stared at my reflection, marveling at how much I'd changed since meeting Ellie.

The bags under my eyes were nearly gone, the hollow look behind them now full of life and love. I looked happy. Probably because I felt happy. Even with the guilt weighing me down, being with Ellie made everything easier. Sure, I still had a killer to catch and had regrets from this case and others, but that wasn't consuming my thoughts now.

She was.

She still hadn't given an answer to coming home with me. But she had to. I needed her with me. I didn't want to morph back into that shell of a man. I needed Ellie like I needed air to survive. She was my lifeline to a true life, one worth living.

The soft fibers of the towel scraped across my raw knuckles, little lines of crimson left in the wake.

Was it terrible that I didn't care if the bastard lived through the night or not? I leashed my rage, which was the only reason I knew I didn't beat him hard enough to inflict too much damage. The worst part was what I did to his ego with my final order.

Step down from police chief and never bother Ellie again.

Beneath the swollen eyes, battered cheeks, and split lip, Swann had blanched.

At the end of the questioning, I was confident Brett wasn't the unsub. A creepy, manipulative asshole, yes. But our unsub? I didn't see it.

A distorted knock from the other room had me rotating from the mirror to the closed bathroom door. After securing a towel around my waist, I stepped into the bedroom, a cloud of steam following me. Ellie smiled from her perch at the end of the bed where she was tying her boots, hair still damp from her own shower.

Another round of demanding knocks shook the door, quickening my steps. Whatever it was couldn't be good. I twisted the knob and yanked the door open.

"We have a problem," Alec said, gradually lowering his fist.

"Now what?" Ellie groaned behind me.

His intense gaze never left mine. "They found Swann's squad car. Abandoned. Five miles from here along an old county road. Door open, like he just vanished into thin air."

"What?" I stated in disbelief. This could not be happening.

"He's gone."

My eyes widened as the implication set in. Either he took what I told him to the extreme, or he was running because he didn't want to get caught.

A soft feminine gasp sounded behind me. "What do you mean, gone?" Ellie whispered, her fingertips pressed against my lower back as if searching for support.

"I mean Brett Swann is now considered a missing person. And there's more." Alec's features tightened. "They searched the squad car for clues to where he might have gone."

"That's a good start," I muttered while massaging my brows.

"You're never going to believe what they found."

Thin arms wrapped around my waist, her full chest now pressed against my side. I placed a comforting hand on her forearm and gave it a slight squeeze. "What did they find?"

Alec's gaze flicked to Ellie, his features solemn.

"Fingers. I'm guessing the most recent victim's."

What the hell?

Chapter 24

I shook my head in dismay. Several droplets of water sprayed from my short hair as I rubbed my hand over my head.

Could I have been that wrong about Brett Swann?

Was Swann, the police chief tasked to protect this town, a serial killer?

25

Ellie

THE WHIRLING of the truck's tires against the rough blacktop filled the otherwise silent cab as we drove toward the police station. Cold seeped from the glass window into my forehead as I watched the dismal scenery pass by.

A search party for Brett Swann.

Police chief, my ex—and a serial killer?

"This doesn't feel right," I said for the thousandth time in the last five minutes. "Sure, Brett is an asshole who doesn't take no for an answer, and he's terrible at his job, but a killer?"

"I agree, but the evidence is all there." Chandler's clear blue eyes reflected in the rearview mirror, meeting my own. "We'll figure it out shortly. But killer or not, he's obsessed with you coming back to him, and with us not having tabs on him, I need you attached to my side or Alec's until we find him."

"Yeah, sure, that makes sense." Was this what all those wives of the serial killers felt, the complete foolishness and embarrassment of knowing the man responsible for heinous crimes, yet you never realized? "Wonder what set him off to ditch his squad car right there in the middle of the road with evidence inside. Why be meticulous to this point, then bam, evidence everywhere?"

"That might be my fault," Chandler admitted. He cleared his throat and adjusted in the driver seat to sit taller. "I was informed of some illicit activity of his, which prompted me to offer him an ultimatum. Either he stepped down from police chief or I'd arrest him."

"Now that, the illegal stuff, I believe over him being a killer. What was the information?" Chandler avoided looking into the back seat. Not good. Dread weighed heavy in the pit of my stomach. "I don't want to know, do I?" I whispered.

"That's up to you. If you want to know, I'll tell you, Ellie, but there's nothing we can do about what happened in the past." He paused. "It was a bluff, about arresting him. I don't have any evidence, just his confession, which I didn't record."

We slowed to take the turn into the crowded police station parking lot. Almost every space was taken with old trucks, a couple tractors and side-by-sides, and one bike. The entire town showed up to help search for Brett, either because he was a danger to the town and to himself or because they were worried about him. A little of both, I surmised, based off the men's faces as the truck crept through the lot, Chandler searching for a place to park.

The moment he cut the engine, we hopped from the truck. Chandler's protective hand pressing against my lower back guided me through the chatting crowd as we maneuvered our way to the entrance. When the double glass doors shut behind us, I inhaled deep through my nose and shook out my trembling hands. With a quick scan of the reception area, I located Ryan in the back corner, talking to a couple officers. He noticed me at the same time and nodded in acknowledgment, his face drawn with worry.

Hands shoved deep in my new coat's pockets, I rocked back on my heels as Ryan excused himself from the conversation and came to stand with me, Alec, and Chandler. Chandler snaked an arm around

Chapter 25

my waist and tugged me an inch closer and therefore an inch farther from where Ryan had paused.

"Anything new since this morning?" Alec asked, crossing his arms over his broad chest as he peered down at Ryan.

"No," Ryan said, his lips dipped in a frown. "This is ridiculous. My brother isn't a killer. There must be a misunderstanding of some kind." Hope dripped from his words as he looked between Alec and Chandler, who shared a look of their own. Pleading eyes locked on me. "Tell them, Ellie. Tell them Brett wouldn't do this."

I bit my lip to keep from saying a single word. I did agree with him, but this wasn't my investigation, and I really didn't want to mess anything up for Chandler and Alec.

"Did you see him last night?" Chandler questioned, flexing the fingers around my waist.

Ryan nodded. "Yeah, he came home after you talked with him. He looked terrible." Chandler's face tightened with a cringe. "I thought he was drunk because he was mumbling to himself about making someone pay, and—" Ryan rolled his lips in and glanced at me, "—about getting Ellie back no matter what."

"Anything else?" The hard tone in Chandler's voice made a shiver bolt down my spine.

"I'm not sure what he meant, or if he even knew what he was talking about, but he said something about tying up loose ends, then left in his cruiser."

Alec cursed. "I sure as hell hope that doesn't mean another victim will die by his hand. Does he have access to another vehicle since we have his cruiser?"

"Our old farm truck is missing," Ryan sheepishly admitted. "I don't know for how long. I don't look in the barn that often, but this morning with him missing, I went to check."

"He could've stashed the truck somewhere yesterday for when he ditched the cruiser, which has a GPS tracker and is easily identifiable." Chandler's brows furrowed, gaze unseeing. "This doesn't make sense. He doesn't fit the profile. We said the unsub would have a menial job, be an underperformer in almost everything in his life.

Brett had a job that gave him power and prestige. And he's a sloppy alcoholic. He couldn't pull all this off without leaving trace evidence behind."

Continuing to mumble to himself, he spun on his heels, wrapped his hand around mine, and led me toward the back of the station. Stopping at a nondescript door, he pushed it open and urged me inside before following right on my heels. Pictures, evidence baggies, notes, and other things I couldn't identify were taped to the far wall, separated into columns.

The victim wall.

Chandler helped me into a chair before standing close to the wall, staring at the victims. I sat in silence, giving him the quiet he needed to process what Ryan revealed about his brother.

"What if I was wrong about one thing?"

The chair creaked as I leaned back. "About what?"

"Sure, Brett had power in the job title, but he really didn't have any power over the one person he wanted." Chin on his shoulder, he cast a weary glance my way. "You. What if that was what made him feel powerless? And in a small town, what power does a police chief really have? Besides being the boss and having a couple officers under you?"

"I could see that, but not in this case." Brushing the ends of a lock of hair against my lower lip, I stared at the basic brown table. "I just can't see it being Brett."

"He has motive, you leaving him. He has the means, a police cruiser that could get him to Waco to pick up the last victim and make it easy for the other victims to feel safe enough to get into the car alone. He's depraved enough to do the physical abuse the victims endured, and he has the strength to stab a long blade through the ribs into the heart."

There was something off in Chandler's tone. Almost like he was trying to convince himself.

"All that does make sense, and for anyone else, I'd say yes. But I know Brett, and I can't see him doing this."

"Me either, but I have to follow the evidence even if my gut is

Chapter 25

telling me we're wrong and that I'm missing something." He paced along the wall, taking in the pictures. "I'm missing something that is so obvious, I can feel it."

I agreed, but that wasn't what he needed in this moment. Standing, I stretched my arms up over my head. "You think he'll come after me?"

"I do."

"But I'm safe here."

"You're safe here with me and Alec." He inhaled deeply and massaged his eyebrows. "But we need to go out with the search party. The sooner we find Brett, the sooner we'll have answers. And if we can find him before he 'ties up loose ends,' maybe we can save a life too."

"Then go," I insisted.

"I'm not leaving you," he snapped. "Sorry, I just don't know how to do what I need to do for the case and keep you safe."

I was holding him back. He didn't say those words, but I could see it in the way he seemed at war with himself.

"Come on," I said. At the door, I pulled it open and waited until he was behind me before going back out into the lobby area.

Alec still stood in the intimidating stance, now giving orders to two officers and a handful of local men. Ryan was nowhere to be seen.

"I want a man watching for a late eighties model hunter green Ford F150 on every corner. Focus around the diner, bar, and Golden Chick since those are the places Ellie works. The rest of us will head up the search party. His brother mentioned a few isolated locations within hiking distance from their house that we'll check out first. We'll split up if we need to cover more ground faster in case there's a victim out there."

"I'm going to stay here," I cut in. Alec and Chandler glared, but I didn't shrink back. "Leave an officer with me, hell, even give me a gun, but I'm staying here. I'll only slow you down out there, and you guys know it. I refuse to be the reason Brett gets away or you don't get to the other victim in time. We need answers, and he's the only one who can give them to us. Go." I gave Chandler's strong arm a push. "I'll be fine."

"Brett would expect us to bring her with us," Alec mused. "Maybe this was his ploy to get her out in the open, take us out, and then disappear with her."

"I'm not leaving you alone," Chandler gritted out through clenched teeth. His jaw flexed and moved as he ground them together.

"This isn't your choice." I pointed at Jake, an officer I knew well and trusted. "You're staying here with me." Jake nodded. "There. Now you can go do your job, find Brett, and I'm safe."

Chandler pursed his lips, but Alec stepped between us before a fight could ensue.

"She's right. Those short little legs will hold us back—"

"Hey," I shouted and smacked his back, hurting my hand more than him.

"The ground is unforgiving out there in the fields we'll have to cross by foot to get to a few of the old barns." He hooked a thumb toward the doors. "Ryan is outside, said he'll go with us as a guide. It's our best option. If any of the locals on the lookout for the truck see it, they can radio it in to the station. I'll even put two locals I trust outside the police station if that makes you feel better."

"It doesn't." Chandler's voice was muffled with Alec standing between us. "But I don't have a better option or a choice, so it seems." Leaning to the side, he peeked around Alec, a single brow raised. "Do you know how to shoot a gun?"

"Um," I said, stalling. Tell the truth that I'd never touched one or lie so he'd give me a gun to protect myself, making him feel more comfortable about leaving me behind?

"I'm taking that as a no."

I gave him and Alec a sheepish shrug.

"We need to get going," Alec barked to those standing around us. "Everyone outside for your assignments."

Eager to help, the small crowd followed Alec out the double glass

Chapter 25

doors, converging with the other locals waiting outside, until it was only me, Chandler, and Officer Jake in the lobby.

"I'll be fine, Chandler." I gave his bicep an encouraging squeeze. "Go. Find Brett, get our answers."

His hot forehead pressed against mine. "I don't trust anyone, not when you're the one in danger. If it's not Brett, the unsub could be anyone. We still have a long list of locals to go through to narrow down. What if it's him?" He cast a narrowed-eye glare that promised death in Jake's direction.

"It's not Jake."

"How can you be so sure?"

"Because I'm gay," Jake voiced from where he leaned against the wall.

I gestured toward the man who'd just proved my point for me.

"Oh," Chandler grumbled.

"That's why I trust him. We'll be fine, Chandler. He'll protect me, and I'll protect myself too."

The corner of his lips dipped in a frown. "I'm not leaving you unarmed." Reaching into his pocket, he pulled out a pocketknife. Flipping my hand palm up, he set the heavy metal into my hand and folded my fingers around the red handle. "If anyone acts suspicious or you feel uncomfortable, stab them here." He pressed two fingers to the side of my neck. "Or here," he whispered, pressing against the inside of my thigh. "For maximum damage."

"Got it." Toes pressed to the linoleum floor, I stretched as high as I could and planted a kiss on his cheek. "Now go, and hurry back."

Before I moved away, Chandler turned his head and pressed his lips to mine in a scorching kiss. When he pulled back, allowing my feet to float back to the floor, my legs felt like rubber.

"Be safe, and don't trust anyone." At the door, he turned, confliction pinching his features. "I love you, Ellie."

My heart stopped at those emotional words neither of us had expressed but clearly both felt.

Then all the love and softness vanished from his gaze when he turned to Jake. "If anything happens to her, you die."

I continued to stare out the glass door long after Chandler and the search party had driven off. A smile crept up my cheeks as heat filled my face.

"He's intense," Jake said. Groaning, he fell into a plastic chair and stretched his legs out long. "Not that I blame him. If someone I loved was the target of a serial killer, I'd probably be the same way."

Nodding absentmindedly, I dropped into the chair opposite Jake and tucked my knees to my chest. As he continued to talk, telling me about this guy he met in Waco, I played with the knife, pulling it open a few hundred times to engrave the motion into my brain. I didn't think Brett was our guy, but that meant our killer was still out there.

Waiting.

Watching.

For the right moment to claim his prize.

Me.

26

Chandler

THE INTENSE PAIN radiating from my chest was the worst I'd ever experienced, and I've been shot multiple times as a Marine. Leaving Ellie at the station felt like I'd ripped my heart straight out of my chest and had my soul split in two. The feeling only worsened the farther we drove away from her, trailing Ryan's beat-up champagne Camry.

Thankfully it was another pleasant day, but the looming clouds signaled the weather might change again soon. The only way this could get worse was if it rained or the damn insistent wind picked up again.

Halfway down a dirt country road, his car barely visible in the dust cloud left in his wake, Ryan pulled over to the shoulder.

The dead grass and crumbling dirt ground under my boots as I strode toward Ryan, who was already making his way across the field we'd stopped alongside. After almost turning my ankle twice, I acknowledged that Alec was right earlier, Ellie would've slowed us down in this terrain. Hell, *I* was slowing us down. The locals seemed to know how to avoid the shin-deep divots without studying the ground, but I was finding every damn one of them.

Even though Alec was right, it didn't make the pain I felt at leaving her behind lessen. Digging my phone out, I glanced at the screen for the tenth time since we started the trek to see if she'd messaged or called.

"She's fine," Alec said beside me, sounding winded.

"I don't like it," I grumbled and shoved my phone into the back pocket of my jeans. "If something happens to her...."

"We're doing everything we can to ensure it won't. Jake is a good officer. He knows not to let anyone close. He'll take care of her."

"But it's not me." There was the rub. Some other fucker was protecting my girl while I was out here getting my ass kicked by dirt. I stumbled again, a string of curses slipping out as I caught myself before falling. "If it's not Swann or Jacob, where does that leave us?"

"With a long list of locals or members inside the Church. We can narrow it all down once we get the DMV results and property maps."

"I hope it's not someone inside The Church. If it is, we'll never find enough evidence for an arrest, much less a conviction. Jacob wouldn't want that kind of press for his *utopia*," I spat the word.

The weight of the case, Ellie being in danger, and the uneven terrain stoked my rising frustration. I was damn good at my job, and I'd solved many cases before this one, so why was this proving so difficult? Was it because the unsub was cleverly hiding in plain sight or because I was letting my personal feelings get in the way of seeing the truth in the evidence?

"We're almost there," Ryan, who'd slowed to wait for us, called out. Me, he had to wait for me. "This is the first one that came to mind. The rancher who owns the land is older and hasn't plowed his fields in years, as you can see." I grumbled my agreement. "The house is just a fifteen-minute walk through there." He pointed to a grove of trees. "It's a bit of a hike but doable for my brother."

"Where are we on finding the truck?" I asked Alec.

"I have people on the lookout for it. If Brett stuck around town, we'll find him." Squinting at the phone in his hand, he held it up high and moved it a little right, then left. "I don't get a damn signal out here."

I checked my phone, hoping mine somehow had better coverage. Nothing. Not a single bar attempting to light up. A sense of foreboding grew in the pit of my stomach, making the unease of leaving Ellie behind intensify.

We hiked the remaining half mile in silence, the stomp of our boots against the hard, dry soil the only noise. Finally reaching the edge of the leaning structure, I motioned for Ryan and the two local men to stay back. My nine-millimeter slid easily from its holster. Beside me, Alec mimicked my motions, withdrawing his own gun. The rough grip pressed into my palm, easing some of the tension that threatened to make my muscles stiff.

The rotted wood structure groaned with the wind; a rusted tin roof panel flapped about, popping against the few remaining pieces. Anticipation raced through my veins, heightening my senses. Every sound, movement, and smell seemed enhanced, offering me an edge in case an armed off-kilter asshole waited inside.

The flaking, rusted lever was cold in my hot palm as I wrapped my fingers around the metal to slide the lock free. Gun ready, I adjusted my grip and nodded to Alec, who dipped his chin, signaling he was good to go.

With a deep breath to calm my racing pulse, I shoved away all the anxiety of leaving Ellie behind and slid the bolt free.

The decrepit hinges complained as I tore the door open, the rust and buildup grinding from years of disuse. I cringed at the sound as I followed Alec in, my hand resting on his upper back. Together we slowly made our way through the barn, clearing each dark corner as we searched.

A mouse scurried along the floor, scratching across the toe of my boot.

"This place is as abandoned as it looks from the outside," Alec muttered, keeping his voice low and even. "No one has been in here in a long time."

"Agreed. This isn't it." I lowered my gun, pointing the barrel to the dirt floor. "This is a dead end."

Holstering our guns, we gave the relic of a barn one last glance to ensure we didn't miss anything. The door once again protested when we emerged into the bright sunlight. An unexpected gust of wind snagged the door out of Alec's hand, slamming it against the rotted frame. The entire structure shuddered, threatening to crumble.

I squinted and shielded my eyes from the late morning sun. In the distance, another barn or structure of some type stood out from the flat landscape.

"That's where Ryan said to go next," one of the locals stated, pointing to where I was already looking.

My gaze snapped to the men, and I lowered my hand. Two local men, not three, stood off to the side. I glanced back toward the vehicles, squinting. Only the rough outline of my truck and one other stood out. Ryan's car was gone.

"Where'd he go?" I asked, suspicion rising at the random quick exit of our only suspect's brother.

"He got a call from Janice, said someone needed him at the clinic. Something about stitches or something." The man raised and lowered his shoulders, the bulky Carhartt coat barely moving with the motion. "He said he'd meet up with us as soon as he was done."

"All right, let's start—"

I cut Alec off with a raised hand. Something wasn't right.

When it clicked, I slid the phone out of my back pocket and checked the screen. Still zero signal. "Alec, do you have a signal yet?" I asked, the worry in my voice clear.

He checked his phone and shook his head. "Nothing, why?"

"If you don't have a signal, and I don't have a signal, how did Ryan get a call?"

All three men blinked in unison, a stunned expression on each of their faces.

My stomach dropped with dread, like a lead weight in the middle of a stormy sea.

"He set us up," I stated, barely keeping my anger in check. How was I so damn blind? Of course he'd help his brother. "He's going to help that fucker take Ellie and run."

"No, no way. He wouldn't do that," one of the other men said, but his tone lacked conviction.

"Ryan isn't like his brother. He's a good man," the other added.

I glanced to Alec, who was silent, scrubbing at his jaw, deep in concentration.

"What do we know about Ryan Swann?" I asked. "Why would he help his brother evade arrest and kidnap Ellie?"

Alec spoke up first. "Single, midforties, dropped out of undergrad to help out after his father died—"

"Well, not exactly." Alec and I turned in unison to the man who spoke. He tugged off his red ball cap and fidgeted with the bill, avoiding our demanding gazes. "That's what we were told, but I knew his daddy well, and Ryan was actually kicked out of school before his daddy's death."

"What?" Alec's tone was menacing. I pressed a forearm to his chest in case he tried to lunge at the clearly intimidated man.

"Yeah, some misunderstanding with a girl. The school kicked him out, but there wasn't enough evidence to convict him of the rape charge. He was hanging out in Waco, getting his EMT certification, when his daddy died, and he came home using that as an excuse."

I didn't wait to hear any more. Not caring about twisting my ankle or even breaking a leg, I tore across the field. Dirt kicked up in the wake of my pounding steps, a second set just seconds behind me, hot on my tail.

"Call that fucking officer and warn him that Ryan is our unsub," I shouted over my shoulder. "Not Brett. Fuck, why didn't I see that? Ellie needs to be somewhere safe and protected at all costs."

"On it," Alec's deep voice rumbled behind me. He cursed, and I knew exactly what he was going to say before the words left his mouth. "I still don't have a signal."

Which meant neither did I.

I glanced at my watch. Fifteen, twenty minutes tops. That was how much of a head start that fucker had on us. I had to get to her, get to Ellie before he did.

All the missing pieces that were disjointed when Brett was our main suspect fell into place.

Middle-aged white guy, dead-end job, felt powerless to change anything. But the message about coming home didn't fit, or how someone like Ryan was able to pick up so many women who wouldn't pull up in the system. And why Ellie? She had been with his brother, not him. Was there some sort of hidden attraction there that he never acted on?

But that didn't matter now. What mattered was getting to the truck, hauling ass back toward town, and alerting everyone in Orin that Ryan was our main suspect.

My heart sank as we drew closer to the truck.

We wouldn't get to her in time, or make the call that could save her.

The fucker slashed all the tires.

Panic shoved aside every other emotion as I stood, fists tight at my side, staring at the deflated tires.

"Now what?" Alec shouted, stopping beside me.

I scanned the surrounding area, but we were too far from town, in a remote field with nothing around us. Except....

"Didn't he say Brett's place was fifteen minutes that way?" I pointed toward the grove of trees Ryan had indicated earlier.

"Yeah, but can we trust him?"

I closed my eyes and tilted my face toward the sky, praying for a miracle.

"No, but we can't take the chance that he accidentally told us the quickest way back. I'll run back the way we came," I stated with zero room for negotiation, "and you cut through the grove of trees." Turning, I grabbed the front of his T-shirt and held it in a tight fist. "We save her no matter the cost, you hear me? She's... she's everything." I pulled him closer and narrowed my eyes. "And if you find that fucker Ryan before I do... he's mine."

With a hard shove that didn't move Alec an inch in the direction he needed to start running, I turned on my heels and sprinted down the flat dirt road.

We would get to her in time.

And once she was in my arms again, I was never letting her go.

She was my forever.

Now to find her and make the asshole who threatened our happiness pay.

27

Ellie

SEVENTY-SEVEN, seventy-eight, seventy-nine.

Seventy-nine ceiling tiles. Yep, I was that bored. Bored and famished. My stomach growled, desperate for nourishment or candy; the grumble seemed to echo in the small area. Jake glanced up from his phone with a sympathetic smile.

"Sorry, Ellie." He sighed, tossing the phone to the chair beside him. "I'm not comfortable with us leaving to get something to eat." Biting his lip, he looked toward the back of the station. "But...." I straightened in the uncomfortable seat with the hope that one word created. "There might be some snacks hidden in Hart's or Swann's desks if you want to rummage through them."

I was out of the chair before he finished talking. Leaving him sitting in the front lobby, I pushed through the side door into the officers' area, which was nothing but a small cluster of well-used desks. The metal drawers of the first desk I tried rattled as I tugged them open one by one scavenging for anything to eat.

If I found candy, even better. Even a simple Tic Tac or strip of gum would help ease the mounting anxiety. I needed my dose of sugar more than ever, but of course I left my purse at the house when we rushed out after the news that Brett was missing and now the main suspect. Coming up empty again, I slammed the drawer shut, the objects atop the desk shaking.

One more place to check. I cast a weary glance toward Brett's office. With a resigned sigh, I weaved between the desks and paused, resting my hand on the office doorknob. I hesitated, though not sure why. It wasn't like I'd find any evidence, right? Well, he *was* stupid enough to leave fingers in his cruiser, so maybe I might. I shivered at the thought of what could be hiding behind the solid door.

Squaring my shoulders, I twisted the knob and pushed. Groping along the wall, I searched for the light switch. Soon the overhead fluorescent bulbs buzzed as they flickered to life. A large desk and chair sat in the middle of the room with two smaller, lower chairs in front.

I huffed and rolled my eyes. Brett really did have an ego issue. That part of the profile seemed to hold true. My curiosity piqued as I surveyed the office, from the disheveled stacks of files in the corner to the messy desk and the old cup of coffee that sat beside a closed laptop.

The laptop held my attention, making it difficult to look away. There could be something on there that could help Alec and Chandler, evidence maybe. The heavy leather rolling chair creaked as I rolled it out from under the desk and gingerly sat in the large seat. Digging the heels of my boots into the floor, I walked the chair forward.

Before cracking the laptop open, I rummaged through the two right-side drawers, then the left in search for food. An old-looking protein bar, an empty bottle of Jack Daniel's, and a half-eaten bag of stale potato chips were all I found. I pressed a hand to my hollow stomach, hoping that would help quell the building ache.

After a cautious peek to the closed office door, I flipped the laptop open. The dark screen came to life, a small password box standing

Chapter 27

out in the middle. Biting my lip, I stared at the blinking cursor. Hopefully Brett used the same basic password for this laptop as he did everything else in his life.

"One, two, three, four," I whispered to myself as I pressed the numbers on the keyboard. I cringed, hoping it wouldn't blare an alarm or something if it was wrong, and hit Enter.

It worked.

A picture of Brett and me from ages ago filled the screen. He was smiling and I was... well, I guess that was a smile. I studied the picture, my focus on me, specifically my gaunt features and the hollow look behind my gaze. It was a vast difference than the woman who stared back at me in the reflection this morning. So much had changed since that picture—hell, in the past two weeks.

I was happy.

That reminded me. Tugging my cell phone from the hidden pocket of my leggings, I pulled up the text string I had with Chandler.

Me: This is a terrible way to say this, but I can't wait.

Me: I love you too.

Me: And yes. Yes to going back with you.

Me: I'm ready to live.

Me: With you.

My cheeks burned with my wide smile as happy tears slipped down. I wiped them away with the back of a hand and cleared my throat of the clogged emotions.

A blue folder sitting on the desktop with my name as the label caught my eye.

Frowning, I double-clicked on the folder. A new box appeared on the screen, several files inside.

Squinting at the screen, I leaned closer.

Why in devil's balls would Brett have several dozen movie files in a folder with my name on it? I hovered the white arrow over the oldest-dated file, hesitating. Did I want to know? Did I *really* want to know? Or would whatever I find cause more harm than good? Sometimes the truth added bars on your cage rather than setting you free.

Jake's muffled voice slipped under the closed door. I stared at the door, expecting it to swing open and be caught red-handed. But it didn't. With a sigh of relief, I refocused on the file I had yet to click on.

With a quick double-tap on the mouse, the video filled the screen. It was dark, a single blurred figure in the distance, but something about the room seemed familiar. With a reluctant click on the Play button the video began.

That room. I knew that room

That girl. I knew that girl.

My breathing stuttered, my heart racing as *my* face came into focus. My skinny naked body strapped to Brett's bed. A menacing laugh rattled the speakers before Brett's naked ass filled the screen as he strode to the bed, whatever he held in his hand dragging behind him along the floor.

Not able to endure one more second, I slammed the laptop shut. Bending forward, I put my head between my legs, attempting to slow my erratic breaths, but that only made the stomach acid that was already mounting to burn along the back of my throat.

Hand squeezing my throat to keep from puking, I inhaled a lungful of air through my nose.

There had to be thirty or more videos in that folder.

Why would he tape me? Tape us?

Horror filled every inch of my body as I bolted upright. What if he sent the videos to others and didn't just use them for his spank bank? Swiping at the touch pad, I pulled up his email, then hovered the white arrow over the Sent folder and clicked. A knowing feeling had me typing out one name into the search bar.

Jacob.

Hundreds of emails filtered through, half with attachments and the other half without. I clicked on an email without an attachment, the date a few weeks after Jacob had exiled me from the community. My eyes widened as I scanned the words.

The fucker traded me.

I fell backward, the chair rolling back an inch with the momentum. Jacob traded me to Brett for protection against Janice's accusation on how she found me and anything I might try to accuse The Church of.

My heart broke. Not because I loved Brett, but I at least trusted him, and this was pure betrayal.

The screen wavered in my vision from unshed tears as I enlarged an email with an attachment and an ominous subject line.

Payment for Use.

For the second time in a matter of minutes, nausea rolled my stomach. I gagged, slapping a hand over my mouth.

A male shout of alarm from the other side of the door had me holding a breath to listen.

Another shout, then a deafening boom that sounded a lot like gunfire—well, the gunfire on TV. But the following silence was what chilled me to the bone. Jake wasn't on the other side of the door yelling everything was okay. Which meant... it wasn't.

I'd seen enough crime shows to know that when something seemed off or sounded wrong, it usually was. Trembling with the swell of fear coursing through my veins, I slipped from the chair and inched beneath the desk.

Knees to my chest, I cowered in the corner, making myself as small as possible. I clasped a hand over my mouth and nose to quiet my heavy breathing. Blood pounded in my ears, yet still the distinctive click of the door opening filtered through. I swallowed back a terror-driven sob.

Brett found me. This was it unless I did something besides hide helplessly beneath the desk of my would-be captor and killer. Witch's tits, he was going to kill me.

Tears leaked from my eyes. I really didn't want to die today.

Soft, menacing footsteps slowly rounded the desk.

My entire body quaked as I slipped the borrowed knife from the waistband of my leggings. As quiet as possible, without slicing my own finger off, I flicked the blade open like I'd practiced and pointed it toward the opening.

The plastic wheels rattled as the chair was shoved away from the desk.

My entire body vibrated with a mix of fear and adrenaline. Shifting, I balanced on the balls of my feet, ready to lunge forward and sink the pointy end of the knife into Brett's eye or neck or ear. Hell, I didn't care as long as I hurt him. I wanted to wound him like those videos had just damaged me. I felt violated, betrayed, and I fucking hated him.

First a knee peeked around the edge of the opening, then a hand appeared, pressing the tips of all five fingers to the floor as if to balance the owner as he prepared to peer under the desk.

I sucked in a breath so loud the people in Waco probably heard it. No doubt creepy-as-Hades Brett did, notifying him I was in fact hiding under the desk.

A battle cry built in my throat, ready to scream with the pent-up terror and hate that filled every inch of me, when an unexpected face popped below the desk and grinned.

Ryan.

I deflated, the knife shaking in my still extended hand as a soul-crushing sob bubbled out from my parted lips.

Ryan's smile didn't falter. "There you are."

"I thought you were him," I said between sobs. "I thought you were Brett here to take me away."

"No, Ellie. Not Brett. Hope you're not disappointed."

I smiled only for it to freeze halfway. There was something off about his entire demeanor. I swiped the unshed tears from my eyes to see him clearly. Alarm bells immediately sounded in my head, telling me to run.

"Where's Jake?" I asked cautiously, keeping my tone light just in case my instincts blurting "red alert" were right. I didn't want him to realize my suspicion.

"Why do you care?" Ryan's eyes narrowed, but his strained smile stayed.

"Um, because he's my friend, and I was just wondering—"

"Oh, I get it. You're fucking him too." The hand not balancing his weight slammed against the desk, making the metal rattle, the resounding boom ringing in my ears. "First my brother, then the guy from Boren and that FBI asshole. Now Officer Jake. You're a damn whore, Ellie. Guess that's what happens when you're trained that way." Closing his eyes, he took a deep inhale like he was calming himself down. "Not that it matters anymore. It's just you and me."

"Ryan, what are you talking about?" My voice shook. "You're my friend."

"No, I'm the one who you overlooked all these years. But not anymore. Come on, we're leaving."

Right. That sounded like a terrible idea.

The metal handle of the knife dug into my clammy palm as I adjusted my grip. I wasn't a victim. I was a survivor, and now, because of Chandler, I had something worth living for.

No, I wouldn't make taking me easy for him.

Even if I died trying.

I huddled farther back, cramming myself tighter into the corner.

"Come on." Ryan's frustrated voice boomed in the small area. With a grunt of annoyance, he stuck his hand into my hidey-hole, fingers stretching to grab on to anything he could use to pull me out against my will.

Not today, Satan.

Not today.

With the knife secured in my tight fist, I lashed out at his hand, slicing and swinging at any part of him I could reach. Finger, artery, palm, I didn't care as long as I inflicted damage. Warm liquid splattered across my hand, a few drops flinging against my cheek from my erratic slicing.

Ryan screeched, the sound piercing through my eardrums. I fought against the urge to cover my ears. Instead I followed his bloody retreating hand, continuing to stab at anything I could. I fell onto my knees, my free hand smacking against the floor and catching my body weight before I could face-plant forward. Ryan collapsed backward, still screaming and cursing my name, leaving the small opening unguarded.

I'd been in situations like this before with Jacob, when I'd done something that required punishment after, and I knew this was my only chance to escape. Even if I couldn't get away, I'd at least be free from the confines of beneath the desk, and that was better than being stuck under here.

Taking the opportunity, I scurried out, keeping my wide eyes on Ryan as I crawled backward.

"You stabbed me," he screamed. "You fucking cut me."

Using the wall for support, I crawled up it, my knees knocking with fear and the surge of adrenaline.

Run. I had to run.

I tripped, a bolt of pain spreading down my bicep where the edge of the metal filing cabinet had nearly punctured the skin. Stumbling toward the door, I let out a cry of frustration when the knob slipped in my sweaty palm.

A shuffle at my back begged me to turn and look, but I stayed focused on the normally simple task of opening the door. A sob of relief passed my trembling lips as the latch clicked, allowing me to swing the door open.

I lurched forward, my hip nailing the edge of one of the desks I'd rummaged through for snacks. My name growled from behind me, the tone loud and furious, almost had my already weak legs buckling under the weight of my terror. But I had to keep going. At the next door, I gripped the knob and turned, yanking at the same time with all the strength I had left.

It flew open, banging against the wall. The noise was almost enough to cover the approaching footsteps.

Almost.

I was running out of time. Bouncing from one wall to the other down the hall, I skidded to a stop when the lobby came into view.

Jake.

I choked on a sob, covering my mouth with my clean hand.

The dark crimson pool surrounding his motionless body stunned me enough that my muscles froze.

I couldn't move even when the pounding footsteps down the hall grew louder.

Couldn't move when a panting chest pressed to my back and hot breath brushed against my ear.

Couldn't move when his sticky hand wrapped around my throat.

"You really shouldn't have done that."

His hand sealed against my ear. With a hard shove, I sailed through the air, the wall coming faster than I could react.

I squeezed my eyes shut, preparing for the impact.

My temple collided with the cinderblock wall.

A burst of pain followed by an almost cry on my lips.

Then nothing but darkness.

Blissful, painless darkness.

28

Chandler

My boots were not made for running at a rapid, lung-hemorrhaging pace. The painful blisters that formed miles back along the soles of my feet were now a raw mess. Even still I continued to sprint toward town, reminding myself over and over again what was at risk if I failed.

The flat, desolate landscape allowed the town to show on the horizon, making it look closer than actuality. Chin to my chest, I pushed through the pain radiating from my feet and tight leg muscles, adding another burst of speed. Every second counted.

Hope ignited at the sight of a dust cloud billowing to the east, a long brown cloud trailing behind a pickup truck cruising down the main highway. It was too far to chase down, but I wouldn't be deterred, not when Ellie's life was on the line.

Phone in hand, hoping the screen would reflect the few rays of sun that escaped the building clouds, I waved both hands high above my head like a crazy-ass fool. My shout for attention came out more like an angry, frustrated bellow than a plea for the truck to stop.

Even with my aches and pains, relief sent a renewed wave of energy when the older model blue truck slowed. I swallowed down the emotions clogging my raw throat. Digging deep, I kicked up my speed another notch and raced toward the now idling truck.

My nostrils flared with each wheezing breath as I approached the vehicle. A man I didn't recognize from around town leaned across the seat and manually rolled down the window. Index finger to the brim of his cowboy hat, he tipped up the front and leveled a steely eyed glare my way.

"You lost, son?" he asked, his accent thick with a Texas drawl.

"I need," I said before sucking in another lungful of air, "to get to town." I reached for my back pocket, the rancher tracking each movement no doubt ready to draw a weapon if needed. Extracting my FBI identification, I held it as steady as I could into the cab. His eyes widened after surveying my badge and papers. "A woman is in danger, and I need to get back to town. Now."

"Hell, son, why didn't you say that first?" he said, his tone chastising. "Get in." Two fingers tucked under the metal pin, he raised the door lock and gestured for me to hop inside. The door wasn't fully closed before he whipped the truck around, the cab jolting as he tore through a field to make the U-turn, and floored it toward town.

"Thank you. Head to the police station." I rolled up the window with one hand and checked the bars on my phone in the other. Still nothing. "Damnit," I cursed. Not wanting to seem ungrateful for the lift, I indiscreetly leaned toward the driver side to eye the speedometer.

"I'm going as fast as I can." He spit a chunk of dark liquid into an old Dr. Pepper bottle.

"I know you are, and I'm grateful for the ride. It's not just any girl," I admitted.

"It's your girl."

"Yes." The sharp ding of an incoming text had my hands flying to the device. Fucking finally, I was somewhere with coverage, even if it

Chapter 28

was only one bar. I scrolled through text messages from my boss, our analyst, and a few others when one name made me pause.

I pressed the message several times before the screen shifted, showing the many texts I missed from Ellie. But that was nearly an hour ago. Pressing the Call icon, I lifted the phone to my ear. The line connected with a loud ring, then another, and another and another. A generic voice mail message picked up, suggesting I leave a message.

Ending the call, I tried again.

And again.

And again.

Each time receiving the same damn message.

Damnit. Flicking to Alec's contact listing, I pressed the Call button, but the line didn't connect. He was still out of service area, then. I held on to the door handle as we flew through two four-way stops and swerved to miss a stray dog lying in the middle of the road. Without slowing, the driver whipped into the station's parking lot.

A distinct click of the slide of a gun engaging caught my ear seconds after he shifted the truck into Park. Slowly I rotated toward the driver side, unsure what I'd find.

"You need backup?" he asked, all business, holding a massive .40-caliber handgun on his lap. "I'm locked and loaded."

A wave of gratitude flooded through me. "No, but thank you." I hopped out, ready to shut the door when he spoke again, making me pause.

"I'll wait out here until you give the all clear, son. If I hear any shots, I'm coming in after you. I know it's your girl and you want to play the hero, but everyone needs backup every now and then."

Nodding in acknowledgment, I slid my own gun from the holster and flicked the safety off.

Muscles tight and inflexible, they ached and pulled as I climbed the two steps to the cement landing, careful to keep each footstep silent. At the glass doors, I paused, my hand suspended over the wide grooved metal handle.

The door opened silently, and I said a mental thank-you to any deity for that small gift. The unmoving body of Officer Jake lay in the middle of the lobby, the tacky puddle of crimson beneath him clearly his own. I held a breath, tuning all my senses into listening for movement, sharp breaths, or whispers, anything that would indicate I wasn't alone.

Nothing.

Through the side door, I tracked an inconsistent path of blood droplets down the hall. Gun leading, I pushed through the door into the officers' work area. In a fluid sweeping motion, I cleared the room. Gun still raised, I tracked the now more constant trail of blood.

At the next door, I snarled at the nameplate.

Repeating the sweeping motion that was ingrained from the Marines and FBI training, I cleared Swann's office. Empty. Slowly lowering the gun, the barrel pointed at the ground but held steady between both hands, I surveyed the room.

A heavy four-drawer filing cabinet had shifted at some point, a few of the folders that looked to have been stacked on top now strewn about the floor with crimson drops on the white pages. Treading around the desk, careful to not disturb the evidence, I studied the large leather chair that was pressed against the wall and a blood splatter along the space where the chair should've been.

My knees protested as I squatted, needing to get closer to the evidence. My heart hammered against my chest with fear at the thought that the blood could be Ellie's. Pursing my lips, I shoved the image of her hurt and scared to the back of my mind. I was no good to her if I couldn't focus and do my damn job.

Leaning forward, I ducked under the desk and used the phone's flashlight to cast away the shadows. Spatters of blood dripped down the sides, but there, in the back, was a void. A small space in the corner. Dipping back out, I glanced over the top of the desk as if I could see through the walls to the lobby.

Jake could've suspected Ryan or maybe just wouldn't let him through to the back. The two argued, loud enough for Ellie to hear. Ryan shot or stabbed the officer, causing an even louder commotion, so probably shot, then. That would've been heard through the entire station, confirming to Ellie that something wasn't right.

Chapter 28

Based on the evidence, the clever girl hid. But she was found. She used the knife I gave her to fend off the attacker. Then….

I stood and scanned the rest of the office.

Guilt and worry warred in my mind, attempting to overtake every thought and divert my focus.

I startled when a sharp ring filled the small office, having forgotten to turn off the ringer due to my urgent need to find Ellie.

"She's gone," I said when I answered, my voice quivering. "Fucking gone."

A heavy pause, Alec's deep exhales vibrating through the earpiece. "I'm still in the middle of nowhere and barely have one bar. Get on the radio and call in reinforcements—"

A thought snagged and built, evolving into a plan.

"What if we didn't?" I mused. My calm tone hid the inner turmoil eating me alive.

"What?" Alec shouted. "Are you fucking crazy? We need help hunting this bastard down."

"Give me a fucking second to think," I snapped. Careful to step over the blood drops, I retraced my earlier steps and slipped into the vacant room where the victim timeline covered the wall.

I scrutinized the evidence with new eyes, knowing the who, thinking maybe I could figure out where he would take Ellie now that he had the one he wanted. The second to last victim stood out, the message on her skin like a beacon.

"Where is home?" I asked.

"Whose?"

"Ryan's. Where is his home? I think that's where he'll take her. He's spiraling. He didn't plan for any of this. Brett disappearing because of me threw off his plan. Now he doesn't have one. Home is where he wanted to take Ellie before, so that's his comfort zone. That's where he'll go to work through what to do next."

"They lived together," Alec said. I pulled the phone from my ear and gaped at the screen.

"You didn't think that was fucking important to mention?" I shouted.

"Now, yeah, I see it was a slight oversight on my part." The guilt in his tone added to my own.

"It's fine. Nothing we can do about it now. Send me the address, and I'll get my analyst to send me an aerial view in case he's moved her to where he took his other victims."

"Help me out with why no backup."

I massaged my brows, the short hairs sliding beneath my thumb and index finger. "He's jumpy, scared," I explained. "If we swarm him, he's likely to take himself out and Ellie too." Just saying it out loud made my stomach roll. *Fucking think, Peters. How can I get Ellie out of this alive and unharmed?* "What if I find him and make him believe we still consider Brett a suspect? Make up a story how we assumed Ryan messed with the trucks and left because Brett put him up to it. That would calm him down, make him think he has time to come up with a plan to get Ellie out of town."

"Why do you think that plan would work? He's a smart motherfucker. He's gone this long without being caught."

He was right. This was a stupid, outlandish plan. But it would work because of one tiny woman.

Ellie.

"Ellie's good at seeing between the lines. She'll realize she needs to keep him calm, placate him. Maybe by helping him make a plan and deflecting the blame to Brett, wherever he is, she'll figure it out. She knows I'm coming for her."

"That's a big stretch. I love Ellie she's a smart girl, but you're putting a lot of faith in her figuring out your plan while under extreme stress, and hell, who knows, maybe even drugged."

I held in my possessive rumble. "He's the one who planted that evidence in Brett's squad car. He's also the one who said Brett came home spewing about tying up loose ends. He already laid that groundwork."

"Makes me wonder if Brett is even alive."

I grunted in agreement. Not that I was distraught about the idea. That was one death that wouldn't add to the growing weight of guilt I carried.

Chapter 28

"Take my truck," Alec said, then cursed loud into the phone. "I have the keys."

I smiled despite it all. "It's fine. I have a ride, and it comes with backup."

"Good. Now, go get your girl back, Chandler. And make that fucker wish he'd never been born."

"On it. I'll call you with any updates." I inhaled deep, steadying my voice. "And Alec?"

"Yeah?"

"If I don't make it, if I have to give myself to save her... tell her that for the first time in my life, I truly lived, because of her."

His shouts were muffled as I lowered the phone and pushed the red End Call button.

Back outside the police station, I let out a sigh of relief when the old rancher was still there, truck idling, hawklike eyes on me.

First get the address, then get Ellie.

A surge of renewed energy pulsed through me.

Time to save my own life by saving hers.

No matter the cost.

29

Ellie

IT WAS either the loud one-sided argument that pulled me to consciousness or the sharp pain spiking between my pinched shoulder blades. A breath hissed through my clenched teeth when I attempted to lift my head. My brain rattled around in my skull at the small movement, making the mind-numbing throbbing worsen.

I'd felt this kind of pain before, at Jacob's hand, when he'd disciplined me for sinning against him or The Church. The headache, rolling nausea, and insistent ringing in my ears all pointed toward a concussion. At least I wasn't dead.

Wait.

Why do I have a concussion?

My lashes stuck together as I peeled my lids apart, blinking several times to clear the haze hindering my vision. Dated light brown kitchen cabinets were the first thing to come into focus. A sense of familiarity pulsed, stirring unease. The galley kitchen with appliances from the eighties and the brown-and-cream linoleum floor also struck me as familiar.

"Brett?" My voice was raspy from either screaming or disuse. I hoped the latter.

"Don't say his fucking name to me." Ryan's voice crackled with the ferocity of his yell.

I followed the anger-filled voice to find him pacing the living room. Fingers interlocked behind his head, mumbling under his breath, Ryan marched from one end of the room to the other. His wild eyes flicked my way with every turn before he mumbled something under his breath again and his focus drifted back to the maroon carpet.

Right. Okay. I'm good. I can handle this. I've seen every episode of Criminal Minds, *watched every serial killer documentary, true crime episode, and memorized every word out of Chandler's mouth like it was profiling scripture since he arrived in Orin.*

I know what's happening.

He was self-destructing. No, that wasn't the word. I searched my memories for the right one.

Spiraling. That was what Chandler used once.

Not that it mattered, because either word meant the same thing.

That I was fucked.

Based on what Chandler profiled, the killer was careful, planned the abductions when no one was around, and even chose victims who couldn't be identified. He also kept the victims for months, which meant he planned his time with the women so others didn't notice he was missing.

Which begged the question: How in Hades did Ryan get away with all that for almost two years without Brett noticing? Unless....

I watched Ryan with a small level of respect, as disgusting as that sounded. I assumed Brett's drinking was self-induced, but what if Ryan either encouraged it or added to his nightly drinks to make him intoxicated?

One thing was for certain, I had to calm him down to give Chandler time to find and save me.

Chapter 29

Right. I can do this. What do I know from the profile and evidence that might help?

Witch's cold cunt.

Me. I'm the key to all this.

Worst. Life. Ever.

No, wait. That wasn't fair. Chandler was right with the life being a book analogy. Jacob was a chapter, as were Brett and Chandler. And now this time with Ryan was a new chapter. A super shitty one. But the previous, the one where Chandler ignited a passion in me I'd never felt before and viewed me as a woman, not an object, that one was pretty great.

The best, really.

Fine.

This. Chapter. Sucked. A. Witch's. Cold. Tit.

Now back to the dilemma.

He wanted me home. Well, I was "home," and he was still freaking the fuck out. Now what?

Then it clicked. Sure, I was home, but I was *taken*, which meant he couldn't keep me here for long until someone, i.e. Chandler or Alec, came along to take me away. Unless I convinced Ryan otherwise.

For this to work, I had to be persuasive. Good thing I had plenty of practice hiding my disgust and rage from men who controlled me.

I grazed the tip of my tongue along my dry lips and attempted to ease the pain that burned like a hot poker between my pinched shoulder blades.

"Thank you," I rasped. Lost in his delusional world, Ryan didn't hear the faint words. I cleared my throat, cringing at the pain it produced. "Ryan," I said louder, catching his attention. "Thank you for saving me."

His feet paused instantly. Those thick dark brows drew in tight.

"I'm scared of Brett." The shake in my voice wasn't added for dramatic effect, it was real adrenaline making my entire body quake. "And you saved me. I'm sorry I hurt you." Dipping my chin, I faked remorse.

Ryan shook his head. "No," he snapped. Closing his eyes, he inhaled deep. "There's no way out now."

"Sure there is," I said, my voice soft and comforting. "We just have to figure out a way to be together, right?"

"I killed my brother for you." He sat on the back of the couch and crossed his arms expectantly.

I swallowed down my revulsion and forced a grateful smile. "Because he hurt me."

Ryan rolled his eyes. Wrong answer, apparently.

"Because he videoed what was mine. I overheard the Fed last night confronting my brother and what he admitted. Those moments were special between you, Brett, and me."

"You?" I squeaked. *Surely I heard him wrong. Please let me have heard him wrong.*

"Come on, Ellie, don't play naïve with me. You knew I was watching."

I didn't. Holy Hades, I didn't. But that was the wrong thing to admit in this moment. I had to build trust. Yeah, yeah, that was it. I had to make him see me as a human again, not a problem to be solved.

"You're right." I looked to the floor before peering up through my lashes. "I knew, and I liked it."

I held down a gag at the proud, cocky-ass smile that contorted his face.

How did I not see this side of him before now? Four years, I'd known him. But not this him. No, this side was, evil... deviant... terrifying.

"It was then that I knew you were the one." He stood and rubbed at the seam of his jeans. "Only with you could I simply watch, with no touching, no pain, and have this"—he cupped himself—"come to life. All the others, none of them could affect me like you."

"I'm very impressed with how you kept this a secret for so long." I gave him my best adoring expression, hoping to cover up my disgust.

"I was taught well." He laughed. "You never knew my father. He was a kind man... to everyone but his family." A dark look passed over his face. "Until one day the anger stopped. It was like a new person had moved into our home. He'd go walking every night, said it was his way to relieve the stress of the job. One night I followed him and, well...." He chuckled. "My father wasn't just walking. I trailed him to the barn I still use today. Peeked through a gap in the boards and watched him with some unfamiliar woman. Every night he went back to her. She never left, always there waiting for him to beat her, then fuck her."

I nodded along, acting riveted with the story instead of trying not to piss my pants with fear.

"One night I took my own walk, an hour before my father, to see what all the fuss was about. That was my first time having sex." He smiled like he was cherishing the memory. "I mimicked what my father did before fucking her. She cried, asking me for help and to let her go. But after, when for the first time in my life my dick was hard enough to do anything with, there was no way I would. I was zipping up my pants when my father came in.

"I just knew he'd be furious with me. But he wasn't. He simply smiled, slapped me on the back, and said, 'Don't tell your mother.' After that, he dropped his pants and fucked her in front of me, beating her as he did until she bled out on the mattress."

There was no holding back. I pitched forward as far as I could and vomited on the floor.

A snarl of disappointment had me snapping my head back up, making the room spin.

"Sorry, I think I have a concussion," I said, adding a tremble to my lower lip. "I feel nauseous."

A flash of concern wrinkled his brow, but it faded as quickly as it appeared.

"I didn't hit you that hard," he said defensively. "If you thought that was bad, just wait."

That would be a hard no for me.

Stall. I had to stall him, get back on track for calming him down, not focusing on the torture he wanted to inflict.

"He sounds like a good man," I said, nearly choking on the words, and it had nothing to do with the rest of my menial stomach contents still trying to escape. "Did he teach you how to find your...?" I looked at him expectantly. I didn't want to say "victims"; that could signal to him that I believed what he did was wrong. Which it was, but pretty sure pointing out to the crazed killer holding me hostage that he was in the wrong was the last thing I needed to do.

"Pets," he finished for me. "And yes, we had to replace that one. First we cleaned together, relishing our moments with the one and planning what we'd do with the next. Then we hunted."

Apt term.

"We'd wait. It takes a lot of patience waiting for the right pet. But eventually the waiting paid off, and one would come walking down the road a little broken, a lot dazed at what they'd talked themselves into."

"The Church," I tested.

"Yes. People come and go from there often, but finding the right one, the one that wouldn't be missed or looked for...." He smiled and shook his head. "I never knew my father was also doing that so the pets couldn't be identified after we were done with them. Not that we ever allowed that. Digging a hole deep enough so the animals didn't dig up the body was easier with two men."

I nodded along, the dutiful submissive pet listening with rapt attention. All while my mind whirled with ideas of how to get the fuck out of the situation. I couldn't just wait like a damn damsel in distress for Alec or Chandler. No, I had to help myself. And keeping him talking seemed to be my best plan of attack for now.

"And the beautiful hair you sent me, that was a gift, right?"

His smile fell, and the disappointed look that settled over his features had my stomach sinking.

"Yes, that day in my office, you said you didn't really like the black, that you missed your old hair." *Fuck, I did say that.* "I was at a bar in Waco, and I saw her. Her hair was just like yours used to be. Long, thick, beautiful blonde, and I knew you'd like it."

"I loved it," I said through clenched teeth.

"Then you left it to go with that Fed." He took a menacing step

Chapter 29

toward me. I fought against the urge to shrink into myself. "You left my gift behind. And you let him touch you, touch what's mine."

And it was amazing.

Again, wasn't saying that out loud.

"You watched us?" I said, smiling like I was happy with the thought.

"From the window. I wanted to see your face when you opened the gift. But you ruined it."

"I'm sorry," I whispered and turned my face downward.

"Don't you see you're the only one who can save me, Ellie?"

"How can I save you?" I asked, truly curious. Maybe I was the one being selfish by not giving in and saving future victims' lives. If I just gave in to him, no one else would get hurt. Wasn't that what I was taught all my life? To give all of myself for others?

"Because this—" He grabbed my hand and held it to the front of his jeans, grinding his semi-hard cock into my palm. "—this only happens with you. I didn't even know it worked without inflicting pain before you. You cured me those two years we were together."

Also known as when he watched his brother and I participate in BDSM from the shadows. Not that Brett was much better, since he'd videoed our intimate moments and gave them to Jacob as payment.

"I hate him," I said, the truth and vindication making my voice louder and hard.

"Who?"

"Your bother. He videoed me. I didn't know. Why?" A single hot tear slipped down my cheek. "Why would he do that?"

"Do you want me to kill Jacob too?" He knelt before me, searching my face, waiting for my answer.

And I debated.

Truly debated.

But I couldn't have that on my conscience. Even if Jacob deserved it. He'd get what was coming to him at some point in life, just not by Ryan's hands because I asked him to kill my husband.

"No, but thank you. You really do love me," I said. Ryan nodded. "Then we need to figure this out, don't we?"

He popped up to stand, pacing around the oval dining table. "We could run," he said to himself. Long, deep lacerations littered his hand, a few still bleeding enough to warrant stitches, but he acted like they weren't there or didn't feel the pain.

"But this is our home," I reminded him. I used the word he'd used. This place was special to him. We couldn't go on the run; I'd never be seen again. I'd never see Chandler again. Just the thought was like a rusted spoon stabbing into my heart.

"They'll come after me," he said. "They'll take you. I won't let that happen." With his uninjured hand, he withdrew a handgun from the small of his back.

Devil's saggy balls.

"They won't," I shouted. "They won't. They still think it's Brett who killed all those... pets. You set it up perfectly." For added effect, I batted my lashes. "They think everything was Brett's doing."

"Not after what I did to the Fed and Ranger."

My stomach rolled. "What did you do?" My words were more of a high-pitched squeak. "We can get out of it, right?"

"I took them outside of town." I swallowed, lingering on his every word. "Led them to a barn I told them Brett might hide in." *If he says he killed them, if he killed Chandler and Alec, I'll do whatever it takes to make him kill me too.* "Faked getting a call, then went back to the cars and slashed their tires so they couldn't follow me."

I let out the breath I was holding with a whoosh. Ryan paused his pacing and stared me down from across the room.

"I'm relieved. That's an easy excuse."

"How?" he demanded.

"You did it because Brett made you." I licked my lips, the words barely having a chance to form in my head before leaving my mouth. "All of this, Brett made you do it. And they'll never find him, right?"

"Right," he said, running a hand through his shaggy light brown hair. "He's in the trunk."

Gross.

"See, there's our plan. When they come here, which I'm guessing they will to look for you and me, then you tell them Brett made you do it all."

"And the dead cop? They have video surveillance in the station."

"It's been down for months," I said quickly. That was a bald-faced lie, but due to the circumstances, I highly doubted all these lies I'd accumulated in the past half hour would be held against me at Judgment Day. "Brett did that too. And brought me here."

"And—"

The rumble of an approaching diesel engine had his mouth snapping shut. Racing to the front window, he used the end of the gun to peer through the thin metal blinds. He cursed and gripped the back of his head, mumbling to himself.

A surge of panic overrode the forming details of my plan. "Who is it?"

"Two people. I think one's that loner rancher who never comes to town but to drive through to the interstate."

"And the other?" My heart thundered. Half of me wanted it to be Chandler, but the other half needed him as far away from this crazy party as possible.

"That Fed you're fucking." Ryan's eyes had a crazed look in them. Pointing the barrel at my chest, he sneered. "I will not let him take you from me. If I die, you die."

"No, please, Ryan," I begged. "It was Brett, remember?" I sobbed. "It was Brett. It was Brett." I whispered it over and over again, hoping it would convince him that he still had a chance to get away with all that he'd done.

"No." He shook his head hard. "This is the end. This is where it all ends for us."

"No," I cried. The truck's loud engine cut off, the rumble dying and leaving the stark silence of the country in its place. "Please, Ryan. Don't do this."

Storming forward, he wrenched me off the chair with a hard tug. I fell against him, unable to move due to something securing my feet to the chair legs. Sealing me to his side, he wrapped an arm around my waist, turning us both so we faced the front door.

I bit my lower lip until a sharp metallic tang hit my tongue to keep my sobs at bay.

A hot prickly cheek sealed against my left side as smooth, cold metal pushed to my right temple.

And we waited.

I watched the brass doorknob, waiting for it to twist.

Waiting for my early death.

I'd survived so much in my life, yet this was the end.

At least I had one good chapter.

I lived once.

Shutting my eyes, I said a silent goodbye to Chandler, to Alec, to Janice and Stan. To the town that took me in when it didn't have to and gave a home to a broken woman who didn't exist.

When I reopened them, the tears had dried.

I was ready.

Ready for this to be the end of my book.

The end of it all.

30

Chandler

Ryan's older Toyota sat in front of us in the driveway. I was right that he would bring Ellie back here where it all began. How he distorted the past, him believing Ellie was his, not his brother's, was still an unknown.

Go in gun at the ready or not? That was my current dilemma. Brandishing the gun, I could irritate an already unstable killer, but not holding one would leave me vulnerable. I weighed the two options as I stared down the front door.

An irritated killer could harm Ellie before I got a shot off.

No gun, then. Even if it left me vulnerable, I wouldn't add to the possibility of her getting hurt.

The decaying cement loosened beneath my steps as I inched toward the front door. The torn screen door protested with a screech as I drew it open. Knuckles raised, I landed three sharp knocks and held a breath.

"Come in," said a familiar female voice from the other side.

I swallowed down the spike of hope hearing her voice had conjured. Brass knob in my grasp, I gave it a hard twist and shoved the door open. It too protested with a groan, popping at the hinges as it swung open.

A stuffed dated living room with a couch, chairs, and matching wood coffee table and end table was what I saw with my first small glimpse into the home. I pressed two fingers to the wood door to widen the opening. Every muscle tensed, freezing me in place when the kitchen came into view.

Ellie's entire body involuntarily trembled, her face a blank mask and held against Ryan, who had an arm constricted around her waist. The metal barrel of a revolver pressed against her temple, Ryan's face sealed to the other side. If he pulled that trigger, there would be no saving either of them.

My fingers twitched with the impulse to seize the gun secured against my lower back, close enough to grab but out of sight. Every emotion flared, swarming my body and mind. I had to calm down, take control of the situation. Inhaling through my nose, I let it out slowly and forced myself to relax.

"Where's Brett?" I asked. "I'll help you and Ellie get out of this. But I need to find him first."

Something like confusion flickered across his face. A quick spark of light that flashed across Ellie's placid face encouraged me to keep going.

"I know he made you do it all, to get her." I nodded to Ellie but didn't take my focus off Ryan. "First the tires and now this. It's okay. We know you're innocent." The gun barrel retreated a fraction. The red circular indention left in its place caused rage to boil in my chest and heat my skin. The fucker would pay for marking her. "Just tell me where he is and we can stop this."

Ryan shook his head. "No, it's too late. It's too late for us." My heart stopped when the gun barrel pushed against her temple again. Ellie's features pinched with pain. "*You'll* take her from me."

"Me?" I scoffed. "I'm leaving tonight."

"What?" he asked, clearly buying into the lie.

Chapter 30

"Yeah, sure. I was sent here to help identify the killer. And we did that—with your help, by the way—so why would I stay? The Rangers will continue searching for Brett, and I'll move on to the next case."

"What about Ellie?" he snapped.

Fuck, I needed to get that gun pointed at me instead of her. I would need to dig deep into my training to talk my way out of this one. If I made him angry at me, attacked something he loved, then maybe, just maybe he'd forget about Ellie and turn his sole focus to me.

What could I use to make him upset at me and not her?

Those blue eyes met mine.

Ellie.

"What about Ellie?" I laughed and crossed my arms, widening my stance. "It was fun, but I'm going home. Getting the hell out of this shithole of a town."

"You love her. I heard you say it," he muttered, though to me or to himself, I couldn't tell.

I twisted my lips into my best cocky smirk. "I've said that to every woman I've fucked. You know, to make them feel better for spreading their legs for just anyone." Fuck, I hated myself for saying this shit, but if it saved her life, I'd pay the consequences. "She wasn't that great though. I've had better."

Lies. All lies.

Ryan stood a little straighter and shifted, putting his body slightly in front of Ellie's.

"She's amazing," he said defensively.

"Really? You know that from experience?" I had no idea if he'd ever slept with her, but pointing that out seemed like a good idea. If he was reminded that he'd never had Ellie the way he wanted, maybe he would dismiss the murder-suicide plan.

"No, but I've seen her. Watched her." He looked at her and sniffed her dark hair. "She's amazing."

"Wouldn't you want to know for yourself? Why should your brother get to have all the fun, leaving you watching in the shadows?"

I gave him a second while he thought over my words. Forcing my focus on anything other than Ellie and the tears that now streamed down her cheeks, I nodded toward the living room.

"Nice place. Seems like a great home."

"It is. We inherited it from my father."

"Where is Brett, Ryan?" I coaxed. "Don't let him get away with what he did to you, to Ellie. You can have her. Just tell me what I can put in a report so I can get the hell out of this town."

My heart hammered as I followed the slow path the gun trailed down her cheek, along the column of her throat, past her shoulder, and finally pointing toward the floor. A relieved whoosh of air escaped when the immediate danger to the woman I loved was removed.

But he still had the gun, and he was still batshit crazy.

Still holding her tight, Ryan stood tall. "He liked going to Waco. I bet that's where you'll find him."

I nodded. "Good, that's good. Would you mind giving me an official statement to put in the report?" I waved a hand with the perception of being nonchalant. "You know, make all this official so I can get on that plane and get the fuck home."

His features relaxed. "Yeah, sure."

"Great. And since Brett's not here, how about you untie Ellie? I know you were only doing that for her safety, right?" He tilted his head. "In case Brett came back and demanded you hand her over to him. You were only trying to save her."

He nodded like that was the best excuse for having a woman's feet tied to a chair and her arms pinned behind her back. It was farfetched, but it was all I could come up with in the moment.

Sweat dripped down the back of my neck and along my temples, slipping down my jaw. Ryan knelt at Ellie's feet and worked at the knot he'd made when securing her to the legs of the chair.

Keeping my movement small and slow, I inched my hand back for my gun.

The loud bang of a car door slamming shut startled me—and Ryan.

Chapter 30

He shot to his feet, having only untied one of her ankles. Frantic, he looked to me, then outside the still open door and back again.

"You're lying!" he bellowed, spit flying. "They're coming for me. You're here for me. You're taking her away from me."

"No, Ryan. I'm here—"

"Shut up," he shouted and stretched forward, grasping for Ellie.

His desperate fingers only brushed the edge of her shirt as she leapt out of his reach, dragging the chair with her foot still secured to the leg. A manic look overtook his face, distorting his features to show the evil that lurked inside.

It took less than a second for my world to shatter. Too fast for me to prevent the inevitable.

The revolver rose to chest height as Ellie continued to stagger away.

Palm wrapped around the cold rough grip of my nine-millimeter, I pulled it around, raising it with my finger already hovering over the trigger.

Simultaneously, two shots boomed, rattling my eardrums.

A tendril of smoke lifted from the end of my barrel as Ryan's body folded to the floor.

Immediate threat neutralized, I leapt toward Ellie, not offering Ryan's body a second glance. My bullet struck exactly where I intended.

Between the eyes.

A quiet cry emanated from her crumbled body. I dropped to the floor beside her, my knees slamming to the linoleum. Rolling her to her back, I held a breath, not sure what to expect. Thin red rivers leaked from between the fingers pressed against her side, trailing over her knuckles and dripping to the floor.

Panic filled her blue eyes as they searched mine.

"I didn't mean it. A single damn word," I rushed. "I'm not going anywhere without you.".

"I know," she rasped. With another pain-laced whimper, she sealed her lids shut, her face contorted in agony.

Taking the hand covering the wound, I peeled it free, then the blood-soaked shirt. I forced a calm mask to settle over my face as I inspected the jagged hole that bubbled with a crimson flood. My smile was strained as I replaced her shirt and pressed hard on the wound.

"It's fine," I lied. "You'll be fine."

The stomp of boots behind me had my anger soaring once again. If that dumbass wouldn't have left the truck, if he would've stayed out of this like I told him, Ellie wouldn't be bleeding out in front of me.

Shoving away the emotions that wouldn't help Ellie in the moment, I used the hand not staunching the wound to toss my cell at the old man.

"Call Alec Bronson. He's the last person who called. Tell him we need a helicopter here. Now. Tell him Ellie is injured."

Knowing he'd do what I commanded, I turned my full attention back to Ellie. Her lower lip trembled like she was either cold or scared. I rubbed the pad of my thumb along the edge, leaving a streak of blood behind.

"You're okay, Ellie." Helplessness ate away at my soul. There was nothing I could do. No hospital close by, no doctor in town who could offer aid. I'd just killed the one person in this fucking town who had any type of medical training.

Her lids dipped, dousing my all-consuming panic with lighter fluid.

"No, stay with me, baby. Keep those beautiful eyes on me, okay?" My eyes burned with the tears I held back. "Ellie, you have to hold on. We'll get you to the hospital, but you have to stay strong for me."

"Chandler," she rasped, coughing, then whimpering. "Chandler. I want you to know...." She bit down on her lip, tears running out of the corners of both eyes. "I want you to know that you were the best chapter. I loved every word, every sentence, every page. You made all this worth it."

"Don't you fucking say that," I snapped. "Don't say that like it's goodbye. It's not. It's not your time. It's not my time. We have more to our story, Ellie. You and me, there's more to be written." Those tears

Chapter 30

I'd held back now dripped down both cheeks, a visual display of my despair. "Didn't you know?"

"Know... what?" Her chest rose and fell with shaky breaths.

"Our story isn't a tragedy, it's a love story. A story people will read about for years wishing they had what we had."

"How does it end?" That pain-filled gaze held mine.

"Happily ever after."

With an almost smile curling her lips, her lids slowly closed.

"Ellie," I begged. "Ellie, please. Please don't leave me." My shoulders shook with each wounded sob from my heart shredding. "Where is that damn helicopter?" I shouted over my shoulder, my voice cracking with the tidal wave of devastation drowning me.

"He doesn't know. Can't get—"

With a raging yell, I scooped Ellie in my arms and turned. The old man stood at the threshold, phone still pressed to his ear.

"Get in the fucking truck. You're driving us as fast as the damn thing can go to Waco. She will live, damnit. She will fucking live."

Inside the truck's cab, I ripped the shirt off my back and pressed it against her seeping wound.

It had been a long time since I prayed, decades maybe, after being forced throughout my fucked-up childhood. But there in the cab of the old truck bouncing down the highway, the woman I loved more than life itself in my arms, I lifted my face to the sky and begged to anyone listening to save her.

Because I knew if she didn't survive this, neither would I.

31

Ellie

BLEACH, cleaning fluid, and... something familiar I couldn't place that filled me with a sense of comfort and love were what first came to mind as I slowly drifted awake from a deep sleep. My body felt heavy, limbs made of metal rather than flesh and bone. A dull ache bloomed from my lower belly but was more of an annoyance than actual pain. Unlike the last moments I had before passing out. The pain of the bullet tearing through me was excruciating; my body slowly growing cold as blood seeped from my wound was something I'd never forget. Then there were those last few moments with Chandler. Witnessing him breaking was a different type of agony. That pain was in my heart, in my soul as if I was sobbing from the inside, devastated at the sight of him so upset because of me.

Chandler.

I inhaled again.

That was the familiar comforting scent. His unique combination of manly soap, deodorant, and a spicy cologne that I committed to memory from sniffing the collar of his borrowed jacket and all the days we'd spent together since. Behind my lids, I searched through the darkness, not quite ready to wake up and face reality just yet.

Somewhere to my right, whispered voices spoke. A quiet rhythmic beeping close to my ear, and something warm wrapped around my hand keeping the chill I felt everywhere else at bay.

The need to find Chandler won over my body's urge to slip back into that peaceful darkness. Peeling my lids open, I blinked, clearing the haze. The small room was unfamiliar, clean, cold almost. My gaze tracked toward the far corner, where Alec and a short man in a white coat stood, both too wrapped up in their conversation to notice my stare.

The heater around my hand tightened. Rolling my head along the pillowcase, I found Chandler sitting beside me, hand engulfing my own. Red streaked the whites of his eyes, dark purple bags hanging beneath. Hair disheveled and skin paler than normal, he looked exhausted.

We both blinked when our gazes locked, neither speaking a word as we stared at the other. His last words played on repeat as we sat in silence. So much was said those final few minutes. All honest declarations, full of emotions and promises.

A slight tremble shook his fingers as he reached for my face, palm delicately cupping my cheek. Happy tears burned behind my eyes.

"There you are, baby," he murmured against my knuckles as he brushed them along his lower lip. "I've missed you."

After a few tries, I swallowed back the lump of unshed tears that clogged my dry throat. "You told me not to give up."

"And you didn't," he said between planting kisses along the inside of my wrist and up my forearm.

"Where am I?" I asked, lids fluttering closed at the tingling sensations left behind at each place he kissed.

"A hospital. In Dallas."

"Dallas?" I squeaked, eyes flaring open. My hair shifted along the pillow as I twisted to see out the windows. Ginormous buildings stretched high toward the sky, hundreds of them clustered so close

Chapter 31

together that I wondered if they touched. Between the buildings, highways packed with cars and trucks zigzagged. One building in particular held my attention, its odd shape and green windows a sheer marvel.

"What does it smell like?" I murmured.

When he didn't respond, I rolled my head back along the pillow, brows raised in expectation. Chandler's focus was still locked on me. I couldn't help the way my cheeks heated beneath his intense focus.

"Smell like?" he mused. An almost smile ticked a corner of his lips. "Like old money, poor decisions, and pollution."

I barked out a laugh at his unexpected description of the famous city, yet I knew if he said it, the words were true. My stomach muscles tensed and pulled with the action, and a searing pain stabbed into my side as a hiss pushed through my clenched teeth. I went to press on the area, hoping to calm the burning pain, but Chandler stopped me, urging my hand back to the bed.

"Don't touch it, but if it hurts, let me know, and I'll get you more pain meds." Sorrow flashed across his face. "You had surgery to get the bullet out and had a few transfusions to help replace the blood you lost. Everything went as planned, and the doctors say you'll be back to normal in a couple days."

"How did I get here, to Dallas?" A million different questions flashed through my thoughts, but that one was the most important.

"I got you to Waco, where a medical team patched you up enough for us to fly you to Dallas."

"Fly?" I squeaked. *I flew. Holy Hades, I flew.*

"A helicopter. Careflight, to be exact."

Awe washed through me. "I'm sad I missed it." I attempted a smile, but my disappointment at not remembering the flight hampered my mood. "So I'm in Dallas. Where exactly?"

"Baylor Medical Center."

I took in the room and all the contraptions beside my bed. Embarrassment flared within me.

"Chandler, I can't pay for this." I sighed. "I don't have enough—"

"Really? You were shot, and that's what you're thinking about." He shook his head, but the heaviness that surrounded him seemed to lift. "Don't worry about any of that, okay? The FBI will foot the bill since you were injured during an altercation with the unsub. But"—he rubbed a hand over his short hair—"I do have a confession. I filled out your paperwork and consent forms for surgery, and I listed your name as Ellie Peters."

I pressed two fingers to his reddening cheekbone. My dry lips stretched into a wide smile. "I like the sound of that."

"Like it?" he huffed with zero frustration behind the sound. "Just *like* it?"

"Scratch that, I love it."

"Hey there, Ellie girl." I shifted along the sheets to turn toward Alec's deep voice. "You gave us a scare. Try not to do anything like that again."

I snorted while Chandler punched Alec in the stomach.

"Promise," I said. "That's nothing I want to go through again." All three of us fell into a heavy silence. "He told me the why, the how." I swallowed and picked at the white blanket pooled at my waist. "Did you find Brett?"

"Ellie, we can do this later—"

A knock at the door interrupted whatever Alec wanted to say next. A woman in maroon scrubs walked through the door, face downturned, studying the clipboard between her hands. A bright smile split across her face when she glanced up, finding me awake.

"You okay to be in here alone?" Chandler's brows were furrowed in concern, lifting slightly when I nodded. "Okay, well, we'll be right outside if you need us." A quick kiss to the top of my head and he stood, arching to stretch his back. Our fingers slid apart as he stepped away, mine dropping to the mattress when he moved out of reach.

"Chandler?" I called out before he made it to the door. He turned, brows raised. "Thank you for saving me."

In two rapid steps, he was back by my side, curved over the hospital bed with his lips pressed to mine in a desperate, all-consuming, deep kiss. It said the intense emotions and feelings we couldn't put into words, pouring it all from one to the other and connecting us on a new level. Guess that was what almost dying and seeing the one you love almost die in your arms did to you. It made you realize nothing else mattered but the one you love and who loved you back.

Something in my hand pinched as I clasped the back of his neck, nails biting into the skin in my desperate need for him to consume me whole. An attention-grabbing cough brought me back to reality, reminding me someone else was in the room.

I smiled, and he grinned in return. He brushed a soft, cherishing kiss to my forehead. "You saved me too."

This time when he walked away, I didn't stop him. He would be right outside like he promised, probably with an ear to the door ensuring I wasn't in danger. This was my first hospital to ever see, let alone be in, and surgery was also another first, but I'd seen enough through TV shows and movies to know the basics of what to expect.

The nurse nodded toward the closed door. "That man didn't leave your side once. We even had to call security to keep him out of the surgery room when you first arrived." That was not surprising in the least. And if I was being honest with myself, it made me love my protective profiler a little more. "I know all this is new to you, so if you have any questions or are uncomfortable, let me know. First, I'll start with checking your vitals, then change out your IV fluids and check your incision. After that, you'll want to get some sleep."

"Didn't I just do that?" I asked as she changed out one of the deflated bags on the metal hook and replaced it with a full one.

"I suppose, but sleep will help you recover faster. Plus, I'm sure you're tired."

As if on cue, I yawned wide, making us both laugh.

Maybe sleep wasn't such a crazy idea, even though I'd just woken up.

Just the thought had my lids drooping and finally falling closed completely after several attempts to keep them open.

Okay, maybe she's right. Just a short nap.

THE ROOM WAS dark except for the bright lights glaring through the window. I squinted to make out the details past the glass. Not a single star was visible in the clear sky, the brilliant artificial light from the buildings keeping them hidden. It was strange, having been in a town where streetlights only existed around the interstate, to see the dark night lit up like it was daytime.

"Ellie."

Turning toward the voice, I searched the dark room. My breath caught at the sight of him sitting across the room. Even with the shadows, his stiff posture and tension were clear. Between his hands was a blue folder, the edges bending under his tight hold.

"Hey," I said, my voice still hoarse with sleep. "What are you doing all the way over there?" All my alarms went off when he failed to answer. "Chandler, what's wrong?"

"I did something, Ellie." I stopped breathing altogether as I waited. Tilting forward, he pressed both elbows atop his thighs and dangled the folder between his knees. "And I can't take it back."

The machine to my right beeped in sync with my rising pulse.

"What did you do?" My voice shook with trepidation. After everything I'd been through, those words held heavy meaning. Did he trade me like Jacob, video me like Brett? Even as those fears swelled, maximizing the worst-case scenario, I knew in my heart that Chandler would never do anything to harm me. To harm us.

Despair leaked from his stare, his tone heavy. "I want you to know I didn't know," he pleaded. "I had no idea it would be this deep, this dark." The chair shifted as he rested back and tapped the folder against his opposite hand. "I thought... hell, I don't know what I thought. It was a long shot."

"What did you do?" I asked again, stronger this time.

"It struck me as odd when I saw your parents, the lack of resemblance between you and them. I just had this gut feeling that something was off, and I followed through with that feeling."

"What did you do?" I shouted, immediately regretting it when my wound pinched, sending bolts of pain radiating from the incision.

"I took a hair sample one night when you were sleeping." I

released a breath. That wasn't so bad. Creepy but not terrible. "I sent the sample to the Dallas FBI office to run DNA." Again, I found myself holding a shallow breath in anticipation. "It's all in here," he said, holding the folder up.

"What's in it?" My voice shook. "Why are you acting so strange? It's freaking me the fuck out."

"You were stolen, Ellie." He shook his head and cursed under his breath. "Fuck, your name isn't even Ellie, or Elizabeth, or Lizzy, or any name you've ever been called."

"What are you talking about?" I balled the rough material of the blanket in my tight fists. "I would know if I had a life before The Church." But that dream, the memories that sometimes surfaced for half a thought before floating away again.... I shook my head in disbelief. "It's wrong."

"You were kidnapped from a water park in Oklahoma City."

"No," I stated.

"You were five, there with your family. You have an older brother and sister."

"No. I don't have any family." My tone held the conviction I didn't feel.

"Ellie." The clear despair on his drawn features and the crack in his pleading voice made me ache to comfort him even though I was heartbroken too. "You have a name, a real birthdate and birth certificate, a social security number."

I slapped a hand over my quivering lips to quiet the building sob. Chandler launched from the chair, coming to sit on the edge of the bed before pulling me into his protective arms. Face tucked against his neck, he held me close, never saying a word as I sobbed, my tears flowing down the column of his throat.

"You have a family who's looked for you, who's never stopped looking for you."

"Really?" I said between sniffles.

"Really, really. The detective over your disappearance logged every call your mother made to him asking if anything new was discovered. Every year on the date of your disappearance."

"What's my name?" I swallowed down my fear. I couldn't hide my head in the sand. This was real. I should've been excited, overjoyed that I was a real person, but more than anything, I was scared. Terrified of this new unknown.

"Maddison Jane Bishop."

"Maddison." I blinked, saying the name over and over in my head, but it didn't feel right. Hand pressed to the center of his chest, I put some distance between us. "No, not Maddison. Maddie."

"You remember?" Lifting the few strands of hair stuck to my cheek, he swiped them behind my ear, his other hand cupping my face.

"Maybe." I nibbled at the edge of my lip. "Do they know about me, what I... where I was?" Shame bloomed, making me feel dirty and used. If they knew what I'd done, what I'd lived through, would they even want me now?

"No." I relaxed against him. Good, that was good until I figured out how I felt about all this. "When I received the report, I instructed everyone who knew to hold off on contacting your parents or the detective. That will be your call if you want them to know about you." Chandler brushed a thumb along my cheekbone. "But there's more."

A half laugh, half cry bubbled past my lips. "What, I'm a millionaire?"

"Better, some might say. You've gained a few years back to your life. You're twenty-three."

My jaw popped open and a hysterical laugh erupted, the revelations and weight of the last few minutes finally catching up with me. "Look at you, robbing the cradle." No idea where that came from, but for some crazed reason, it was the funniest thing I'd ever heard. Tears streamed down my bunched cheeks. Hand to my bandages, I attempted to keep my stitches together as I laughed and laughed before breaking completely and collapsing against Chandler, sobbing once again.

Careful of my incision, he held me tight, whispering how strong I was, how I'd survive this just like I had everything else in my life. He spoke in my ear all the things about me he found amazing, and sexy, and beautiful.

After who knew how long of me crying in his arms, the tears slowed. Stroking my hair behind an ear, he tipped my chin up, forcing me to look up to him. "Do you realize what this means?"

Using the sleeve of my soft cotton hospital gown, I wiped at my eyes and nose. "I'm a real person?" I joked.

"You've always been a real person, Ellie. You're the most real person I've ever met. But I'm talking about your age and how it affects The Church. I'm suspecting you were taken that day specifically for The Church, meaning someone within those gates kidnapped a five-year-old child."

I sucked in a breath at the implication of that statement. "There could be others."

Chandler dipped his chin in acknowledgment. "And if you decide to move forward with all this, allowing the FBI to run with your kidnapping, we have the evidence to arrest Jacob."

"What?" My voice dipped with doubt.

"You weren't eighteen, Ellie. When he forced you to marry him. You were underage, without parental consent and against your will. There isn't a judge in this state who wouldn't sign that arrest warrant."

I blinked at Chandler, processing what he said. If I decided to move forward, that bastard of a man could be behind bars. I could be free of him, truly free, finally.

There wasn't a choice, not really. I loved that Chandler gave me the option, but there was no way I could say no. Not when I could possibly save other victims behind those gates and help find their real families.

"I'm in. That bastard needs to pay for what he took from me, what they all took from me." Sitting up straighter, I gripped Chandler's shoulders. "What do you need from me?"

APPARENTLY ALMOST DYING OPENED the floodgates to the tears I'd held back my entire life. It was one of the things Jacob hated, that I could control my emotions to hide any physical reactions to his games. Well, being shot broke down my walls *and* meeting my real parents.

The tears hadn't stopped since the two walked through the hospital room door. I expected it to be awkward, having to explain where I'd been, but it was the opposite. Their steps weren't tentative, no hesitancy slowing their enthusiastic shouts of relief the moment our eyes met.

My dad—Steve, I quickly found out—wrapped me in a bear hug, his shoulders shaking with joy-filled sobs. My mom, Kathy, just held my cheeks between her small hands, memorizing my features while silent tears leaked down her smiling face.

It wasn't awkward at all.

It was perfect.

After an hour, Steve excused himself to gather his emotions in private. That was twenty minutes ago. Now Kathy clung to me like a koala bear, arms looped around my neck, keeping me close in her tight hold. A soft sniffle echoed in my ear before she pulled back to study my face again. Her smile was mine—or mine was hers, I guess. Matching blue eyes, same petite face and button nose, which was red from the box of tissue we'd already cried through. And of course the thick blonde hair. Well, mine was still dyed, but if I had my natural color, it would match hers minus the brilliant streaks of silver that sometimes caught the fluorescent light.

Biting back her grin, she shifted her gaze to look over my shoulder. More tears pooled in her lower lids as she pressed three fingers to her trembling lips.

"Thank you," she whispered, her throat clogged with emotion like mine. "Thank you for saving my baby and bringing her home."

"She saved herself long before I came along." I leaned back against Chandler's chest, savoring the warmth that seeped from him through my soft long-sleeve T-shirt.

"I need to call—" She flicked her gaze to the ceiling, her eyes searching as if the names were written on the tiles. "—well, everyone.

Our family, everyone who helped look for you originally, and who's continued to search since."

Chandler held up a hand, stopping her. "We need you to hold off on telling anyone about Maddison." I held back a wince at the sound of the foreign name on his lips. "If the people who took her are tipped off, they could run. I'd like us to make the formal arrest and have the ones responsible in custody before you make any calls."

"Right, of course, sorry. That makes sense, and I don't want to jeopardize the chance of making that asshole pay." She winced. "Excuse my language." She patted my hand. "Now, I'm going to go check on my husband, and, well, collect myself a little too. We've dreamed of this day for so long. It's a miracle. *You're* a miracle." My returning smile was brittle. She didn't need to know Jacob had said similar things and just thinking I was special now made my stomach sour. "I'll be back in a little while."

"She's safe with me." Chandler's chest vibrated with the words, tickling along my spine.

"I know she is." With another near asphyxiating hug, she walked to the door, turning around before slipping into the hall. "I love you, Maddie." The moment the door closed, an elated scream belted down the hall.

Chandler chuckled and wrapped his arms around my waist, careful of my injury. Twisting around, I pressed my cheek to his chest. We sat on the edge of the bed for several minutes in contemplative silence, letting the last couple hours soak through.

"When will the arrest be made?" I asked, resting my chin on his sternum.

He pressed a soft kiss to the end of my nose. "Alec's headed there now with all the warrants and reinforcements in case of resistance. Once Jacob is arrested, they'll begin investigating the community as a whole."

I released a slow breath. "After today I'll be free?"

"You're free, Maddie."

I pulled a face. "Please stop saying that. It might be my legal name, but in here"—I pointed to my heart—"I'm Ellie. The girl who knew deep down there was more waiting for her on the other side of the fence, the girl who twice left the life she knew, breaking free of the men desperate to dominate her. I'm the girl who gets the happily ever after with her hero."

He chuckled, rubbing the back of his hand along my cheek. "I'm no hero. You *were* shot, after all."

"Sure, but it would've been worse if you hadn't talked Ryan down initially. You saved me, Chandler Peters. You helped me live."

Closing the small distance between us, I planted a kiss to his lower lip. With a contented sigh, I relaxed against him, nuzzling his neck until I was tucked beneath his jaw. My lids grew heavy from the emotional exhaustion and the warmth of his skin.

"About DC." My eyes snapped open at the hesitation in his tone. With a firm grip on the back of my neck, he pulled back, putting us face-to-face. "I think you need to stay here."

"What?" I exclaimed, scooting back an inch on the bed to put more distance between us. "You don't want me to go with you?"

He offered a sad smile. "Of course I want you with me. The thought of leaving you"—he rubbed a fist against his sternum—"it physically hurts. But, Ellie, you need time with your real family. Catch up on everything you missed. Meet your siblings, spend time with your parents, who seem really great, hell, celebrate Thanksgiving next week surrounded by your real family. If I were to take you now, when you've just found all this, it would be selfish of me. As much as I want you by my side, which will happen one day soon, I think you'd regret not taking some time to breathe."

"But I don't want to breathe without you," I confessed. Stretching past Chandler to the bedside table, I snatched a peppermint from the candy stash he'd surprised me with earlier that day.

"It's not goodbye. We'll never be done. You and me, we're forever, remember? Think of the time apart as a pause. A breather for you to discover who you are outside of Orin, Texas, away from Jacob and Brett, away from me. I'll wait for you." Tilting to the side, he withdrew a long white envelope from the back pocket of his jeans and placed it in the space between us. "Inside you'll find a first-class, one-way

Chapter 31

plane ticket to Washington, DC. To be used anytime. Also my address, access code, and a key to my condo. For when you're ready to start a new chapter. *Our* chapter."

I sniffled and wiped away a stray tear with the back of my hand. I didn't want to agree with him, but deep down, I knew he was right. I needed some time here, wanted to breathe the air as a free woman, a real person with a real family. Maybe give my internal bruises a little time to heal, maybe even find a little bit of this Maddie I'd buried deep inside myself where no one could find her.

I nodded in agreement but kept my lips sealed, unable to say a word without crying all over again.

"Listen, I don't leave until tomorrow." A knuckle pressed beneath my chin, Chandler lifted my face to meet his. "And with it being my last night here, I'd really like to spend it with you." The bed jostled and creaked when he stood. Searching through a backpack that sat along the floor, he held up his iPad and gave it a hopeful look. "How about a *Mindhunter* marathon?"

More tears leaked out of my eyes against my will. Not only was he sexy, smart, and all mine, he understood me.

"Yes, I'd love that," I somehow said around the ball of unshed tears burning my throat.

With a childlike grin, he toed off his shoes and stripped down to his undershirt. As he emptied his pockets, I shimmied beneath the layers of blankets, holding one side open as an invitation for him to crawl in beside me. After a few adjustments of the pillows and him tucking one arm under my head, we finally found a comfortable position.

Halfway through the intro to episode one, I turned my head, pressing my cheek to the pillow to take in his handsome face.

"What?" he questioned, cutting his eyes my way.

"I think I love you," I whispered as I searched for the right words. "But I'm not so sure. It feels more than that, like my heart might burst with everything I feel when I'm around you. So I'm lying here wondering, what comes after love? What goes beyond that emotion? Because that's what I feel for you."

turning, he mirrored me, our noses brushing. "I beyond love you too, Ellie. I forever love you."

And just like that, I knew.

I knew my happily ever after had started.

And I never wanted this chapter to end.

32

Chandler

Forearm against the frigid glass, I surveyed the wintery scene from the high perch of my condo. Fresh glittering snow blanketed the park across the street and covered tops of other nearby high-rises. The streets, however, were stark black lines through the white wonderland after being salted and plowed sometime early this morning. Snow continued to float from the sky, gusts of wind producing small snowstorms to swirl along the covered balcony before mixing with the other flakes.

I took a long pull from the beer dangling between my fingers and turned from the serene view. Next to me stood a fresh evergreen, fully decorated and nearly touching the high ceiling. It was a beautiful tree, one I splurged on yesterday. My mood dipped further at the sight of the new red skirt beneath the grand tree, empty of gifts. I took another long drink of the beer as I took in the sad, beautiful tree. The fire across the room warmed the space, keeping out the winter chill.

The lights blinked, a gold ornament reflecting their shine. It should've made me happy, but I felt more lost than ever before. It was a picture-perfect Christmas day with a beautiful tree in a cozy condo, yet I was alone, again.

Perched on the arm of the long leather couch, I released a despondent exhale and downed what little remained of the beer. Balancing the empty bottle on my knee, I chastised myself for doing all this, driven by nothing but hope, a one-off chance that I might not spend this holiday, like so many others before, alone. I never decorated for Christmas, seeing no point considering I wouldn't be enjoying it. But this year I hoped that a blue-eyed beauty would walk through the condo door in the ultimate Christmas present.

I glanced at the closed door again. I found myself doing that every few minutes or so.

The last time we spoke, she'd sounded happy, which made me happy. She was having a great time with her real family, getting to know each of them while also discovering where she fit into their lives. I wasn't worried that she'd forgotten me or had doubts. I was just fucking tired of being alone.

After having her for that short period, I understood what all I'd missed out on in life by not having someone special to share it with.

I huffed, telling myself to stop moping, and stood, groaning as I stretched both arms overhead.

The bottle clinked and clanged against the other bottles when I tossed it in the recycling bin. Knowing only a steady intake of alcohol would keep me from hopping on a plane and flying to Texas, I opened the fridge for another beer only to find the shelf empty. Grumbling a slew of curses at my lazy ass for not picking up more yesterday while I was out, I slammed the fridge door shut. Retrieving my thick winter coat off the hanger by the front door, I scooped my keys and wallet out of the bowl on the side table and begrudgingly headed out to face the winter storm for booze.

Twenty minutes later, key held tight between my freezing fingers, I twisted the lock and shoved the door open. The bottles rattled in protest as I placed the case just inside the door to strip out of my coat. Snow that had collected atop my short hair melted in the heat of my apartment, causing icy rivers to race down my temples and the back of my neck, dipping beneath the collar of my sweatshirt.

Grumbling under my breath about moving somewhere that never got snow, I turned from the front door, edges of my coat tight in my grasp as I tugged it off my shoulders and froze.

"Hey, Chandler. I'm a little late."

She looked exactly as I remembered her, except now the short hair that was jet-black with blonde roots was now a cute shade of pastel pink. Noticing what held my attention, she tucked a few pieces behind her ear.

"Late?" That was all I could say. Even after hoping all day she'd show up and be the best Christmas present I'd ever received, all words vanished from my vocabulary. Giving myself a second, I ran a hand over my hair, sprinkling the wall and floor with specks of water.

"I tried to be here this morning, when you woke up." She motioned to the floor-to-ceiling windows that displayed the still raging snowstorm. "I wanted it to be a surprise. I hope it's okay that I just showed up. Maybe I should've called or—"

Dropping the coat, ignoring everything but my urgent desire to hold the woman who stole my heart and owned my soul, I strode with purpose to where she stood in the middle of the living room. I didn't stop when I reached her. She squealed in surprise as I scooped her up, her legs immediately wrapping around my waist.

The wall rattled, a picture threatening to fall to the floor from the disturbance as I pushed her back against it. Not having the words to tell her how much I missed her and wanted her here, I kissed her with all I had, allowing her to devour the weight of loneliness I'd harbored since we parted last month.

Her short nails scoured along my scalp and down my neck. Our tongues danced, taking from each other exactly what we needed to feel whole again. By the time we pulled apart, my dick threatened to pop out of my damn jeans, and she was breathless.

"Wow," she panted. "I missed you too."

"Tell me, Ellie, are you here to stay?" I leaned forward, sealing our foreheads together. "If not, then I'm moving to Texas. I can't do that again. I—"

"I'm here to stay, Chandler. You're never getting rid of me." Placing both of her small hands on my cheeks, she urged me back an inch. "Scars, bruises, and all. I'm here for as long as you'll have me."

Heart hammering, threatening to pound right out of my chest, I considered her words. She was it for me, forever, and it seemed she felt the same way.

It took a few tugs on her ankles, but I finally unwrapped her legs from my waist and slowly lowered her to the floor. "Stay right there." I turned to the tree I spent hours decorating yesterday and withdrew a single red velvet box from the branches.

Rotating back to face her, I held it between us.

"Let me more than love you. For the rest of my life, let me be your everything and you be mine. Be my one person I can count on for life, who always has my back and more than loves me back despite my own issues and scars." Dropping to one knee, I peeled back the lid. A small hand flew up to cover her gaping mouth. "Marry me?"

It felt like eternity before she answered. "I don't love you despite your scars, Chandler. I more than love you because they match my own. Yes, I'll marry you."

With an exited shout, I leapt from the floor, wrapped my arms around her waist, and lifted her off the ground so we were nose to nose.

"You said yes," I said, my cheeks burning from my broad smile. "You're mine. You said you'd be mine." My voice dipped a little at the thought. All mine, no restrictions.

She bit the edge of her lip and looked up through her dark lashes. "Yours to do with as you please." A naughty sparkle lit behind her blue eyes.

I nipped at her lower lip, more than ready to do as I pleased.

Forever.

How in the hell had I gotten this lucky?

Chapter 32

As I carried her to my bedroom, I decided I didn't care how it happened. I would spend every moment for the rest of my life being thankful for what we had together. That even us, a little broken and lost, could find a happily ever after.

Forever.

EPILOGUE

Ellie

Despite the street crowded with pedestrians, milling about from shop to shop on foot or racing straight down the middle, weaving between bodies on bicycles, I paused. The sea of people parted to move around, a few grumbling under their breaths about lazy Americans, but I didn't care what they said or what they thought, because ultimately they were a blip on my radar. I'd never see them again.

That was the oddest part about leaving Orin. Seeing faces, meeting people you wouldn't see day after day after day. Like now, all the tourists snapping photos and purchasing souvenirs probably didn't even notice me like I did them, because to them, I didn't matter.

What a glorious thought.

This was what freedom felt like. I could scream in the streets, cause everyone to look at me, and tomorrow it wouldn't matter. Well, except to the man standing behind me, keeping a protective watch as I tilted my face to the late afternoon sun and closed my eyes.

I loved the way the sun felt against my skin in different parts of rld. For some reason, the heat mixed with the new environment made me feel more alive than ever.

A hand snaked around my waist, tugging me back an inch, sealing my back to his.

My wound, long ago healed, tugged like my skin was just a little too tight in that one spot, but after living with it for five months I hardly noticed the pain anymore.

"Want to grab something to eat, Mrs. Peters?" Chandler whispered into my ear.

I smiled at the sun. "Another apple strudel? But I want to run into this shop really quick." I inclined my head to the small souvenir shop with racks of postcards stationed outside the door.

"I'll grab your strudel and—"

I arched a brow. "Get two. Last time you ate half of mine."

"Lies," he joked. "Fine. I'll get two strudels and"—stretching his arm out in front of me, he pointed toward a stone wall that others sat upon, staring at the rolling river on the other side—"I'll meet you over there."

The metal rack squeaked with each rotation as I inspected every postcard available. Some were funny, things I could find back home, which wasn't exactly what I was looking for. The last turn displayed the row of scenic postcards in front of me.

Bingo.

Thirteen in all, each beautiful in their own way. Some displaying the nearby Alps, the others with quaint Swiss villages similar to the one I received that very night my path crossed with the man who altered my destiny. For several minutes, I debated which one was *the one*, unable to choose my favorite.

"Get them all, Ellie." I jumped at the breath ghosting past my ear. Chandler chuckled as he stepped beside me.

"I can't," I whispered for some privacy. "You know that."

Even though he gave me access to his accounts the moment we said, "I do," I still had a difficult time not overthinking every penny spent. Those two years working my ass off and living on nothing created a difficult mentality to break.

"I like that one." He pushed a finger to the one I was leaning toward too, leaving a smear of—

"Chandler Peters, did you eat my strudel?" I accused. He hid his grin and shrugged. "You owe me two now."

Wrapping both arms around my waist, he pulled me to his chest. "How about I buy you every postcard in your hand and then buy you three strudels as penance?" Bending forward, he placed his lips against the shell of my ear. "And then tonight I'll eat my favorite meal of all: you."

"Deal," I said breathlessly.

He tugged the postcards from my fingers and strode to the cash register. Minutes later, we were back on the street making our way through the crowd. Sitting me on the stone wall where we'd originally planned to meet, he handed me the thin brown bag and a pen. "I'll be right back."

As I watched his ass as he walked toward the small pastry shop, a content sigh passed my lips. I shook my head, a few blonde locks floating across my line of vision on a soft, cool breeze.

Free. I was free. With Jacob behind bars, and there for the unforeseeable future, and the Swann brothers dead, I had no one else to fear. I was free to live and that was exactly what I planned to do from here on out.

Pulling out the postcards, I found the one I wanted and uncapped the pen. Holding the end to my lip, I considered my surroundings, taking in every sense and storing it in my memory.

Smiling, I pressed the pen to the paper and began writing.

Dear Janice,

Switzerland is fantastic. The people are kind and warm, the air that kind of soft and cool that brushes against your skin like an almost kiss. Below me the river rushes, white caps forming on larger waves. It's no doubt never seen a drought in its existence. The pastries are fresh, and everything is made with butter, which makes every bite delicious.

h you were here.
Ellie

PS – It smells like new beginnings, pine, and freshly melted snow.
PPS – I'm pregnant.

Want more Chandler and Ellie? Sign up for my newsletter HERE to receive a deleted sexy scene delivered right to your inbox!

Loved Mine to Save? Make sure you've read the first book in the Protection series, Mine to Protect.

ABOUT THE AUTHOR

Kennedy L. Mitchell lives outside Dallas with her husband, son and two very large goldendoodles. She began writing in 2016 after a fight with her husband (You can read the fight almost verbatim in Falling for the Chance) and has no plans of stopping.

She would love to hear from you via any of the platforms below or her website www.kennedylmitchell.com You can also stay up to date on future releases through her newsletter or by joining her Facebook readers group - Kennedy's Book Boyfriend Support Group.

Thank you for reading.

ALSO BY KENNEDY L. MITCHELL

Standalone:

Falling for the Chance

A Covert Affair

Finding Fate

Memories of Us

Protection Series: Interconnected Standalone

Mine to Protect

Mine to Save

More Than a Threat Series: A Bodyguard Romantic Suspense

More Than a Threat

More Than a Risk

More Than a Hope (Coming 2021)

Power Play Series: A Protector Romantic Suspense

Power Play

Power Twist

Power Switch

Power Surge

Power Term

ACKNOWLEDGMENTS

I feel foolish that it took me THIS long to publish Chandler's story. But it's here and I LOVE these two so much. Even though you had a wait a while this story turned out exactly as I wanted it to. So, thank you for being patient with me!

There would be zero Kennedy L. Mitchell books if it weren't for my main support group, my tribe, my alpha readers and besties. Thank you to Em, Chris, and Kristin for encouraging me when I needed it, telling me sweet things like 'you'd make an excellent cult leader', and putting up with the zillion self doubting texts. You three have supported me from the beginning and I cannot thank you enough.

Once a book is written then the hard work starts for all those who make the novel readable! If you guys saw my manuscript before my amazing editor, Kristin, got her hands on it you'd wonder if I even made it through elementary school. Thank you Kristin for making my words shine while keeping my voice in each paragraph.

And of course Sarah my amazing proof reader (who's reading this and cringing since she didn't proof this part - sorry Sarah!) thank you for finding all those missing words and helping make my book flawless.

ladies at Wildfire Marketing went above and beyond with this book. Pushing ARC sign up, encouraging bloggers to help spread the word, and of course holding my hand and giving helpful suggestions along the way.

Last but not least I want to thank YOU. Yes, YOU! Because you took a chance on this series, on this book, on an author who's never made a list, isn't the talk of FB and has zero interpersonal skills. Thank you for reading Ellie and Chandler's story.

Printed in Great Britain
by Amazon